FREE FALL

Murphy overrode the airlock's safeties and took several deep breaths. They were on the far side of the second planet. She had to go now, before she crossed back into visual with the station.

The acceleration was only a gentle pull, maybe a quarter gee. She should use a tether, but Siskoll wouldn't have time to reel it in before he reached the station and a loose line would raise questions.

She hand-over-handed her way down to the *Gambit*'s level, saving the jets for an emergency.

When she reached the first singleship, she activated her shoe magnets. A toe button controlled the grab release of the electromagnet. Place. Release. Place right foot. Release left. Place. Release. Place—

Her right foot released before her left one caught. Her hand slipped.

The singleship's steel hull skidded under her right foot. She lost contact with the accelerating ship.

She fired the jets. For an endless second she hung in the same reference frame as the girders, spending precious fuel to hold her position, until the jets compensated and she crept up on a girder.

Suddenly, the jets faltered. The display read empty.

Come on. She willed the jets to fire again. Nothing . . .

"*Murphy's Gambit* is the real thing: adamantine-hard science fiction with heart. Syne Mitchell is a rare author—as equally deft with special relativity and biochemistry as she is with sculpting real characters and delivering a ripping good read."

—Eric S. Nylund, author of *Signal to Noise*

MURPHY'S GAMBIT

Syne Mitchell

A ROC BOOK

ROC
Published by New American Library, a division of
Penguin Putnam Inc., 375 Hudson Street,
New York, New York 10014, U.S.A.
Penguin Books Ltd, 27 Wrights Lane,
London W8 5TZ, England
Penguin Books Australia Ltd, Ringwood,
Victoria, Australia
Penguin Books Canada Ltd, 10 Alcorn Avenue,
Toronto, Ontario, Canada M4V 3B2
Penguin Books (N.Z.) Ltd, 182–190 Wairau Road,
Auckland 10, New Zealand

Penguin Books Ltd, Registered Offices:
Harmondsworth, Middlesex, England

First published by Roc, an imprint of New American Library,
a division of Penguin Putnam Inc.

First Printing, November 2000
10 9 8 7 6 5 4 3 2 1

Cover art by Matt Stawicki

RoC REGISTERED TRADEMARK—MARCA REGISTRADA

Printed in the United States of America

PUBLISHER'S NOTE
This is a work of fiction. Names, characters, places, and incidents either
are the product of the author's imagination or are used fictitiously,
and any resemblance to actual persons, living or dead, business establishments, events or locales is entirely coincidental.

BOOKS ARE AVAILABLE AT QUANTITY DISCOUNTS WHEN USED TO PROMOTE
PRODUCTS OR SERVICES. FOR INFORMATION PLEASE WRITE TO PREMIUM
MARKETING DIVISION, PENGUIN PUTNAM INC., 375 HUDSON STREET, NEW
YORK, NEW YORK 10014.

A first book carries a large burden of gratitude. This book is dedicated to:

My parents, Dr. Bryce and Dr. Robert Mitchell, for raising me to be courageous enough to follow my dreams.

Jennifer Jackson and Jennifer Heddle, for believing in the book and for their excellent suggestions to improve it.

Dr. Mike Brotherton and Leah Cutter, for reading and critiquing an early version of the work, even at risk of life and toe.

Beverly Blanton, because in third grade I promised I would.

All the friends who have encouraged me since then, especially Julie Kitzmiller.

And most of all, Eric—for early morning coffee and endless encouragement. For sharp-eyed critiques and unstinting advice. For inspiring by example. For book-tour adventures past . . . and those yet to come. You have my gratitude and love.

PART 1

"An object at rest tends to stay at rest . . . until acted upon by an outside force."

—Mechanics, Book of Newton 1:1

CHAPTER
1

Lieutenant Thiadora Murphy stood at attention. It was typical of Colonel Osborne to summon her to his office and then keep her waiting. Another way to show the floater her place. Despite six years planetside and her excellent record, that was still how he thought of her.

Her eyes fixed straight ahead, resting on a Topping model of an Avocet 457 Destroyer. The stellar-class ship was depicted with Bussard-Jeans scoops extended, circling a tiny Jovian planet.

The office door sheathed open behind her, and Murphy snapped to tighter attention.

Colonel Osborne walked in with a man she didn't recognize. The stranger was dressed like a civilian: his suit was black synth-silk, cut in smoothly tailored lines. Murphy's stomach tightened. Military intelligence? If Osborne had fabricated a link between her and the floater insurrection at Cago-chi station, he could get her expelled, or worse, convicted of terrorism.

The stranger stopped in front of Murphy. He was good-looking in a prosperous way. His golden-brown skin glowed with health. Shiny auburn hair slicked back from widow's peaks at his temples. There were hard, uncompromising secrets in his gray eyes.

He leaned forward and studied Murphy's face. Murphy knew what he was seeing: wide-set brown eyes, thin lips perched over a too-square jaw. His eyes lingered over the tattooed equations that peeked out from her bangs: the delicate script of Heisenberg's uncertainty principle, the bold lines of Newton's laws, the cuneiform of relativistic mass acceleration. Her floater's marks.

"You don't want Murphy," Osborne said. "She's a floater. Her father was an anti-corporation agitator. With the current resurgence of the rebellion, you couldn't trust her with any sensitive missions. And all that time in weightlessness, with exposure to floater diseases; she's not in top physical condition.

"Lieutenant Haverfield, on the other hand, is an excellent prospect. A man you can trust, and his piloting scores are virtually the same."

The stranger flipped open a palmtop and consulted it. "We are aware of Murphy's background. In fact, that is why we are interested in her."

Oh, gods. Murphy's lips compressed. He *was* going to question her about the rebellion. Seventy disenfranchised floaters capture a manufacturing station, and suddenly her loyalties were suspect. Why couldn't the floaters have waited another six weeks, until she graduated?

"At ease," the stranger said.

Murphy swung into a wide stance.

The man reached into his inner jacket pocket and removed a small plastic disk. "Has Colonel Osbourne told you who I am?" he asked.

Murphy met his eyes. "No, sir."

"My name is Williams, Sean Williams. I'm here to evaluate you." He took her left hand and thumped the disk against her middle finger. When he pulled it away, a dark spot of blood welled up. The disk changed color to a pinky-red. He set it on the corner of Osborne's desk and tapped it. The disk spun.

Osborne said, "I tell you that Haverfield—"

The blood-unit beeped. Williams picked up the disk and pushed it into the palmtop computer. His eyes scanned the screen. As he read, his mouth spread into satisfied smugness. "Haverfield may also be tested," he said, "but Lieutenant Murphy must go through the simulation." Williams tucked the palmtop into his jacket pocket. "My employer insists."

Employer, not commander? Murphy's chest loosened. Williams wasn't military intelligence after all.

Osborne's mouth worked, but he scowled and said, "As you wish."

Murphy's eyebrows rose. Osborne backing down? Williams's employer must have authority over the military. A chill prickled the back of her neck. That meant a major corporate-political interest, one that sat on the council governing interstellar trade and traffic. The kind that considered people like her expendable.

"Dismissed," Osborne barked.

Murphy saluted and exited the colonel's office. As she turned, she snuck another glance at Williams. He was watching her. Their eyes met, and he smiled—like an alligator.

Murphy returned to the barracks and found Talibah Hamadi lounging on the top bunk of their shared quarters. She wore cadet uniform pants and a crisp white shirt unbuttoned to show off a long strand of nonregulation gold and titanium beads. Tali's right foot dangled off the edge of the bed. She listened to a recording, her foot tapping a jazz rhythm against the air.

Murphy closed the door behind her and threw her jacket over one of the chairs in front of the fold-down desks. Then she flopped onto the lower bunk.

Tali popped the speakers out of her ears and leaned over the edge of the bunk to look down at Murphy. "What did Osborne call you in for? To make sure you got your day's allotment of grief?" She wrinkled her pert nose. "What is it with him?"

Murphy shrugged. "Since they've taken him off active duty, I'm the closest thing to a revolutionary he's got to fight."

Pulling black braids out of her face, Tali said, "A few dozen floaters take over one station, and it's a revolution? Right. It's like the Companies being afraid of an uprising of *janitors*." She broke off. "I didn't mean—"

The corner of Murphy's mouth twisted into a half smile. "I know. Some of your best friends are floaters." She waved away Tali's apology. "That's all right. It's a horrible life. That's why I joined the CEA to better myself."

Tali bit her lower lip. "So what did Osborne want?"

Murphy pulled off her cap and dropped it on the table. "A civilian's on-planet." She scratched her scalp, fluffing her brown chin-length hair. "He wants to test me in a simulation."

"Oh?" Tali's eyebrows shot up. "And?"

Murphy shrugged. "That's all he said." Then she grinned and looked askance at the terminal on Tali's side of the desk. "I was hoping you'd tell me. You mean with your creative networking, there's something you don't know?"

"Ha!" Tali leapt off of the bunk in a fluid motion and danced to her side of their shared desk. She tapped on the screen. Her brown hands flew over the panel. "Not for long. Just watch me."

Murphy tugged on her roommate's shoulder, suddenly worried. "No. Forget it. Commandant Harbrolt threatened to cut off your financial aid after your last hack."

The security log-on screen reflected in Tali's black eyes. She flicked her hand dismissively. "Only if I get caught."

Bands of guilt tightened around Murphy's chest. She hadn't meant for Tali to take her joke about hacking seriously—or had she? Had some small part of her been hoping Tali would take up the challenge? She shouldn't have said anything. "Don't do that. I'll know what he wants tomorrow morning."

Tali didn't answer. Her eyes were locked on the flat screen, hands twitching in manipulation of the virtual controls.

Murphy grabbed Tali's shoulder again and shook it.

"Stop it. Whatever's going on, it's not worth the risk of you getting caught."

Tali shrugged her hand off.

Murphy knew from long association that once set on a problem, Tali was relentless. Nothing short of a nuclear blast could keep Tali away from a puzzle.

With a last uneasy glance at her friend, Murphy put on her jacket and slipped out the barracks door.

Reddish-gray sky shone through the high-impact plastic of the tunnel between the barracks and mess hall domes. The landscape beyond the domes was barren. To the east, the hills bordering Jagg's Canyon looked like a row of giant knuckles, the rock worn smooth by millennia of atmospheric turbulence.

Wind swept the powdery dust that covered the planet into cirrus streaks, streaming out between the hills. Looked like another dome-thumper swirling out of the canyon. Murphy's eyes flicked nervously toward the emergency breathing equipment. Stupid reflex. A leftover from her floater childhood. Ares had an atmosphere. A person could breathe it for hours with only minor bronchial irritation. But that knowledge couldn't shake the fears ingrained in her since childhood.

After looking to make sure that no one was around, Murphy opened the emergency pack and checked the filters and air tanks.

When she was done, she continued on to the mess hall. It was filled with students getting trays, ordering food, and gossiping. At one table, engineering students fight-tested flavored gelatin, measuring the inclination at which the cubes fell from their palms.

Murphy's skin tensed as she entered the room. She'd been at the University six years, and still—

"Hey, jellyfish!"

Murphy glanced in the direction of the voice. A group of seated freshmen goggled innocently at her. Murphy exhaled to calm herself. You'd think the students would have gotten over her floater background by now—but no, each first-year class had to hassle her all over again. It made no sense. She'd been here six years; the only thing floater about her was her marks. Murphy turned toward the food trays.

The same mocking voice said, "Been to any floater orgies lately, jellyfish?"

"Why?" Murphy shouted back over her shoulder. "You can't get any on the ground?"

"So how was your fa-ther?" The voice jeered back. Then in a stage-whisper to his companions: "Small floater communities, you know . . . like to keep it in the family."

This was it. Murphy turned on them. The innocent looks devolved into smirks, then concern as she strode up to the table and grabbed the nearest freshman by the lapels of his flight suit.

"My father's lost, rocketing past the galactic rim. Want to join him?" Murphy leaned in until her face was three inches from the young man's nose. "For six years I've endured punks like you. Why? Are your lives so small and pathetic that the only way you can feel big is to put someone else down?" She wanted to jerk him out of his seat and shake him, but her body wasn't up to it. Six years on Ares hadn't made up for her weightless childhood. If this turned into a real fight, she'd get pounded.

His pals were getting out of their seats.

The boy she'd gripped muttered, "No—no, sir. It wasn't me."

But Murphy wasn't listening. "I'm three times the pilot you'll ever be. All your taunts and insults don't change that. I've made something of my life. In six weeks I'll be an officer of the Collective Enforcement Agency. I'm not a floater—not anymore."

A leather-gloved hand settled on Murphy's shoulder. "Lieutenant Murphy, release Cadet Wolford."

Murphy's shoulders tightened. She recognized the voice. In the six years she'd been here, cadet taunts, and her temper, had made her all too familiar with the University's MPs. She released the young man, turned, and saluted.

The black-uniformed MP was Taniguchi, no admirer of hers, but no enemy, either.

"Is it too much to ask that you get through one lunch without pummeling a first-year student?"

"Sir, he—"

"You are the senior classman. It is your duty to display an example of decorum and self-control. You've been listening to the same inane catcalls for six years now, I'd think you'd be immune to them by now."

Murphy flushed, angry at his one-sided reprimand. "Yes, sir."

The MP extracted her promise that she'd try to get through the next six weeks until graduation without further incident. Murphy saluted and turned back to the food machines. She grabbed two packets and left the cafeteria, eating her burrito as she walked.

When Murphy returned to the barracks, Tali was still working. She leaned forward, elbows on the desk, her forehead pressed against the top of the screen. She whispered commands furtively.

Murphy placed a packaged cabbage-and-cheddar pirozhki next to the screen. "Luck?"

"No." Tali leaned back and rubbed her eyes. "There was a shuttle up from Gottsdamerung station yesterday, but the logs are sealed as tight as Osborne's sphincter."

Murphy sat on the bottom bunk, across from the desk. "You weren't able to crack the shuttle logs? You never had trouble before."

Tali tore open the pirozhki's wrapper with her teeth. The smell of cabbage filled the dorm room. "There's some serious corporate moves going on."

"Which company's involved?"

"I couldn't decipher that. They're using sophisticated encryption. But it looks like a founding company. One of the big twelve."

Why would one of the twelve Companies on the ruling council of the Collective be interested in her? The Collective governed interstellar trade and traffic,

and passed the laws the CEA existed to enforce. But
they never interfered with the CEA directly. Not
until now.

Murphy kicked off her boots. Curiouser and curiouser.

Murphy reported to the flight simulation hangar the
next day at six hundred hours. The dimly lit hangar
was filled with cockpits from all makes of ships in the
fleet. Lieutenant Haverfield was waiting with Colonel
Osborne and Williams. Murphy recognized Haverfield
from flight training. A stocky, red-haired student, he
was the second-highest-rated pilot in the University.
Murphy had edged him out for first place.

As she approached, Haverfield's pale gaze sized
her up.

The four of them walked through the cavernous
room, boots echoing in the early morning silence, On
which ship would she be tested? What skills was the
civilian looking for? As they walked past each machine, the list narrowed.

At the end of the hangar, Osborne palmed a door.
The closet normally held maintenance equipment.
Murphy knew the room from hours of repair duty.

The stale air smelled of aluminum shavings and axle
grease. Osborne touched a wall panel and turned on
the lights. The welders and lubrication bots were gone.
They'd been replaced by a matte-gray cube. Four meters square, it was twice the size of most simulators
and took up most of the space in the maintenance
closet. The cube was featureless except for six metal
steps that led up to an airlock hatch.

Murphy looked over at Haverfield. He raised his
red-blond eyebrows, mirroring her surprise. A new
simulator?

"Welcome," said Williams, lounging against the
simulator. "You two are the best pilots at the University. This simulation, however, will tax the limits of
your ability. If you perform well, certain . . . opportu-

nities will become available to you." He slapped the
simulator with his palm. "Who wants to go first?"

Murphy stepped forward. "Sir?"

Osborne said, "What is your problem, Lieutenant?"

"Sir, you haven't briefed us on the craft. How are
we supposed to fly a ship we know nothing about?
Sir."

"Information about the simulator," Williams said,
"is proprietary. All I can say is: in addition to your
reflexes and piloting skills, we are examining how
quickly you interpret and adapt to unfamiliar
controls."

Murphy's lips compressed. It didn't make any sense;
even a test pilot would be briefed on operations, know
how the ship was supposed to work.

"Sir!" Haverfield said. "I'm ready to fly this thing,
sir!"

Osborne grinned. To Williams he said, "That's why
I recommended Lieutenant Haverfield. His uncompromising respect for authority." Osborne glanced side-
long at Murphy. "Haverfield's a pilot you can trust."

Williams's right eyebrow rose. "We shall see, Colonel. We shall see."

Haverfield squared his shoulders and marched up
the stairs, spun open the hatch, and opened the inner
airlock door.

Inside, the simulator was dimly lit. The screens, if
any, were off. Murphy saw nothing but the twinkle of
yellow status lights. Then Haverfield crawled into the
pilot's seat and disappeared into the simulator's dark
interior.

Williams closed the hatch behind Haverfield. He
pulled a portable screen out of an inner jacket pocket
and spoke: "Begin simulation."

"That's all?" Osborne asked.

Murphy shared the colonel's confusion. A simulation was interactive: a team of technicians and instructors monitored and responded to the pilot's state.

Williams smiled without warmth. "Automated. AIs
control his environment and monitor progress. The

simulation is also proprietary: the fewer people involved, the better."

For long minutes, the trainer rocked and swiveled.
Then a low sound, like stressed metal, emanated from
inside— No, a man's scream. The cube shuddered, and
the airlock and hatch popped open.

A blast of hot air hit Murphy in the face, carrying
the smell of burnt hair and urine. She lunged forward
to help, but Osborne shoved her aside and dove into
the trainer.

Murphy tumbled to the concrete floor. Damn her
weakness. She gritted her teeth against both pain and
humiliation. Female and floater. Six years planetside
hadn't made up for her first sixteen years of life spent
in microgravity. Stiffly, Murphy pushed herself off the
ground. She felt her arms and legs for injury. There'd
be bruises tomorrow, but nothing felt broken.

Osborne exited the simulator, carrying Haverfield
over his shoulder. He lowered the lieutenant to the
floor. "You all right, boy?"

Haverfield croaked, "Sir, yes, sir." He sat up and
coughed. The hair on the left side of his head was
singed, and his face was blistered. His eyes, at the
same level as Murphy's, were wide open and terrified.

Williams spoke to his screen again. "Reset simulation." The hatches closed automatically, and the cube
heated until it glowed a dull red. The maintenance
room grew warmer.

A minute later, the red faded and was gone. The
civilian placed his palm against the trainer. "Ready
for our next candidate."

Murphy studied the simulator uneasily. What had
Haverfield faced in there? His burns were serious. If
she screwed up—could she die? Panic fluttered in her
stomach. Was this Osborne's plan to get rid of her?
He had opposed her career every step of the way.
Now that she was only weeks away from graduation,
how far would he go to prevent her from commanding
a CEA vessel?

Murphy forced herself to breathe. It couldn't be a

trap. Osborne hadn't wanted her to be tested. He'd recommended Haverfield. Besides, she wasn't a floater anymore; she couldn't be made to disappear without questions being asked. *Relax*.

Murphy straightened her shoulders. "Sir, I am ready to begin the simulation."

Osborne waved her in.

She walked up the stairs and paused. "Sir, is there a suit?"

Williams's attention focused on her. "Why do you ask?"

"Sir, this airlock. I thought the simulation might include suit training, for verisimilitude, sir."

In truth, she had a hard time walking through any airlock, even a simulation, without double-checking her helmet seals, thanks to Aunt Maisie's training.

"Excellent question," Williams said, making a note on his hand-held, "but a suit is not required."

Murphy nodded and continued up the stairs. Once inside, she closed the hatch. It was a relief to shut Osborne and the others out. The opposite wall of the closet-sized room contained a panel. It was similar to airlock controls she had used as a child, but the screen was labeled with unfamiliar black characters. They were hollow shapes: triangles, polygons, and circles. The inner and outer edges of each shape were embellished with organic-looking spikes and spirals. Strange. Why would a Company build a prototype and label its controls in an unreadable script?

She cycled the airlock and stepped into the room beyond.

The dim flicker of status lights lit up a spherical room a meter and a half in diameter. The walls were inlaid with mosaic touchpads. Murphy had never seen anything like it. The controls were arranged in all directions with no regard for up or down.

In the center of the cramped room was an enormous crash couch. The seat was attached by a steel bar that ran through the pivot of the seat and back and into the curving walls, allowing the couch to swing in the direction of acceleration.

Murphy strapped herself in and leaned forward to examine the ship's controls. Some, like the velocity strip, were standard; others, completely alien. There seemed to be two sets of engine panels. Murphy stared at the text underneath each one. The delicate black script was gibberish.

She noticed a repeating pattern in some of the icons. Tiny triangles arranged in designs like those on playing cards. One. Two. Three. Numbers. Had to be. But why not use the Arabic characters? She examined the tiles closer. The most number of triangles on any one control was seven. Octal? Sweat prickled on Murphy's back. There was something eerie about this ship. What kind of game was Williams playing?

In front of the pilot's ergo, pie-shaped fiber-optic screens framed a hemispherical depression. Was that also a screen?

Murphy touched what she hoped were the integrated fiber-optic controls. IFO screens were simplicity in design, fiber-optic threads that ran from the hull of the ship to flat-panel displays in the cabin. They worked even when power went out, funneling in light from all sides of the ship.

Views of space filled the IFO screens, showing hard, untwinkling stars behind and on each side, and a red hydrogen nebula ahead. The central depression illuminated. It showed her a 360-degree view, as if she were looking through a distorted fish-eye lens. The point directly behind her stretched along the circumference of the display.

If this was a prototype, it was light-years beyond anything Murphy had ever seen.

A silver point glittered in the IFOs.

Murphy fumbled with the controls, searching for magnification. There. Three ships approaching fast.

The hulls were old Avocet 34CX mining trawlers—hulking rectangular ships with fission engines. Old brute-force Orion types. The top half of each ship had been cut away, mining cranes replaced by ion cannons and ship piercers.

Revolutionaries. Had to be. A test of her politics?

Osborne must have told them about her father. Damn. Would she ever escape his dissident shadow?

The ships were at twenty-five hundred meters and closing fast.

Murphy scanned the tiled controls for communications. How was she supposed to run a simulation when she didn't know where or what anything was? Finding it finally, Murphy tapped in the universal ship-to-ship frequency and said, "This is . . ." What were her call letters? Fake it. "This is CEA test ship to the three trawlers. Stand down your weapons and transmit identification codes."

A salvo of ions hit her ship broadside in answer; the simulator slammed Murphy to the left.

So much for protocol.

Murphy scanned the unfamiliar controls. She didn't see anything that looked like a weapon.

Ship piercers launched from two of the trawlers. But two piercers only defined a plane, and Murphy had grown up thinking in volumes. She touched the throttle strip—that at least was familiar—and the strange craft darted away, perpendicular to the incoming piercers.

Simulated acceleration made her sway on the ergo.

She corkscrewed down and back, to get behind the trawlers and—what? There weren't any weapons. She had the drop on both ships, and no idea how to attack. Bluff it out. Murphy spoke into the com, "Surrender, or I will be forced to fire."

No reply. The ion cannons glowed as they heated for another salvo.

Murphy increased engine power. It took her a moment to realize something was different. These weren't the controls she'd used last time. She'd activated the second set.

A stream of white-hot ions fired in slow motion

toward her ship. Then the IFOs filled with reddish-orange hell.

The cannon impact Murphy had braced herself for never came. The red glare on the IFOs didn't fade. The stars were gone. In their place were tangerine-colored convection cells, hot gases that rose and fell, cycling against the IFOs.

The cabin temperature leaped ten degrees. What was going on? This simulation didn't make any sense—hadn't from the beginning. Murphy touched the engine controls again, reversing her actions. The red-orange atmosphere displayed by the IFOs undulated, but Murphy remained trapped.

Sweat dripped between her shoulder blades and from under her small breasts. It was getting hard to breathe.

She tried the first set of engine controls—no response. Her eyes blurred. She estimated the cabin temperature at over fifty degrees centigrade. If she didn't get out of here soon, she'd broil. And she had no illusions about Osborne leaping to her rescue.

Desperate, Murphy tried every control. She slid her fingers along touchpads, spoke to computer screens, tapped icons. Holographic displays popped up and disappeared at random. Their green and blue gridlines overlapped in a chaotic display.

The heat was becoming unbearable, making it difficult to think. She bit back an urge to scream. No. Won't give Osborne the satisfaction. What kind of training was this? No instructions. No explanation. Can't even read the gods-damned script!

Murphy swung her fist through the holographic displays and pounded the controls.

The simulator shuddered, and then the plasma hell was gone, replaced by unfamiliar stars, pinpoints of light in ebony velvet.

Everything went black.

A cold wave of air hit Murphy's face, evaporating the sweat and chilling her. The blue-white fluorescents of the maintenance room glared through the airlock.

Williams reached in and offered his hand. Murphy grasped it and he pulled her out.

"Excellent," he said, clasping her wrist. "That was excellent."

It was? She wasn't sure what she'd done. Murphy shivered in the relative cold of the maintenance room. The sudden change in temperature nauseated her.

Haverfield stood against the wall, wrapped in a blanket from one of the medipaks in the simulator room, shivering.

The civilian beamed. "What did I tell you, Osborne? She performed as well as predicted." He clapped Murphy on the shoulder. "We have great things in store for you."

Osborne's face was stone. "What about Haverfield?"

Williams turned and regarded the junior officer. "He may go. Murphy's the pilot we want. We have no need of him."

Haverfield's eyes narrowed. But he didn't look at Williams; he glared at Murphy.

The civilian held out a blanket to Murphy. "Get cleaned up, eat breakfast, and meet me in Osborne's office at eight hundred hours."

"Sir, I have class at—"

Osborne brushed aside her argument. "This is more important."

Murphy ran into Haverfield later as he was coming out of the infirmary. She'd taken the long way back to the barracks after her post-quantum theory class to check on him.

His face was red and puffy. A pink sim-skin patch engulfed his right cheek. His jacket was slung loosely over shoulder bandages. When he caught sight of her, he stopped and stared.

Murphy held out her hand. "No hard feelings?" She hoped he wouldn't hold a grudge against her for outperforming him. Haverfield was a good pilot, and they might have to work together in their military careers.

He stared at her hand a moment, his eyes focusing

on the too-thin palm and delicate fingers. Then he took it in a firm shake. "No hard feelings. You got lucky this morning, and I won't hold that against you."

Murphy frowned. "It wasn't luck."

"What was it, then?"

Murphy shook her head in disgust and turned to leave.

He grabbed Murphy's shoulder. "I didn't mean that as an insult." His face was earnest. "I want to know. What did you do in that simulation that I didn't? Why did you pass and I fail?"

Murphy relaxed. She understood needing to know—and being too proud to ask for help. She leaned against the wall and studied her fingertips, remembering. "I'm not sure. The interior of the ship was strange—but also familiar. Ships attacked me, then—"

"Haverfield, this the floater who beat you in that flight sim?" A trio of young men, dressed in fatigues, sauntered down the hall toward them. The one in front stared at the tattoos peeking out from her hairline. Slicked-back brown hair topped the long angular features of his face. The label on his flight suit read: JENKS.

"Shut up," said Haverfield.

Jenks cocked his head, studying Murphy's form. "There isn't much to her. Looks like a bag of sticks. She's a pilot? How does she take the gees?"

Murphy's lips curled back. "Better than a flaccid button-pusher like you. I heard you peed your flight suit during the Möbius course."

Haverfield's arm checked Jenks's lunge toward Murphy. "She's a fine pilot," Haverfield grumbled. "One of the best at the University."

"Better than you?" Jenks asked with mock disbelief. "Better than the incomparable Haverfield?"

Haverfield's face darkened. "I didn't say that."

"Then, why'd she pound your butt like a gong in that sim?"

A second classmate chimed in, "I've heard the University's token floater is some kind of piloting prodigy. A real freak. Apparently it runs in her family."

The conversation was now going downhill fast, and any further disciplinary actions on Murphy's record might influence her commission. "Be seeing you," she told Haverfield and backed away down the hall.

He was still arguing with his companions when she turned the corner.

When Murphy entered Osborne's office, Williams rose from the desk and shook her hand. He'd exchanged his gray suit for one of shimmering navy. His hand was warm and rich-man's soft. He smelled of expensive cologne.

They were alone in the room. Osborne, apparently, hadn't been invited.

Williams said, "I am a recruiting agent." He gestured to a chair. "Please. Sit."

Murphy folded her lanky body onto the molded plastic.

Williams walked to her side of the desk and sat on the edge of the tempered glass. "Your performance in the simulation was exemplary. My employers wish to hire you. A permanent position as a pilot. The terms are most generous."

Murphy wondered who offered those terms. She'd enlisted with the military as a way to better herself without working for a company that exploited floaters. She didn't want to live as a floater, but she didn't want to have a hand in oppressing them, either. "Thank you," she said. "But I already have a career with the CEA."

Williams ran his hands through his auburn hair, slicking it back. "I don't think you understand the magnitude of this offer." He pulled a portable screen out of his jacket pocket and tapped open a file, then held the reader out to her.

Murphy glanced at the contract. The employer was listed as "a member corporation of the Collective." So it *was* one of the big twelve, the megacorporations that ran the galactic government. Seventy-five years ago, the Plutocrat wars had ended in a settlement: Local governments handled planetary matters, but space habitations and interstellar issues came under the purview of the Collective.

But she was still on-planet, in training for the CEA. Williams's Company was stepping outside of its authority by contacting her. Murphy asked, "Which Company would I be working for?"

Williams brushed imaginary lint off his shoulder. "That's tactical information and will be revealed after you have signed. The employer is not important. Read the terms of the agreement."

She did. The money was amazing—but she'd still be working for a Company. Her mind flashed back to the sixteen-hour workdays, leaking reactors, and slave wages she had fought so hard to escape. Even though she would be skilled labor, it didn't sit well. She couldn't see herself working for an entity that treated her people as a disposable resource. "It's quite generous, but—"

"You must accept." He laughed nervously. "You'd be crazy to turn down this offer. There would be repercussions." He met her eyes. "For both of us."

Murphy cocked her head. "Are you threatening me?"

"No, no. Merely making you aware of all pertinent facts." He held forth a portable screen. "May I have your palm print?"

"No," Murphy said firmly. "The CEA gave me a scholarship; they lifted me out of floater life. The military gave me hope when I most needed it, gave me something to strive for. I won't work for a Company, no matter how well paid. I want to enforce the law, to serve justice."

Williams's left eyebrow arched sardonically. "And you think working for the CEA will accomplish that?"

"Yes." She gestured at her too-thin arms and under-muscled legs. "It wasn't easy being the first, the only, floater to attend the University. I suffered ten months of centrifugal conditioning just to be able to stand on this planet. Over the last six years I've endured prejudice, instructors' low expectations, and hazing." She stood. "I am about to graduate with honors. I don't know if you can understand how much that means to me, but I'm not going to walk away from it."

His brow wrinkled with concern. "You won't reconsider?"

Murphy's tone softened. "I'm sorry, but my decision is final." She turned to leave.

"Wait!" Williams pressed a datacube into her hand. "If you change your mind, or discover that military service is not all you believe it to be, contact me."

Murphy pressed her lips together. Never, she wanted to say. She wouldn't be bought back into Company service. Not after fighting her whole life to be free. She wasn't a floater anymore, so poor that she had to trust fate and Company promises for the food she ate and the air she breathed. With a military career, she'd pay her own way—and bring to justice any Company that dared break the law in her jurisdiction.

She wanted to tell Williams this, to throw the datacube in his face. But to avoid further argument, she nodded and slipped it into her jacket.

That night, Murphy huddled in her bunk, the crisp white sheets pulled up to her chin. The storm she'd seen brewing yesterday had fulfilled its promise. She wished Tali didn't have night watch. Another clang rattled the University's dome, and she shivered.

Intellectually, Murphy knew there was atmosphere outside the dome. Ares's gravitational pull held a thin covering of sulfur-tainted air. When a breach occurred, students and staff collected in the main hall and waited for the repair crew to patch the dome.

She knew she wasn't in danger, but her gut didn't buy it. A floater childhood had taught her how fragile life could be. Murphy didn't share her fellow students faith in an atmosphere.

Another clang. Murphy's heart clenched. She wrapped

the sheets tighter around herself. If she closed her eyes, she could pretend it was a pressure suit.

Someone pounded on the door.

Murphy jumped. She panted a moment before answering, "Come in."

Jenks rushed in. His dark hair was tousled, his eyes wild. He fell on his knees beside her bunk. "You've got to save him—it's my fault, if anything happens to him."

Murphy drew back against the wall. "What happened?"

"Haverfield stole a shuttle and took it into the storm."

"In this storm? Is he insane?"

"The storm's why he went. To prove himself," Jenks said. "Me and some of the guys were ribbing him about the sim—we didn't mean any harm by it— we were talking about your piloting record, and I laughed and said that you could've flown through a class-V storm like this. I dared him to. I didn't expect him to take me seriously—but he did. He's flying to Jagg's Canyon to prove he's better than you."

"Oh, gods."

Jagg's Canyon shot straight out of the planetoid's crust, the result of a grazing blow from the rock that used to be Ares's moon. The walls were gray stone, a kilometer high and half a kilometer wide. High-pressure shears blasted up from the canyon wall, crushing atmospheric craft against the dense cliffs. In the time she had been here, it had killed four cadets.

Jagg's was dangerous enough in clear weather, but in a class-V storm—lethal.

"I lost radio contact eight minutes ago," Jenks said.

In the silence that followed, the storm roared against the station's dome.

"Then, he's dead," she said. "Jagg's smashed him flat." Her throat tightened with remorse. What part, however passive, had she played in the impulse that led to Haverfield's doom?

"No," Jenks said. "He made it down. His leg's broken, but he's alive."

"What?" Murphy leapt to the com. "Then we have to notify ground rescue."

Jenks's hand came down on hers, stopping her from placing the call. "Ground rescue won't fly in this. The winds are at three hundred kilometers per hour and all atmospheric craft have been grounded." Jenks drew a long breath. "His ship is split in half, and there's no life support. His lungs will be parboiled by the time ground rescue could reach him by crawler. You're his only hope. No one can fly through those winds. No one but you."

Murphy pulled her hand away from his and backed up a step. "You want me to attempt a rescue that ground control, with all their training and equipment, won't?"

"Ground control has the equipment, but they don't have your skill. You fly better than most people breathe."

Murphy considered his words. She was good—but good enough to fly Jagg's through a class-V storm? A thrill of fear and challenge fluttered in her stomach. For a moment she wanted to make the attempt, for the same stupid reason that had sent Haverfield out there, just to see if she could. Then sense reasserted itself. "I can't go against regulations. Not this close to graduation. There're enough people around here who want to see me bumped as it is."

Jenks's expression sobered. "Prichett told me you wouldn't help. But you have to—you're the only pilot at the University with the skill to save him."

Murphy was torn. Part of her was afraid of the storm and the potential consequences to her career, and part of her was gratified by the compliment.

Jenks pressed on. "You've flown in high-wind conditions before—the records say that you flew through a class-IV storm last winter. The weather turned bad during a training exercise, and you were the only one who could get through the storm to summon ground rescue."

"Yes, but that was different. My instructor ordered me to go for help. Here, I don't have any authority to attempt a rescue. I'd have to contact the control tower and ask them for clearance."

"They won't let you fly—it's too dangerous." He frowned. "You're going to let a man die because you're afraid of regulations? I'd think anyone who'd fight the system and become the first floater to attend CMU would have the courage to bend a few rules. Especially when a man's life is at stake."

Jenks's accusation hit her like a blow. He was right. She wouldn't have been the first floater to attend the University if she hadn't been willing to break with convention. Could she now turn away from saving a man's life because she was afraid of a reprimand?

"I don't have a ship," she protested.

"Yes you do," Jenks said. "My father gave me a sportster as an early graduation present. It's a solid ship, fast and maneuverable, an Avocet Phaeton. You've got to do it, Murphy. His life is in your hands."

Murphy listened to the wind screaming against the dome. She'd turned her back on floater life to make something of herself in the grounder world. Why should she risk that to help a smart-ass pilot she didn't even like?

Then again, if she saved Haverfield, she would no longer be considered lower class, a floater, a throw-away worker, a shadow of her father's legend. Just this once, she could do something Colonel Osborne would have to respect. Just this once, she'd be a hero.

"He's running out of air. Murphy, please."

"Shit. This is the stupidest stunt . . ." She sighed. "I'll do it."

"That's great!" Jenks grinned and he pumped her hand. "That's really great of you. I knew you wouldn't let us down."

Murphy smiled, but halfheartedly. She was the only person who could save Haverfield, but that didn't stop a pang of misgiving—and fear. She'd never flown in a class-V storm, no one had, without crashing, especially not in a rich man's toy car. But wasn't doing what had to be done—in spite of the fear—what courage was all about?

The private garage was empty, illuminated only by amber safety lights set into the wall at chest height. The roar of the storm was deafening against the bay doors.

The Avocet Phaeton was a sweet atmospheric vehicle. Sleek wings swept back from a wasp-shaped body. A nest of chromed exhaust pipes swarmed around the wheels and back of the car. Its detailing gleamed black and silver.

"Rich," she said as she climbed into its velvet upholstery.

Jenks leaned in and handed her a scrap of paper. "These are the coordinates Haverfield gave when he crashed." He swallowed. "Thanks for doing this, Murphy. I know he's unbearably proud, but he doesn't deserve to die for it."

"So why didn't you stop him?"

He reddened. "I didn't think he really meant to do it. I didn't know he was gone until he called in." After a pause, Jenks grasped her shoulder. "You'll never know how much this means to me, Murphy."

"I haven't brought him back yet." She shrugged his hand off, embarrassed, and Jenks stepped away from the Phaeton.

She eased the ship up to the bay doors on low power. Murphy wouldn't apply full thrust until she taxied. She wanted to put as much of the storm as she could between her and the control tower before she powered up. Jenks opened the bay door from the wall panel controls.

Chaos waited outside. Tan and gray whorls of dust limited visibility to ten meters. Balls of sulfur-laden water the size and shape of Murphy's thumb cut streaks through the dust.

The ship pitched and yawed when the winds hit the open bay. She applied forward thrust to keep the Phaeton from flipping back onto its left wing. The ship vibrated as its engines fought the blast, then it crept out of the hangar.

A high-velocity crosswind tilted the craft onto two wheels. Murphy angled into the wind and revved the engine.

She fought to stay upright. The wind grabbed the Phaeton and lifted it into the air. Turbulence tossed the ship back down, and she opened the throttle farther to gain altitude.

Murphy watched the instruments as she fought the driving headwind, until the ship stabilized.

She breathed out, centering herself, and relaxed into an alternate perspective, the one she had grown up in. To a floater there was no up, no down; just close and far away. Floaters thought in three dimensions. The ground was just another wall.

The craft dipped toward the horizon.

She pulled back. Gravity. Murphy balanced the two perspectives: a floater's ability to intuit three dimensions, and a grounder's constant awareness of the gravitational field. Her talent navigated that edge. Her edge.

She angled toward Jagg's Canyon.

A sizzling pop spattered off her right wing. Lightning strike. The air exploded with thunder. Deafened, Murphy fought to keep the ship level.

"Praise Faraday," she prayed automatically. Farther off, a second boom of thunder reverberated in her stomach.

A high wind cut across her left wing. The pressure dropped on that side and suddenly the craft inverted. A loose stylus fell toward the ceiling. There was a clatter from the back of the ship as items shifted in the stow-boxes.

Murphy rolled the Phaeton. The altimeter dropped to two hundred meters, one hundred, fifty.

A stone outcropping jutted out of the haze. Murphy

banked hard to the right and poured on the throttle
to gain altitude. Another stone spike cut the dust, sixty
meters high. Murphy fought the stick and dodged left.
The Phaeton clipped the rock. Sparks flew from the
right wingtip.

"Stabilize, goddamn it," Murphy swore.

The Phaeton wobbled and caught. With the wingtip
gone, it listed to the right.

The slate-colored cliffs of Jagg's Canyon bisected
the horizon in front of her. She corrected her velocity
vector and headed for Haverfield's coordinates.

High pressure shears threw dust and debris up from
the canyon floor. It crashed over the rim in an opaque
wave. She was going to need more momentum than
the sportster's small engine could supply to break
through those winds.

Murphy inverted the craft, on purpose this time, and
the ground rolled crazily in the window. For a second,
she lost her floater's perspective and nearly panicked.
Then the ground was just a wall again.

Inverted, the airfoils sucked the Phaeton toward the
ground. It dove, trading altitude for speed. Her attention flicked back and forth between the altimeter and
the velocity readouts.

The ship shuddered when she hit the wall of dust.
Her window turned brown, all visibility gone. She had
only the altimeter and the transponder to keep her
from crashing into the ground or the canyon walls.

When the transponder said she was directly over
the canyon, she rolled the Phaeton into a straight dive.
Her vision tunneled as the acceleration slammed her
back into the seat. A rock spanged off her left wing,
and Murphy's heart nearly stopped. It wasn't the canyon wall. Not yet.

Suddenly the canyon floor burst into view. She was
below the wind shear.

Her Phaeton dropped below the canyon rim, seconds before the updrafts plowed it toward the cliff
face. It shuddered as wind shear off the canyon walls

threatened to flip the craft once more, and Murphy fought to right the ship.

The engine stalled.

The sportster dropped like a stone. *One-one-thousand, Two-one-thousand.* The ground rushed up. *Three-one-thousand.* Murphy flicked the starter. *Four-one-thousand.* The engine sputtered. *Five-one-thousand.* Caught. *Six-one-thousand.* Murphy pushed the throttle full in and pulled the craft out of its dive. The ground rushed by thirty meters below.

The air was calm inside the canyon. Murphy breathed a deep sigh of relief and turned the sportster in a tight spiral over Haverfield's coordinates.

The ground was empty.

Did Jenks miscalculate? She widened her search pattern. Was Haverfield's transponder faulty? Unrelieved gray stone met the horizon. A cold dread filtered in from the back of her mind and dripped down her spine.

She pushed the thought away. Jenks must have given her the wrong coordinates. He'd been scared. He must have transposed digits. Hand shaking, she flipped open the com.

There was no connection. Only static. The signal couldn't get through the storm and the canyon walls.

The winds above the canyon rim howled with increasing velocity. No one else could make it through the storm. If she turned back now and Haverfield was in the canyon, he would die.

And she'd be a failure. Again.

Murphy had to find him. She had already gone against search-and-rescue protocol, by putting her own life in jeopardy to find Haverfield, but she had no choice. She searched up and down the canyon floor, scanning every meter of ground.

Nothing. He wasn't there.

With no options left, she ran the Phaeton down to the shallow entrance of the canyon and back into the storm. The winds were picking up speed. This was no time for stealth. She drove the ship higher, trying to rise above the storm.

The Phaeton broke out of the soot-colored haze into clear sky. The storm below her looked like a solid horizon. The clouds roiled beneath her like a restless landscape.

Two gnats broke out of a cloud on her left. They moved fast, cutting the vapor into streamers behind them. Murphy swallowed. Even at this distance she recognized the green and black markings of the University police.

"Private craft, N9UDSEW3," a man's voice called over the hailing frequency. "You are flying a stolen vehicle in an unauthorized airspace. Identify your pilot."

Murphy's heart stopped. She closed her eyes and inhaled. "Lieutenant Thiadora Murphy. I commandeered this vessel for a rescue mission."

"There is no record of a rescue attempt. Who is in danger?"

"Lieutenant Haverfield, sir."

There was a pause. "The tower says Haverfield reported for watch duty thirty minutes ago."

The police scouters followed the Phaeton down. Murphy taxied it to the hangar through puddles of sulfurous water. A heavy rain spattered against the windshield, leaving tan streaks across the glass.

Two MPs were questioning Jenks. When she taxied in to the hangar and opened the cockpit, Jenks turned and pointed.

"That's her," Jenks said. "That's the woman who stole my Phaeton."

CHAPTER 2

When Murphy climbed down from the shuttle, three MPs were waiting. One aimed a needler-rifle at her. The second crawled into the Phaeton.

Murphy put her hands on top of her head and said, "What the hell—"

"We'll ask the questions," the third MP said. He passed a fist-sized scanner over her. He nodded to the first MP, "She's clean."

"*She* may be," said the MP in the vehicle, "but look at this." He stood up, holding a gyro-rifle.

It whined like a wasp as he moved it, internal gyroscopes holding it on target. The matte-black surface was scarred with nicks and scuff marks. Murphy had used such weapons in training exercises. They were designed for low-gee combat.

"There's five crates of these in the stow-boxes," the MP said. He looked at Murphy. "Who did you plan to meet out there?"

"No one. Jenks told me Haverfield had crashed in the storm. He loaned me the Phaeton so I could rescue him. I don't know anything about the guns."

"Sure you don't," said the man holding the contraband. He called to Jenks, "Lieutenant, these your guns?"

Jenks shook his head. "No, sir. Never saw them before."

"He's lying!" Murphy said. She made a move toward Jenks and was caught short by the MP who'd tracked her with his needler. "Jenks, tell them the truth."

The MP holding her arm shook her and nodded toward the door. "Save it for the court-martial."

And with that, the three MPs led her to a detainment cell in the administrative wing.

The room was not unlike her barracks. It had the same prefabricated floor plan: bed and desk extruded from the walls. The only difference was the electronics weren't installed. A white plastic panel was set into the desk where the screen should be. Even the light controls were outside of the room.

"You'll have a chance to clean up in the morning before the council hears your case," one MP said. With no more preamble than that, the door shut and Murphy was left in darkness.

She felt her way to the bed and lay down, punched the mattress. She'd been set up.

But by whom? And why? By Haverfield, as revenge for outperforming him in the simulation? By Osborne, to keep her from graduating? By Jenks, for some reason of his own? Was it because she was a floater? Murphy tried to put her background behind her, but people still assumed she was dirty, frail, diseased, and immoral. The insults were a constant in her life. But no one had ever tried to discredit her before.

Or had Williams done it to punish her for not accepting his offer? Had his money been enough to buy Jenks's and Haverfield's collusion?

Murphy rubbed the tight cords in the back of her neck. That was crazy, paranoid, floater thinking. Corporations didn't go out of their way to destroy people. There must be a simpler explanation.

She rolled over. How would she explain herself to the council? If they believed Jenks's story—that she was a rebel collaborator—she would be indentured, or worse. With the recent insurrections, the council would be obliged to make an example of her. Murphy shook her head to clear it. Can't think that way, she'd make them understand what really happened. Her

life's ambition was to make something of herself, to
be a CEA officer. Somehow, she would convince them
that she'd been set up.

But what then? She had taken a ship out without
ground clearance. Even if she proved she hadn't stolen
it and knew nothing about the guns, she'd still broken
the rules. It would affect her commission. She could
kiss off the first-lieutenant's position she'd wangled on
the *Juno VI*. Likely they'd have her spend the next
two years flying transport. Her lips compressed.

She'd make Jenks pay for every second.

In the morning the MPs brought her a clean uniform and breakfast consisting of a biscuit and cup of
coffee. After she had eaten, they escorted her to the
council room.

A large molded-glass table dominated the chamber.
It was the color of smoke and shaped like a parabola.
Before each of the seven seats, a screen was set into
its surface.

A second small table stood at its focus. Murphy was
led to the rightmost of three seats. Moments later,
Jenks and Haverfield sat down beside her.

Murphy leaned over and whispered, "You're going
to explain everything Jenks, you understand?"

Jenks smiled blandly. "Of course I will."

Murphy leaned over farther and spoke to Haverfield. "Do you know what's going on? Are you
involved?"

Haverfield looked straight ahead and did not respond.

The council arrived. She, Jenks, and Haverfield
stood as the commandant and three instructors filed
behind the curved table and sat down.

Osborne watched Murphy as he took his seat, a hint
of triumph on his florid face.

Harbrolt, the University's headmaster, was a stocky
woman with cropped gray hair. Her brown eyes glittered with authority. Murphy had only met her briefly,
at commencement and again when she was awarded

her first-pilot's medals. The commandant had a reputation for being hard, but fair.

The other two members of the council were Wickmont, a propulsion scientist, and Ng, a grizzled veteran of the border wars. Murphy had taken navigation and military ethics from Wickmont. She counted him as a friend. Ng, she knew only by reputation. He'd closed down the McNally pirating ring in '06 and helped with the sting that got Kiplinger Environmental ousted from the council. She hoped he didn't share Osborne's prejudices against floaters.

When Commandant Harbrolt spoke, her resonant voice filled the room. "Lieutenant Murphy, the charges against you are grave. You have the right to retain counsel. Do you wish to exercise that right?"

The balance in her account wouldn't pay for a two-minute off-world phone call to an attorney, much less buy representation. "No, sir. I will abide by the council's decision."

Osborne rose to his feet and consulted the data screen in front of him. "Lieutenant Thiadora Murphy, you stand accused of stealing a private vehicle, flying without clearance, and possession of stolen arms."

"Sir, I didn't ste—"

Harbrolt glared at Murphy. "Order. You will remain quiet as the charges are read."

Murphy's cheeks heated. She subsided back into her chair.

Harbrolt waved to Osborne. "Continue."

Osborne puffed out his chest and said, "This proceeding will provide evidence to show that at four hundred hours twenty-three minutes, an encoded transmission was sent from the University to an unregistered ship orbiting Gottsdamerung. Eight minutes later, Lieutenant Murphy took a private vehicle into the storm, without permission from its owner, and in possession of five crates of rifles. It is my belief that Murphy was not acting alone. I will prove her actions were part of a larger conspiracy to sabotage the station."

Murphy fumed. Surely the council could see through those lies. It didn't make any sense. Rebels? Crates of guns? If she really was a traitor, there were other things she could do that would help the rebels more. But making that point wouldn't help her case.

"Fortunately," Osborne continued, "Lieutenant Jenks was on watch that night and noticed Murphy's unauthorized access of the hangar. If he had not done so, Murphy's actions, under cover of the storm, might have gone completely undetected." Osborne looked at Murphy significantly. "And who is to say that last night's performance was the first time such goings-on have occurred? I have often cautioned the board against the advisability of letting into our ranks a person of . . . suspect allegiances."

Murphy shot to her feet. "That is a lie—"

Harbrolt banged her gavel again. "Lieutenant Murphy. You will be given a chance to address Colonel Osborne's accusations. For now, hold your seat. Such outbursts do not help your case."

Murphy sunk back into her seat, reluctantly. Her face was hot. Jenks wouldn't meet her eyes.

"I object." Professor Wickmont pounded his bony fist on the table. "Colonel Osborne is indulging in speculation. The facts are that a ship was taken out into last night's storm. The motivations of the pilot and her connection to the weapons found on board have not been established."

Harbrolt nodded. "Sustained. Colonel Osborne, please restrict your comments to statements of fact."

"Fact," Osborne said, "Lieutenant Murphy, fully in knowledge of University procedures and flight regulations, willfully took a vehicle out into a storm without authorization. Fact, we have a sworn statement from the owner of that vehicle that Lieutenant Murphy did so without his authorization. Fact, when the ship and Lieutenant Murphy were recovered, several crates of stolen rifles were found on board. Those items alone are damning. Add to that Lieutenant Murphy's background and political ties, and," he spread his hands before the council, "the picture is clear." Osborne inclined his head. "That is all."

Harbrolt directed her laser-sharp gaze at Murphy and said, "The charges against you are grave. Do you have anything to say in your defense?"

"Yes, sir. The truth is very different from the story presented by Colonel Osborne. I did take a ship out without ground clearancc. Yes, I should be punished for that. But Jenks begged me to take the ship out, and the guns . . ." Murphy shook her head, wide-eyed. "I knew nothing about them."

Ng leaned forward on the smoke-gray glass and asked, "If you were not running guns, why, then, did you go out into the storm?"

Murphy mct his gaze squarely. "To save Lieutenant Haverfield's life. Jenks broke into my room last night and told me Haverfield had stolen a flight trainer and gone into the storm. That Haverfield was upset after I outperformed him in a simulation and wanted to prove he was a better pilot than I. But he crashed. I went out into the storm to save him."

Osborne's face showed exaggerated surprise. "Why didn't you follow procedure and notify ground rescue?"

Murphy's face reddened. "Ground rescue couldn't have flown through a class-V storm. The way Jenks told it, the canopy of Haverfield's trainer was shattered. If someone didn't fly out there and rescue him, Haverfield's lungs would have cooked. I was the only one who could do it."

Osborne's tone was sarcastic. "You believed that you, alone in a private car, would be more effective than ground rescue, with all their equipment and training?"

"Yes, sir."

"You must have a high opinion of your abilities," said Ng, steepling his gnarled fingers.

"Yes, sir," Murphy said, staring ahead.

Osborne continued, "If Jenks came to your room last night and pleaded with you to go out into the storm and save his friend, why would he then turn around and report his aircraft stolen?"

"I don't know, sir." She looked askance at Jenks. "I'd like the answer to that myself."

Harbrolt leaned forward on her elbows. "Lieutenant Jenks, did you at any time last night go to Lieutenant Murphy's quarters?"

"No, sir. I ate dinner in the mess hall, showered, and reported to my midnight watch at the tower."

Murphy whirled on Jenks. "That's a lie." Her voice rose in volume. "Tell the truth or I'll—"

"Lieutenant Murphy!" The commandant's voice cut through her anger like a knife. "You will respect these proceedings or I will have you removed."

Murphy lowered to her seat and studied Jenks's face. His breathing was relaxed, his face calm. Why was he setting her up? Because he hated floaters?

Or was Williams pulling the strings? Did he plan to ruin her military career so that she'd have to accept his offer?

Harbrolt asked Jenks, "Did anything unusual occur during your watch?"

"Yes, sir. At four hundred hours I noticed one of the hangar doors in the private garage was opening. That's when I discovered my Phaeton had been stolen. Happened right on the monitor while I was watching. With the storm, Murphy must have supposed the watch would be busy observing weather conditions and wouldn't notice a missing—"

"Objection," Wickmont said. "Assumes motives not in evidence."

"Sustained," declared Harbrolt. "Lieutenant, please restrict your statements to matters of fact."

"Yes, sir. Anyway, I saw the hangar door open on the monitor. I reoriented the cameras to check the ships. That's when I discovered that a private car— my car—was gone."

"What did you do after that?" Harbrolt asked.

"I called security."

Osborne broke in. "Jenks, what do you make of

Lieutenant Murphy's story that you came to her room and prompted her to take your ship out into the storm?"

"It doesn't make any sense. I don't know how she expected anyone to believe it."

Osborne directed his attention to Haverfield. "Lieutenant. Did you at any time last night steal a shuttle and go out into the storm?"

Haverfield glanced sideways at Murphy. He licked his lips. "No, sir."

"Did you tell Lieutenant Jenks that you were going to steal a shuttle and go out into the storm?"

"No, sir."

"Can you account for your whereabouts last night?"

"Yes, sir. I was in the student lounge with Dorsey and Wong, playing Strategeon. Then I went on watch."

"Thank you, Lieutenant." Osborne nodded at Haverfield and sat down.

Harbrolt asked, "Colonel Wickmont, have you finished investigating the security log for the tower?"

"If I may?" He gestured at the wall behind Murphy. Harbrolt nodded.

Wickmont transferred the tower's security log to the wall. Murphy turned to watch.

Jenks sat alone in the tower, recording wind speed and direction, when something off-screen caught his attention. Moments later he jumped up, checked several screens, spoke a few commands, and dialed security.

Wickmont's thin face was serious. "This log was recorded at two hundred fourteen hours, precisely when Lieutenant Murphy left the hangar. I have reviewed the entire log. At no time did Jenks leave his post."

"Do you have a rebuttal?" Harbrolt asked Murphy.

How could this be happening? Murphy held out her hands palm up. "The log must have been modified. I tell you the truth: Jenks came to my room last night. He pleaded with me to take his car out in the storm."

"Are you suggesting that a junior-grade lieutenant

would have the knowledge and resources to break into the security system, record a false log, and edit it seamlessly into the file?" Osborne asked.

Tali could have done it as a second-year cadet, but of course Murphy couldn't say that. "Check my room's security tapes. It'll show he was there."

Osborne leaned forward, almost smiling. "Funny you suggest that. The recorder for your room malfunctioned last night. The data files are corrupt. You wouldn't know anything about that, would you? Perhaps your friends in the rebellion—"

"Enough," Harbrolt interrupted. "Is there further evidence to present?"

"If you would let me check the tower's video log," Murphy said, "I'm sure I could find evidence of tampering."

"Find it," Osborne asked, "or create it?"

Murphy bit back a reply.

"The files you question have been exhaustively examined," Harbrolt said. "No such tampering is in evidence."

Osborne was right. Jenks didn't have the skill to alter the security log, but then, maybe he wasn't working alone. She thought of Sean Williams as she stared at Osborne. One wanted her, the other wanted her gone.

Osborne met her gaze, leaned back, and sucked his teeth.

She wanted to speak out, voice her suspicions. But no. He was an instructor, with tenure. A groundless accusation would only hurt her case. She needed evidence.

"Are there closing statements from the floor?" Harbrolt asked.

Murphy stood. She closed her eyes to center herself, breathed out. Then she faced the council.

"I did fly into the storm without authorization. I don't deny that. But my intentions were the best possible. I believed that a fellow lieutenant's life was in danger. And I believed only I could save him. Why

Jenks misled me, I don't know. All I have are theories that I can't prove. I don't know who tampered with the security video. I only hope that the council will find answers to these questions before it renders a decision." She sat down.

"Any closing statements from the council?"

Osborne took the podium. "I would like to remind the council that Lieutenant Murphy was accepted into the University over my strong objections. No one more than I hoped she would overcome the disadvantages of her floater upbringing. However, her actions reinforce the fact that a culture without a solid moral reference cannot produce a suitable candidate. Her freely admitted situational ethics prove this. She is a danger to this institution. At best, the events of last night were irresponsible. At worst, Lieutenant Murphy is a rebel sympathizer."

Wickmont held up his forefinger. "That has yet to be proven. Murphy's politics are not on trial here. Her father may have been a leader in the rebel community, but that does not mean—"

Osborne bellowed, "How can we train and equip a potential enemy of the Collective in the latest warship technology?"

"Colonel Osborne, your views on that subject are well-known." The commandant's voice was sharp. "You will maintain order in this council or I will have you removed. Are there any other closing statements?"

Wickmont stood, his slender frame leaning forward, as if into a headwind. "I ask that Lieutenant Murphy's record be taken into account when this council renders its decision. I have taught her in several classes and found her to be a talented student. She is the highest-ranked pilot the University has ever produced. It would be a shame if such a promising career were cut short by one impetuous act."

Harbrolt's lips tightened. "There is no room in the CEA for impiety. But your request is noted." She stood and tapped the screen in front of her. "The council will discuss this matter and reconvene at eight hundred hours with a decision." The rest of the council rose and left.

A black-helmeted MP returned Murphy to her cell.

Murphy rubbed her temples as she sat on the bunk waiting. Her case was now a matter of politics. A handful of disenfranchised floaters had just captured a Telesto Inc. terraforming station in the Tau Ceti system. With a new rebellion underway and this infraction on her record, the staff of the University would never trust her with command of a military vessel, even if she wasn't convicted of treason. At best, she would end up with command of a transport, and ferry techs from one station to the next for the rest of her career. At worst . . . Murphy's mind shied away from what would happen to her if she were convicted of treason, but she forced herself to face it. At worst, if Osborne's version of the story was believed, she could be permanently indentured . . . or executed.

She sat in the small room for six hours. Other than excursions to the rest room and lunch, there was nothing to do. Except worry. At eighteen hundred hours, an MP brought her dinner.

"What's taking so long?"

The man set the tray down on the desk. "They've been arguing all day. The vote's deadlocked."

"Could you bring me a portable screen? I'm going mad with boredom."

The MP smiled. "I'll see what I can do."

Minutes later, the door slid open a crack, and Tali poked her head in.

"Thank Newton! How'd you—"

"—Shhsst." Tali slipped inside. "I'm not exactly supposed to be here."

"How'd you find out where I was being held?"

Tali perched on top of the desk, cross-legged. "The news is all over campus. I know Harris, I got him to let me in. Did you really steal a fighter and strafe the power plant?"

Murphy groaned.

"Didn't sound like you. What happened?"

"Jenks came to my room last night with a fabricated story about Haverfield crashing in the storm—he'd gone out to prove he was as good a pilot as me—and I was the only one who could save him. I fell for it and took a ship out. When I got back, Jenks claimed I stole his ship."

Tali whistled.

"There's more. The ship was filled with stolen rifles. The story is I'm part of the floater revolution and have been plotting to destroy the Gottsdamerung launcher."

"Ouch."

"Yeah, ouch. Osborne's on the council, and he's howling for blood. You've got to get to Jenks and convince him to tell the truth. Or Haverfield. I think he's involved, too."

Tali traced the curve of her eyebrow with a fingernail. "That's going to be difficult. They're off-world."

"What? They can't leave. The council hasn't finished its investigation."

"Saw them go myself. I was working the terminal. Jenks, Haverfield, and a man in a synth-silk suit got on a private ship."

"The man have auburn hair?"

Tali cocked her head. "How'd you know?"

Murphy groaned. So the civilian had taken Haverfield to fill the test-pilot's position. But that didn't make any sense. If Haverfield had been accepted as her replacement, what was Williams's motivation for setting her up? And where did Jenks fit into the picture? Murphy pinched the bridge of her nose. "What's going on here?"

"Sounds like serious scapegoat time for you. Got any ideas?"

"My only chance is that Wickmont will prove the tower's security record was altered. But everyone's convinced there's no way a junior-grade lieutenant could have broken into the monitoring system."

Tali rolled her eyes. "Fat lot they know. Don't worry. I'll put a bug in Wickmont's ear. Tell him about the civilian and that simulation. He'll look at the video again. Once we prove the tower's log was altered, you'll be home free."

"If," Murphy said.

"When. Hey, I almost forgot. I brought something for you." Tali lifted her shirt. Nestled against the coffee-colored skin of her belly was a silver rectangle. She hauled it out and offered the palm-sized book to Murphy.

The cover was stainless steel and printed in raised letters was the title: *The Gods of Physics*.

Murphy's eyes widened. "Where'd you get a floater's bible?"

Tali shrugged. "I have friends. It was supposed to be your graduation present, but I thought you might need it now."

"Well, you can keep it. I don't believe in that superstitious nonsense."

"Take it. This place isn't exactly brimming with entertainment. Read it for a laugh. You can hide it under the mattress."

Murphy touched the cool metal cover. There were real pages inside, made of plastic with raised lettering, so the words could be read even if the power went out. Or, as floaters liked to say, especially if the power went out.

Tali leapt off the desk and landed on the balls of her feet. "I'd better go before Harris gets in trouble." She hugged Murphy tightly. "Don't worry. I'm on the case."

Murphy sighed and lifted the cover of the bible. The pages of the holo-book fell open. An animated image on the left showed two middle-aged men, smiling and clasping each other's shoulders. On the right was a caption: Pons and Fleischman, patron saints of lost causes.

The next morning the MPs brought her full dress uniform.

The council was waiting for her, already seated, when she was led before them.

Murphy stood for their decision. The magnetic backings of her wing leader gold star and first-pilot medals were cold through her thin microfiber undershirt. She scanned the faces of the council members. Wickmont's face looked pinched and weary. Osborne shifted restlessly in his seat, eyes glancing at the council members beside him. Harbrolt was as unchangeable as sculpted titanium.

Commandant Harbrolt rose. She tapped the screen in front of her once, then spoke. "Lieutenant Thiadora Murphy, there is insufficient evidence to prove you were involved in a conspiracy with a rebel faction. That is the only thing standing between you and criminal prosecution." The commandant's eyes pinned Murphy, as if she were about to dissect Murphy's soul.

"This court, however, has concluded that you are guilty of stealing private and University equipment, flying without access, and destroying evidence. For these crimes, this council has reached the only reasonable decision: expulsion."

The word detonated in Murphy's chest.

"Furthermore, your transcripts will be sealed. It will be as if you never passed through these halls. Judging from the events that have occurred, it would be better for all if you never had."

"You can't do this," Murphy protested. "The University is my life, everything I've worked for."

Harbrolt fixed her gaze on Murphy. "Ms. Murphy, when you entered the University you took an oath to abide by its constitution and regulations. You broke that oath and must face the consequences. You have twenty-six hours to collect your possessions and vacate the premises."

One day. The hole in Murphy's gut ripped wider. "I thought that if I didn't go out into the storm, Haverfield would die. Isn't that worth anything?"

"Yes." Harbrolt answered, unblinking. "It is worth your commission."

The commandant rapped on the screen three times and the file closed. The light from the screen winked out. The council rose and filed past Murphy.

She had a desperate impulse to grab the instructors, shake them, make them understand. She couldn't let her life's goal slip through her fingers, not this close to graduation. But it did, carried out by the officers, as they walked out of the room.

They left her with nothing. They took the ten months of physical therapy she had undergone just to apply. They took the six years of eighteen-hour days and the all-night study sessions. They took every insult she had weathered, every accomplishment she had fought to achieve.

They left her a shipless floater.

"Expelled?" Tali almost fell off the desk. "With your record, they expelled you?"

"They didn't believe my story."

Tali pounded the edge of the desk with her fist. "We'll nail Jenks's hide to the wall! I don't care what Harbrolt does to me, I'm going to tell them—"

"You won't do anything. This is my problem."

Tali scraped her dark hair back from her temples. "It's my problem, too. You're the best wing-mate I ever had. We were going to serve together."

"I'm the one who fell into Haverfield's trap. You—"

"—I won't stay here if they expel you. I'm going to tell—"

Murphy grabbed her friend's shoulders. "No. Listen to me. I was set up. Jenks couldn't have done it alone. Someone higher, maybe Osborne, set me up. I know you want to help. But it won't do any good."

Tali shrugged off Murphy's hands and sighed. "What are you going to do?"

"Contract floater. It's all I'm qualified for."

"What? Are you suicidal? Contract floaters have a life expectancy of what—fourteen years? What about the radiation, or the new viral diseases that thrive in zero-gee? Even if those don't kill you, you'll get space adaptation syndrome. Once you've got SAS you'll never work on a gravity ship, never be able to set foot on a planet again."

"No gee ship is going to hire a floater."

"But you've proven you can work in gravity. Hell, your ability to think in three dimensions makes you a better extra-planetary pilot than any grounder. Space is your natural environment! You've built up your gravity tolerance and can do things that would kill any other floater. Any company that looks at your record—"

"My record's been sealed." Murphy swallowed. "The only thing a company checking up on me will find is that I attended the University and was expelled."

Murphy looked around at the room she had shared with Tali for the last six years. The left wall was covered with awards for piloting skill: time trials, acrobatic maneuvers. Except for high-gee dives, she'd taken first in every event.

They meant nothing.

She had set out to prove that floaters could be more than cheap replacements for mechanicals. Her success would have shown that floaters were not emotionally unstable health risks. She was supposed to be the first floater to graduate from the University, the first to enter the Collective Enforcement Agency. But she'd failed.

Now the University would use her example to keep the next floater out.

At eight hundred hours the next morning, two MPs arrived at her barracks door to escort her off the base.

Murphy tugged on the waistband of her only civilian clothing. The floater's microfiber jumpsuit was tight around her waist and too long in the sleeves and pants. Her body had adapted to seven-eighths gee.

No part of her old life fit her anymore.

"I haven't said good-bye."

The MP's black faceplate was inscrutable. "There's no time. The shuttle leaves in seven minutes."

Murphy threw her few possessions into her large olive-green duffel bag. She looked at the pile of data-cubes full of six years of meticulous notes. They belonged to a University student. She left them for Tali.

Wickmont was waiting for her in the terminal. He stopped the MPs with a gesture. To Murphy he said, "I'm sorry about the decision. I went over the logs again. There's nothing, no evidence of tampering."

"I'm not sure it would have made any difference. They wanted me out, so I'm out."

"The University's losing a fine pilot."

Murphy flicked her head back toward the dome. "Tell them that."

A sad smile crossed his lips. "I did."

The pain that Murphy had stuffed deep inside began to well up. "What do you want? I've got a shuttle to catch."

Wickmont opened his hand. "I've coded you a letter of recommendation. I wish you well."

She stared at the thumbnail-sized prismatic cube. She wanted to dash it to the ground and grind it under her heel. It was too little, too late. But self-preservation took over. She took the cube and stuffed it into her pocket.

CHAPTER 3

Six thousand meters across, Gottsdamerung spaceport filled the forward screen. Three concentric rings encircled the vast globe of its power plant. The launch cannon and its booms and cranes were silhouetted against the sun like the black legs of a spider. Tension cables and access tubes stretched between the station's rings. The tiny irregular shapes of docked ships looked like flies caught in the power plant's web.

The nearest inhabited star system was three point four light-years away. With faster-than-light travel still an engineer's dream, Gottsdamerung's space-folding launcher was the only way out of the system. The symbols of the twelve member corporations of the Collective dotted the station's sides: Gallger's atomic shells, ISR's binary star, Avocet's melded A&V, Canodyne's double helixes, and others that curved into shadow.

From her window seat, Murphy watched the station's rotation appear to slow as the shuttle matched angular velocity. Electromagnetic grapples shot out from the ship, locking to the surface of the ring. Automatic wenches reeled in the tethers and completed the shuttle's hard dock. Murphy was light-headed for a moment while her body adjusted to the eight-tenths gee.

The University had provided her with a two-week visa for the station. She waited until the other passengers had cleared through the airlock, then slipped her visa and health certificate into the airlock's reader.

"Greetings Thiadora Murphy," a cheerful voice said. "You are registered for fourteen days. During that time you will be able to access the station's facilities. Enjoy your stay." A fine line of print at the bottom read: AIR AND WASTE, PAID.

The airlock cycled Murphy through with a hissing finality. It was the last barrier between her and the civilian world. She hefted her duffel bag onto her shoulder and entered the station.

She did not look back.

The outer ring was full of traffic: grounders in business suits, neon-colored body stockings, and CEA uniforms crowded the corridor. Both walls were filled with commerce: offices, trade goods, a gym, and hotels. Murphy glanced at a holo display. Her lips tightened. A room for an hour would cost a third of her savings.

She saw a man leaning against a news kiosk. His attention alternated between reading a portable screen and scanning incoming passengers. He was tall and dressed in a nondescript suit, his black hair cut almost floater short.

When he saw Murphy, he tucked the reader into a lapel pocket and walked over to her.

"You Thiadora Murphy?" he asked.

"Maybe." Murphy studied his face. "Who wants to know?"

He held out his hand. "I represent Gallger Galactic. We have an offer for you. Have you had lunch?"

Murphy'd had enough of Companies to last her a lifetime. But funds were tight, and a free lunch was a free lunch. "Lead on," she said.

He led her to an elevator set into one of the station's spokes. "Middle level," he said. The door closed, and they were sucked up the access tube. As they rose, gravity lessened. She rolled her neck as muscles loosened. The tube was dotted with windows.

They flashed past stars and the tan planetoid that, for the last six years, had been her home.

He took her to a restaurant in the mid-level. The half-gee was just enough to keep the vegetables in the wok. Bean sprouts and tofu arced in a lazy parabola.

The chef looked up. Startling blue eyes stared out of epicanthic folds. She waved them to a nearby table. The table screen lit up with a menu and drink advertisements as they wrapped their legs around the ergonomic. The bent-eight shape had been adapted for gravity use by the addition of a seat. Murphy wrapped her legs around the padded metal and leaned forward to tap out an order on the screen. The food was wheeled over minutes later by a robot that tested her companion's credit card and found it worthy.

After four mouthfuls of shredded cabbage and red peppers, Murphy asked, "What do you want?"

"You. Gallger Galactic has followed your training. We're impressed and want to offer you a job."

"How'd you know I'd be here?" Murphy's brows lowered. "My records were sealed."

The man smiled. "As a major contributor to the University's funding, Gallger receives certain liberties—including access to the records of exceptional students." He pulled a palm-sized data screen out of his pocket and slid it across the table. The number it displayed was four times the annual wages of a contract floater.

"That's just to start. After you've completed your pilot's certificate, it'll go up to a hundred thousand. Performance bonuses are offered semiannually."

"What would I be doing?"

"Piloting experimental spacecraft."

"Gallger builds launchers. When did they start prototyping ships?" And how would Avocet Industries, the galaxy's largest shipbuilder, feel about the competition?

The man steepled his fingers. "A wise business diversifies its sources of revenue."

Something in his gesture, his tone of voice, reminded her of Williams, the civilian who had visited the University. "Was the custom simulator a model for your prototype?"

He met her eyes, blinked. "I don't know what you're talking about."

But she'd already seen it. A moment of wariness that slipped out between eye blinks. It hung in the air between them like a retinal afterimage, superimposed over the studied innocence of his expression.

It all clicked together. An undergraduate couldn't have altered the net deck's logs, but it would have been simple for a corporate hacker.

Murphy said, "Gallger sent the simulator to the University. And when I wouldn't accept your offer of employment, you took steps to make sure I wouldn't have any choice." Her eyes narrowed. "You set me up."

"Please sit down, we have terms to discuss—"

Murphy pushed her chair back. "No. We don't." Her hands worked, clenching and unclenching. "You destroyed my career."

"But we're offering you another one—a better one."

Murphy ached to beat his face in. "I would rather die in a floater slave camp than work for your *effing* corporation." She turned and strode away.

"Call me," the man shouted after her. "You'll feel differently in fourteen days."

Murphy pulled the datacube Williams had given her out of her jacket pocket and hurled it at the table.

"Give that to your partner. I won't need it."

She brooded over Gallger's threat as she climbed into the access tube. If she couldn't find work before her money and visa ran out, the station would indenture her and sell her contract. Gallger could pick her up cheap.

Murphy shook off her fear. She was a crack pilot, and Gottsdamerung, a major hub of interstellar trade, was the best place to pick up a contract. The job-nets would have a position for her.

*   *   *

The only rental she could afford was a sleep sack in the floaters' quarters next to the hub. The room was shaped like a cylindrical shell. The opposing walls were only three meters apart, but curved for kilometers around the power plant in the station's hub. Polyethylene mesh sleeping bags lined every available surface.

She had to climb to reach 348-C. Her fingers grabbed the mesh of other people's bags. Someone grunted, and Murphy murmured an apology.

She stuffed her possessions into the sack then wriggled in. The olive-green plastic smelled of disinfectant and sweat.

The waste heat from the launcher was oppressive. Each launch consumed sixty-five thousand terawatts. The main reactor leaked, what the station termed, "an acceptable level of radiation." Murphy was issued a film badge to monitor her exposure when she paid. It reminded her of Osborne's joke when she first arrived at the University, "Floater baldness: it's not fashion, it's the radiation." Gottsdamerung could have added more shielding, but the people who slept next to the hub weren't worth the expense.

This is only temporary, she told herself. Tomorrow, she'd get a job.

Nine days later, Murphy was broke. She'd applied for twelve piloting jobs; eight of those were filled when she called, and two never returned her messages. The eleventh was incorrectly filed. They needed a heavy-worlder. The last position took one look at her and disconnected.

People milled past Murphy into shops, cafés, and entertainment lounges. Employed people. She envied their calm assurance that there'd be more money next payday. Her funds were dwindling away to nothing.

Piloting was the only skilled profession she knew, but this was no time to be picky. With a grimace, she tapped the public kiosk and opened the manual labor listings.

She applied for twenty-three positions: light clerical work, food service, even janitorial. Each one turned her down flat as soon as she told them her name.

What was she on Gottsdamerung, poison? Then she remembered the Gallger's confidence that she would call. With a sinking dread she began to suspect he had pulled strings to keep her unemployed.

One job was left, mucking out algae tanks in hydroponics. She'd done that for her Aunt Maisie. It was smelly, backbreaking work, but not as dangerous as sewage recyc or reactor maintenance. For that companies bought the service of indentured criminals. She dialed the job access code into the public kiosk.

A wide-faced bald man appeared on screen. He dabbed sweat off his forehead with a gray handkerchief that had once been white. "Yeah?" he asked.

"I'm calling about the hydroponics position. It still open?"

He glanced over his shoulder and counted silently, his lips moving. "Yeah, I could use a couple more bodies. You used a power shovel before?"

Murphy admitted that she had and detailed the maintenance work she'd done.

He listened without interest, chewing on the inside of his cheek. "All right. You'll do. Name and station ID?"

That was sticky. This was the point where all the other prospective employers had shut her down. There was also the matter of her visa. It expired tomorrow, and without employment, she wouldn't be able to get an extension. "Thia Halliday," she said, using her mother's maiden name. "I don't have a station identifier yet, I just arrived this morning."

The man's eyes hooded, but he didn't look surprised. "No ID, I only pay half. And not even that if there's any trouble with the law." He stared at her. "Is there?"

"No, of course not."

"Of course not," he echoed and read an address off to her. "Show up in half an hour, and we'll get you suited up in waders and a respirator."

She used her last cash to buy a protein bar from the grocery. Her grumbling stomach hoped she'd be able to talk her boss into an advance on her half wages.

The address led her to a dingy office underneath one of the spokes. The windows were steamed by humidity escaping from the greenhouse door at the end of the hall. The air was warm and close and smelled of phosphate.

The office was barely wide enough to contain the desk and the hulking man who sat behind it. Overlapping charts and printouts were tacked to every wall.

When she walked in the man shooed her away. "Can't use you after all, girlie. Get out."

Murphy put her palms on his desk and leaned over him. "You made me an offer. You can't just brush me off."

"Looked you up, girlie. False name and no ID made me curious. So I flashed your image during our conversation and checked the photo files. You're listed as a known agitator."

"I'm no rebel. I've never—"

"The record says you're bad news. I've worked with muck long enough to know not to go stirring it up." He waved the back of his hand at her dismissively and went back to his reports.

Murphy's hands tightened on the edges of his desk. "Please. I'm out of money. The record is wrong. I won't cause trouble. I *need* this job. I'll work for quarter wages."

He looked up. "Save me the sob story. Even if you worked for free, it's too big a risk to hire you. Get out before I call station security."

Murphy returned his challenging stare, but it was no use. She couldn't force him to hire her. And she couldn't afford to be picked up by station security. She had less than twenty-four hours to find employment.

When she got back to the shuttle station, she checked the job kiosk. There were no new listings. Something would open up tomorrow. It had to. She was running out of options.

But how to make it through the evening without being picked up as an indigent? She couldn't even afford a sleep sack in the spacer quarters.

She spent the night walking, her duffle bag hoisted over her shoulder, looking like she had somewhere to go. Occasionally, she'd sit down in a public place: shuttle terminal, fast-food cafeteria, the lobby of a hotel. But never for long, as the security AIs were watching. She catnapped, twitching awake anytime a person walked by.

At three a.m., desperate for sleep, Murphy scrawled "out of order" on the outside of a public bathroom and locked herself in. The floor was hard and cold. She clutched her olive-gray duffle bag to her chest, and fell asleep.

She woke up to bright lights and a mechanical jangling. A metal arm plucked at her sleeve.

"Do you require medical assistance?" a synthesized voice asked.

Murphy sat bolt upright and found herself face-to-screen with a maintenance robot. Its six arms clicked nervously, as if unsure how to fix her.

"No, I'm all right," Murphy said, standing up and lifting her gear to her shoulder. "I just slipped and fell. Must have knocked myself out for a moment."

The robot paused, no doubt conferring with an AI about how to proceed. That or it was calling the police.

Murphy didn't wait to find out. She walked swiftly away from the bathroom and caught an elevator to the mid-rim level.

It was six a.m. when Murphy checked the job boards. Her visa had expired at midnight, so she couldn't log onto the public kiosk—the machine would destroy her visa and alert the station police. Instead

Murphy lingered near the kiosk, sneaking glances at the listings when other people read them.

There were no new jobs. Exhausted, she leaned against the kiosk. Her back ached from lack of sleep, and her stomach grumbled.

Murphy's mind paced through her options. She could steal a credit card and maybe buy her way off the station before she was caught. The thought made her ill. Her life's dream had been to enforce and uphold the law, she wouldn't break it.

Call her mother and ask for launch fare? Jenevie was a free-trader. She had disowned her daughter when Murphy announced she was joining the military. The CEA had hounded Jenevie ever since Murphy's father left. That her daughter had joined the CEA was too big a betrayal. Even if Murphy could locate Jenevie's ship, she wouldn't help.

Uncle Arch and Aunt Maisie might send money for launch fare home to Formalhaunt. But what waited for her there? Just the knowledge she was a failure and the marital machinations of her aunts. Like Jenevie, they'd despised Murphy's decision to enlist with the CEA. No. She couldn't crawl back to them a failure.

Her only other option was Gallger. But that idea made her blood run hot. Gallger had ruined her military career, stranded her on a station without a job, then slandered her in the station records so no one else would hire her. She'd as soon slit her throat as work for them.

For a moment, she considered this last idea. Why not? She'd lost everything else. Murphy scrubbed her face with her hands. I'm tired, she thought, I can't be thinking this way.

Motion distracted Murphy from her morbid thoughts. Two station policemen in starched blue uniforms walked briskly toward her.

Murphy pushed to her feet and picked up her bag. There was no mistake; their eyes were locked on her, and they were coming her way.

Her visa had expired. If she was caught, she'd be indentured. Her services would be sold to the highest bidder, and Murphy knew who would buy.

She threw her duffle bag at the policeman on the left. He caught it and stumbled with its weight. The second braced a taser in both hands and commanded, "Halt!"

Murphy ran. She zigzagged through pedestrians and public kiosks, shoving people aside as the policemen chased her.

Adrenaline pumped through Murphy as she ran, but her body was tired and hungry. She tripped.

Someone grabbed her wrist and jerked her into a side passage. A door sheathed shut behind her.

When Murphy's eyes adjusted to the gloom, she made out the dim outline of a maintenance passageway, and a man in a dark business suit.

"Who—"

He clapped a hand over her mouth. "Not here," he whispered, "they might hear us." He pulled her farther into the tunnel.

It opened into the back kitchen of a coffee shop. Her savior purchased two cups of stimulants and led Murphy to a booth tucked into the corner.

On the promenade outside Murphy heard the cops shouting her name.

"Thanks," she said. "For the java, and the helping hand."

"It is not altruism." He took a steaming sip of chai. "My employer wishes to make you an offer."

Murphy stiffened. "I won't work for Gallger." She stood up. "You might as well turn me in right now."

Something that might have been amusement lit the man's eyes. "My employer will be most happy to hear that. He is not a Gallger."

Murphy sat down again, puzzled. "Then, who?"

The man handed her a business card.

When Murphy touched it, the tiny screen sparkled with dancing golden pixels. They resolved into a melded "A" and "V," the manufacturer's mark on

almost every ship built in the last twenty-five years.
The symbol faded, replaced by a chubby bald man
with piercing black eyes. Animated currency symbols
from a thousand worlds ringed his brow like a crown,
spinning in slow procession. It was a face she had seen
many times in news broadcasts. Damon Avocet, the
CEO of Avocet Industries.

"Damon Avocet? What does he want with me?"

"Mr. Avocet will answer any further questions—if
he so chooses."

Like all major corporations, Avocet Industries
maintained an office in Gottsdamerung, the capital
system. Avocet's was in the outer ring of Gottsdamerung station. The ceiling was three meters high and the
steel floor was brushed in swirling patterns. A hallway
large enough to park three shuttles end-to-end led to
Avocet's office. The opulence and wasted space an-
noyed Murphy. The door itself was the final insult.
The golden A-V symbol was inlaid on a two-meter
slab of solid teak. The money it had taken to grow
and ship that door would have supported twenty
floaters for a year.

Her escort palmed open the door, but he did not
follow her in. The door shut behind her, and Murphy
was left alone with one of the richest men in the galaxy: Damon Avocet.

His face was the same as it had appeared on the
business card: smooth, unwrinkled, inviting except for
the glittering black eyes. If you ignored the eyes, he
was Buddha in a pressure chair.

The chair covered his body from mid-chest down.
The pressure kept his fragile organs from shifting
under gravity's influence. Hairlike tubes carried meds
to his neck and shoulders. With the suit, Avocet could
tolerate near-gee gravity for up to eight hours. Murphy had never seen a pressure chair up close before.
They were expensive.

"I didn't know you were a floater," she said.

"Not many people do." He stared at her forehead,

her crew markings, the delicate script of the founding postulates of quantum mechanics peeking out from under her crewcut. "Why do you hide your marks?"

"Probably the same reason your office address is on the outer rim. You wouldn't need that chair if you were located in the hub."

"Ah, yes, a certain pretense is required." He glanced at her unbraced legs. "Your conditioning is remarkable."

Her eyebrows rose. "Is that why you wanted to see me? To admire my conditioning?"

"No. I need your piloting skills. But the trip I have in mind is very challenging. Frankly"—his eyes appraised her—"I'm not sure you're up to it."

Murphy's face heated. "I was the top-ranked pilot in my class at the University. I flew a singleship from the time that I was four until I turned sixteen. If it has forward thrust, I can fly it. What's the job?"

Avocet smiled. "That is negotiable. It may be that I have many jobs for you. Right now I need someone to retrieve . . . sensitive goods and deliver them to one of my research stations."

"I won't smuggle for you."

"I don't expect you to."

"I'm not sure I trust you."

"You don't have to. Just work for me." Avocet rubbed the tips of his fingers together. "Really you have no choice. Your visa is expired. If you walk out of that door unemployed, you'll be arrested and sentenced to indentured servitude. Then I'll buy your contract from the station. Either way, I win."

Murphy stared at Avocet a long time. He was right. And whatever he wanted it had to be better than working for Gallger. "In that case, I accept."

His smile grew to epic proportions. "Excellent."

At eight hundred hours a private shuttle ferried her to Avocet's ship, hovering in synchronous orbit with Gottsdamerung station. Wedge-shaped, it was as large as the hub itself.

Avocet met her at the airlock. In zero-gee, he was graceful. His ribs were barrel wide and his waist, wasp thin. Years of living without gravity had caused his internal organs to pull up into his chest.

One hand braced on a cross beam, he pulled her out of the airlock—then flipped her. She tumbled end-over-end, then extended her legs and caught the wall.

"Not bad," he said.

"Was that a test?"

He laughed. "One of many. Come to my office. I want my medical staff to examine you before we sign contracts."

He led her into a tube car, explaining that the medical labs were twenty-eight levels away from the airlock. The first moments were confusing as she precessed in the car: floor, wall, ceiling, floor. Then she broke through six years of grounder preconceptions about a fixed up and down. In zero-gee, there was only near and far, and motion was constant. Aches she hadn't noticed before disappeared, leaving her muscles curiously supple.

It was a strange feeling. This ease of motion wasn't home anymore. She felt like a grounder day-tripping in weightlessness.

They exited the car and pulled along handholds down a long corridor. Avocet palmed the lock of a door, and it opened onto a medical laboratory.

An examination table hung in the middle of the room, suspended by cables and braces. Three technicians swarmed over the facility, checking readouts and making adjustments.

The lab had been planned with a floater's sensibilities; every available surface was covered with equipment. The room looked like a geode, with medical gear crusted like crystals along its inner surface. The examination table was an inexplicable green pearl, thrust into its center.

A medical technician asked Murphy to remove her clothes. Her skin pebbled in the cool air. He lifted up her hair in back, and the cold line of an autoshaver caressed her nape. Murphy batted his hand away. "The hair stays."

The tech looked at Avocet for guidance. "The neural inductors won't work with her hair in the way."

"Murphy, let the man do his job."

Her lips compressed in a tight line. "I don't want to look like a floater."

"That's what you are." He locked his black eyes on hers. "Besides, I want to see your marks. Make sure you're all that my intelligence agents said you were."

Murphy flushed. So even the great Avocet was subject to floater superstitions. "You're hiring me, not my lineage. I won't do it." Her hair was the last link to her University days, the only indication that she had risen above her floater origins. Without it, people would mark her low status with a glance, and dismiss her as easily.

Avocet folded his arms over his wide chest. "You should reconsider your position. I don't hire disobedient staff. If you don't do exactly as I say, I'll feed you to the Gottsdamerung police."

Murphy saw the determined glint in Avocet's eye and had no doubt he would do exactly that. Her night on the run had left her too exhausted to fight him. "You win," she growled, and bowed her head.

Her thick brown curls were sucked into the clear plastic vacuum tube attached to the autoshaver. When he was done, her head was cold. She ran her hand over its smooth, surface.

Avocet stared at the marks over her left temple, the delicate lines of Heisenberg's uncertainty principal: $\Delta x \Delta p \geq h/4\pi$. His eyebrows rose. "So, you *are* the daughter of Ferris Murphy."

Murphy glared. "My father's nothing to do with me." She squeezed through the neck of a conductive, elastic bodysuit. A hood of the same material pulled tight over her head and zipped to the collar. The cloth felt like cold latex against her skin, yet was porous enough to breathe through. Without another word the technicians tethered her to the examination table.

* * *

An hour later, perforated and sore, Murphy un-strapped herself. "Is my physical condition satisfactory?"

The medical technician glanced up from a palm screen of statistics. "Extraordinary. Your reflex re-sponses are off the scale. Comprehension of spatial images is remarkable."

Avocet floated through the doorway. "All done?" He scanned the technician's report. "Excellent. It's no wonder that you did so well at the University."

Murphy winced. It was a fresh wound. She ran her hand over her smooth scalp and asked, "So what's my first assignment?"

"You will fly an experimental ship to my research station around Barnard's star."

"Sounds easy."

"It will be," Avocet's black eyes glittered, "unless the owners find out."

CHAPTER
4

"I won't do anything criminal." Murphy rolled the bodysuit down past her hips.

Avocet handed Murphy her clothes. "It's not illegal . . . exactly. An employee of one of my rivals has discovered free enterprise. I paid for the ship."

Murphy stepped into her overalls. "But the person who sold you the ship doesn't own it." She puzzled over the implications. Why would Avocet, the largest manufacturer of space-faring vessels in the Collective, need to steal a spaceship? Murphy shrugged a shirt over her shoulders. "I won't pirate for you."

Avocet glanced around the room at the medical staff. "Come to my office. I need your palm print on a few documents. We'll discuss the details there. Once you see what's at stake, you'll put aside your outmoded ethics."

She doubted it. Murphy watched him watch the technicians. He didn't trust his staff with the details.

When she finished dressing, they drifted up three levels to a hallway terminating in a door. Avocet palmed the lock.

The office was spartan: bare gray walls and sheet metal furniture, the room barely large enough to hold the two of them. Avocet's desk stuck out from the left wall. A guest ergonomic was welded to the front of the desk. Murphy wrapped her legs around its figure-eight shape and floated above it. The ergo was more anchor than seat. The only sign of wealth was the screen in his desk. It was high VR holographic resolution, Datronic.

He turned to the computer. The embedded microcamera in the corner of the screen picked up the motion and activated the language application.

Avocet said, "Open a contract, standard employment, first term, research rider, today's date." Text scrolled across the screen. To Murphy he said, "I'm going to need your full legal name."

"Thiadora Murphy."

The contract appeared instantly. Avocet asked, "How's the spelling?"

Murphy tapped the edge of the screen nearest her, and the text flipped to her orientation. "Perfect. But I'm not signing anything until you tell me what I'll be doing."

Avocet folded his arms and looked at her. "You are the most stubborn creature."

"I'm not stealing any ship."

"You're not still holding onto that outdated floater code of ethics? I thought you'd rejected all that. Besides, it can hardly apply here. No one depends on this ship for their livelihood. It's just a possession."

"I was an officer-in-training of the CEA. I enforced the law, I won't break it."

Avocet's smile became less playful. "You're about to become an employee of Avocet Industries. And the only law around here is what I say. After this one . . . indelicate act, your duties will consist of test-piloting my ships. Nothing more. I assure you, I have no intention of wasting your talents as a"—he smiled at the term—"pirate."

Murphy said nothing.

"What if I told you the ship in question belongs to Gallger?"

Murphy's eyes narrowed. Gallger. The strange simulation. Was there a connection?

"It would be a chance to strike back at the company that destroyed your military career."

"Tell me more about this ship," she demanded.

"Not until you're my employee." Avocet pressed his right palm against the reader. It chimed. "Your turn."

She scanned the text. One line stood out. Her eyebrows rose. "Five years?"

"A standard term for first-time employment. There are the usual loyalty clauses, confidentiality warrantees, all boilerplate."

"But five years?"

Avocet sighed. "This is not a floater market-grapple. And you're in no position to bargain. Five years *is* a long time, but I give bonuses for exemplary work. You can use these to buy back your contract."

"I want to read the rest of the terms." Murphy craned her head to read the text, which was oriented to Avocet.

"There's no time to waste with this. I need you flying that ship tomorrow morning. You don't have any choice. There's not enough money in your accounts to pay for a shuttle back to the station. And you're not so pretty that I'd keep you on my ship as decoration." He paused while his threat sank in. "Palm it."

With misgivings, she touched the cool surface of the reader. It gave slightly, recording the contours of her palm in addition to her fingerprints.

When it was done, Avocet said, "Good. Encrypt and archive." The computer whirred softly. Avocet smiled with satisfaction.

"What I'm about to discuss with you is confidential. There's an extra clause in the research rider that upgrades leaking industrial secrets to a capital crime."

Murphy's lips pulled down at the corners.

Avocet waved his hand dismissively. "It's standard for any employee involved with prototype development. You can read the details later."

"What else did I 'agree' to?" She flicked the back of her hand against the screen. "Indentured servitude would be better than this."

He leaned forward. "Shall I tell you about the ship,

or do you want me to have you arrested for breach of contract?"

Murphy folded her arms and glared at him.

"Good." He leaned back. "An employee of a rival corporation contacted me three weeks ago. He sent documentation on a derelict ship that his work group discovered. For an exorbitant fee, he offered to misroute records and add the vessel to my next shipment of trade-ins."

"Won't your friend be caught when the switch is discovered?"

Avocet smiled slyly. "I think he plans to retire before that happens."

Murphy's brow furrowed. That wouldn't keep the corporation from filing charges. The CEA would put a trace on his accounts. How much money would it take for a person to give up his identity and spend the rest of his life in hiding?

"The ship was abandoned," Avocet said. "There was no pilot on board, only ashes floating around the command room. It was unregistered. No call sign, nothing. Gallger code-named it the *Gambit*." He tapped his screen.

A projection of the ship rotated above his desk. The image was as long as Murphy's body.

The lateral cross section was a black sphere. Four ridges connected the poles.

It looked real—and intriguing. Murphy's hands opened. She wanted to hold it, explore its contours with her fingers.

Avocet touched a keypad, and a second hologram displayed the interior. Inside, the pilot's couch was ringed with IFOs. Whoever flew it would feel like they were suspended in space.

The room was the twin of Gallger's simulation. Murphy was starting to feel she was doomed to fly that ship.

She kept her voice level. "What kind of vessel is it?" She cocked her head, studying the projection.

"The design's inefficient for shipping. The engines take up more than half the cargo space."

Avocet smiled. "There's more." A second tap and the hull of the ship stripped away. What she had mistaken for one, was actually two engines. Heavy radiation shielding formed a bulkhead between them.

Murphy walked forward and touched the holo-image with a finger. "Two engines? What's the point of the small forward engine?"

"It supplies power to the ship and drives the thrusters," Avocet said.

She looked back at Avocet. "No way a fission plant that size could power a ship."

Avocet steepled his fingers. "Ah, but that's the best part, it's not fission, it's fusion."

Murphy sucked in a breath. "On a ship that small? That'd be an incredible expense and power drain. Where's it get fuel? Is that what the second drive does, runs the fusion plant?"

"No. My crew tells me the fusion plant is entirely self-sustaining. The lateral ridges fold out. They look like Bussard collectors, but they're too small to be effective. The only way they'd be any use is if you were traveling through dense gas or plasma. The fusion plant is powered off the organic waste recycler. It's the most efficient design I've ever seen. That technology alone could revolutionize space travel."

Murphy gazed at the projection. It was unbelievable. "Where did the ship come from?"

"No one knows. It's not like anything being built in the Collective. I know, I see my competitors' designs before they do." He tapped his desk screen and scanned a report. "There's more. When the salvage team started the engines, the hull temperature climbed to ten thousand degrees in seconds. The pilot died.

"My enterprising friend recovered the black box and erased two seconds from its log. He told his team that it was corrupted by the power surge. In those two seconds, the pilot's personal recorder shows a radioactive wasteland: no stars, no planets, no large masses of any kind. Interesting, no?"

The heat she'd experienced in the simulator. Flying this thing would put her back in that kind of danger, with no escape hatch. She pursed her lips. "An error in the ship's recorder?"

Avocet shook his head, a knowing smile tweaking his lips. "My scientists believe the ship experienced a dimensional shift."

Murphy looked at Avocet, but he wasn't joking. "Impossible. Multiple universes are only theory."

"Until now. During those two seconds, the ship disappeared."

The thought made her body tingle with excitement. The possible uses of dimensional travel were astounding. You could jump to a compact universe and travel a small distance in it, but on return, the resulting translation might be thousands of light-years. Instantaneously.

Her theoretical propulsion professor had explained it as two dots on a ballooon. The uninflated balloon is the alternate universe. Blowing up the balloon is the translation back to this universe. The dots don't move, but they become farther apart.

With this ship, she could explore places no human had ever seen, without a launcher, without depending on the Collective and its transportation web. For the first time in her life, she wanted to steal. Not for Avocet, but from Avocet.

That avarice must have shown on her face. Avocet said, "I see you understand my interest in the ship."

Murphy forced herself to speak calmly. "If the *Gambit* is as amazing as you say, Gallger will be watching it around the clock. No salvager is going to be able to misroute it."

"According to our anonymous friend, Gallger is transporting the *Gambit* to a private research station. It's being carried in the belly-hold of a cargo tug. Both for secrecy and because they don't have a pilot they trust to fly her."

Murphy thought of Haverfield and Williams's disappointment with his performance. "You mean they don't have me."

"Exactly. *I* have you."

Murphy didn't like the sound of that.

"Gallger's using minimal security to move the *Gambit* because they don't want to attract the attention of rival corporations"—Avocet smiled—"like Avocet Industries.

"In thirty-two hours there's a launch to Rigel Kentaurus. There you will rendezvous with James Siskoll. He runs a handler at the station. From there, you will travel to the company's Onneil platform. Every month they order new ships from my yards to maintain their fleet. Our friend has bribed the crew of the transport, to switch the *Gambit* with one of our trade-ins.

"You'll replace Siskoll's partner, load the *Gambit* into the handler with the rest of the ships, then, midway to the launch station, you and the *Gambit* unload. Fly her to prearranged coordinates, where I'll have my own cargo tug waiting. We'll load her in the belly-hold and continue to the station." He smiled. "Then we'll use Gallger's own launcher to steal its ship."

Murphy spent the evening on Avocet's ship, studying the *Gambit*'s schematics. In the morning, Avocet provided her with an Avocet Industries flight suit and papers for a new identity as copilot to a cargo ship. Using her new credentials, she booked a space on the next launch to Kentaurus.

Murphy took the gel tank near the front window. She wanted a good view when the ship launched. Her last jump had been to the University, six years ago. Even with the support of a gel tank, she had blacked out during the acceleration. Tali said the simulations at the University were like comparing a good-night kiss to a Roman orgy. Murphy hoped the last six years had made her strong enough to experience a launch.

The stars in the forward window didn't look right. She stared at them a long moment before she realized they weren't twinkling. There was no atmosphere to block their light. These were the stars she'd grown up with: uncompromising and intense, and they were strange to her.

The ship received clearance and backed into the open end of the cone. Booms and cranes locked it into position. Once it was in place, the launcher generated space-folding fields along its hull. The ship vibrated, ready to leap across the rent in space before it closed.

All the output of the power plant in the station's core was routed through the launcher. The entire station dimmed.

The launcher opened space; the ship exploded through the gap.

Pressure slammed Murphy into the crash couch. The back of her head sank into the gel. Her lips pulled back from her teeth. The high gee flattened her retinas and her vision blurred. She forced herself to look at the stars as they blue-shifted and collected into a disk, then shrank to a pinpoint. When it had almost disappeared, it expanded again. The stars reddened, then settled into their normal spectrum.

Sirius was in a new position, stretching Canis Major into an elongated configuration. Andromeda, two million light-years away, was unchanged. Murphy oriented the three-dimensional star map in her head and traced the route, estimating the distance. They had traveled ten light-years in three minutes.

Instantaneously the rent behind them at Gottsdamerung collapsed, leaving no physical trace of the launch or its destination, only a computer record in the launch log. And Murphy suspected Avocet would have that last jump-destination altered.

"Welcome to Kentaurus Station," a voice said over the com. "We hope your stay is a pleasant one."

Rigel Kentaurus was a yellow star, much like Sol, except that it had a dim orange companion star, Beta Centauri. Kentaurus Station circled its namesake with a period of four hundred standard days. It served as a cargo transfer point for the myriad of colonies cropping up on planets in the system.

The habitable ring was dwarfed by the axial scaffolding of docking ports. Hundreds of ships were locked into the lattice of green girders, waiting for cranes to load cargo. Tiny figures in hard suits jetted between the ships. Transport tubes pulsed between the habitable regions and the passenger ships like umbilical cords, feeding cheap labor into the station.

Murphy unbelted herself from the crash couch and tottered up the aisle to join in the crush heading for the airlock. When it cycled, Murphy peeled herself away from the dockers and busi-men, who had come to tour the station, and followed the yellow markers to the pilot's lounge. She'd seen one blurry flat sim of Siskoll and hoped she would recognize him.

The lounge was a dark, low-ceilinged room that stretched into shadow. It smelled of intoxicants: the cloying scents of rum and scotch warred with the burning-steel tang of hype and blitzo. Two men in the corner were strapped head-to-head in an interactive VR game. Neither of them was Siskoll. A plump woman disconnected from the inhaler of a hype-tube and jittered over to Murphy.

"What we got here?" Bleached-blond points exploded from her scalp. If it had not been gelled into hard spikes, her hair would have fallen to her shoulders. Her thin lips were pushed into a perpetual pout, and her irises vibrated erratically in bright eyes.

The five pilots not engaged in VR looked over at them.

The woman scanned Murphy, then frowned at her bald scalp and her markings. "A floater in three-quarters gee? You lost, honey?"

Murphy clenched her hands. She didn't have time for this. "I'm looking for Siskoll."

"Oh, honey, he won't have nothing to do with you—he ain't no jellyfish poker."

Murphy wanted to put her elbow into the woman's twitching face. Show her this jellyfish was hard.

A man in the back of the room stood up. He was two meters tall, and built like he'd spent all his time on heavy-gravity planets. He wore canvas pants and a too-tight white T-shirt that accentuated arms as thick as Murphy's waist. His face was wide and lined with the residue of inhalant smoke. Gray eyes cringed above his cheekbones. "I'm Siskoll. You Murphy?"

"Siskoll honey, you surprise me. I knew you were depraved, but this?" The woman leaned in until Murphy could smell her rotten back teeth. "I had me a floater man once." She licked her lips, and made a popping noise. "Snapped him like a twig."

That was it. Murphy swung. Her fist connected just under one heavily rouged cheekbone. The woman's head snapped back, and her eyes widened.

Murphy's follow-through carried them both to the floor. She rolled off the woman's spongy body and sprang to her feet.

Siskoll grabbed Murphy's right arm and twisted it behind her back. "Nice inconspicuous entrance," he whispered in her ear. "Very nice."

Three men in the back stood up. One twitched his head at the conflict; the other two nodded and started forward.

Murphy jerked in Siskoll's grasp.

The woman dabbed blood from the corner of her mouth. She tasted it, and smiled. "Oooh, feisty little jellyfish. You gonna tether her, Siskoll? If you do, invite me and the boys. We'd love to be in on that party."

Siskoll propelled Murphy out of the lounge, steered her into a side hallway and threw her up against a wall. "Didn't Avocet tell you to keep this quiet? The last thing we want to do is stick in anyone's memory." He flipped the back of his hand at her bald head. "So what do you do? Start punching up the locals, looking like the goddamned SAS poster child."

"She started it. And you can thank Avocet for the haircut. You want to call him and tell him the deal is off?"

The man flicked gray hair off his forehead and looked down the hall. "No. Just stay in the hauler till we load up. After that, you're on your own."

"Suits me."

Siskoll took her to the hauler, a smaller, portable version of the station's docks. A cube of green scaffolding large enough to hold sixteen singleships separated the one-man cabin from the fission reactor. The engine was small for the craft, speed sacrificed for economy.

The cabin was cramped. Inside, it was painted the same gray as Siskoll's hair and eyes, as if the color had leached into him over the years. Murphy's head barely cleared the ceiling. Siskoll slumped inside, bending at the waist to fit. The cabin smelled of stale sweat and ethanol.

"There's no shower, and the toilet's zero-gee." He spoke without looking at her. "Can you use a male attachment?"

"If I have to."

"Okay, then, I'm going back to the station. See you in eight hours." He pulled a pile of dirty white shirts off the crash couch and smoothed the cracked vinyl. "Make yourself at home," he said, and left.

Make herself at home. That was the problem. The first fourteen years of her life, before the University, had been spent in cabins exactly like this. If she closed her eyes, she was on Uncle Bertram's ship. It even smelled the same. Murphy flopped down on the couch.

"Unauthorized pilot. System locked," said a cool mechanical voice.

Why install security on this heap? Its best protection was that no one would want it. She kicked her feet onto the controls and the warning sounded again. Gods hope the *Gambit* was better than this.

Siskoll returned ten hours later. The airlock's chime woke Murphy from a light sleep. His hair was canted to the right, and the lines on his face were deeper.

He took the pilot's seat, hands roaming over the

controls. "You as good in zero-gee as those marks on your forehead?"

"Yes."

"All right. When we get to Gallger, you go EVA and load the ships. When you're done, slip into the *Gambit*. Your suit's heat signature should be too small for Gallger to register."

The hull shivered as the docking magnets holding the hauler to the station released. Siskoll slid his thumb along the throttle strip, and the hauler lumbered into space.

Four hours later, the stubby cylinder of Gallger's shipyards came into view. Fifteen singleships were docked on the nearest end. The black bead of the *Gambit* was nestled in the center, obscured by a press of ships.

"This is how it works," he said. "A tug brings the singleship up and rough positions it. You, wearing a hard suit and drive pack, maneuver it into place and dock it with electromagnets set into the girders."

"Why don't I just fly the ships in?"

Siskoll snorted. "Too dangerous. Gallger doesn't trade them in until they're falling apart. They squeeze every second of usefulness out of the ships; forget the pilot's safety. Why should they care? There's always another damn-fool floater willing to break his neck for a few dollars." He looked at Murphy and cleared his throat. "You know what I mean."

Yes. She did.

Murphy pulled herself to the back of the ship, where the spacesuits were recharging. She unlocked hers from the cabinet and began checking it. Her fingers moved automatically through the routine, leaving her mind free to reflect. What was she doing? Stealing was wrong—a ship even more so. She looked out the airlock porthole at the ships, the *Gambit* hidden among them like a black pearl. Murphy sighed with both longing and regret as she slipped into her suit. It was past the point where she could back out. The only path lay ahead.

Murphy cycled the airlock and drifted out into space.

She had to remind herself not to stare at the *Gambit*. The ship was beautiful, a smooth black sphere among the rough angles and steel. Looking at it, however, was dangerous; she might draw attention to it, and she needed all her concentration to load the singleships.

Each ship was a thousand times her mass. It took five minutes of pulling and tugging to start the first one into motion, and another five minutes to stop it. Calculating the turnaround point between propelling and braking was tricky. One mistake and the ship would crash into the scaffolding, its inertia ripping the lattice apart.

She loaded up the *Gambit* last, locking it underneath the engines in back. It was partially hidden there, and only secured to two girders, not four. One pulse, and the locking magnets would release. The hauler would continue to accelerate, leaving the *Gambit* free in space.

"Get back here," Siskoll's voice crackled through the helmet's speakers.

"But—" Murphy looked longingly at *Gambit*'s airlock. So close.

"Gallger's command is touchy," Siskoll said. "They're watching you. You have to come back."

She tapped the suit's jets. The projection on the inside of her faceplate indicated the suit's propellant was down to ten percent. She hoped Siskoll had extra, otherwise there wouldn't be enough to get her back to the *Gambit*.

She jetted the length of the hauler, the fuel indicator sinking steadily. When she reached the cabin, it was on reserve, the indicator blinking. She cut it off, and coasted the rest of the way to the airlock.

When it finished cycling she launched herself to the control couch, braking with her left hand on the headrest. Her face was inches away from Siskoll's. "How the hell am I supposed to pilot the *Gambit* if I'm in here?"

Siskoll's gaze was glued to the screen as if he could divine the company's intentions from the movements and orientations of the tiny ship icons. "Gallger suspects something—they've been asking a lot of questions, sticking to tighter protocol." He rubbed his jaw. "I can't stop the hauler enroute. The station's control tower will register any time discrepancy. But if we arrive with fifteen ships, customs is going to be all over us because the manifest only shows fourteen." He reached for the com. "They've got us."

Murphy grabbed his arm. "No. Don't surrender. I'll climb back there during acceleration."

Siskoll looked over his shoulder at her, his eyes wide with incredulity. "You're going to climb over the outside of an accelerating ship? That's insane. The suit's jets don't have enough thrust to compensate."

"I'll be accelerating at the same rate as everything else."

Their eyes locked. "Yeah, so long as you hang on."

"Then, I just won't let go."

"WARNING. THE SHIP IS ACCELERATING. PLEASE WAIT FOR CONSTANT VELOCITY."

Murphy overrode the airlock's safeties and took several deep breaths. They were on the far side of the second planet. She had to go now, before the handler crossed back into visual with the station.

The acceleration was only a gentle pull, maybe a quarter-gee. She should use a tether, but Siskoll wouldn't have time to reel it in before he reached the station and a loose line would raise questions.

Without a tether, though, any mistake would send her hurtling off the ship. Even in a heavily monitored system, a hard suit's signature would be impossible to find. Not that there'd be anyone looking. She didn't have any illusions about Siskoll flying to her rescue, and Avocet would cut his losses.

In the four-by-four grid of the ship hauler, the *Gam-*

bit was one level down and four away. She'd have to crawl over three singleships in order to reach the *Gambit*'s hatch.

She hand-over-handed her way down to the *Gambit*'s level, saving the jets for an emergency. She'd siphoned what she could from Siskoll's suit, but it hadn't been much.

When she reached the first singleship on the *Gambit*'s level, she activated her shoe magnets. A toe button controlled the grab release of the electromagnet. Place. Release. Place right foot. Release left.

Three singleships to climb over to reach the *Gambit*. Sixty meters to safety. Above and all around her, the stars were bright and impossibly clear. The only sound was her ragged breathing.

Place. Release. Place—

Her right foot released before her left one caught. The singleship's steel hull skidded under her right foot. Her hand slipped and she lost contact with the accelerating ship. Girders passed over her head as the ship carrier continued to increase speed.

Murphy toed the controls again and stretched her right foot toward the singleship. The magnet failed.

A horizontal girder sped past on her left, just missing her helmet.

She fired the jets. For an endless second she hung in the same reference frame as the girders, spending precious fuel to hold her position. Then the jets compensated, and she crept up on the girder.

And the jets faltered. The display read empty. *Come on.* She willed the jets to fire again. Nothing. Not even a spark.

Murphy was now a hand's breadth from the girder. Inertia drove her the last five centimeters. She wrapped her arms around the steel column. That was close, too close.

While she'd lost contact, two singleships had slid past her. Only forty meters lay between her and the emptiness of space. If she hadn't been able to grab the girder, she'd have fallen out of the back of the ship carrier. Murphy panted, catching her breath, and contemplated the endless space that had almost swallowed her.

Her jets were completely expended. One more slip and she might be lost. Her heart pounded in her ears.

This was a stupid way to die, playing pirate for Avocet Industries. As soon as she reached Barnard's star, she'd quit. She'd find a way to break the contract. Right now, being indentured didn't sound so bad.

Her arm tensed as she pulled her left leg forward. Only one more singleship between her and the *Gambit*. The muscles in her abdomen cramped with the effort to place her foot on its hull. She toed the button, and her left foot caught. But to reach the *Gambit*'s hatch, she needed to cross a girderless span of hull. How could she get there with one working shoe, depleted jets, no handholds, and acceleration's relentless pull?

She couldn't. Jumping would be suicide. She'd failed again. Her father was right to run away. You can't fight a Company. They're too big.

Siskoll's voice crackled over the intraship frequency. "What's the delay? We're out of time."

Tears of frustration stung her eyes as she looked at the *Gambit*'s hatch. So close. Twenty meters away was a chance to strike back at Gallger, the chance to fly a ship so advanced that not even Avocet understood it. Damn it. She had to get to that ship . . . or die trying.

Because if she failed this time, what did she have to left to live for?

And she was sick to death of failing.

"One of my boots shorted out. I'm going to jump for it."

"You're going to wha—"

Murphy shut off the radio. No distractions.

She tensed, eyeballed distance and trajectory, and kicked off.

The last ship passed under her. Too fast. She reached out with her left foot, the magnet activated, but it was too far from the hull. A weak tug as the magnet tried to connect, but its force wasn't enough to overcome her inertia.

She drifted over the *Gambit*. The hatch slid by, tantalizingly close to her hand, then was gone. The *Gambit* was the last ship in this row. When she slipped past it, she'd be left behind. No hope of rescue.

Her head and shoulders drifted past the end of the carrier, into the emptiness of space.

Desperate, Murphy scrambled with her arms and legs. Instinct compelled her to struggle against air pressure that wasn't there.

Bravado abandoned her. In that moment she wanted only to live. She stretched her left leg wide, willing the magnet to break the laws of physics and catch, damn you, catch.

A shock ran up her leg. She looked down and saw her left foot was wedged between the *Gambit*'s hull and a girder.

Suspended by her ankle, Murphy dangled behind the ship carrier and stared face-first into starry oblivion.

For a long moment, tendons and metal strained. Then her momentum was overcome, the pressure eased. Bending from the waist, she tried to grab the girder. Too far. She bent her knee.

Pain exploded up her calf. She gasped and swung back into space.

Holding her knee, she pulled herself up and clutched the structural support. Her foot twisted at a ugly angle, but for the moment it didn't matter.

She was alive.

Murphy moved her toes; the bones in her ankle ground together. She bit the inside of her cheek against the pain and pried her foot out from under the support that had saved her life.

There were two handholds positioned on either side of the *Gambit*'s airlock, seven meters away. There was nothing to hold onto between her and them. Murphy braced her good foot against the beam, took a deep breath, and pushed off, leaping against acceleration back toward the *Gambit*.

The hull of the *Gambit* passed under her, appearing to slow as the carrier's acceleration countered the velocity of Murphy's leap. The airlock drew closer and closer. Murphy's chest tightened. Missing this grab could be the end of her life.

She reached across her body for the hatch—and reaction rotated her torso away. Shit. The handle was going to pass by too far on her left. She pulled her hand back; her body spun back into position. The hatch passed her head and shoulders. Her fingers tensed to feel the bump of the grips through thick gloves.

Pressure brushed her fingertips.

She clenched her hand. The two middle fingers caught. Muscles in Murphy's shoulders pulled into tight cords as she strained to close her fist around the grip. The fingers absorbed her forward momentum. The ship's acceleration did the rest.

The grip slipped into her palm.

Murphy clutched it like life itself. She wrapped her wrist around the handhold, jamming her hand between it and the hull. With her right hand she hit the controls. The airlock sheathed open, and Murphy pulled herself inside.

She tested the air with her suit. Perfect. No harmful bacteria, no antigens. None of the viruses that thrived in zero-gee. With a sigh of relief, she pulled off her helmet and looked around.

Her breath caught. The faint green light of status indicators shimmered off the glossy walls of a spherical room. Touchpad mosaics decorated every surface, oriented in random directions. Tantalizingly illegible black script scrolled by on a dozen screens.

It was beautiful. Alien, and yet somehow, Murphy felt like she'd come home.

Gallger's simulation had only shown her the cockpit. The complexity of the ship, in full size, was amazing.

But she'd explore it later, now she had to get away before Gallger caught her.

Murphy strapped herself into the crash couch in the center of the room. It was thickly padded with a cobalt gel that oozed into the curves of her body.

She hoped she'd do a better job flying it this time; there was no one waiting outside the hatch to bail her out.

She touched a control on the wall before her, and the cabin lit up. Pie-shaped IFOs showed girders and free space below. Her suit's clock indicated she had four minutes left to get *Gambit* free. Longer than that and the delivery station might spot her or she'd miss her rendezvous with Avocet's transport.

She sent a low-powered transmission to Siskoll. "Cut me loose."

At first she wasn't sure the message had gotten through, then a clank vibrated up through the ergo as Siskoll released the docking magnets.

"Done. You're on your own, floater."

Murphy dropped the ship with a foot tap on the upper thrusters. The hauler slid overhead like the shadow of a shark.

There had been pain when she pressed the control, and she could feel her ankle swelling. She leaned toward her foot to loosen the clamps on her boot, when a shuffling noise interrupted her.

Murphy turned.

A man crouched in the doorway to the galley. Blond curls blossomed from his head like a marigold. He wore navy blue coveralls with a Gallger Galactic patch on one shoulder. His hand flew to his mouth, and he convulsed with nausea.

Before Murphy could say a word, he disappeared into the back of the ship. A spy? Was he armed? Her heart pounded in time with her ankle. Had he sabotaged the ship?

She froze the controls into a straight trajectory to Beta Centauri, Rigel Kentaurus's companion star. The plan was to slow-boat to the coordinates where Avocet's cargo tug waited and then catch the launcher to Barnard's star. But Avocet hadn't said anything about stowaways.

She prayed to Einstein that he hadn't brought a gun aboard. Even if she could find the breach repair kit in time, she wasn't prepared to fly a patched ship.

Murphy pulled herself slowly into the galley, which was lit by the green status lights on the refrigeration unit. The man huddled in midair, holding a plastic bag to his mouth.

"Who the hell are you?" she asked.

"Kyle," he croaked, extending a hand. "I sold the *Gambit* to Avocet."

"You were supposed to stay on the station. If you disappear, Gallger will know something's up."

Kyle's brow furrowed. "Gallger is aware of the theft already. I couldn't remain. Besides"—his gaze shifted from her face—"you have larger problems than me right now." He pointed past her to the cockpit.

The ship's aft screens were lit up. Four armored cruisers were trailing them, each one three times as big as the *Gambit*. They bore the atomic orbitals of Gallger Galactic.

The com buzzed. ". . . of the singleship *Gambit*, you are in possession of a stolen ship. Power down and prepare to be boarded."

Murphy jammed herself into the crash couch, increased thrust to the engines—

And her hands hovered over the console. What did the symbols mean? Some of the controls were obvious, like the throttle strip and the gyros. But there was a second panel of engine controls. Which was the main drive? Should she activate both? Would the ship's electronics overload?

The warships were closing in. "Your position has been given to the CEA. You have no hope of escape. Surrender peacefully or we will fire."

Kyle leaned over her shoulder. "A bluff. Gallger won't risk damaging the *Gambit*, it's too valuable. Accelerate us out of here."

Murphy shoved him back with her free hand. "That's what I'm trying to do."

Hell with it. She powered up everything. She wasn't going to be arrested for piracy two weeks after her expulsion.

The ships behind closed to five hundred meters.

The *Gambit*'s engines kicked in with a shudder.

Two hundred fifty meters. She could read the call signs off their bow.

Murphy slid her fingers along both throttle strips increasing power to the propulsion systems. Indecipherable blue characters scrolled across the screen. They turned green, then started blinking. What did that mean?

One hundred seventy-five meters. The ion cannons on the warships glowed a deep red. When they heated to white, Gallger could fire.

Murphy tapped the screen.

A surge of acceleration thwacked her head against the headrest. Her skull flattened.

A second later Kyle impacted the back wall.

The stars slid together like dust on an oil slick. Streamers of light streaked the viewscreen. Murphy's vision blurred. The stars tunneled. All light compressed to a single point. The dot wavered—and went out.

CHAPTER 5

Murphy felt the heat first—the cabin was an oven. Her head pounded in time with her ankle. Atmospherics whined. She gasped and drew in a searing breath, then opened her eyes.

The light in the cabin pulsed orange-red. Murphy checked the integrated fiber optics. In all directions, the view was unchanging: motes of gold danced in magnetic eddies. Fear left little time to be amazed. The *Gambit* was streaming through plasma, and the temperature was rising.

Eight clicks ratcheted from the rear of the ship, and a third of the IFO ports went black. Murphy looked along the hull. The lateral ridges had folded out into the sharp fins of undersized Bussard collectors.

Kyle groaned behind her. "Where are we?"

"I don't know, but we can't stay here."

"The *Gambit*'s original pilot had to be vacuumed out of the air," Kyle said. "He was burned to ashes."

"I don't intend to follow his example. There's got to be a way to return to normal space." She had shifted back in the simulator. But how had she done it?

Licking sweat from her upper lip, she activated controls in a panic, looking for anything familiar. The blue laser lines of a holographic display blossomed into a spherical grid. A finger-length *Gambit* appeared at its apex. It was one of the displays she'd seen just before the simulation ended.

Metal pinged as the hull expanded unevenly. If the ship breached, Kyle was dead. It was too late for him to suit up. She checked the seals of her helmet, then looked at the plasma hell outside. Convective cells bloomed and roiled against the ship's surface. Who was she fooling? If the hull went they'd both die.

The *Gambit* icon in the holo display blinked. What did that mean? She reached out her hand. The icon turned green and projected onto her finger. She pulled back to examine it. The ship lurched. Murphy was thrown forward, smacking her chest against the console. She moved her hand out of the holo display, and the icon stopped flashing. It had rotated twenty degrees from the apex. Plasma writhed against the aft screens. They were accelerating backward.

Gingerly she touched the icon again. This time when it projected onto her hand, she crept it back to the top. The ship slowed, then stopped.

The hologram was a navigational system. Moving the icon along the surface of the sphere affected direction and velocity. What would happen if she moved it radially, off the sphere? Had Gallger's pilots tried that? Unlikely. Grounders thought in two dimensions, along surfaces.

She moved the icon to the dead center of the sphere. More of the triangle-numbers appeared. Coordinates? Where had they come from? Murphy hadn't programmed a destination.

The plasma swirled in on itself, retracting to a red pinpoint in the forward screen. The rest of the IFOs went black. The Bussard collectors groaned. Indicators clearly labeled in unreadable text flashed amber. Vibrations sent shocks of pain through her ankle. Cross-braces shrieked in metal agony as the ship's hull flexed.

The red pinpoint in the viewscreen stretched into an orange circle, growing quickly and set on a collision course with the ship. It blue-shifted as it expanded— to yellow, white—and then it blossomed into a field of stars.

Murphy fluttered the braking thrusters with her left hand. The engines whined louder. The ship slowed. The IFO displays showed endless blackness and stars. As far as she could tell, the *Gambit* was back in normal space.

Kyle clung to an emergency oxy-pak mounted on the wall. "We survived?" Drops of sweat jiggled in the air around him.

Murphy rubbed clenched muscles along the back of her neck, and exhaled in relief and exhaustion. "So far."

A blue cross-section of the *Gambit* appeared in the air before her. Angry red lines fissured the outer hull. One of the Bussard collectors had been torn away. Numbers that could have been the ship's internal and external temperatures were dropping rapidly. No breach alarms, though—the inner hull was intact.

Murphy touched one of the fissures. It expanded. Beneath it was an engine schematic and lines of unreadable red text.

Out of the corner of her eye, she thought she saw human text. But when Murphy focused on the script, the characters were gibberish. Her mind was playing tricks on her.

She rubbed her eyes in frustration. How could she pilot a ship when she couldn't even read the status displays?

She checked their position by looking at the stars in the IFOs. The configurations were subtly altered. Her stomach clenched. Constellations wouldn't shift this much unless the *Gambit* had jumped dozens of light-years.

"Forget Newton," she breathed. Her hands flew across the navigational panel. The text was still gibberish, but she was able to translate the spherical coordinates.

"Well?" Kyle asked.

"Avocet was right. The *Gambit* self-launches." She closed her eyes and rubbed them until she saw sparks. "We've just jumped more than forty-three light-years."

Murphy stared at the changed stars in amazement. She imagined a universe filled with ships like this one. Distance would be irrelevant, and launchers unnecessary. She felt a strong proprietary urge. For a moment she contemplated keeping the ship for herself, disappearing into the big black.

But that would be wasteful. This ship should be studied, reverse-engineered, and duplicated. With ships like this, floaters could jump anywhere, without permission from the Collective or paying exorbitant launch fees.

The insistent throbbing of her ankle brought her back to reality. The adrenaline of her escape was wearing off. Her entire body ached from heat and acceleration. She was going to feel like hell in the morning.

Murphy verified that the ship's position was not in any immediate danger. Or at least, she hoped that's what the alien controls were telling her. She asked, "There a med kit on board?"

Kyle pulled a Velcro box off the wall, with a *rrrupt* and threw it to her in a clumsy motion. He didn't compensate for the reaction of his throw and blundered into the wall behind him.

She popped the seals on her boot and said, "You haven't spent much time in zero-gee."

"No," he answered distractedly. Kyle pulled himself to an IFO and looked out at the unfamiliar starscape. "Did Gallger see us jump?"

"They saw something." Murphy eased her foot out. Sudden pain made her eyes water. She clung to the arms of the captain's chair until she could see again.

"You all right?" he asked.

"It's nothing. Just got a little banged up getting on board." She wasn't going to admit weakness in front of Kyle until she had a better idea whose side he was playing on. She turned so the back of the captain's chair hid her foot from his view.

Her ankle was bruised eggplant brownish-purple. The swelling ballooned the top of her foot seamlessly into her shin. The sight made her queasy. To distract them both, she asked, "So, what did you do for Gallger? You got any more information about how this ship works?"

Kyle continued staring out the IFO. "Just what I put in Avocet's report. The *Gambit* was my ticket out. I didn't think it could really launch." His voice was disconsolate. "Gallger will kill me when they understand the magnitude of what I've stolen."

Grimacing, Murphy opened the medipack. The kit contained rolls of medicated bandages, skin patches, a flexible MRI, an infectious disease tester, and tubes of insta-cast. Murphy unrolled the ten-centimeter-wide strip of the MRI, wrapped it gingerly around her ankle, and set it to slow sweep. "You have anything to do with the preset coordinates?"

He turned toward her. "What?"

"When we launched, a set of coordinates flashed into the navigational display. I didn't put them there. Did you?"

"It must have been the Gallger engineers." Kyle's eyes became huge. "They know where we are. They'll be here soon, we've got to—"

"Easy. We can't afford to jump to conclusions. Maybe it was the Gallger boys, maybe not. First let's find out where we are and what shape the ship's in. Then we'll decide what to do. You got a portable?"

"Yes." He unzipped a chest pocket and removed a compact black clamshell. Gallger must pay their employees well, it looked like the latest Datronic model.

"Good. Look up these coordinates on a star map." She recited the numbers that had flashed by during the launch.

While he was busy, Murphy checked the MRI. Magnetic fields generated in waves across its width. A low-resolution image formed on the outside of the flexible strip.

She didn't see any breaks. The dark line across the

front might be a hairline fracture, but nothing that needed a cast. Murphy tapped an anti-inflammatory patch over her ankle, then ground her teeth together as she wrapped the ankle tightly with a silicon-cotton bandage.

She eased her boot back on. Sweat broke out on her forehead as she zipped up the seals, but better a little pain than a breached suit if something happened to the *Gambit*. She purged the air inside her suit and repressurized, ran through the integrity tests twice to make sure the seals were solid. Kyle looked up from his portable reader. "We're in the Ross 671 star system. There used to be a pharmaceutical manufacturing station here, Canodyne 4265, but it was shut down. The system's abandoned now."

"Closest inhabited star system?"

"Twenty-two point six light-years away."

"We got enough food and water on board to long-trip it if we have to?"

Kyle shook his head. "A couple of weeks, no more." He looked out the IFO, as if expecting company. "We've got to get out of here. It can't be a coincidence that we jumped to this system out of all the infinite reaches of space. Gallger must have preset the launch coordinates. They'll find us."

"You better hope they do. The outer hull's breached, and it looks like one of the engine systems is damaged. We *can't* launch with the ship in this condition, and I don't know if we can repair it. I'd rather be captured and convicted of theft than starve to death in an abandoned system."

"You don't understand. Gallger owns ninety percent of the launchers in the galaxy. Its linchpin technology is how the Collective controls interstellar traffic. The technology on this ship would certainly bankrupt Gallger, and could even destabilize the Collective. And I sold it to a buyer with the means and motive to mass-produce self-launching ships. In their eyes, I'm a traitor. That's a capital crime. I won't be working my time off as an indentured—I'll be dead."

Murphy studied his face, decided he was serious. "All right, I'll look at the engine system. But before I EVA and try the insanely stupid move of trying to repair an engine I know nothing about, I'm going to eat. In the last fourteen hours, the only thing I've had is a stale energy bar I cadged off a tow-man." And while she was cooking, the pain-patch on her ankle might kick in. She'd need all her focus to go EVA, with only a spacesuit between her and the void.

Murphy pushed herself out of the captain's chair with her palms and groaned. "I'm going to the galley, and you're coming with me."

Kyle cocked an eyebrow at her. "I'm no chef."

"Let's just say that you've already betrayed one company." Murphy stared at him. "I'm not leaving you alone in the control room."

"You're that paranoid?"

"I'm that cautious."

Kyle shrugged and they floated out of the room.

Past the airlock was a suit cabinet. Two of the four stations were filled. The first suit, Kyle's she supposed, was haphazardly tethered to the wall. The catheters hadn't been closed off and urine bulged from a plastic tube. Murphy wrinkled her upper lip in disgust. In space, your suit was your life. Abusing it was like eating radioactive waste.

The second suit made her pause. Its body was a flexible white material without seams or joints. The helmet was a streamlined black bubble. The gloves and boots were, by contrast to the rest of the suit, bulky. They were twice normal size.

"Where'd this come from?" she asked Kyle, pointing at the suit.

"I don't know. It was on the ship when Gallger salvaged it."

Interesting. She'd have to take a closer look after she ate and inspected the engines.

They continued through a circular hole in the wall and entered the living quarters. In a five-meter-wide space was the galley, composed of a rehydrating microwave, water hose, and food racks; sleeping quarters, a sack tethered to the wall; and a zero-gee toilet built into the wall. Murphy pulled vertical boards out of the pantry and inspected the stores velcroed to either side in plastic packets. It was full, supplies for two weeks . . . or a month for one person.

She poked a freeze-dried packet. "Package meals." She grimaced and pushed the shelf back into place.

The hole in the floor continued. Murphy poked her head through and saw maintenance panels, oxy-and-water recyc, and a closed bulkhead marked in illegible script.

"What's on the other side?" she asked, pointing.

"Four hundred cubic meters of empty space. Enough cargo room for a small shipping concern if they carried high-profit loads."

Or information. The only way to affect faster-than-light communication was to launch datachips. The three-kilometer-wide net required to intercept the incoming chips was hardly discrete. This ship, small as it was, could slip into a system undetected. The *Gambit* would be ideal for a courier . . . or a spy.

She didn't mention this to Kyle. He'd already proven himself a corporate traitor, and she didn't want to give him any more information to sell.

In the galley, Kyle pulled out a rack and flipped, somersaulting out of control. "Damn." He wriggled about in the air, making his situation worse.

"Stop struggling," Murphy said. "Tap the walls to center yourself. Don't make any sudden movements." She grabbed a handhold with her left hand and extended her right.

Kyle grabbed it like a drowning man.

Murphy hauled him to her. "How did you become a salvager if you can't maneuver in zero-gee?"

Kyle clung to the wall. His face was tinged green. He gulped. "Gallger uses centripetal gravity for its fleet. It's affordable. Why would anyone risk their health long-term in microgravity?"

Murphy pushed off toward the pantry. "Someone

has to work the crystallography and pharmaceutical plants, do space construction and assembly." She pulled two insta-packets of marinara pasta off the board. "There are some things you can do only in null-gee. And no employer's ever seen a need to provide a separate spinning barracks for the crews. The cost would cut into their profits." She jabbed a waterline into each pasta packet, hydrating the powdered sauce. She said, "Once a floater is fully conditioned to weightlessness, there's no going back."

Kyle said, "Zero-gee workers who exercise for five hours a day can preserve their bone and muscle mass. Scientists knew that in the twentieth century. Floaters are obsolete. They should integrate into normal society."

She ignored his assumption of what was normal. "When you're working eighteen-hour days for slave wages, who has five extra hours a day? Companies don't pay you to work out."

"You don't have space adaptation syndrome."

She slammed both packets into the microwave and turned to face him. "I'm a special case. The uncle who raised me runs his own business, so there was money and time for me to exercise. Even with years of preparation, it took me ten months of centrifuge training to stand full gee."

"Whatever."

The oven pinged. Murphy took out the food. The bags were steaming. She held the hot plastic by a corner.

Kyle let go of his handhold and carefully eased over to the kitchen areas. He wedged himself between the counter and the cabinet to pull two bowls free from their Velcro fasteners. Murphy wrapped her legs around his waist, tearing open a packet.

His eyes widened and he sputtered. "Get off me." He shoved her away.

Kyle bounced off the near wall. Murphy spun, hot marinara leaking in a steaming arc from the open bag. A hot blob adhered to her cheek, surface tension locking the burning sauce to her face. She scraped it away with the flat of her palm. Livid, she bobbled to a stop in front of Kyle. "You idiot! I was putting us in the same frame of reference so you could fill the bowls."

"You must think I'm naive. I've heard about your floater orgies. No thanks."

Murphy locked her left leg around the ergonomic and caught Kyle's shoulder. "A *floater* would have flushed you on sight: you're a drain on the atmospherics, the food supply, and your flailings in zero-gee are dangerous. *I* didn't because I'm University educated. I spent six years training to protect useless people like you. But"—she tightened her grip—"I am the captain of this ship. You will do what I say, when I say, without question, or I will stuff you into your inadequately maintained suit and blast you into the big dark. Is that clear?"

Kyle struggled, trying to pry her hands loose. He was stronger than she, but he wasn't braced. The only thing that moved was his body, whipping back and forth at the end of her arm. Murphy shook him.

"Is that clear?"

He went limp and choked, "Quite."

"Then go clean up your suit. It's disgusting." Murphy shoved them apart. "I'll be in the control room." She wanted to bash his face in. The rungs of the ladder were cold and hard under her left hand. She balanced the bowl and pushed off—with both feet.

Her ankle screamed in electric blue tones. Stupid move. Dumb.

She caught the lip of the bowl in her teeth and grabbed the ladder with both hands. She pushed off from her palms, braking with her left foot on the couch, and eased in behind the controls to eat. Her hands shook.

Damn Kyle anyway. He shouldn't be here. What business did a grounder have in space?

Murphy froze.

The thought echoed in her head like an inverse harmonic of Osborne's bigotry. She was ashamed. Of all people, she should know better. Kyle didn't want to be there. She shouldn't let his incompetence upset her.

There were more important things to worry about, like how to get back to known space.

She scanned the star systems. No sign of the old pharmaceutical plant, not even the remains of an exploration launcher, just a few asteroids circling a lonely star.

She looked at the distant points of light. This space had existed since the beginning of time, untouched by humans. A cold ache settled behind her ribs. The emptiness reminded her of her father, a man who had decided that exploration was more important than his wife, or his five-year-old daughter.

She had vague memories of him, a tall laughing man with eyes so dark blue you couldn't see the pupils. Everyone deferred to him, called him "The Murphy." She was the Murphy now, and he was twenty-years gone, lost among stars farther than these.

Murphy wiped her nose on her sleeve. She took another bite of pasta marinara and wished she had thought to grab cutlery. She sucked red sauce from between her fingers.

Impact rocked the ship.

Murphy's hand danced, not quite touching the controls. It was wrong to touch instruments with greasy hands.

Another blow sent the ship spinning. The right edge of the pilot's chair slammed into her rib cage. She grabbed the armrest and struggled against the sudden acceleration to reach the controls.

Her fingers slipped across the throttle strip and eased the ship around. One good thing about floater taboos—they deferred to necessity.

"What was that?" Kyle clung to the rungs of the ladder. His hair was canted to one side by centripetal force.

"That's what I'm trying to find out." She fired the left thrusters and slowed the rotation, then scanned the IFOs. A mass moved into view on the front screen. It was a third of the *Gambit*'s mass, an organic collage of spare parts and manufacturing scrap. The left side was spiked with satellite antennae. The right was melted in spots. The center, holding the deformed mass together, seemed to be an Avocet 4-11 emergency lifeboat.

A metal disk ejected from a dark winking eye. A gray line arced from the collage to the *Gambit*.

"A grapple magnet," Kyle said. The ship shook as it connected. "They intend to capture us."

"We'll see about that." Murphy slid her finger along the throttle, easing the engines up. The line pulled tight.

A man flickered onto the screen. Biophysical equations were scrawled in thick black curlicues over his heavy eyebrows.

"Heya, *Gambit*." The eyebrows raised when he saw her. "You're powering down, or a thermal charge shoves right up your exhaust tube. We may be small, but our aim is true."

"They can't be serious," Kyle said. "A detonation at this range would destroy both ships."

Murphy studied the stranger's face. It was bloated with full SAS, but the neck beneath was skeletal. "You may be overestimating the value of life in this particular corner of the galaxy," she said to Kyle. "Besides, he got out here somehow. He may know a way back." She tapped the throttle slightly and set the engines on idle.

The man on the screen glowered. "All the way down. Full power off."

Murphy touched the symbols on her forehead. "You take me for a *gronuger*? Idle's all you get. I'm not hostile. Yet."

The other floater licked his teeth, considering. "Crazy fem." He clicked off the com.

"Well. He's taking us home to meet Mama."

"What is a *gronuger*?" Kyle asked.

"Non-floater." She nodded at the pile of junk towing the *Gambit*. "You're about to get a crash course in floater culture."

CHAPTER
6

The lifeboat reeled its grapple magnet in, pulling the tiny bubble of metal closer to the *Gambit*. "Open the bay," the floater said. "This range, my weapons won't miss."

Murphy studied his set expression on the screen. Her gaze traveled along his jawbone, to the heavy black marks that ringed his skull. Viral RNA diagrams and bacterial growth equations.

The bumblebee ship docked to the *Gambit*'s airlock. "Open up," he repeated.

"Who are you?" Murphy asked. "Why do you need to board my ship?"

The floater bowed grandly. "Call me Spanner. Here to pilot us into dock."

She ground her teeth. "No one flies the *Gambit* but me. You can ride piggyback, but I stay in command. I'm coming in for talk, not search and seizure."

"We're no fat company-owned station. There's no rotation to spare with a sloppy dock. Open the wasting bulkhead."

She jerked her index finger at her forehead. "These aren't birthmarks."

Spanner sneered. "Any *gronuger* can be marked." His eyes flickered sideways. "Who's the man?"

Kyle. Damn. She was hoping to keep him a surprise.

"Cargo. No one you need to worry about," she told Spanner. "I'm taking us in."

" 'Sa tough dock for a ship this size. Open the airlock and let me pilot, or this ship'll be wreckage."

"You eager to throw away your life? Shoot at this range, and it'll engulf us both." She met his gaze. "I was the top-ranked pilot at the University for the last six years. Flew the Möbius course in three point four seconds and didn't touch a rock. I can take us in."

Spanner appraised her, one eyebrow raised. "You're one hard-hulled fem." Coordinates wiped his face from the screen. Murphy was left staring at blue numerals. Seconds later the lifeboat disconnected from the *Gambit*.

"What do you mean: I'm cargo?" Kyle asked.

"Let me do the talking. You don't understand floater culture. I'm not going to let your big mouth and grounder ways get us killed."

"Oh, and how long have you been away from floater society? Five years? Six? You escaped at the first opportunity. I may be ignorant of floater customs, but you rejected them." He pointed his finger at her. "So don't treat me as second class."

"I didn't ask you to come aboard my ship—"

"This isn't your ship. It's mine."

Murphy's eyes widened.

"If it wasn't for me, you and Avocet would be oblivious this ship existed. I stole it, and I sold it—only I haven't been paid yet." He straightened. "So it's still my ship. The way I see it, you work for me."

"Listen to me," Murphy growled. "The only thing between you and hard vacuum is my goodwill. And right now that's running a little thin."

"Don't threaten me." He scanned her thin olive-skinned body. "I could snap you in half like a silicon wafer."

Murphy struck with both hands: her left, balled into a fist, connected with Kyle's face; the right slapped the wall, counteracting her rotation.

Kyle spun like a top. He flailed in the air, trying to grab something to slow his turning.

Hitting him was a calculated risk, but if he didn't

learn who commanded the *Gambit* and soon—he might try to overpower her. The truth was, with the strength advantages of being male and a grounder, he probably could. And then who would fly the ship? Ambiguity would endanger them both.

His feet caught in the emergency air tanks, slamming his body into the wall. He drifted groggily.

Murphy grabbed his hand and pulled his face to hers. "Strength means nothing without control." She shook him, and they vibrated in and out like two ends of a spring. "I don't care who you were, or what deal you made. My only concern now, and for the foreseeable future, is to get us and this ship back to Avocet. Intact. If you want to be a part of that, you'll do what I say. Understand?"

They stared at each other a long moment, her brown eyes boring into his blue. He looked away first.

What was Kyle thinking? He'd committed theft to take the ship. Would he commit murder to keep it? She wished she had Tali's knack for understanding people.

His muscular body rotated slowly in the air. Blond hair exploded from his head. It looked ridiculous. But how would he look in gravity, with all that fine pale-gold hair settled about his shoulders? Not bad, she supposed.

She decided to give him a second chance. He couldn't pilot the ship. If he killed her, he had no way to return and collect his money from Avocet.

Besides, if she spaced him now, it would make Spanner's people suspicious.

They spent the next three minutes following the floater's coordinates in silence.

"What did you do on the salvager?" she asked Kyle.

After a pause he said, "Filed reports and communication logs."

"Good. Why don't you take over the com? See if you can locate any signals. Maybe we can learn something about our destination."

Kyle nodded, a gesture that, in zero-gee, rocked his entire body.

He was like a new recruit. Left to his own devices, he'd make trouble. If he felt useful, he'd be less likely to cause disruption. Up here, she could keep an eye on him. She wasn't ready to trust him alone, downstairs, with the suits.

Seconds later, he had the communications diagnostic display up and was searching the bandwidths. "You're a fast learner," she said.

Kyle shrugged. "I served on the reconnaissance team that boarded the *Gambit*. I used these controls to communicate with the salvager."

The com chimed. He touched the controls, and a green wave trace vibrated in the air in front of them. "A transmission," he said, ". . . and another. He's probably reporting to the station. I'm picking up scatter from the beam profile. Shall I transfer it to the speakers?"

Murphy nodded. Kyle operated the controls until they were surrounded by a static roar.

Murphy tapped a speaker. "Sounds like white noise."

"Filtering." Kyle flicked his fingers across the com screen. He brought up a diagram of the wave packet. He selectively cut some peaks and amplified others, then tweaked the gain. The sound dimmed into a murmur, a purposeful rumbling.

"Where'd you learn to do that?"

"Salvage. We would often detect and unscramble the last communications of an inoperable ship. By that means we could obtain most of the security codes, and avoid burning the locks."

"Those signals must have traveled hundreds of parsecs before salvage found the derelict. How did you locate the signals? How did you match them to their ship?"

"Standard procedure: Gallger dispatches a salvage unit as soon as an accident report arrives. Some of the crew are usually still alive. Salvage positions nearby and monitors. Easy."

Murphy nodded. "So you wait while the rescue team recovers the crew."

"No." Kyle looked at her oddly. "Gallger sends no rescue ship. We just jump in-system and . . . wait."

Murphy's eyes widened. "You don't help them? You sit there and listen to them die?"

"A salvager doesn't have the resources to support extra personnel," Kyle said. "If we took them on board, everyone would die. Gallger sends us for the equipment, nothing more."

"What about the people?"

Kyle shrugged. "Not profitable."

"That's sick."

"It's the way Companies work."

Murphy knew she shouldn't be surprised. She'd grown up knowing the Companies valued money more than lives. She rubbed her eyes. "What are they saying?"

Kyle touched the screen, and the murmur increased in volume. A blend of clipped accented voices, clashed, broken by static.

". . . from where?"

". . . *Gambit* . . . no call sign . . . Fem claims . . . floater . . . marked."

"Spies . . ."

". . . eats, 'plies? . . ."

"Ship's . . . refit . . ."

". . . 'scued."

The sound disappeared. Kyle played with the com. The noise returned but was an incoherent wave of static. "The angle's changed. I've lost the signal."

"Damn. I wish they'd given us a clue how they got out here."

Three hours later, a multiple-shipwreck appeared in the forward IFOs: four Avocet miner tugs slammed together, nose first, into a roughly spherical asteroid. They angled in, like a child's pinwheel. The spaces between their elongated bulks were bridged by girders, lifeboats, parts of asteroids, and general mechanical debris. The entire structure was no more than a half kilometer across.

Murphy clocked the rotation. Three-quarters turn per minute. There'd be a little over a tenth of a gee at the rim.

"That can't be our destination," Kyle said. "No one could survive on that."

"You'd be surprised what desperate people can do." She pointed at the blue-and-white Gallger symbols on the side of the miner tugs. "I wouldn't mention your former employer."

Spanner flickered into view. "Dock to tug 443. Match spin to outer rim, near the engines. Airlock's on the tug's side, third of the way in, inside the webbing, so angle in between the tugs. Keep your angular momentum in perfect synch, or you'll crash."

Adrenaline buzzed along Murphy's shoulder blades. She'd burn the *Gambit* before she'd let that arrogant son-of-a-*gronuger* touch her controls. "I can do it." She had to; if their hosts learned what the *Gambit* was capable of, she and Kyle wouldn't last the sleep-cycle.

"You better. Threaten the station, and they'll burn the engines on us. Salvage'd be just as profitable for the station." He glanced past her at the advanced controls in the background. "Maybe more so."

Don't get your hopes up. Murphy reached over Kyle and clicked the com off. "You'd better strap in," she said, studying the approach. "There'll be some angular acceleration."

Spanner's threat was an empty one. If they had fuel for a burn, they'd have spun the station up farther. One-tenth-gee wasn't enough to prevent first-order SAS. Besides, a burn that big would generate a lot of radiation for the people inside. Still, if she wasn't all the way up to the station's full spin, the *Gambit* would be crushed against the tug.

She'd never docked the *Gambit* before. Which controls were the docking magnets? Did the ship *have* docking magnets? With Spanner watching, she smiled confidently, flexed her knuckles, and slid her fingertips millimeters along the throttle strip. She'd have to figure it out as she went.

Though the characters were indecipherable, numerals were recognizable patterns of triangles. The ship's spherical and station-relative coordinates were laid out in the same pattern as other ships she'd flown.

She inclined the ship into a radial trajectory around the station. One pass. Two. The ship handled like a dream, fast and responsive. In seconds, she was nearly aligned. The mass of twisted metal and rocks grew larger and slowed in the IFOs as *Gambit* neared synch. Then the station stopped. For a long gleaming moment, *Gambit* hovered in synchronous orbit. Then the station rotated—in reverse. She was coming in too fast. Murphy fluttered the braking thrusters, trying to get enough lift for a fourth pass. She was too close. Enough burn to raise her orbit would radiate the people inside. She could break the trajectory, tangent off, and start all over. But that would show her inexperience. She didn't want them to know she was unfamiliar with the ship. No. She had to dock perfectly, the first time.

"Too close," Spanner's voice rose from the com. "Break away."

Murphy clicked him off.

"Murphy . . ." said Kyle.

"I'm going to dock on this pass. Now, shut up, I need to concentrate."

The IFOs filled her vision. The reverse roll of the station increased. She could read the numbers stenciled on access panels of the mining tug. She licked her upper lip, tasting salt. Her hands danced over the thruster controls. Pulse. Evaluate. Pulse. Only the controls under her fingers and the view in the IFOs existed. All else was gone.

She slipped the ship below the circumference cut by the tug's engines. *Gambit* was between the tugs now, unsynched. The web of girders grew in the hull-side

IFOs. Only a narrow channel was kept clear for docking lifeboats. *Gambit* was going to be a tight fit.

Something buzzed in her ear, but she ignored it. Almost in synch. Flutter the braking thrusters. Evaluate. All motion stopped. Synch.

Sound crashed in on Murphy like a wave too long denied the shore. Kyle and Spanner screamed at her. Proximity alarms blared. She exhaled, letting it wash over her.

She still needed to mate the airlocks. The thruster pulses would have to be perfectly balanced. Any variation or perturbation would dash them against the web of girders spanning the tugs.

Murphy didn't breathe. Extending her fingers to the controls, she became the ship. Wiggling and twisting. Scraping once. Murphy felt sparks in the IFO flare along her ribs. *Gambit* hovered above the airlock. The connection of the docking magnets slammed into the ship like the first thrust of intercourse. Tension—then release. Murphy exhaled.

For a moment no one said anything. Only the bleating of alarms cut the air.

"We made it," said Kyle.

"I said break off," Spanner's voice was hoarse. "Who do you think you are—a Murphy?"

She smirked. "Thiadora Murphy, at your service." Waste. Why did she say that? Knocking Spanner down a peg wasn't worth dealing with that old superstition.

Spanner's eyes went wide. Whites showed around his nearly black irises. "No spoofing about The Murphy," Spanner whispered. "Some here knew him." His hands flew across his com, opening channels. "Meet in the airlock. Fifteen minutes. Stay suited. Don't know you well enough yet to share air." He disappeared.

Kyle stared at the blank screen. "He called you 'a Murphy.' What does that mean?"

She glanced away. "It's a stupid floater superstition. A relation of mine survived some stunts in the early days of the revolution—got a reputation for being lucky." Murphy pushed off toward the galley. "Come on. We'd better suit up. Who knows how often that kludged-together station ruptures."

As she passed through the galley, Murphy grabbed an armful of pasta packets.

"Why are you taking those?" Kyle asked.

"To make friends with the natives."

Kyle followed her to the airlock, took his Gallger 340-B down, and started fumbling with it. Murphy made a mental note to train him how to fast-suit. If the hull breached, he wouldn't have time to drain the catheters and pull each leg on separately.

She checked the status report on her suit. The batteries were dead. She checked the circuit. Shit. A short in the oxygen regeneration cycle had bled the batteries dry. There wasn't time to fix it.

She could use Kyle's suit, but then she'd have to leave him alone in the ship. It was unlikely he'd figure out the piloting controls—but she didn't trust him not to try. The only thing better than selling a ship once was selling it twice.

Her eyes fell on the other suit, the one found with the *Gambit*. She touched the white fabric of its body. It was thick like rubber, and the gloves were enormous. Would her hands fit? Instead of boots, there were glove-like appendages for each foot. Each toe had a separate sheath. What kind of person used their toes in a suit?

Experimentally, she slipped her hand into a glove. It was snug. Rubbery nubs lined the inside. She wiggled her fingers. The glove jerked in reaction. When she flexed her palm forward, the glove moved back as if she had pressed against something solid. How was it moving? There wasn't any visible propulsion. Intrigued, she slipped on the rest of the suit.

The socks and body of the suit were lined with more nubbed sensors. Her limbs flexed without restraint. The range of motion was like nothing she'd ever worn before. Despite the suit's bulk, it was like wearing thick synth-skin.

When she contracted her hand quickly, it stopped as if she had grabbed a solid object. A slow contraction allowed her to close her fist. Was the sleeve contracting or was this an outside effect? She didn't see any jets or electromagnets. Floating in the center of the room, she pushed sharply against the air in front of her. She moved backward.

Incredible. Would it work in vacuum?

She slipped the helmet on. It was clear from her peripheral vision forward, with sensors in the back. There was a profusion of tongue controls. She touched one, and a display reflected on the inside of the helmet.

She pressed another and the faceplate bent, focusing like a lens. When she moved the control to the left or right, the focal point changed. Far objects came into view, close objects were magnified. She'd never heard of a flexible helmet. It couldn't be vacuum-proof.

Theoretically, though, she'd only be in hard vacuum for seconds. The two airlocks were mated. She would void the *Gambit*'s lock, step through to the other side, and wait for pressure to build up. The suit only had to last for those brief moments.

She would evacuate the lock slowly. If the suit leaked, she'd have time to stop the cycle.

Kyle finished the last of his connections. "Why are you wearing that suit?"

"Don't have any choice," Murphy said, transferring her few possesions—a knife, the floater's bible—to the new suit. "Mine's got a short."

Murphy bit her lip as she watched the pressure display of the lock cycle. The suit held.

The lock on the other side opened and filled. Murphy tested the air. If she understood the suit's display, the air was marginal, high in carbon dioxide, but breathable.

Spanner, suited in an obsolete Gallger hard suit that had been patched several times, came forward and clasped her forearms. He touched helmets with her. "Well met to Canodyne 4265."

Kyle cocked his head at the Company name. "Canodyne? The old medical research station?"

"No. Manufacturing. We synthed drugs with crystal structures that only grow in zero-gee. Now"—the floater shrugged—"we survive." His gaze lingered on Murphy's unusual spacesuit.

Murphy interrupted his appraisal. "These are for your station." She held out the dozen insta-food packets she had brought.

Spanner snatched them from her hand. He flexed the heat disk of one and massaged the packet furiously. With a suspicious glance at Murphy and Kyle, Spanner popped his helmet seals long enough to attach the packet inside his helmet and suck on the straw. After a moment he sighed. "Haven't had red sauce in years. Tomatoes didn't take in hydroponics." He stowed the rest of the packets in a mesh pocket on the outside of his suit and rechecked his seals. "This way," he said.

Murphy restrained him with her hand. "I want a guarantee my ship won't be tampered with while I'm talking."

Spanner pressed both hands to his chest in a wounded gesture. "Even desperate, we don't forget the Code. Your ship is safe while we talk. After that"—he shrugged—"depends on what is said."

The lights in the airlock flickered. Spanner's head jerked up. "Not now," he pleaded, "wait." The bulbs went out.

"What was that?" Murphy whispered in the darkness.

Spanner clicked on his helmet light. His bobbing head threw wild shadows. "Blackout. It happens. Be up by the time we meet the crew in central."

"Only one crew?" Murphy asked.

Spanner's reply was long in coming. "All that's left." He pushed off through the cavernous cargo bay. "Follow me."

The electronics there were dead, too. Shadows danced in the corners. It was all she could do to not look at them. She felt watched.

"What make's your suit?" Spanner asked without looking back.

"I'll explain when we meet your people," Murphy said. "No use repeating myself."

Spanner grunted.

They reached the far side of the cargo bay, and Spanner typed a code into the bulkhead's keypad. It irised open, revealing a gray access tube that was half again the diameter of her suit. Tight.

Over the speakers, she heard Kyle swallow.

There was a whump as the air generators came back online. The fluorescents flickered and caught, bathing the bay in green-tinged light.

"About time," Spanner muttered.

Murphy asked, "How long has your crew been here?"

"Five years." Spanner pushed Kyle and Murphy past him, into the tube, and climbed in after them.

Murphy stopped, pressing the gloves of her suit along opposite sides of the wall until she slowed. She touched her faceplate to Spanner's so they could talk without using helmet speakers.

"Can't you leave? Don't you have a launcher?"

Spanner grimaced. "Company shut down the launcher to trap rebels hiding in-system. Done it before, but the last time they detonated charges. Total loss.

"Even if we'd materials to rebuild the ship launcher, there's no power to drive it. *Waste*, even the data-launcher browns-out the station for three minutes." He studied the symbols above her brow. "Now, tell me, why're you here?"

She met his near-black eyes. There was desperation there, and something else. "I'll save that for my explanation to your crew."

His lips tensed, and he pulled away from her. "This way," he said brusquely, pushing past Kyle.

Kyle gave her a questioning look. Murphy shook her head. Even with the fractional gravity, her whole body shimmied in reaction.

The tunnel changed to rough-hewn rock welded and melted to the metal. Light washed out of the corridor ahead and drenched them.

Spanner led them past a hydroponics rack, where kelp and spinach were layered with banks of lights, then took them through to a second mining tug. He stopped in the control room and pulled up beside them. "Security'll scan you for weapons, then we go in. Don't try to de-suit. No telling what diseases you're carrying. Crew's survived one outbreak; won't risk another one. If the meet goes well, we'll blood-scan you. No use wasting a testor only to kick you out. For now, keep your seals closed. First sign of trouble, and security caps you." He looked at Murphy. "Understand?"

"Yes." It was a common precaution. Some bacteria responded to zero-gee by growing to plague proportions. And new strains of viruses had evolved in the past decade that thrived only in weightlessness. Those facts, combined with the way radiation and weightlessness hindered the immune system, caused disease to take many lives in zero-gee. Millions of floaters and space workers had died before quarantine rules had slowed the diseases down.

Spanner opened a reinforced door and signaled to a man and woman wearing industrial exoskeletons. A cage work of metal rods covered a normal suit. The joints were powerful gear mechanisms, compounding the wearer's force.

Kyle held his helmet against hers. "What does he mean, 'cap us'?"

"A type of epoxy shot from a cannon. It's used to reinforce domes. The fluid has a high surface tension and creeps to cover whatever it touches. It hardens in seconds. In a dome, it spreads itself millimeters thin, strengthening the structure. Over a suited human, it's two meters thick. Once you're capped, you stay capped until your cooling systems fail. Then you broil in your own juices."

The couple in exoskeletons ran hand scanners over

Murphy and Kyle. They frowned at Murphy, then spoke helmet-to-helmet with Spanner. He stared at them; the couple returned the look. Finally Murphy and Kyle were ushered into the central chamber.

Carved out of solid asteroid, the spherical room was twenty meters in diameter, with pitted gray stone walls. Except for the ten-meter-wide screen along one wall, floaters clung to every surface: ceiling, walls, floor. They all wore suits with the helmets dangling loose, a testament to the station's instability—or the radiation.

Radiation and weightlessness warred to accelerate and retard aging, respectively. To Murphy's eyes, all of the floaters looked in their forties, or older. Spanner, in his mid-thirties, was one of the youngest.

Wait. There. A child clung to its mother's leg. It was small, barely seventy centimeters long, yet the face looked four or five years old. Though bald, there were no markings on its head. It had not been designated a person. Murphy saw why: the head was undersized, and the lips were slack. Its eyes were dull and devoid of intelligence.

Spanner followed her gaze. "Lil's fault. Station's doctor, she should've known better than to carry without a proper rock. Kid was born four months after the Company blew the launcher. No resources for spin-up or proper radiation shielding." His lips tightened. "Still, the crew didn't ask for an abort. Chance was he might Murphy out okay." Spanner glanced sideways at the child. "But he didn't. Something should be done about him. He drains resources. But"—he looked at the small, gray-eyed woman—"her man died from plague two months before the child was born. When she went to put down the kid, she couldn't. Last link to the one she lost. Since then, no one's had the heart to take the kid from her."

He turned his attention to the other floaters. "Gift from our guests," he said, and flung the food packets into the assembled crowd.

"Don't," Lil shouted, "might be poison."

No one heeded her warning. Floaters lashed out like solar flare-ups and grabbed the packets. For three minutes the only sounds were the pops of heat disks and gurgles of chewing.

Between the smacks and swallows, the floaters asked questions. In a crew meeting, anyone could ask anything.

"Which company launched you?"

"Why are you here—"

"—Food was—"

"—Who are you?"

Murphy braced her feet around a head-sized out-cropping of reddish stone, and held up her hands.

"My name is Thiadora Murphy." Her stomach roiled at the confession, but bragging to Spanner had already let the air out of the airlock.

The room hushed. People shifted to get a better view of her faceplate.

"Lies," shouted a woman tattooed with Carnot heat-cycle equations. "View her companion's suit. A Gallger model. She brings more lies from the Compa-nies who left us to die. She's no Murphy."

The rumbling grew. Lil rose, pushing off the wall. Neighboring floaters grabbed her feet to keep her from drifting into the sphere. Trailing her child behind her, she said, "Perhaps Gallger sent her to rescue us."

A tall fair-skinned man answered. "Gallger? Sent her to drain the last dregs of nutrients from our twitching corpses more like. How's she to rescue us in that tiny ship of hers? She's a spy"—he glanced at Murphy—"and a poor one at that."

A honey-skinned man with cheekbones as sharp and round as saw blades held up his hands. In a moment the room was silent.

"Who's that?" Murphy asked softly.

"Yanni," Spanner said. "He's our tech. Only one left."

The yellow man turned his dark brown eyes on Murphy. His entire scalp was stenciled with green-and-gold circuit diagrams. He asked, "Which launcher sent you? The jump signature was strange."

Murphy hesitated. If she told them the truth about the *Gambit*'s self-launching capabilities . . . Code or no Code, there were some temptations too strong to resist. She didn't want the ship stolen before she could deliver it to Avocet.

The woman with Carnot equations jeered, "Answer him, you Gallger spy!"

Murphy ignored the woman. "What do you mean, strange?"

He lifted his chin in her direction but spoke to the crowd. "When her ship launched in, the signature was too compact, as if what jumped her folded space more than normal." He met her gaze. Light flashed off the gold connections tattooed on his head. "Tell us, which launcher sent you?"

Murphy glanced at Kyle, his lips pressed so thin that white showed around the corners of his mouth. He twitched his head: "No."

Everyone in the room was watching her. There was no way to avoid an answer. Her eyes met Spanner's, and he crooked an eyebrow at her. Murphy licked her lips. It was foolish to tell the truth—but a lie could be fatal.

Before she changed her mind, Murphy kicked off. Inertia carried her into the hollow center of the spherical room. The security guards tracked her with the cap-cannon. "I didn't use a launcher," she said, looking into the narrowing eyes of the tech. "The *Gambit* self-launches."

Silence, except for the rustle of floaters exchanging puzzled and uneasy glances.

A disgusted grunt from Kyle. "Idiot."

Yanni cocked his head to the left, "How—"

His question was interrupted by the boiling hiss of static. The wall screen flickered to life, showing a man in his mid-twenties, wearing acceleration equations. He looked scared. "More company just launched in. There's an Enforcer off tug 443." His image was replaced by a large ship, bearing green-and-black CEA markings.

An enormous black grid of power cells and machinery loomed behind the CEA ship. As she watched, parabolic sails unfolded and turned toward the sun. Murphy's throat constricted. An exploration launcher, expensive and disposable, used for one-way travel back from distant systems.

The Enforcer drew closer to the *Gambit*. Murphy's blood pounded in her ears. How had they found her?

The Enforcer opened its lower cargo hold, descending on the *Gambit*, engulfing it. With a terrible wrenching that shook the entire structure, the *Gambit* tore free, trailing part of the mining tug's hull. Low-pressure warnings blared throughout the station. Bulkheads clanged home.

Murphy reached out to the screen, her empty hands clawing at the air.

The ship closed the cargo doors, sealing in the *Gambit*, then blasted over to the black grid. The exploration launcher glowed blue-white, folding space around the Enforcer. With a flash of blinding light, the ship disappeared.

CHAPTER
7

It was gone.

The black grid of the exploration launcher was empty.

Murphy turned her gaze to the rent torn in the station's hull by the *Gambit*'s theft. Twisted girders rippled with stress fractures. She felt like the station, empty and broken by the strain of the week's events. Breach alarms shrieked in time with her pulse.

Floaters climbed over and around her, rushing to emergency stations. They checked their helmet seals as they went. Murphy reached to test hers. Why bother? Without the *Gambit* she had nothing. No career. No ship. No future. She was a waste of air.

The alarm vibrated through her body, demanding action, but she couldn't answer it. She wasn't part of this carefully choreographed repair drill. Anything she did would be in the way. She was as ineffective as a grounder.

Within seconds, she and Kyle were alone in the central chamber, their potential threat ignored for the real catastrophe of a hull breach.

Her helmet speakers buzzed in her ears. She increased the volume. Communications glutted the helmet frequencies. Aural chaos.

—sealed?—Bulkheads home—welder in place and—leak in four-eight-nine —Medical fac, check—Ohm-and-Maxwell! Why'd they— Lil, floor thirteen—We'll have to cut—On my way—Left fourteen degrees—

If she knew these people, she'd be able to pick out voices, follow trains of thought. Loneliness ached in her chest. It was yet another reminder that she didn't belong here . . . or anywhere.

The screen monitored the repair crew's efforts. Eight floaters maneuvered a wall of sheet metal into place. Two techs powered up sputter-ion welders.

The video wall pulsed with static. Trumpeting fanfare crackled across all frequencies, disrupting station communications. On the display, the crew's repair efforts were replaced by white stars dancing on an indigo sky. The stars whirled and resolved into the atomic orbitals of Gallger Galactic. The music swelled, and the logo morphed into a golden-haired woman. Two streamers of teal synth-silk crossed her breastbone, twined around the right side of her neck, and reappeared above her left ear.

"No," Kyle whispered, his face pale. "Not her."

"Good news, floaters." A smile lit the woman's face—except for her eyes. They were single-digit Kelvin cold. "There is work for you in the Delta Eridani system. Gallger Galactic has provided you with a pre-programmed launcher that will deliver you to the worker's station. You will be placed on active status and begin drawing wages immediately. Gallger Galactic needs you."

"Who is that?" Murphy asked.

"Vivien Gallger, the new CEO," Kyle said. "She'd dissect her mother if it was profitable."

The transmission continued. "You must jump within the next twenty-four hours. After that, the limited-term batteries will start to degrade, and Gallger Galactic cannot be held liable for any injuries or damages. Any attempt to change the launch coordinates will cause the launcher to self-destruct." The smile brightened and she repeated the company motto: "Gallger leads the industry with its vision." The dancing stars returned, swirled into the center of the screen, and winked out.

"She knows I'm here," Kyle whispered.

"She couldn't."

His eyes were haunted. "She knows."

Murphy stared at the black grid of the launcher looming in the IFOs. Why had Gallger left a working launcher behind? They could have set it to destruct after they launched away with the *Gambit*. Why risk news of a self-launching ship getting out?

The repair crew flashed back on screen. The wall of metal listed. Floaters gestured wildly, hand signals replacing the preempted frequencies.

Voices returned: "What the hell was that?—'nore it, position the damn plate—Section 49, A, check—Status in hydropon 12, we've lost a lot—Hold her, Hold her, got it—Not as bad as we thought, Engineering 5—"

As she listened, the different parts of the station checked in, reporting status. The station was an organic whole: floaters, antibodies repairing damage; communications, the lightning-fast flicker of nerves.

"No way to finish repairs this sleep-cycle," Spanner transmitted. "My station's locked down. I'll dock the strangers in my quarters."

Lil responded, her voice as flat as a mistuned com, "Crew, let's regroup next sleep-cycle."

Murphy stared at the display. Two floaters used sputter-ion welders to fasten the wall of sheet metal over the rent.

How had Gallger known where to find them? They couldn't have tracked the ship through jump. Had they preset the launch coordinates as Kyle suspected?

Murphy didn't think so. If Gallger had understood the launch controls well enough to set a destination, they'd have known the Gambit was capable of self-launch and it would have been so well guarded that a fleet of Avocet's ships couldn't have stolen it.

No. Someone had told Gallger they were here.

Her glance slid sideways to Kyle.

Kyle was slumped in midair, his wide, blank eyes fixed on the screen. "I'm doomed. Without Avocet's money . . . what will I do? I can't go back to Gallger. Vivien's revenge . . ." He shuddered.

Murphy trusted Kyle's greed. If he'd sold Murphy out, he'd be spending the money, not stuck on a dying station.

She stared at the white-suited bodies, welding the patch. It had to be one of the floaters.

Spanner pulled himself into the room, flipped once before tucking his feet into the rock. "Here to—"

Murphy grabbed his arm. "You promised my ship would be safe."

He stared at her a long moment. "You're running from Gallger. One of the big twelve. How's abandoned Canodyne 4265 to protect you from that?"

"We lost them in the jump. They couldn't have found us unless somebody here told them."

"Does not parse. Who here'd be loyal to Gallger?"

Kyle unfurled and kicked himself over to Murphy and Spanner. "You said the data launcher drains all power for three minutes."

Murphy straightened. "When we boarded—"

"The lights flickered," Kyle finished.

"Could have been anything," Spanner protested. "Station browns out when we run the recycler, for Bohr's sake."

"Five minutes with the communication logs," Kyle said, "and I can tell you whether a message was sent. Gallger conceals a recorder in the com system."

Spanner snorted, "You think we don't know? Disabled those when the Company dropped us."

"I doubt that," Kyle said. "Gallger hides multiple pickups. You found one, maybe two, but I doubt you eliminated them all."

Spanner stared hard at Kyle, frowning. "How d'you know so much about Gallger's tricks?"

Kyle met his gaze. "I worked communications." He shrugged. "Perhaps the transmission was sent by a traitor, perhaps by an automated report system. I don't know. There's one way to find out."

*   *   *

The communications room was embedded in the scaffolding between two mining tugs. It smelled of mildew. Dust covered the controls and the floor. Each step sent tendrils spiraling into the air. The motes hung in graceful loops; the one-tenth-gee settled the particles slowly. Three of the walls were covered in diagnostics and directional controls for the data launcher. On the other wall, four empty chairs faced a bank of low terminals against a backdrop of IFOs.

"Haven't used the transmitter in years," Spanner said. "Supposed to be the cornerstone of our plant, but last message we got was Canodyne detonating the launcher to trap the rebels in-system."

"Why didn't you call for help?" Murphy asked.

"Wasted too much power. Tried a few times. Other companies didn't see a profit in it. CEA judged the action an internal company problem. Not their jurisdiction."

The two-kilometer-wide receiving web filled the IFOs. Murphy spotted the last transmission's puncture: a tiny pinpoint of light against the black fabric. Com-webs didn't have enough tensile strength to stop the datachips launched in at near-relativistic speeds. Instead, the chips punched through the web, delivering their message in a single, parallel, burst.

Launching datachips between solar systems was the only way to accomplish faster-than-light communication . . . with the current technology. Murphy cursed herself again. There was no telling what secrets the *Gambit* would have revealed. No telling what advantages Gallger gained from possessing it.

Kyle settled into the ergonomic, swaying slightly as he found his center of gravity. Statistics crawled across the screen. The last hit was seventeen minutes ago.

"Gallger's message," Spanner said.

Kyle touched the controls. "We need the outgoing log." A second display appeared, a black bar across it. "Display," Kyle ordered. The next box was blank.

"See," Spanner said, "still disabled."

Kyle tapped in a code. Nothing happened. He tried

another, then a third. The display scrolled with numbers and names dated three years ago: interstellar communications, intership, even interhelmet frequencies.

"Last three years, they've heard everything?" Spanner asked.

"Not immediately. The information is recorded automatically, but someone has to transmit it. Launching a chip takes too much power to go unnoticed. It must have piggybacked on a normal report to Canodyne."

"We've had no contact with them for four years. Crew decided."

"Nothing?" Murphy asked. "No unexplained power fluctuations?"

Spanner shrugged. "Power flickers all the time. Normal for boot-rigging."

Kyle jumped to the end of the log and found a transmission dated two hours ago. "Someone's been talking to them. Gallger has recognition software that automatically tags voice transmissions. Unless the message was typed, I can identify the user." He entered a code, and a second display superimposed over the first. "Who is Lillian Burnkeft?"

"Lil?" Spanner frowned. "Makes no sense. Canodyne's slow-killing her crew. Her husband's dead, child disabled as a result. Why would she report to them?"

Murphy's jaw clenched. "That's what we'll ask her at tomorrow's meeting."

The central room was empty when they arrived the next morning. Spanner left them with security personnel while he checked in with his station.

Floaters filtered in, groups of two and three, talking. They stopped their conversation and stared when they passed Murphy.

Lil entered with two others. Her son's arms clung to her waist, his face pressed into the small of her back. His stunted legs trailed behind her like coattails.

Murphy's blood pressure rose. Lil had betrayed her,

had helped Gallger snatch the *Gambit*. Her hands clenched, aching to snap Lil's frail neck.

Lil met Murphy's gaze. Her gray eyes narrowed.

The room was half full when Spanner returned. "The tech's on his way back from the launcher."

Yanni entered the room. His face was haggard. A swipe of grease marked the bridge of his nose.

"All gathered?" Yanni asked the crowd.

A man with blue-black skin answered him, "All that could leave posts. The others monitor."

"Reports on the station's status?"

"Structure's stable. Lost a lot of atmosphere—twenty-four thousand cubic meters—before the bulkheads sealed."

"Why'd Gallger attack?"

"Her ship," Lil said. "Gallger wanted it."

"How'd they scan it was here?" Yanni asked. "Gallger couldn't track her through launch, normal or otherwise."

"They didn't need to," Murphy said, looking at Lil. "Someone on this station told them the ship was here."

"None here bed down with Gallger."

"Show them," Murphy told Kyle.

He called up the communication logs on the widescreen IFOs. "The data launcher was not fully disabled," he said. "There is a record of the last transmission—eight hours ago, made by Lillian Burnkeft." The screen mirrored his words. "When she sent that message, Gallger also received a recording of all the electronic communications on this station for the past three years."

Accusing faces turned toward the slender woman.

She clutched her son tighter to her side. "I did it for us. For all of us," she said. "Gallger's our only hope of rescue. I had to convince them."

"You told them about the *Gambit*," Murphy said through clenched teeth.

"Yes," Lil said. "Gallger announced a ship with those call letters was *jooked* from their shipyards."

"Her ship was friendly-docked," Spanner said. "You betrayed the Code."

"What good has the Code done us? Five years I've watched this colony decline. We don't have the bio-mass for a closed system. This station is a starfish reab-sorbing its arms to stay alive. In a year, maybe two, we'll be dead. I'm the doctor. It's my duty to protect the health of the crew. I can't watch us die anymore—I won't."

"You fool," Murphy spat. "That ship could have ended floater wage-slavery. It could have saved us."

"How? You'd carry us all in that tiny ship? Fly us—to where? Who would take us?"

"Are you blind? The ship had self-contained launch. With its technology, floaters could travel freely be-tween stars. Slavery to the companies would end. You couldn't lock a floater into a system and tell them to work for the company or starve." Adrenaline coursed through Murphy's veins. She ached to wring sense into the tiny woman. "Now Gallger's got the *Gambit*. They'll suppress its technology. It would ruin their mo-nopoly on inter-system travel."

"How many decades until these miracle ships are ready? My people are dying now. Besides, how do we know any of this is true?" Lil asked. "All we have is your word. You claim to have self-launched. You claim to be a Murphy. For all we know, you work for the CEA, sent to test our loyalty to the Collective. Spanner's judgment may be clouded by a fresh face. Mine isn't."

"This"—Murphy pushed off, shooting across the room. She kicked out with her feet and stopped, dead calm, in the center—"is how you know." She slammed both hands against a wall that wasn't there and floated backward. A kick to her left, and she spun. A kick to her right, and she stopped. "This suit was on the *Gam-bit* when it was found."

The tech studied Murphy. "No jets. How's it sense movement? Mercury switches?" He shook his head in disbelief. "Have to be molecular. Built into the cloth maybe."

"I don't know how the suit works," Murphy said, "but I can take it to a tech who could find out. Because of your shortsightedness"—she stabbed a finger at Lil, causing them both to drift backward—"I can't do that with the *Gambit*."

"There's no guarantee a tech would be able to back-engineer the drive in that ship," Lil argued. "And if they did, we've no time or resources to build one. Gallger offers us work, solid promises—"

"Solid as their support for the manufacturing plant?" Spanner asked.

"You sure there'll be a station waiting for you?" Murphy said. "I haven't heard of any colonization in Delta Eridani."

Lil waved the question away. "Gallger constantly builds new stations. Many aren't mapped."

"Why would Gallger risk news of the *Gambit* getting out?" Murphy pushed, her pulse rising. "The launcher may be a trap."

"Thought of that," Yanni said. "I scanned it. The coordinates are clean."

"Perhaps Gallger isn't the monster you imagine," Lil said. "In their transmission they told us the *Gambit* was stolen from their shipyards. Perhaps they'd have produced self-launching ships by now if you hadn't taken their prototype."

"It wasn't a prototype," Murphy protested. "That ship was salvage."

"From whom? Who in the whole universe would develop a self-launching singleship and abandon it?"

"It wasn't abandoned, the pilot was ashes. Kyle told me. He was on the ship that salvaged—"

"You have proof?" Lil asked.

Did she? Murphy glanced at Kyle. She had only his word, and he didn't act or talk much like a salvager.

"No," Lil said, "just his word. Word of a man who betrayed his company. How much did he profit by helping you steal that ship?"

Lil's point hit home. Murphy had entered the University to escape floater life, to do something worthwhile. How had she ended up a ship thief?

"No time for this," Yanni interrupted. He pulled out a portable screen and consulted it. "Batteries are degrading. They're currently at eighty-six percent. Longer this decision takes, less energy there'll be for the jump." He took a deep breath. "Good news is— with some efficiency tweaks—looks like there'll be enough power for two jumps. But we have to move quickly.

"We can't change the coordinates of the first jump," he continued, "they're hardwired. But I was able to program an additional destination by kludging on a second controller. Crude hack, but I think it'll work. Whatever your feelings about Lil's breaking the Code, the end result is we have a launcher. We can go anywhere we want. But we have to act in the next two hours."

"This is our chance," Lil proclaimed, "Gallger needs us—"

"As slaves," Spanner hissed. "We're nothing to them but biological machines. Company left us here to die. You want to work for them now?"

"Where else to go?" asked a square-jawed man. "Who would take us in, support us?"

"Rebels would," Spanner argued. "Let's fight the companies, not beg for their scraps."

"If rebels still exist," Lil said, "they've less resources than us. Will a handful of discontents on a few decaying ships welcome thirty-eight more mouths to feed, thirty-eight more lungs to inflate?"

Spanner looked at Murphy. "What's the current state of the revolution?"

"Rumors are all I've heard. An attack on a company station at Tau Ceti, sabotage against the companies."

"How would you find them?" a woman asked.

"Latigos," Spanner said. " 'Sa hub station. Major launch port. Lots of traffic in and out. And there're two other systems with launchers within slow-trip range, for overflow. Makes it hard to track visitors. If rebels still exist, they'll have contacts there."

"If they exist," Lil repeated. "If they take you. Otherwise, you'll be recycled like so much waste."

"Enough," Yanni said. "There's no time. We must vote."

Floaters crawled over each other, hand-over-hand, talking in low whispers, arguing.

"What are they doing?" Kyle asked.

"Voting," Murphy said. "When they decide which argument they agree with, they cluster around the person who made it."

"Why are so many siding with Lillian, if she's proved herself a traitor and broken floater law?"

"They're not voting for the person, just the idea. Besides, station physician is a place of honor in floater culture. Her illegal acts were to protect the health of the station. That mitigates them somewh—"

"Hurry and vote," Spanner interrupted, "it's nearly done."

"We get to vote?" Kyle asked. "We're outsiders. We've been here less than a day."

"Does that change the fact that your skin is on the line?" Murphy replied. "You've got an interest in the outcome—you get to vote. In a society as mobile as spacers, everyone's got full voting rights all the time."

"Quickly," Spanner urged.

Murphy and Kyle took places next to Spanner. Latigos was dangerous, but traveling to a Gallger station would be suicidal.

Two others besides Murphy and Kyle clasped hands with Spanner. Twenty-eight of the floaters clustered around Lil. The remaining five clung to a thin man with nitrate-cycle formulas ringing his bald scalp.

Lil spoke above the murmur. "Most want to follow the sensible course. Why risk our lives in an underpowered jump?" She looked at Yanni beside her.

"It's true," the tech said. "One jump's safer." He pulled Lil close to him. "But we can't deny those who don't want to go to Gallger. We can do two jumps."

"It's too dangerous," Lil protested.

The two floaters put their helmets together, arguing quietly.

"Convince them," Spanner whispered to Murphy. "Lil's got support, she might be able to block a second jump."

"Me?"

"You're a Murphy—finagle them."

No chance. If she could bamboozle her way out of a filter bag, she wouldn't have ended up in this godsforsaken end of the universe. Still . . . she looked at Lil, smug among her circle of supporters. In Murphy, a reserve of self-doubt snapped and drained away. She had been thrown out of the University, had *jooked* the *Gambit*, but Lil had betrayed the Code. Murphy straightened and raised her voice. "You cringe as if the Companies owned space. Is this any way for floaters to act?"

The crowd around Lil looked up, and for a terrifying moment, Murphy couldn't think of anything to say, but her mouth rambled on. "Space was settled by people willing to take risks."

She rebelled against the next words, but they were her best chance to sway the crowd. "My father, Ferris Murphy, wouldn't lick Gallger's boot after he'd been left for dead. He'd grind his own in their faces and spit on what was left."

The floaters murmured, some loosening their grip on Lil.

"She's Murphy's daughter," Spanner said. "Listen to her."

"We've only her word on that," Lil protested.

"You knew the Murphy when he was here, Lil," Spanner said. "She's his image. See the marks on her brow. Who but a Murphy'd tempt fate by wearing probability equations?"

"Yes, look at her. She's a *gronuger*, her body is heavily muscled, her face thin."

"I've been training," Murphy said, "at the University, in full-gee."

"My point exactly," Lil crowed. "Would a Murphy train at the University, preparing to be a CEA officer and the Companies's hound?"

"I've trained to protect—" Murphy stopped. To protect who? Lil had a point. Although the CEA was an independent agency, it enforced laws passed by the founding Corporations. Laws which, no doubt, favored those Corporations. The realization shamed her. She'd imagined herself running down smugglers and pirates, punishing law breakers. But the CEA also squelched rebellions and evicted floaters from their ships. In her rush to escape life as a floater, she'd never let herself consider that she would have perpetuated that fate on others.

Spanner answered the question Murphy left hanging. "To protect floaters by knowing the enemy. Murphy's father sent her to the University to learn CEA tactics, so rebels could outmaneuver them."

Murphy's ears burned from the lie. What was Spanner thinking? No one would believe that. But the floaters around Lil were listening.

Spanner continued, "We must stop the Collective. Go back to the days when local govs ruled the systems and interstellar lanes were free—"

"Still a rebel, Spanner?" Lil interrupted, shaking her head. "You were a bad bit of cargo. We should have never cycled the lock for you. Your call to battle is idiotic. We're workers and chemists, not revolutionaries. We earn our way by creating, not destroying. Gallger is known to us. These so-called rebels, if they exist, aren't."

"No more time for debate," Yanni said. "We must decide now."

Two floaters moved from Lil's group to Spanner's. Twenty-six went with Lil and five still crowded around the man bearing hydroponic equations.

"Marsh, who're you with?" Lil asked.

"No one. For twelve years this station has been my home. I'm staying."

"That's suicide. You haven't resources to survive more than eighteen months."

"For the first time in my life, I'm not a slave," he said. "This station is the only place I'm free. I wouldn't survive more than eighteen months anywhere else."

Spanner stared at him. "You sure?"

"More than I've ever been in my life."

Lil spoke, her voice resonating with triumph. "You can't jump to the rebels, Spanner. Yanni is going to Gallger with me. There'll be no one to calibrate controls for a second launch."

From behind her, Yanni said, "I'll stay."

"But—" Lil started.

Yanni touched his helmet to hers and whispered, "They need me."

The two floaters stared at each other a moment. Then Lil asked, "Will I see you again?"

"Tesla willing," Yanni said. He kissed the small woman, lingering a moment past friendship, and pushed off to join Spanner's group.

"It's decided," Spanner said. "There'll be two launches."

"Gallger group launches first," Lil said. "There're more of us."

"Agreed."

"I'll ready the launcher," Yanni said. "Be ready to leave in an hour."

The floaters going with Lil left the room in groups of threes and fours, talking among themselves about their preparations. Yanni hung in the air, limp. Murphy heard him whisper a small prayer: "Need drives me, and this must get done."

She touched the tech's shoulder.

Yanni clasped her hand. "Best ready ourselves for the second launch. If we wait, no telling what resources'll be left."

Spanner asked Marsh, "You sure? You could join us."

He opened his hands. "No other way. Perhaps with the bio-load lessened, we can stabilize."

"You'll have no doctor or tech."

"We'll manage. But"—a smile curled the edges of his mouth—"if you're ever in the area with extra supplies . . ."

Both men laughed at the oxymoron.

It took half an hour for the twenty-seven floaters to load into five lifeboats. Designed for four people each, the lifeboats were packed beyond capacity. Two boats were left. Spanner's group would take one. The other would stay with the station.

Murphy watched the jump from a tug's IFO. Colors fluoresced along the length of the black grid as it folded space and shot the lifeboats into nothingness. Seconds later the flash came, a wave of pure white light. Murphy threw her arm over her face. When she looked out, the lifeboats were gone. Kyle was rubbing his eyes.

She took his hands away and looked at his contracted pupils. "Haven't you ever watched a launch before?"

He pulled out of her grasp. "Not through an unfiltered window."

Filtered windows were expensive. Surely Gallger didn't spend that kind of money on salvage ships. Her brows knitted. "When did you—"

A second flash erupted from the launcher. Green status lights on the control box winked out.

"Waste!" Yanni shoved toward the airlock, clicking his helmet into place. "I'm going out there. I've got to fix that short before the batteries drain."

"I'll go," Spanner said.

"No. Get the others ready and follow me out. If I can patch this, we'll have to jump immediately." He disappeared around a corner.

Yanni reported the damage from the launcher while the others loaded into Spanner's lifeboat. "Down to forty percent of predicted power. Looks like Gallger had a bleeder circuit to empty the batteries after the first launch."

"Batteries are dead?" Spanner asked.

"Not completely," Yanni replied. "The bleeder circuit is fried. That was the second flash we saw. My guess is since the first launch used less than half power, the overload damaged the bleeder circuit. It's good, otherwise the batteries would be completely drained."

"Can we still launch?"

"Iffy. I'm going to use just the center of the grid to generate the launch field. That'll use less power. This thing was designed to launch an eight-man exploration ship. Even at reduced capacity, it should be able to fold space enough to accommodate us."

Spanner angled his lifeboat into the center of the launch cone. There was nothing to do but wait. Interminable moments passed.

Yanni cracked open the controller box and reconfigured the bypasses for the launch structure. He changed some of the software commands and rechecked the readings. "Well, that's done it."

"Is it going to work?" Spanner asked.

"Only one way to find out. Let's hope Murphy's on your side in this."

It was a common saying, but Murphy felt the others' eyes on her. She hated being an icon of their superstition. People expected her to be able to change their luck, because of her name.

"Get in here, let's go," Spanner said.

There was a pause before Yanni responded. His voice sounded tired. "Can't. I've patched the launcher to work on half-grid, but I don't have a remote for the controller—it's burned out, and I've no time to build a new one. I'll stay behind and program the launch by hand."

"I can't let you—"

"Not a matter for discussion." He hit a switch.

The lifeboat illuminated.

"Good trip—" Yanni's transmission blurred into static. The lifeboat trembled. The buzzing walls vibrated through the soles of Murphy's feet.

In the IFOs, the controller flashed. Blue sparks exploded from the gray metal casing. Yanni spasmed—

A blast of white light enveloped the ship.

CHAPTER
8

Blue-white light engulfed the ship, blasting details into glare. Murphy squeezed her eyes shut, but it wasn't enough. Light flashed through her eyelids, and a red glare spiked into her skull. Her faceplate cross-polarized and snapped her into darkness.

The lifeboat kicked forward with violent force. Murphy's ergonomic snapped. The lifeboat continued accelerating—she didn't.

She collided with other bodies in midair. Her head smacked into someone's chest. A helmet hit her knee. She slammed into the back wall.

Murphy wasn't alone. The surface behind her was lumpy, soft, and moving. An elbow dug into her ribs, someone's feet pressed against her shoulder.

Her body throbbed with each heartbeat.

Why this huge acceleration? The launcher had been at half capacity, and had been recalibrated for a lifeboat's mass—no, wait. It had been set for *Lil's* group, five lifeboats. The first launch went wrong, so Yanni didn't have time to change the calibration.

Instead of two gees, they were accelerating at ten.

Pressure on her corneas caused points of light to bloom in the darkness. Murphy squirmed, her spine grinding over the elbow behind her. Focusing on the swimming brilliances, she willed herself not to black out. Ten gees was a strain for gravity-adapted humans. How would the floaters, with their reduced blood volume and atrophied cardiac muscles fare?

A minute later, the braking thrusters cut on. The ship reached constant velocity and the pressure eased. Murphy pulled her head away from the wall. Bodies bounced off her gently when she pushed off toward the front of the lifeboat. She shook one, and got no response.

She waited for her helmet to unpolarize. It didn't. What was wrong? Launch flash lasted only a second. She tongued the controls to remove the polarization. Her helmet didn't respond. Was it malfunctioning? She touched the seals, then stopped, sweating. She had almost breached her seals in a ship with questionable hull integrity. Stupid! Had she forgotten everything while she was at the University? Had she acquired a grounder's arrogance that the universe was tailored to her survival? She exhaled slowly. She needed to think.

If the helmet wasn't malfunctioning, then the cabin was still flooded with light. Turning off the IFOs would allow her helmet to unpolarize.

"Spanner?" She transmitted over helmet frequencies. "Anyone there?"

No answer. The only sound was her own ragged breathing.

Murphy pushed off from the wall. Mistake. The darkness disoriented her. Without gravity, she had no frame of reference. She was lost.

She quelled an urge to flail about wildly, forced herself to breathe deeply. Must not panic. Think like a floater. Make slow, careful, moves.

Murphy waved her hands through the air—and touched a jagged surface. What was it? She eased her hands down it, praying she wouldn't rip her suit. Her hands touched padding, felt along the edges—a seat cushion. The broken surface must be a chair back, shattered by the launch force. Moving from seat to seat, Murphy pulled herself toward the front of the lifeboat.

Someone moaned over her helmet speakers. Kyle. Had to be. His body, like hers, could handle the acceleration better than the floaters. She hoped there were no serious injuries.

Spanner was still in the pilot's chair when she felt her way to the command seat. Reinforced for acceleration, it hadn't collapsed. His body was limp. She touched her helmet to his. "Spanner?"

No answer.

Fear blossomed in her belly. Had the launch killed the floaters? Would they live to escape Gallger?

She felt the smooth control panel through her gloves. Where were the controls? She'd been trained at the University to pilot lifeboats, but not by touch.

This was an Avocet Mark Seven. A picture came: Tali laughing and setting the IFOs on random scan during a training exercise. Images of stars and ships and the University's home planet flashed on the screen. Tali's fingers were—on the upper-right corner.

Murphy pantomimed turning off the IFOs, touching the screen. It didn't work. She reached higher on the right side of the screen and repeated the gestures.

Her helmet unpolarized, leaving her in near-darkness. The only illumination came from their helmet lights. The constant motion of the drifting floaters threw random patterns of light on the walls.

Spanner was breathing.

Kyle was a meter to her left, hunched over, his helmet tucked into his belly. She reached out and touched his shoulder.

He unfurled. His lips and face were pale, nearly translucent blue. "The light is gone." He sighed heavily. "We're alive."

"For the moment. Help me check the others."

The floaters listed in the air, not responding to their surroundings. One woman's arm floated at an impossible angle. It was hard for Murphy to tell if they were breathing with all the motion in the cabin, floaters and broken plastic drifting in all directions. Murphy grabbed an unconscious man and held him at arm's length. His chest rose and fell, but rapidly and shallowly. Shock. Why wasn't his suit medicating him out of it? Then she realized, the colony hadn't been resupplied in five years. Between induced stress and long work hours, the supply of stimulants and relaxants in their suits must be used up. She debated opening his suit to slap a stim-patch on him and bring him around.

"This one is bleeding into his helmet."

"Waste." She'd have to breach suit on that one.

Kyle was awkwardly trying to hold onto the wounded man while keeping them both from bouncing into anything. He was doing everything with his hands. In space, grounder preconceptions left him crippled.

Murphy wrapped her legs around the man, holding him steady while she worked. The nameplate on his jumpsuit said: CARMADY. Blood, black in the low light, creeped along the inside of his faceplate.

"Get the medipak." Murphy was breaking a cardinal rule: secure the ship before the crew. She didn't know the lifeboat's current position and vector, but if she didn't attend to the wounded, they would die. Space was big, and very empty. She hoped it would continue to be big and empty enough to hide them a little longer.

Kyle tore the kit from the wall with a Velcro rasp.

Murphy unlocked the floater's helmet. Bits of metal and plastic and spheres of blood wafted out.

Her gloved fingers probed Carmady's scalp. It was pulped above his left ear. Shards of plastic jutted out of the ruined flesh. Inertia had slammed his fragile skull into his helmet speaker. Both were shattered.

Murphy wrapped exoskel around his head. The thin layers melted together, heating from an exothermic reaction that fused the polymer into a shell thin enough to fit under the floater's helmet, and strong enough to protect his head from further injury.

At the controls Spanner groaned. "Yanni?"

Murphy wasn't sure what to say. An image of the tech, body arced with electricity, flashed through her mind. "We're out of launch. He got it done."

". . . urned off the IFOs?" Spanner moaned and reached for the controls. Light lanced Murphy's eyes, pain blossomed in the back of her head. She heard Spanner grunt, then the light was gone, leaving a white wall afterimage blasted onto her retina.

"Who . . . ched my controls?" Spanner asked.

"Had to," Murphy said, "you were out."

"Don't do . . ." He reeled in his seat. His feet lost their grip on the ergonomic, and he swung out of the pilot's chair and hung inverted, white-knuckled, over the control panel.

Through the fading haze on her retinas, Murphy threw a stim-patch to Kyle. "Here, bolster our fearless leader. Someone needs to pilot this thing."

Kyle plucked it out of the air. "You floaters are more concerned with your ships than your lives."

"Vacuum doesn't give second chances." As she spoke the aphorism, Murphy realized Kyle had meant her, too. It jarred her. Not that he had called her a floater; that had happened countless times at the University. It was that now, once again, it was true. She had better start thinking like one, or she and all the people who depended on her were going to die.

Kyle touched the lock on Spanner's helmet.

The floater snapped awake, grabbed Kyle, and held him against the wall. Spanner's bony arm trembled.

Wide-eyed, Kyle offered him the stim-patch.

"Don't touch a floater's seals," Spanner said, glaring. "Next one might slice first and ask questions later." He snatched the patch away from Kyle. "We're not safe from breach." He clenched and unclenched his red-rimmed eyes, shuddered. "I'll make do."

"Where the hell are we?" Murphy asked.

Spanner checked the navigational readouts in front of him. A wild grin split his face into two halves. Then he cracked the IFOs to let in the merest light. The screen glowed an ominous blue. Etched against the cobalt was the black outline of a spinning hoop. Six spokes connected the rim to a tapered shaft as long as the station was wide. Tiny ships swarmed between the shaft and the outer rim of the hoop.

Latigos.

"That can't be," Murphy said, her eyes widening in disbelief. "The com's dead silent. We can't be near a populated area."

Spanner tapped the com near the upper right corner. Static resolved into a thousand voices: "This is RTF784-QS permission—up about two-and-a-half meters, hold, hold—going ta take me best two girls to third show, then after, we make—never calibrate another intake valve, it'll be too soon." The busy sounds of a working station.

"Sa' weird, during the accident, the com switched off," Spanner said.

Guilt burned the lining of Murphy's stomach. She must have disabled the com on her first attempt to shut off the IFOs. Her error had been compounded when she failed to check the lifeboat's coordinates. While she was administering to the crew, the ship had been flying blind through a populated zone. It was a miracle they hadn't been spotted or captured by station-security ships. Murphy stuffed the feeling down. Mistakes happened. She'd make sure that this one never happened again.

A large rectangular ship on the IFO screen caught her eye. It was a construction of six metal plates, loosely connected together at right angles. Each face was identical to the one across from it. There were two enormous square plates, two long rectangles, and two small squares. The sets were bolted together by threaded rods at the corners. Jets on the edges of the plates maneuvered the craft and kept the interwoven rods from colliding. On three of the plates, where the rods met, were square enclosures the size of singleships. They didn't look like personnel cabins. What was this ship? An adjustable cargo platform? As she watched, it broke from the outgoing stream of ships and tugs, and vectored straight toward them.

"CEA," Spanner growled.

"I thought you said this was a rebel station," said Kyle.

"Floaters owned stations, we wouldn't need a revo-

lution," Spanner shot back, over his shoulder. "Latigos is only a contact point. Rebels I knew five years
ago traded here for supplies."

Murphy interrupted, "That's not CEA—"

"Salvager." Kyle's voice resonated with an effortless
authority that made Murphy stare and again wonder
if there was more to Kyle than she knew.

He continued, "The station must have hailed the
lifeboat while our communications were down. When
the lifeboat failed to respond, it was classified as
metallic-content debris. That's a robotic salvage-
compactor."

The front plate opened, readying to scoop the lifeboat into its center.

"Have to get out of its path." Spanner reached for
the controls.

Kyle grabbed his arm, held it inches above the control panel. "No. There's a better way—"

The skin around Spanner's lips was tight and pale.
"Let go of me—let go of my *ship*, *gronuger*."

Kyle held the struggling floater with little effort.
"We can pretend to be wreckage and ride the salvager
to the station." He tapped the com off.

Spanner's lips turned white. His free hand slipped
below his seat.

The gaping maw of the oncoming ship loomed
larger in the forward screen. Murphy asked, "Don't
salvagers dismantle and compact the debris before
they reach the station?"

"No, they—"

"I said, let go!" Spanner's hand slashed up and
across Kyle's chest. The concealed knife sliced Kyle's
suit. He jerked back, releasing his hold on the floater,
and grabbed his chest in shock. The cabin was pressurized, but as Spanner said, the hull was not safe from
breach.

Murphy grabbed for Spanner, yelling to Kyle at the
same time, "Patch kit's on the far wall."

Spanner slipped under her arms and aimed a spinning kick at her head. Murphy caught the foot and

pulled him closer, increasing their rotation. "He's a *gronuger*. He didn't know touching your controls was taboo. He doesn't know the Code."

He placed his other foot on her helmet and tried to break her grip. But even her thin arms were more than a match for the atrophied muscles of his skeletal legs.

"Ignorance's no excuse. Not for space. Not for me. Let me go, you *shi'eel*."

Impact shook the lifeboat. Inertia held the unconscious drifting floaters in place while the walls of the lifeboat rattled and buffeted them. The walls creaked.

"You said salvagers didn't dismantle the ship until they reached the station," Murphy said.

Kyle almost dropped the tube of patch-epoxy. An uneven ribbon of pink gel was half drawn across his chest. "It's not standard procedure."

Spanner growled, threw Murphy's unresisting hands off, and grabbed the controls. "Stupid *gronuger*, idiotic fem. This's a border outpost. We can't be the only small ship to try to sneak on-station." He used his left hand to lash down, while his right tried to maneuver the ship around. "If we've no clearance, we've no right to station air. They don't want diseases or terrorists brought on board. I'd guess crushing small salvage is an easy way to turn trouble into resources."

Murphy glanced at the IFO screens. She could see plates in each one. The salvager surrounded the lifeboat, compressing it into a cubical cross section. The ship's hull creaked. The sides were caving in where the plates pushed, the corners were stretching out. Sparks jumped from the airlock as the circuitry stretched. The metal above the door rippled with strain. Murphy glanced at Carmady, whose helmet seal wasn't closed.

The hull breached.

With a wrenching sound, the top of the airlock door twisted outward. The atmosphere in the lifeboat exploded through the crack, tearing the rent into a chasm. Loose objects in the ship were pushed toward the breach by the escaping air, including Murphy, Kyle, and the unconscious floaters.

Murphy grabbed Carmady and tried to seal his helmet. She fumbled with the latch, cursing and bracing her legs against the pilot's chair to avoid the breach.

As suddenly as a burst balloon, the pressure vanished. All of the atmosphere in the lifeboat had expelled in a single explosion. Kyle dangled toward the rift in the hull, his arms wrapped around the legs of an ergonomic.

Being on the far side from the rent was probably the only thing that saved his life. Two of the unconscious floaters were gone. A third had landed crossways across the rent and was jammed in the hole, knees and neck protruding from space.

Murphy looked at Carmady in her arms. His eyes were open, staring, shriveled with dehydration. She'd killed him, as surely as Spanner had tried to kill Kyle. Her instincts were dulled by six years of living with grounders. She hadn't been able to survive in the University's world, and now she was no longer fit to survive in space. She stared into the dead man's eyes.

Spanner grabbed her shoulder, hard. "Leave him. We've got to exit before the compactor crushes us." He pressed his lips together, flicking a glance at Kyle. "Even that *gronuger*. 'Sa no way for a human to die."

The man wedged in the breach was dead. His suit had torn on the jagged metal, and his back was folded at an impossible angle.

"Jonesy. Not you, too," Spanner said, his voice leaden. He and Murphy pulled the dead floater back into the lifeboat.

The hull whined and fissured. Other edges of the now near-cubical lifeboat cracked. The sides were collapsing. The hole above the airlock was starting to close as the walls of the lifeboat smashed closer together.

Murphy pushed Kyle through to space-side, holding onto to him. "You got a hold?"

He grunted assent.

She let go and nodded for Spanner to go next.

The floater looked past her at the dead bodies of his friends. He ignored her when she shook his arm. Shock.

Murphy grabbed the edge of the rent and kicked Spanner out. He whirled into space. Instinct took over and his arms and legs shot out, seeking purchase. He caught himself on the twisted metal, glared once over his shoulder at Murphy, and then climbed.

Murphy pulled herself through the opening in the ship's hull and crawled after him.

Inside the lifeboat, the IFOs magnification had added to Latigos Prime's intensity and caused Murphy's helmet to fully cross-polarize to compensate. Outside, in the sun's natural light, her helmet was able to handle the incoming light by partially polarizing. The sun still glowed like a blue coal in the corner of her field of vision, but by looking away from it, her eyes adjusted. She saw Kyle waving to her from the other side of the rectangular compression plate. The gap between the plates was closing. Murphy and Spanner scrambled up the face of the plate, using the magnetic soles of their boots.

On the other side, Kyle clung to maintenance handholds, his boots wedged under them. He was tucked against one of the four large boxes on the face of the plate. The rods connecting the plate to its twin were turning; presumably the construct housed a crank assembly.

Spanner panted. "When they reclaim the lifeboat, someone's sure to see us. Got to find a way onto Latigos." He stared over at the hub of the station.

"We'd never make a free-jump from here," Murphy said. "Not enough force, and the velocity vector is tricky. Besides, they'll be looking for the lifeboat's pilot."

"Won't the floating bodies convince them we perished when the ship breached?" Kyle asked.

Spanner's mouth worked, but he didn't say anything. Space, big as it was, left little room for sentiment.

"I doubt they'll count on that," Murphy said. "It's standard procedure to look for survivors."

Kyle's eyes narrowed, and he stared at the hulking machine compacting the remains of the lifeboat. "What if we ride inside the salvager itself?"

Murphy followed his gaze up the crank mechanism. There wasn't even a control screen, presumably the salvagers were automated or operated by waldo from the station. "Is that possible?" she asked.

"This appears to be a Rutledge class IV salvager." Kyle frowned. "Or a similar model. There's an access panel for servicing the crank assemblies. If we can open it, there's room for one, maybe two people."

"And me?" Spanner asked, his voice harsh over the helmet com. "What will I do?"

Kyle stared at the floater. "I suppose," he said slowly, "we'll have to open two panels."

Murphy grabbed Spanner's arm. "We don't have time for this. Every second we stand here makes it more likely station security will pick up our heat signatures, and we're here without boarding visas. Unless we want to be indentured, we'd better get moving."

Murphy followed Kyle up the wall until the three of them reached the maintenance panel. It was set flush into the salvager's wall, with only a millimeter seam.

Kyle touched the nearly invisible join. He spluttered, "Th-This must be a new model. The Rutledges I worked on had a wider opening."

"Your plan must've been used before," Spanner said.

"Waste." Murphy fought down the impulse to pound her fist against the panel; it would only throw her into space. There had to be a way to make this work.

Latigos loomed larger. New details were visible: the elevators that rode along the shafts of the station, tiny work crews, and a CEA patrol ship heading their way.

Murphy grabbed Kyle with her free arm. "On the model you used, how did the access panels open?"

"Maintenance schedules were preprogrammed."

"What happened if the salvager malfunctioned, or was damaged enroute?"

Kyle thought a moment. "There is a command frequency that the main ship uses to transmit instructions to the salvagers."

Her grip on Kyle tightened. "Do you know the frequency?"

"Sa' no use," Spanner said. "Knowing the channel doesn't give us the codes."

"He's correct," Kyle said. "Without the command codes, there's nothing I can do."

Murphy stared at the salvager. It had compressed the lifeboat into a tightly packed cube. Shadows and sunlight striped the extruded edges of the once lifeboat. Intense blue-white light glared off the metal. Small protrusions created triangles of absolute darkness. The threaded rods were fully tightened, holding the wreckage in place. Her gaze followed the shafts back to an angular shadow on the inside plate of the larger squares. She sucked in a quick breath. "What if we hide in there?"

"The press rides along that shaft," Kyle said. "If it retracts, we'll be crushed."

Her mouth tightened. "Then we'll get out before that happens."

"Crazy fem, how we're going to get past the patrol?" Spanner was wedged into the hiding place behind Murphy, his helmet touching hers. They weren't transmitting anymore, as there was too much risk the CEA officers investigating the wreck would pick up a scattered signal.

Murphy set her helmet to the CEA patrol frequency and scanned the expanse ahead for signs of investigators.

". . . another one. Ugh, the . . . acceleration really tore . . ."

Murphy ducked back as two suited CEA officers crested into view. The transmission cleared.

"What I don't understand is how a lifeboat got this far. We didn't see the carrier ship."

"Crazy floaters. What've they got to rebel against anyway? What's worth risking their lives for?"

"Who knows what a floater thinks? We've got a report to file. You see any signs of life?"

The first voice chuckled. "Not unless it's bacteria. Log it as a full mortality accident and let's get this salvage to processing."

Kyle's helmet clonked into hers. "They're going to retract the plates."

"I know."

With a loud clunk, the crank started to turn. Murphy felt the vibration through the soles of her suit. The plate moved towards them.

The station was still too far away to risk a jump.

Murphy looked at the oversize gloves of her spacesuit. Could she use its inertialess properties to get them to the station? Maybe. But the force it exerted was small. She guessed the designers intended it for fine control, not propulsion. And it was slow, leaving them an easy target to be spotted by station security. There was also the question whether it would work with Kyle's and Spanner's additional mass. Too risky. She needed a faster, surer, way of getting to Latigos.

But how? There was only the salvagers, the compacted lifeboat, and the two-man harness the troopers had ridden from the patrol ship. She looked at the harness, then at the troopers. They were busy, reading mass and density measurements off the salvager's display. As soon as they were done, they'd take the harness and leave.

There wasn't time for subtlety.

Murphy cocked her head in the direction of the harness.

Spanner nodded.

Kyle was horrified. He argued soundlessly, forgetting they couldn't hear him with the helmet speakers turned off.

Then Murphy clicked on her magnetic soles and ran. Pain from her wounded ankle shot up her leg; she pushed it away. Running in mag shoes was an exercise in control. Pick your front foot up too high, and the magnet might not catch; too low, and you wouldn't build up speed.

She was half way to the harness when she remembered—Kyle!

Sick with guilt, she glanced back to see Spanner running, Kyle locked around his shoulders. Her helmet speaker crackled.

"Hey!" one of the patrol said.

"Stop them!"

Murphy punched in the default access code for CEA harnesses. She hoped it hadn't changed since she'd left the University. The default was meant to allow emergency access to officers in need. This certainly wasn't what the CEA had intended, but Murphy had never been in greater need.

The security plate unlocked and rolled back, giving her access to the controls.

She released the docking magnets and powered up the harness. The two troopers were trying to run across the compacted lifeboat. They were clumsy and unfamiliar in zero-gee. She marveled at the University's assumption that floaters were unsuitable for law enforcement, even in space.

Spanner and Kyle strapped in beside her.

"Hope you know what you're doing, Murphy," Spanner said. With a sudden feeling of exposure, she lifted off from the salvager. Their only chance was to get to the station and lose themselves in the crowd. There was no turning back.

CHAPTER

9

Latigos's wheel free-orbited the local sun. Spokes extended past its rim, dotted with docked ships. Murphy accelerated the harness and aimed for a dock near the hub. A more difficult landing than the rim, but if there were rebels on-station, that's where they'd be—in the low-gee floater's quarters. The back of Murphy's neck prickled with expected cannon fire. The harness was unarmored; if they were hit, they were dead.

The CEA ship between her and the station was backlit with brilliant blue light. The cannons remained dim. Both relief and suspicion flooded Murphy. Did the CEA want them alive?

She squeezed hard on the left T-shaped handle. The jets on the right of the harness fired, pivoting the harness left. With both hands she compressed the accelerators in the handles and then rotated her fists sideways. The harness arced around the salvager.

Once they were out of the sight line, Murphy glanced back at Spanner and Kyle. They were crushed into straps intended for a single passenger. Spanner faced forward, jammed against the handholds. Kyle was backward, pressed between the seat and Spanner's back.

The rectangular viewscreen between the accelerator handles flickered with movement. Four harnesses darted around the salvager from every side, each with a single rider.

They were angling in to trap her. And unless she

moved fast, they'd succeed. The other pilots had a better thrust-to-mass ratio.

Murphy strangled both accelerators until her knuckles popped, ignoring the rapidly diminishing fuel bar. She opened her cramping left hand and rotated her right, spiraling into a narrow right turn. The harness snapped around a repair platform welded to the hub of the space station's wheel. Floaters drifted around the site, working in slow, safe movements. Helmets turned as she, pursued by the CEA officers, passed over the crew.

One floater's fist raised in salute.

Murphy frowned as she turned the harness toward the station's hub. She wasn't a rebel. The last six years of her life had been spent denying her origins. She didn't deserve his respect.

Her helmet speakers crackled. "Surrender or we'll fire."

If they hadn't fired when they had a clear shot, they wouldn't shoot this close to the station. She ignored the tinny voice.

A luxury yacht spun in the station's hub dock, increasing its rotation to match Latigos's spin. Murphy darted toward it.

The harness's propulsion sputtered twice, jerking in gentle pulses as the jets intermittently failed. Murphy glanced at the fuel bar—only a thread remained.

The four CEA harnesses were closing in. They split into groups of two, angling in from the left and the right.

Murphy rotated both T-shaped handles palm up and compressed the accelerators. Heat shot up her cramping forearms. Her harness dove forward, passing between the two harnesses trying to cut her off.

They crossed behind her, diving to avoid a collision with the two harnesses following her.

Murphy darted around the luxury yacht, her harness hidden by its gleaming silver bulk.

She scanned the yacht beneath her, searching its sleek lines for a refuge. The viewing port dominated

the front of the ship, glittering like a cabochon diamond set into the convex cone of the yacht's body.

There. She piloted the harness toward a gap between the yacht and the station. She pointed at the
ladder bolted to the side of the yacht, and Spanner
squeezed her shoulder in agreement. Murphy pivoted
the harness to the cargo airlock.

When the harness was within two meters of the
lock, Murphy popped the harness's straps and pressed
the heel of her hands against the brakes below the T-
handles. The reverse jets fired. Inertia carried them
to the metal handholds welded near the seam of the
cargo airlock.

She absorbed the brunt of the impact by flexing her
knees and slipping the toe of her boot under a handhold to keep from bouncing back into space.

Heat shot up her leg as her wounded ankle compressed. Sweat bubbled on her forehead as she
grabbed a rung with her left hand. Spanner and Kyle
clung to a set of rungs above her.

Foot throbbing, Murphy set the harness's autopilot
to fly into an off-station solar collector. The blinding
sun that backlit the collector would wash details into
glare. With luck, station security wouldn't be able to
make out that it was unmanned.

The harness's jets fired, temporarily blinding Murphy. When she looked again, eyes tearing, the harness
was a shrinking dot of light. Sunlight glinted off its
frame and merged with the glow from its jets. The
white speck of the harness dove towards a miniature
sun: the blue brilliance of Latigos, focused and magnified by the solar collector.

The four CEA officers changed course to follow her
harness. If they didn't spot the ruse, it would take
them forty-five hundred meters to intercept the empty
harness, giving her group about seven minutes to get
inside.

The three of them put their helmets together.

The yacht drifted closer to the station, spinning
faster to match the motion of the dock. Every few

minutes the construction platform crested into view, rose, and then sank behind the horizon of the liner again.

Kyle clunked his helmet into hers. "Can we jump to that?"

Jump. She envied the grounder his humanicentric assumptions that the universe was a safe place. Even with the inertialess properties of the suit she wore—which gave her a prayer of tweaking their initial direction and speed—to leap from a spinning ship to a platform more than fifty meters away was insane.

But they might not have a choice. Murphy's arms already ached with the effort of holding on, and the yacht was still spinning up. If they didn't jump soon, they would be hurled off.

Spanner's face was pale, but he nodded.

With the CEA's attention fixated on her harness, it might be possible for something as small as three suits to slip by unnoticed.

A glance passed between her and Spanner. He pointed at her.

Murphy nodded once. She was the obvious choice to shove off. Kyle didn't have the skill, and Spanner didn't have the strength.

With her free hand, she clipped Kyle and Spanner to the equipment loops at the waist of her suit.

Spanner and Kyle clung to her legs. She held the three of them to the yacht, her arms straining with the extra mass. She slid her feet out from under the rungs, ready to release the handgrips and let the liner's centripetal acceleration hurl them toward the station. Murphy waited for the platform to crest into view, then checked her suit's clock. Fifty-eight seconds later, it crested back into view. She needed to jump the instant the platform crested. The liner's centripetal acceleration would hurl them off tangentially. If she didn't jump then, they'd be hurled past the platform, into space, or depending on their trajectory, into the heart of Latigos's sun. Even if her suit was completely

fueled, it would take too long to reverse the inertia
they'd get from the yacht.

Fifty-four seconds for a rotation, knock off two for
reaction time. The platform crested into view again.
Murphy started her suit's timer.

. . . forty-nine, fifty, fifty-one, fifty-two . . .

Her hands wouldn't let go. Every fiber in her body
protested. To let go was death. The platform rose,
passed overhead, and sank out of view. Inside her helmet, Murphy tasted iron-tinged fear. The station
crested. Breathing rapidly, she started the timer again.
Try not to think about it. Don't think. She poured
every ounce of her being into the numbers flashing on
the inner surface of her helmet, glowing green numerals on a black background. Don't think about it, her
undermind whispered, just do.

. . . fifty-one, fifty-two . . .

She let go.

Centripetal acceleration hurled them toward the
construction platform. Her heart pounded, but it was
too late to do anything now.

They were in trouble.

The yacht had been accelerating its spin while she
delayed. As it neared synch with the station, the relative motion of the platform slowed. It had crested too
late. They were going to shoot over it, too fast for the
suit's jets or inertialess system to reverse their direction. Shooting across the plane of the station, they
crossed a spoke's path as it swept out area in its eter-
nal cycle. The metal beam eclipsed the station—grew
larger until Murphy could see nothing else—there
were only seconds of life left—

No!

Fear overrode her floater instincts. Murphy struck
her fists against the void.

And they stopped. As if inertia was a figment of
Newton's imagination. The suit! It worked! Even with
Kyle and Spanner's extra mass, it worked. It wasn't
just for light positioning, it was a fully functional propulsion system. Beating against the emptiness in front

of her, Murphy and her passengers drifted backward. A laugh bubbled out of her chest. They could *walk* to the platform! It was absurd, the laws of physics and space, tamed to a grounder's preconceptions.

Kicking against the void, she built up enough inertia for the three of them to drift towards the repair platform.

Her helmet crackled with a loud multifrequency broadcast. "All crews return to the station immediately. Subversives are in the area. Repeat—return to the station immediately."

When they were within one hundred meters of the repair platform, Murphy beat her fists to the left, so they slipped right. The maneuver hid their approach behind a transformer assembly.

A floater crew was packing their gear when Murphy landed. The three of them watched the suited workers file toward the airlock. Safety lay inside, and the chance for Spanner to send a message to his rebel contacts. They had to find a way to sneak on board.

Then she saw the floater who had saluted them.

She read his identifier off his suit, then tongued the com to a low-range frequency. "Worker 982X4W."

The floater looked around.

"Over by the stanchions. You saluted us earlier. Will you help us now?"

The helmet pivoted, focused on their hiding spot.

He broadcast, "No," but opened and clenched his fist repeatedly.

Kyle touched his helmet to Murphy's. "What's he doing with his hand?"

"It's an old work-crew signal. Used when radio communication goes out. It means he'll help us."

Two more of the crew went into the cycle. The rebel floater stepped back, then pantomimed trouble with his magnetic soles. "They won't release," he transmitted. "Go on without me."

The floater popped off the magnet embedded in his right shoe. As he rose, the small finger of his left hand

pointed at the magnet. Then he slipped into the airlock, on the heels of the second-to-last floater.

They waited two minutes, the seconds stretching
into hours, until the construction crew was well away
from the airlock.

After a visual scan of the area, they climbed up.
The magnetic sole was stuck to the platform. When
Murphy pried it loose, an ID badge floated free.

She grabbed it and clipped it to her own suit,
amazed at the daring generosity of the floater who
had helped them. Losing a work badge would cost
him a week's pay—could cost him his contract.

She approached the airlock, brandishing the badge
on her chest at the reader. The airlock opened. Spanner and Kyle slipped through behind her before the
door closed.

The airlock was built for sixteen occupants. A
screen in the wall displayed air percentage, work assignments, and station time.

When the lock finished its cycle, they stepped
through into a service hallway. Roughly shaped flexcrete arced down, creating a wide tunnel. Murphy had
to stoop her shoulders to keep from hitting the ceiling.

The chute to the outer rim was opposite the locks,
its frame painted a distinguishing bright blue. Arrows
indicated paths to the locker rooms, floater habitation
decks, and the lounge.

Four airlocks down the hall whined and disgorged
twelve floaters each. Murphy glanced at the crowd.

If they stayed, they'd be recognized as outsiders,
especially her and Kyle. In a floater community, even
one as large as Latigos, everyone knew everyone. And
her suit was distinctive, it would be remembered. She
couldn't rely on all the floaters she met to be as help-
ful as the rebel they'd met outside. Money was a language that spoke to people of all classes. The only
safe place for her and Kyle was the public areas . . .
the full-gee grounder areas.

Spanner was a problem. After five years in the

weightless conditions on Canodyne 4265, he'd never survive a return to full gravity.

Spanner caught her gaze. "Go ahead," he mouthed, nodding toward the chute door, "I'll return this." He unclipped the work badge from her chest, tapped the chute door to open it, and pushed swiftly away. Murphy watched Spanner float into the group of suited bodies.

There wasn't any more time to think. She and Kyle had to get through the chute door before it closed, locking them out.

The chute fell all the way to the rim, sloping slightly to compensate for the station's rotation. The inside was two meters in diameter and smooth, except for the handholds that ran all the way down. This end, near the center, was in microgravity. As they climbed down the ladder, the pull of centripetal acceleration increased.

Chute-jumping was a game to students at the University. They'd push off at the zero-gee end and accelerate toward the rim, grabbing the ladder at the last moment or slamming into the decel-pad at the end of the chute.

But floaters like Murphy were afraid of chutes. Falling produced cognitive dissonance in people raised in space. To them, there was no up and down—only here and there. The chute defied that preconception. Space-adapted floaters who fell died from shock or aneurysm before they hit bottom.

Murphy climbed slowly, her hands gripping the steel rungs like twin vises. Gravity settled on her as she climbed, like a sandbag lowered onto her shoulders. She breathed hard, fogging her helmet for a second before the suit filtered the excess vapor.

Standing on the wobbling orange plastic crash bag, Murphy examined the door cut into the bottom of the well. There were no guards; physiology alone kept floaters out of the grounder areas. But set into the wall was a credit reader.

Trapped at the bottom of the well. No credit to get

into the station, and sure to be recognized as an outsider if they went back up, Murphy slumped, fell, and sat down hard on the crash pad. It bobbled in response.

"Get off that before someone else jumps." Kyle had taken his helmet off and was struggling with his gloves. His voice was muffled through Murphy's helmet.

He unzipped his suit and removed a Gallger credit card.

"Are you sure that's a good idea?" Murphy asked.

Ignoring her, he swiped it through the reader. "Executive card. Untraceable. If you're going to be a grounder," Kyle said with a small smile, "you must learn a few survival rules. First lesson, never go abroad without a source of funds."

The door sheathed open.

Kyle waved expansively. "Welcome to my world."

A blast of light poured out of the door. Eyes tearing, Murphy turned away. "What is *that*?"

"'Sun City.' Latigos used to be a solar research facility. Now it's a recreational destination."

Through her partially polarized helmet, Murphy saw a blue-washed boulevard. The ceiling rose to the transparent arch of the outside rim of the station. It was a criminal waste of space. Ships could have been built under the grandiose high ceiling.

Murphy stepped out into the glare, and was met by a strange parade of grounders. They were varied and exotic, unlike anything she'd ever seen. A rich couple, naked except for delicate chains that pierced their flesh at asynchronous points and linked them together, walked next to figures shrouded head to foot in enveloping black robes. A woman passed them whose entire body was tattooed with multicolored metallic dragon scales. Gliders, rich grounders who wore collapsible microfiber wings to play in zero-gee for a day at a time, mingled with grubby merchanteers in rubber overalls and sweat-stained nu-cotton shirts.

Four CEA officers pushed through the crowd, heading straight for them. She grabbed Kyle's arm and pulled him into a swirl of tourists. Her feet felt like lead, and within a few meters her heart was pounding.

As she pushed through the crowd, her throat burned, each breath tearing out of her as she struggled to take in the next. Suddenly, there wasn't enough oxygen. Firefly-speckled darkness closed in on her vision.

Someone's arm wrapped around her waist, half carrying her. She was helped onto a bench.

"I think we've eluded them—temporarily," Kyle said. "We've got to get you out of that suit, it's too recognizable."

Murphy unlocked her helmet and let it dangle between her shoulder blades. The light hit her head like a mallet. Her skull pounded. She spent long moments breathing before she opened her eyes. Squinting, her eyelashes diffracted the light, throwing rainbows across her cornea.

As she stripped off the rest of her suit, Murphy whispered, "How can people live in this light?"

A violet-haired woman turned in Murphy's direction. Her eyes were solid black. As she passed into the shadow of a juice vendor's stall, emerald irises emerged from the black surface under her lids.

Photosensitive contacts. Up ahead on the concourse was a contacts stand. A mountain of a woman perched behind the stall, wearing reading glasses. Her head was tilted back, scanning the text scrolling on the inside of the lenses.

Kyle pulled Murphy toward the booth.

The woman leaned forward as they approached. The text on her glasses vanished. A flash of pale blue eyes, then the contacts darkened and her eyelids filled with blackness. The vendor smiled, taking in their squint and discomfort.

"First time on Latigos, friends?"

Murphy shifted uncomfortably.

"No," Kyle lied. "Of course not. We just misplaced our contacts."

The woman licked her lips. "That was a mistake . . ."

She looked at each of them, then at the spacesuit bundled under Murphy's arm.

Something in her smug expression chilled Murphy. The woman knew they were lying. Surely the CEA had posted alerts for strangers. Would she turn them in?

The woman smiled slyly. ". . . an expensive mistake to come to Latigos unprepared."

"How much?" Murphy asked.

"Fifty for the contacts. Ten thousand for my . . . discretion."

"That's robbery," Murphy choked.

The woman shrugged, looked out into the crowd for a moment, then waved a meaty hand. A CEA officer broke from the group around the chute door and moved in the direction of the vendor's stand.

Kyle slid his credit card across to the woman.

The guard zeroed in on the vendor. "Yes?" He glowered at Murphy and Kyle. "Why did you signal?"

The woman swiped the card through the reader, checked the verification. "Just being friendly. It a crime, being friendly?"

His eyes narrowed, and he glared at Murphy's stubbled scalp. He jerked a thumb at Murphy and Kyle. "You know these two?"

The vendor tapped a large sum into the credit transfer. When it cleared, she smiled. "My best customers. Known them for years."

"Why aren't they wearing lenses?"

"Let them dry out overnight." She pulled out four cracked films. "Careless of them, but good business for me." She leaned across the desk to Murphy. "What's this, your third pair?"

Murphy nodded.

The vendor winked at the security officer. "You know how young mixed-weight couples are. Too busy exploring the possibilities to look after their gear."

Kyle's credit bought them a room on the rim. It wasn't spacious, but nicer than fugitives on the run would be expected to rent.

Two thin beds projected out of one wall, stacked one above the other. On the opposite wall was a com screen. In the corner was a hygiene stool with a flip-top lid, water tube, and towelette dispenser.

Murphy unbundled her spacesuit, checked the air and water reserves. The waste bag was only a quarter full, she could empty it later. There wasn't a recharge socket. Gods knew how the thing was powered. She stood it against the wall, seals open, so that she could jump into it if the station breached.

Her suit attended to, Murphy examined her body. She was covered with the accumulation of three days' worth of sweat and grime. Her skin was tacky, her white tank top and leggings were tinged gray, and she stank.

She sponge-bathed using the water tube, then lumbered to the bottom bunk and collapsed. The fall into gravity had tired her. A giant hand compressed her against the bed. Her ankle ached.

Kyle looked better. He'd only been weightless for one day—not three—and gravity suited him. His corona of hair fell in a wave to his shoulders. Feet solid on the ground, his motions were controlled, graceful.

Walking easily, Kyle peeled off his suit and left it crumpled in the corner. He stooped to twiddle the com to the news channel. Then he sauntered back to the bed, pushed Murphy's legs aside, and sat on the lower bunk.

They caught the tail end of the interstellar news. It was finishing up with an announcement that four more stations had been captured by floaters. The bored-looking anchor, a computer-generated androgyne, was apparently unconcerned about the revolution. It was limited to distant stations, the news sprite explained, and would be soon quelled by the CEA.

Murphy had heard the arguments before. Floaters didn't have the resources or coordination to mount a successful revolt. It was impossible to win against an adversary that controlled space travel. At the CEA's request Gallger Galactic could shut down rebel-controlled launchers, stranding the entire population in-system. Few colonies were self-sustaining. All the Collective had to do was wait out the end of the revolution.

The newscast displayed statistics, and Murphy sucked in a breath. The casualties had quadrupled during the last year. Inside the University she'd been insulated by her studies—she had no idea things were so bad. These days the rebellion was killing more floaters than the plagues.

The transmission was interrupted by an important announcement.

The anchor's computer-generated face morphed into that of a middle-aged CEA officer with steel-gray hair that fell like sheet metal to her shoulders. Her lips were thin and chapped. She did not look pleased.

"An hour ago, a rebel ship was detected in the area. It concealed itself from the ship-recognition system and attempted to infiltrate Latigos station. All but three rebels have been apprehended. A reward of ten thousand credits is offered for any information leading to the capture of these subversives." The CEA officer's face faded to a bright background.

Footage of their escape on the harness played, probably taken from a helmet-recorder. It was a back view. Kyle and Spanner's suits were generic, and didn't offer a lot to use as identification. Murphy's, however, with its bulky hand and foot gloves, was distinctive. She'd have to be careful about wearing it.

Murphy grimaced at the newscast. "They make it sound like a full-sized cruiser snuck through their defenses, not a lifeboat."

Kyle shrugged. "The Collective lies, the CEA lies. What of it?"

"The CEA is supposed to uphold the law."

Kyle's mouth twitched in what might have been a suppressed smile. "Your University ideals aren't worth much in the real world."

She opened her mouth to argue—

"Oh, no," Kyle interrupted, looking past her.

Murphy turned. Her first-year cadet picture filled the screen. It was an advertisement; the logo in the corner was Avocet Industries's stylized "A" and "V."

In the picture, her scalp was smooth and her eyes ringed by dark smudges from the weight-therapy. Except for the uniform, she looked the same now. It was as if six years of her life had never happened.

"—and accomplices. Ex-Lieutenant Thiadora Murphy can be identified by tattoos of the Heisenberg uncertainty principle on her scalp. For information leading to apprehension, a reward of one hundred fifty thousand—"

Kyle pointed at the screen. "What'll we do about that?"

Murphy felt like she'd been kicked in the stomach. Avocet had to know she wouldn't break her contract.

Avocet's paid announcement continued, switching to a shot of the *Gambit* that could only have been taken during its theft from the Gallger shipyards.

Murphy sat down hard on the lower bunk. "How can he do that? I was stealing the ship *for* him!"

Kyle placed a warm hand on her shoulder. "Apparently, he concluded otherwise. From his perspective it must look like we sold out to Gallger for a higher price. What amazes me is that he bought galaxy-wide coverage for the bulletin." Kyle was silent for a moment, calculating. "Eighteen thousand com launches, even with reduced advertising rates—he's spending millions to find you."

There was a second consequence of the message Avocet had run. She wondered if Avocet had considered it. Telling a universe full of floaters that a Murphy had *jooked* a ship—breaking the Code's most sacred law—would be like telling the Collective they were losing money. It was sure to produce a reaction. "We've got to get a message to Avocet, and tell him the truth."

"He would never believe us. I've already betrayed one Company; I am not a credible source." A wan smile passed his pale features. "And, you—you're a rebel."

Her last bastion against the void had turned against her. What could she do to restore Avocet's faith in her? "We have to recapture the *Gambit*." Her heart pounded at the thought of having to face Gallger again—but she couldn't see any other way out of the situation.

"Are you insane? I won't go back there. I've spent my entire life attempting to escape."

"What else are you going to do? Avocet hasn't paid you."

"How would you and I steal a ship from a multistellar corporation?"

"That's the beauty of it. We're such a small target, they'll never see us coming." Murphy felt her pulse race. It was dangerous, probably impossible. But if she left the *Gambit* in Gallger's hands they'd bury its technology, find whoever created the ship, and ensure that self-launching ships only reached the public when Gallger was good and ready, if ever. Since Murphy had no idea how to locate the original builders, she had to recover the *Gambit*. It was the only thing that would save her.

But how was she going to locate the ship? Gallger was sure to secret it in a hidden system. "How much do you know about Gallger?" she asked Kyle.

He studied her a moment, his face as still as stone. Then, apparently reaching some decision, he said, "A fair amount."

"Could you get into their communications systems, locate the *Gambit*?"

He thought about that one a moment. "They must have changed the security codes since my defection. Still, I did put in a few backdoors before I left, as insurance . . ." He shook his head. "No it's too risky. I'd have to be at a Gallger com."

Murphy's eyes widened. Even that was more than she'd hoped for. Kyle, if that was his real name, was no salvager. At the very least, he was a highly placed corporate spy. "Will you help me?"

Kyle's mouth worked, like he wanted to scream or to spit. He stood up, walked to the door. Put his hand on the knob. Stopped. Turned to face her. Stopped. Ran both hands through his tangle of hair and then walked over and sat on the bed beside her. Sighed explosively. "Shit."

"That's great!" She pounded him on the back.

He groaned.

Murphy seated herself in front of the com and touched the transmit icon on the upper left screen.

"What are you doing?" Kyle asked

"I need to send a message to Avocet. Tell him what really happened."

"You can't call him directly. He has a bounty on our heads. Avocet is sure to track any incoming communications. Remember, he hasn't forgiven us yet."

"I know, that's why I'm placing this call in a very circuitous route." She keyed in the initial letters of the address. The silver and blue screen of the University appeared. The stylized wings still sent a pang through Murphy. She was getting farther and farther from her dream. Would she ever find anything to replace it?

She finished the address. Tali's image, a frozen first lieutenant in full-dress uniform filled the screen. Even with her face set in the serious scowl of a formal picture, her brown eyes danced with amusement. The address had been confirmed—a chip in the com launcher waited to record Murphy's message.

She hit a second icon, paying for extra encryption. Kyle reversed the command.

Murphy's head snapped up, "What are you do—"

"Your message will be more secure if you don't encrypt it. It would be a red flag for anyone checking for communications to and from old contacts of yours."

"How do you know?"

He shrugged. "It's what I would look for."

So he *was* a spy. That would explain his skill with

communications and his education. But it didn't explain his lack of space-skills. A spy, but one limited to full gravity? It seemed a grave handicap, but then, grounders were constantly dismissing the importance of space.

Murphy shut down the com. Communications were recorded on chips and launched, there being no other way to send faster-than-light transmissions. She could send a package almost as swiftly as a message. She ran over to her suit and opened the inner pocket. It was still there. She held up her discovery to Kyle. "Can you encrypt a message on this?"

He stared blankly at the palm-sized floater's bible.

The message cube sent with the bible said only, in Murphy's voice, that the holo-book had been damaged and needed repairs, and that Murphy would pick it up when Tali was done. Kyle changed the record-date on the chip to confuse anyone who might intercept it. When the holo-book opened, a garbled version of the video played.

But there was a second, encrypted message that Tali would only find in the process of repairing the book. It was buried under the program that controlled the holo-book's timing functions. That message explained that Murphy was in trouble and asked her to forward an encrypted message to Avocet Industries.

"Will she find it?" Kyle asked.

"If there's a hidden message, Tali will ferret it out."

"Many things could prevent this from reaching her."

"Have you got a better plan?"

A pounding at the door interrupted his reply. Murphy and Kyle exchanged a tense glance. The room was a single, barren cubicle. There was no place to hide.

"Lay down in the top bunk," Kyle whispered. "If they see you, I'll tell them you're ill."

Tucked as tightly as possible into the join of bunk and wall, Murphy could still see the corner of the door. Kyle's shoulders tensed. He smoothed his blond hair back and checked his left pants' pocket. Then he pressed a palm against the door. The tiny viewscreen activated. Kyle's head blocked the image, but she saw the grounder relax and open the door.

It was Spanner, in a gravity chair. The chair took up most of the available floor space. It was an older model and had seen a lot of use. Hoses were patched with duct tape, and the arms were worn through the chrome patina to the titanium underneath. The floater was panting with strain despite the supporting pressure from all sides. Sweat beaded his smooth scalp and upper lip.

Kyle motioned the chair into the room, looked up and down the corridor, and shut the door quickly behind Spanner.

Murphy dropped from the top bunk. One hand pointed at the chair. "Where did you—?"

Spanner gasped and then spoke, "It's on loan. Couldn't wait to electronic-contact you, wasn't sure you'd follow a messenger. Spoke to local resistance. Floater-owned frigate's on the far side of the sun, coming here to resupply. They're anxious to meet Murphy, once I described her marks. We must hurry, there's a reward out for you."

"We know," Murphy said. "One hundred fifty thousand."

Spanner looked surprised. "No. *Two* hundred thousand is what's being offered by Gallger Galactic."

CHAPTER 10

"Gallger?" Murphy leapt from the top bunk and clicked the news screen off. "*Two* of the Companies have posted a reward for us?" Her stomach clenched. If they started a bidding war, the whole galaxy would be looking for her. With that kind of money on her head, who could she trust?

Murphy turned the news screen back on and flipped through the channels.

"Spanner, how was the Gallger reward notice worded?" she asked. "Was Kyle mentioned?"

The floater looked off into space for a moment. "No. He wasn't."

For some reason Gallger wanted *her* back, but didn't care about Kyle, the employee who'd betrayed them. Interesting.

"Have to get out of here," Spanner said. "If I can find you, others will."

"How did you locate us?" Kyle asked. "My credit card is untraceable."

"Credit card?" Spanner shrugged. "I just described you to the clerk."

Murphy shook her head in disbelief. "You described us when there was a price on our heads?"

"Didn't know," Spanner said. "Saw the newscast on the hotel elevator's screen."

The door chimed. A short man with sandy-blond hair appeared on the screen set at eye level in the door.

"Who is that?" Kyle asked.

Spanner looked and then groaned. "The clerk."

Murphy tapped the center of the screen and slid her finger along the edge, widening the angle of view it displayed.

The lump of somebody's shoulder clipped the lower-right hand corner. A foot showed in the left. "He brought friends."

The door chimed again.

"What should we do?" Kyle asked.

"If we don't answer the door, they'll let themselves in. Spanner?"

He shook his head. "I've got no weapons."

Murphy said, "Spanner, distract them. Kyle and I will hide on either side of the door. We'll hit them when they come in."

"What?" Kyle said. "I've never struck a—"

The door opened. Three men strode in.

Murphy clenched both hands into one big fist—connected with the temple of the guy on the clerk's right. He went down.

The guy on the clerk's left was big. He wore black rubber pants, red-and-white suspenders, and a purple bowler hat. His hair hung in greasy yellow dreadlocks.

Kyle swung at him, and connected with his jaw. The man, almost a head taller than Kyle, shrugged off the blow and returned the favor. There was a sickening crack. Kyle's head snapped back, and he dropped.

The clerk locked the door. "Get the rest of them."

The big man lumbered forward, his left hand gripping a taser.

Waste. Murphy looked around for something she could use. Spanner, trapped in the chair that was keeping him alive, wasn't maneuverable enough to help. Her eyes glanced at the groaning body of the man she had felled. On the floor, in front of his outstretched hand, was a second taser.

She leapt, dodging under the big man's wide swing. The clerk jumped back, colliding with his protector. The big man shoved the clerk behind him. In that second, Murphy grabbed the fallen weapon and jumped away.

Eyes on her opponent, she thumbed the taser up to maximum charge.

The big man circled her, his dreadlocks swinging as he lumbered forward, arms extended. He drove her closer to the beds, farther from the exit.

She jumped backward, catching her opponent off guard, and kicked off of the top bunk and toward him. It was a beautiful maneuver, and would have worked—in zero gravity.

Murphy crashed into the big guy's waist. A hot electric jolt ripped through her shoulder blades, thrashing her limbs. Her hands clenched. She jerked and contorted, tasted ozone in her mouth.

She heard the whine of Spanner's gravity chair accelerating, then a crunch. The taser stopped.

Lifting her rubbery arm, she shoved her taser into her attacker's calf.

Maximum charge arced through the big man. His bowler hat flung off as seizures rippled through his body. She wrapped herself around the trunk of his thigh and held the taser on him. For long seconds he slammed them both against the steel floor. Then he went out. Murphy looked up.

Spanner's chair leaked fluid and the side of his face was swelling, but he had bought her enough time.

She'd thank him later. The clerk was running for the door.

Her legs wouldn't cooperate. They stumbled instead of running. The clerk was at the door, when a pale hand grabbed his ankle. He kicked at Kyle. Murphy hit him with the taser. Unlike the big man, the clerk was out in seconds.

She helped Kyle to his feet and handed him the big man's taser.

"Are you hurt?" he asked.

Her head felt fried from the inside. Her limbs were rubbery and twitched of their own accord. "I'll do," she said. "Spanner?"

His words were slurred, his lip was split and swelling. "Patched the hydraulic leak, don't know if it will hold."

"Long enough to meet the friends who lent you that chair?"

He nodded.

They pulled the bodies away from the door, throwing the two smaller men on the bunk beds. They pushed the large man into a corner. Murphy hit all three with another taser jolt.

Kyle suited up. His helmet provided a small amount of anonymity. Murphy donned the big guy's bowler hat and shrugged into the clerk's jacket. She carried her suit over her shoulder, wrapped in one of the hotel's sheets.

The front desk was empty when they passed it.

They quickened their pace. Murphy's legs were coming back online, but her hands still twitched at odd moments.

Crowds of grounders parted as Spanner plunged his chair through them. Murphy's face burned as she walked. Would she be recognized? She waited for the shout, for arms to grab her.

They reached the spoke without incident. A large elevator ferried goods between the rim and the cargo ships docked on the hub. The platform was guarded by a station security officer.

"Friction," Spanner swore.

"I'll handle this," Kyle whispered. "Follow my lead."

She searched his face for his intentions, but they were hidden, locked behind the tight set of his jaw and blue eyes gone suddenly dark.

Spanner shook his head. "There's another service spoke."

"It'll be watched, too," Kyle said. "I can handle this—if you'll allow me."

Murphy nodded, deciding suddenly. "This is his world, let him play it."

Spanner scowled.

"I'll speak to the guard," Kyle said. "When I gesture, you two approach. Murphy, act despondent and don't step more than a meter away from Spanner's chair at any time—Spanner, grin like you've won a lottery."

"We could better follow your plan if we knew what it was."

Kyle chewed his lip. "I can't tell you that, the details are . . . embarrassing. Please trust me." He raked his hair out of his face with his fingers, licked his lips, and strode forward. The guard intercepted him, and they talked.

Spanner watched the interaction intently, focusing on their faces. Murphy guessed what he was doing. Reading lips. It was a skill some floaters acquired. It allowed them to communicate in vacuum without speakers or direct helmet contact.

Whatever they were saying, it didn't please Spanner. Before she could ask the chair-bound floater what was going on, Kyle waved for them to approach.

Spanner kept his face impassive as he crept the chair forward. Murphy followed, staying close. It was easier for her to play her part. Her worried expression echoed her internal state.

Her fear escalated when the security officer brought out a retinal scanner. She glanced at Kyle. He nodded imperceptibly. Murphy let herself be scanned. The guard had seen her, knew who she was. The retina check was merely a formality, but still, she wondered what kind of con Kyle was running, and whether he was playing on her side.

"Murphy, Thiadora. She checks out all right. Rebel. Ship thief. Guess that'll teach the CEA not to pull recruits from floaters."

Kyle chuckled conspiratorially. Murphy could feel Spanner's hatred grow, burning like a fusion reactor next to her left arm.

"Your ID?" the guard asked. Kyle handed his credit card over to the man. The CEA officer ran it into his reader. Examined the screen. His eyes widened, and he saluted.

"A pass, please," Kyle said quietly.

The guard hastily issued them a transport permit for the docking levels. "There you go, sir. That will prevent you from being bothered to show your ID again."

"Thank you," Kyle said, inclining his head. "I will report your efficiency to your supervisor."

The guard beamed and saluted again.

Kyle ushered Spanner and Murphy into the cargo lift. Murphy wanted to ask Kyle what he'd shown the guard, but a five-man loading crew shared the lift with them. They looked as if they'd just come off shift. Their coveralls were dark with sweat, and they stank.

Kyle stared straight ahead, not meeting Murphy's eyes.

As they rose, Murphy felt a tug on her shoulder. She looked down, and Spanner leaned close to her. Moving only her eyes, she glanced sideways at Kyle. He either hadn't noticed, or was ignoring them.

"Bounty hunter," Spanner whispered.

"No," she murmured.

"Told the guard he was turning us in."

"No," she repeated. But doubted the word as she said it. Kyle had been hiding his identity ever since she met him. But why would a bounty hunter steal a ship and sell it to a rival company, unless . . . it was an elaborate trap. For who? Her? Why would he bother?

"Don't trust him," Spanner mouthed.

Under her breath Murphy said, "He got us through the guard post."

"This time."

Murphy looked away, unwilling to continue the conversation.

As they rose toward the center of the station, gravity lessened. Kyle drifted, his face puffy. Spanner grunted as fluid flowed into his face and tightened the skin of his split lip.

Murphy was both relieved and worried. Her limbs

stopped aching in weightlessness. The pressure that had been a low-level annoyance all day, eased. Microgravity seduced her tired muscles. But if she adapted, she'd be trapped in a floater's life. Her mind tightened as her body relaxed. Atrophy haunted her like a thief, stealing her peace of mind along with her strength.

At the top, workers drifted in and unbelted shipping boxes, pushing them toward the door. In slow motion, garish boxes of tourism chips floated from the freight elevator to ships that would transport them across the galaxy.

Once the cargo was unloaded, Kyle kicked off toward the door. He grabbed the handle attached to the wall, and waited for the others to join him. It wasn't graceful, but he was learning.

Spanner activated the electromagnets on the treads of his chair and crawled forward. Murphy kicked, caught Kyle's hand, and waited for Spanner to join them. Outside the cargo drop, a nervous teenage boy with pale skin and a long angular nose waited. The marks on his brow were a summation of the moments of inertia of three conical rods. So far, the series only included second-order terms. Probably a junior engineer or an apprentice tech. The boy jumped when Spanner came out of the hold. He must be their contact.

The nervous boy silently attended to Spanner. Like a pupae emerging from a cocoon, the older man disconnected himself from the chair. Trailing plastic tubes and electronic monitors, he stretched his arms, hovering.

The boy disconnected probes from Spanner and stowed them on the chair; then popped the center of the seat and collapsed the chair to half its width. He drove it into one of twelve large lockers built into the wall, and stowed it.

The boy sealed the locker, substituting a retinal imitator when the locker whistled for ID. The Lucite ball had the same index of refraction as vitreous humor and someone else's retinal print embedded in the back of the plastic. Imitators were also highly illegal.

The boy motioned for them to follow him.

They walked past the cafeteria and a set of euphoriant establishments. Abruptly he turned, leading them into a tunnel that ended in an unpainted door set flush into the wall. The back door to a bar?

"Where—" she started to ask.

"No questions," Spanner hissed under his breath.

Murphy was still staring at the door when the wall behind her sheathed open. It was black, pinpoints of LEDs the only light. There was no path, just pipes and crossbars. It smelled of dust and grease.

Their guide stepped through, and they followed. The door behind them closed seamlessly, leaving them in darkness. Murphy's breath caught. Was this an ambush? Then a bright light blinded her.

When her vision adjusted, she saw a pair of middle-aged floaters hovering before them, a man and a woman, in their fifties. The woman held an arclight, her thumb on the switch that would boost it to cutting strength.

Their guide was gone.

The couple wore quick suits, thin microfiber mesh that filtered toxins and viruses from the air. They were less bulky than a standard suit, only a few micrometers thicker than heavy synth-silk. But the fabric was strong enough and passed air slowly enough that it could protect a person in vacuum for up to five minutes.

The man drifted closer, his limbs twisted in ways that would never bear weight. His head, huge and round, dwarfed his wasp-waisted torso.

Space-born.

How had he survived? Floater women usually gestated and gave birth in thick-walled asteroids with at least minimal gravity. The radiation and low gee of space produced horrible birth defects: weak hearts, curving bones, reduced blood volumes, profound mental retardation. Murphy was amazed his mother had carried him to term. She regarded the gleam in his eye. Unlike Lil's son, this space-born had Murphy'd out okay.

"That her?" the man asked, returning her appraisal. He looked at Spanner. "Feynman and Pollack, what the hell happened to your face?"

Spanner's words were thick. "Ran into trouble getting out." He waved at Murphy. "Louis, meet Thiadora Murphy."

"Has the look of him," Louis agreed.

"That means nothing," the woman said, her arclight never once wavering from Murphy's face. "The companies would choose such a one to trap us." Her face was obscured by the golden mesh of her quick suit, but the tone in her voice was clear.

"Spanner said you wanted to talk to me," said Murphy.

"Speaks," said the woman. "Brazen little thing."

"Elma, at that age, you would have taken both our heads off by now," the twisted man said. "She looks veritable to me. Let's get her on board."

"Not before we confirm her identity," Elma said.

From a zippered pack hung around his waist, Louis removed three clear plastic rectangles the size of Murphy's thumb. Stiff transparent fibers a centimeter long sprouted from one of the large faces.

"What's that?" Murphy asked.

"Blood test. Can't take you on board if you're carrying something." He plucked at his quick suit. "These aren't for fashion."

Spanner held his arm out. The twisted man pushed toward Spanner, grappling him around the waist. They drifted, locked together, as he lowered the rectangle to the crook of Spanner's elbow. The tiny fibers sank into his flesh and filled with red-black blood.

Murphy was next. There was no pain, but the sight of the filaments disappearing into her arm unnerved her, making her queasy. It was over in seconds.

Kyle stepped backward, or tried to. Forgetting he was in zero-gee, he flailed, increasing his motion. "No. I won't—"

The man shrugged. "No test, no trip."

Murphy grabbed his arm and pulled him close to her. "Where else are you going to go?" she hissed in his ear. "It's just a blood test for bacterial and viral infections."

His eyes locked with hers, but did not give away his thoughts. "You'd better hope that's all it is," he whispered.

Louis regarded Kyle with interest, and Murphy wondered if he, too, could read lips.

"Please." She held out a hand. The man passed her the sampler, and she touched it to Kyle's inner arm. He stared at the translucent leech as it filled with his blood. It wasn't queasiness that showed on his face, but fear. Why did this bother him so much?

When the three samples were complete, their host pressed the first one, Spanner's, into a palm-sized analyzer that he pulled out of yet another of the many pockets on his belt. A white pinpoint appeared on the surface of the rectangle as the blood drained out of a single hair-thin vial.

Seconds later, the screen displayed: "Clean."

"That's all you needed for the test?" Murphy asked. "Why take the extra blood?"

"One for sickness," Louis said. "The rest for DNA scan. You say you're Murphy's daughter, but we must know for sure."

"You testing me, too?" Spanner asked.

"Can't be too sure, my friend. The CEA's morphed agents before. We test everyone, these days."

Murphy looked over at Kyle. His lips were compressed to a thin white line.

None of them were infected with anything serious, at least, as Elma laconically put it, not yet. The pair of floaters ushered them through the maintenance corridors, letting Murphy and her companions lead, so that Elma and her arclight could cover their movements.

The group emerged from the maintenance passage back into the station proper. Shuttles were docked to a windowed tube, like the spiraling spines of an agave cactus.

"The *Negotiator*'s too big to dock directly," Louis said. "We'll shuttle to her and verify your ID there. Then we'll discuss alternatives."

The shuttle was a McKinley 380. Murphy hadn't known there were any of those still in service. The controls were antique: LEDs and membrane switches. The chrome was thin in spots, and the polyfiber seats were frayed around the edges.

It hadn't been designed for five passengers. Murphy, Kyle, and Spanner clung to equipment tethers on the back wall while Louis and Elma piloted the shuttle.

The floater couple worked in silent communion. A shuttle this old didn't have synchronized station release algorithms. It had to be undocked manually. Their fingers skimmed the controls in front of them. As soon as one activated thrusters, the other compensated. Back and forth, like couples in a minuet, their hands flew across the controls. Murphy admired their skill.

The acceleration out to the rebel's ship was less than half-gee, but Louis gasped and for a second, Elma took over the controls completely. When they reached the turnover point, he dabbed his beaded forehead and returned to work.

The ship was a midsize cruiser with a 360-degree ion cannon tower on the top of the flat disk of the hull. Like the shuttle, it was old but well maintained. No Company insignia graced its sides. Louis and Elma must be free-floaters, those who'd bought, or finagled, their contracts back.

"How did you justify the cannon?" Murphy asked. "It takes special dispensation for civilians to purchase armament."

Louis tapped his chest and pointed at Elma. "We're L&E Shipping, specializing in rare commodities and electronics." He winked at Murphy. "The weapons are in case we are attacked by revolutionaries."

Elma scowled at him. Whether it was the information he was revealing, or his enthusiasm for talking to a younger woman, Murphy couldn't say. "Not another word until they check out. They may not be the friends you take them for."

The floaters docked in the shuttle bay with quick efficiency. Locks slid home and an umbilical tube ran through the evacuated hold to the atmospheric portion of the ship. No one in their right minds would waste air on a shuttle bay. While they waited for the umbilical to pressurize, Murphy studied Elma through the haze of her quick suit.

She had been beautiful once, before age and radiation had stolen the elasticity from her skin. Wrinkles framed her large dark eyes.

Elma caught Murphy's stare, scowled, then said, "Lock's open. You first."

Murphy sealed her helmet and waited for the others to seal theirs. No floater alive trusted pressure gauges, or any instrumentation, farther than they had to.

Murphy opened the door to the umbilical and climbed through the orange plastic tube, pulling herself along by ribs inset at each meter. Spanner and Kyle followed.

The door to the ship was locked. They waited at the far end of the tube while Louis and Elma secured and powered down the shuttle. Louis crawled past them while Elma held the arclight on them. He keyed the palm reader, and they entered the ship.

Murphy was struck with a sudden sense of homesickness. The white-enameled metal walls, the oval bulkhead doors every few yards, the recycled air, all reminded Murphy of cruisers she'd traveled on as a child. There was nothing to indicate they were on a rebel ship. The absolute normalcy of it must be part of the camouflage.

"Take them to medical and check them out," Elma said, pulling off the hood of her quick suit. "I'll warm the reactors." Profit-and-loss equations decorated her wrinkled scalp. She held out the arclight for Louis.

He shook his head. "How'm I going to handle that while I run the medical tests?"

Elma scowled. "We can't trust them."

"We've known Spanner for years."

"If that's him."

"Elm . . ."

She licked her lips and stared at Murphy and the others. "I'll watch from control. If anything happens to Louis—anything, I'll evacuate the room. Got that?" She kicked violently upward, and was gone.

"Don't mind Elma," Louis said, hooking the warped bone of his forearm around one of the pull-alongs. "She's had a hard life."

And he hadn't?

The medical room was pale blue and dominated by an empty coffin-sized life tank in the center of the room. Louis opened one of the hundreds of drawers built into the wall nearest the door. A sliding compartment held the DNA sequencer. It locked into place when Louis thumbed a button on the handle. Then he pressed Spanner's blood chit into a depression in the lower half of the box.

The rectangle drained, returning to blood-flecked transparency. Louis removed the plastic vial and pushed it into a disposal chute.

The sequencer whirred. Inside it, Spanner's DNA was broken and reacted with base strands, building up a profile that could be matched with public records.

A screen on the far wall lit up. Half a minute later, a picture of a grounder in his early twenties filled the screen. Curly black hair dangled over the shaved sides of his head. The name below the picture said: Andropolous Spanostani, MD, Ph.D.—bioengineer, specialty: bacterial and viral genetics.

"You were a scientist?" Kyle asked.

"A grounder?" said Murphy. "Why would you become a rebel?"

Spanner looked at the picture on the wall. He touched the bacterial-growth equations on his forehead and was silent. Seconds passed. " 'Sa long story," he said at last.

"You reading all this?" Louis asked the ceiling.

Elma's disembodied voice echoed off the walls, "Yes, so he's Spanner. Test the other two."

Murphy's cube went in next. Her University records loaded up. She winced at the bright fervor of her junior year picture.

"Birth record," Louis said.

The uniformed Murphy was replaced by a wrinkled red-faced infant. Her parents were listed, Mother: Jenevie Constance Halliday; Father: Ferris Murphy.

"That enough for you?" Louis asked the walls.

"Hardly," the disembodied Elma scoffed. "Those records came straight out of the CEA's files. I want a DNA profile before I take her to the grapple and declare she's Murphy's daughter."

"Establish a link to Latigos's data-nets."

"Already done."

"Computer: Genetic extrapolation, from current data. Compare with Murphy, Ferris-2853A."

The baby's image faded, replaced by two horizontal multihued lines, colors representing the different codons. They scrolled by impossibly fast, blurring into white. Where a match was made, both strands turned black. The top line was labeled her genetic code. The bottom line, Ferris Murphy's.

The computer finished its analysis: "Ninety-seven percent probability of paternal identity."

Louis discarded Murphy's cube and prepared to insert Kyle's.

The grounder shifted forward, hand outstretched. "Is that necessary? You've already determined I'm free of disease, and I claim no relation to a famous figure."

"Something to hide, *gronuger*?" Elma's voice asked.

"No, of course not. But we are wasting time."

"Ours to waste," Louis said, sliding the blood sample home.

The computer searched the on-board medical files. Long moments passed. "No record," its toneless voice announced. "Switching to station database."

Everyone in the room looked at Kyle. He stared at the floor.

The screen remained dark. "No record."

"You don't exist?" Murphy asked.

"That's just Latigos's mirror site. We'll check Galactic Central," Louis said. "Elma?"

"On it," she replied. "Just slipped the request onto an outgoing datachip."

"What do we do now?" Spanner asked.

Louis opened a locker near the door, and removed an arclight. He aimed the weapon at Kyle. "We wait."

Spanner and Louis conversed lightly while waiting for Galactic to respond. Spanner stood at a distance, under cover of the other man's weapon. While Louis was distracted, Murphy whispered to Kyle, "Why isn't there any record of you?"

Kyle glanced at the pickup in the ceiling that projected Elma's voice. He tapped absently on the wall, then leaned over, his lips tickling Murphy's ear. "I deleted my records before I left. As a precaution."

A half hour later the com bleeped. "We've a report back from Galactic," said Elma.

The screen flickered, but remained dark. "No record," said the computer.

That was impressive. The Galactic records were safeguarded by the Collective itself. No one had ever succeeded in breaking into their security—until now.

Kyle sighed, obviously relieved.

"But," Elma said, "I also pulled down archive files from Belgua-Morrisey station."

"That station was deactivated eight years ago," Murphy said.

"And since their files haven't been online, they aren't susceptible to corruption." Elma's voice was smug. "Louis, I think you'll find this very interesting."

The floater lifted his weapon.

An image of a twelve-year-old boy displayed on screen. Wide blue eyes stared mournfully through a riot of chin-length curls. The expression was relaxed, but sad, as if sorrow was its natural state. The face was round with baby fat, but unmistakably Kyle's.

"Damn," he whispered.

The name across the bottom of the screen was printed in large block letters: JONATHAN KYLE GALLGER.

PART 2

"All things tend toward a state of disorder."
    —Thermodynamics, Book of Entropy 1:12

CHAPTER 11

Jonathan Kyle Gallger. Murphy froze, her mind click-ing details into place. She remembered a small news item, the opening of a station. The CEO of Gallger Galactic, Jonathan Gallger, cut the ribbon over the airlock. He'd been a tall man with graying hair. Kyle must be his son. It explained the executive card and Kyle's unfamiliarity with space.

Gallger had dogged her heels ever since she had left the University. What kind of trick were they play-ing now? Her chest tightened. She'd taken him in, trusted him.

Kyle slumped in midair. He stared at his empty hands, a little boy caught. His eyes were hollow with despair. The childhood picture displayed wall-sized be-hind him was haunted, not the image of a beloved son.

As someone who'd spent her whole life trying to escape her past, she suddenly understood. He was run-ning from Gallger, just as he said. She didn't blame him for not telling her about his connection to Gallger. In his place she would have kept quiet, too. It was dangerous information.

Louis's body trembled with rage. "How could you bring him aboard and not tell us? You endangered our ship, lied to us. Why?"

Spanner glanced at Kyle. "I didn't—"

"I trusted you!" Louis shouted. For a long moment, the only sound in the room was the low background hum of pumps and life-support systems.

Kyle spoke without lifting his head. "I left Gallger. When I have the money Avocet owes me, I'll disappear. No one will ever know I was on this ship."

"Ha!" Elma's voice crackled over the ceiling speaker. "Who'd give up their claim to a corporation that controls one-sixth of the galaxy's wealth?"

"I didn't own Gallger, it owned me."

The speaker projected Elma's sharp laughter. "Oh, poor baby. Crushing the galaxy in your hand wasn't the fun you thought it'd be?"

"Gallger's been chasing us for two weeks," Murphy said. "They shot at the *Gambit* while he was aboard. He doesn't control Gallger any more than we do. If he did, would he risk his life just to capture a few rebels?"

"He's the Gallger heir!" Elma protested.

Murphy said, "That doesn't mean anything. Just because you're someone's heir, doesn't mean they love you—it doesn't mean they share control with you while they're alive." Murphy pointed at Kyle. "He saved me and Spanner; got us through a guard post on the spoke. I may not know Jonathan Kyle Gallger, but I know Kyle. He's my crew, and you don't touch him."

Spanner and Louis stared at her.

"What're you saying, Murphy?" Spanner whispered.

"I claim him as crew." It was the only way to protect him. Louis and Elma would respect the Code. The ritual words clicked into place. "His actions are mine, his friends are mine, his enemies are mine." She added, "If you harm him, there will be war between our ships."

"Murphy," Spanner whispered, "you don't have a ship."

She strained for a breath, her chest burned. "I will," she said. "I'm getting the *Gambit* back, with or without you." Stars glittered in her peripheral vision. Darkness boiled after them, tunneling her sight.

Louis crumpled, his slack body drifting into a half-fetal curl.

Murphy stared at his pale sweating face. She tried to suck in a breath, but her lungs strained at the air. Spanner and Kyle panted. The subtle hum of pumps vibrated the soles of her feet and the palms of her hands through the metal floor.

Vacuum pumps.

Elma was evacuating the air out of the medical bay.

Murphy kicked, propelling herself toward the exit. She caught the door, palmed the lock. Nothing happened.

Murphy gulped for oxygen. Vision shrank to a pinpoint. "Elma!" It came out as a hoarse whisper.

"Hush, honey." Elma's voice was a parody of consolation.

Murphy's head pounded. She inhaled and tasted sweat and the musty smell of uncycled air. Her feet connected with one wall of her small prison, her left hand the other. Her right hand touched something warm. In the dim red glow of emergency lighting, she saw it was Spanner's shoulder. She shook him awake.

They were jammed into a closet-sized room with only a tiny air vent. On the opposite wall was a door— no handle. It must open from the outside.

There were no handholds, nothing to cling to. To avoid contact, they braced hands and feet into opposite corners. Even with that, elbows and ankles clinked in embarrassing familiarity. Spanner didn't seem to share Murphy's discomfort, only respected it.

"Why didn't you say he was a Gallger?" Spanner asked.

"I didn't know." Even to her ears, it was a hollow excuse. She'd known he was no salvager. Why hadn't she pressed him for the truth? Murphy examined the walls of their prison, but they held no answers.

"You didn't know? You claimed crew with a man you know nothing about? He's a *gronuger*; probably doesn't even know what crew-claim means."

"I know Kyle. He couldn't have been in control of Gallger. It just doesn't fit."

"How can you say that about a stranger?"

Murphy swallowed. "Some people choose to put their past behind them. I understand that. People can change their destiny." She touched the marks on her brow. "Aside from these, and my name, I'm no more a floater than you are . . . Dr. Spanostani."

He winced.

"What are they going to do with Kyle?" she asked.

"Louis'll do the questioning," Spanner said. "He'll use drugs. Doesn't have the strength or temperament for torture. Elma'll plot how to use Kyle for best profit."

"And us?"

"Depends on what Kyle says, how dangerous it is to keep us alive. Louis and Elma haven't survived this long by taking chances." A memory flickered behind his eyes.

"How did you meet them?"

"Let's not launch there."

"You have a more pressing engagement? I need to know who these people are, so I can predict what they'll do."

Spanner stared at a point beyond her right shoulder. "My scientific research . . . troubled me. The Company I worked for offered me more money, better living quarters, anything to keep me. I refused. They made it clear that leaving would not be good for my health." He shrugged. "Joining the rebels was the only way I could break free."

"What were you doing?"

His lips compressed. "Viral research. For Gallger."

"You hated fighting viruses so much, that you turned down wealth and comfort to join the rebels?"

"Didn't fight viruses." He met her eyes. "I engineered them. My laboratory built genetically targeted bioweapons, viruses that are only active when the host has certain gene-sequences in their DNA. Some labs built viruses to kill agricultural pests." He licked his lips and looked away. "My group developed for the human genome."

"Why would a transportation company need bio-weapons?"

"Upper management was looking to expand their operations." His voice was harsh and sarcastic. "I threatened to quit. Management informed me that leaving would be fatal. I escaped and joined the rebel floaters. They were the only people that hated the Companies more than I did. Hoped that the enemy of my enemy would be my friend." He rubbed his eyes. "The Beluga crew took me in, listened to my story, and resolved to help me fight the Companies. But they weren't strong enough to protect me when Gallger tracked me down. The station they shared with Morrisey—"

"Was stricken by a plague."

She saw how Gallger would play it. It was almost too easy. Engineer a virus and release it in a self-contained biosystem. When the inhabitants start to flee, the Collective quarantines the station. Gallger could develop a cure if the disease got out of control—it's easier to find the answer when you know the question. Gallger comes out of the incident a hero—makes a tidy profit on vaccine sales—and the inconvenient masses trouble Gallger no more.

"Why didn't you tell the media?"

"Make myself an easier target? No. I found a wife among the Belugas." He touched his tattooed forehead. "Took the marks of my profession and settled down to design waste-processing bacteria for the rest of my life. We hollowed out an 'stroid. She gave birth to my daughter there.

"Then Gallger found me." His voice tightened. "I took our shuttle and ran, thinking if I was gone, Jan and Mari would be safe." He released a shuddering breath. "I was wrong. Gallger attacked the ring, destroyed the atmospheric generators on our 'stroid, ruptured the hull.

"Hours later I finally ditched the Harrier-Drones. When I returned, power was out. Walked through the wreckage, only light is coming from stars and my hel-

met. Found them together, in the emergency airlock—
only part of the 'stroid that would still hold air. Smart
was my Jan." His voice choked off.

Murphy reached out a comforting hand.

Spanner knocked her gesture away. "You wanted
to hear it—so listen!" He wiped the back of his hand
across his face and continued in a hoarse voice.

"Oxygen regenerator in the baby's suit was charred.
Jan'd rigged her suit to breathe for both of them. At
some point, it hadn't been enough. Jan turned her
valve off. Spliced her batteries into Mari's system to
give the baby more time. I found her body wrapped
around the baby's, frozen. Baby was so still. Perfect
and pink. Tried to resuscitate her. Filled the airlock
by venting from my suit—pushed air into Mari's nose
and mouth. Injected her with adrenaline. Nothing.
When I touched her tiny body, it was still warm. Must
have died minutes before I found them."

Murphy's chest ached. Floater life was so fragile.
"What did you do?"

"Tried to destroy Gallger. Designed weapons again,
but this time to a purpose. I wanted every last person
in that Company dead.

"Some early successes. The CEO of Gallger died
from one of my bugs. Then they found me. The rebels
and I launched from system to system, always a jump
ahead of Gallger. Till they caught up with us—at Canodyne 4265."

"Gallger bought and marooned an entire manufacturing station just to stop you? Canodyne let them?"

"Ya. All Companies sleep together." He held his
face in both hands, drifting free of his braced position.
Tears bubbled out from behind his fingers.

Murphy took him in her arms and rubbed his back.
She could feel his ribs. Deep inside her, a dull ache
pounded.

"I killed them all," he said. "Jan, Mari, the colony,
the floaters who protected me. But that's not the worst
of it. Before Gallger chased me out of hiding, I investigated a disease one rebel contracted on Beluga during

the first labor strike. The virus used the same RNA sequences I'd used on the CEO. Gallger was exploiting my research. My hatred had given them what they wanted—weapons." He clenched his hands into fists. "Gods know how many have died because of me."

Steel bands of realization tightened around Murphy's chest. It was hard to breathe. "The floater plagues?"

His voice was a ghost's last whisper. "Viruses custom designed to thrive in weightlessness. The pinnacle of my research."

Millions dead. Floater society fragmented as people could no longer transfer easily from ship to ship. No one trusted anyone anymore.

There was nothing she could say to ease his guilt. She held him while he cried.

Murphy jerked awake when the door opened. Light and sweet air flushed the room. She untangled her limbs from Spanner, realizing they must have fallen asleep while she comforted him.

Kyle clung to the doorway. His eyes were ringed with black circles, and his face was pale. Elma was a few steps behind him, her eyes hard, hands on her arclight.

"Spanner!" the older woman barked, "we want to talk to you."

The floater rubbed his face with his hands, then scratched his bare scalp. His eyes were puffy.

"Come on." She dragged at his arm, bracing her feet against the doorjamb so that she'd haul him out, instead of his inertia hauling her in.

"Hey!" Murphy said, "I haven't had a drink in hours. I'm thirsty, and I need to go to the bathroom."

Elma pushed Kyle through the door. "You'll keep." The door sheathed shut.

Murphy's eyes readjusted to the dim lighting. She fumbled against Kyle, awkwardly touching stomach and thighs and arms. She pushed herself into the corner again.

Kyle braced his body away from hers. Straining. They didn't touch, but it hardly seemed worth the effort.

"Sorry to interrupt . . ." he slurred, staring at her in the gloom.

"What?" Then she realized she and Spanner had been tangled together when the door opened. She knew how a grounder would interpret that. "I was just comforting him."

"Of course you were."

There was something hard in his voice. Was this the real Kyle? Was the bumbling grounder she knew just a mask?

"No matter," he said. "My feelings are no concern. I've no claim on you."

Her head snapped up, "What?"

"Damn." He rubbed his face. "I didn't intend to say that."

"What happened?"

"They took me to the medical room and strapped me to a wall. Then they injected me with something. It was strong. Mnemonic blocks it had taken me years to develop fell like dominoes. I couldn't stop the flood of words. They asked me questions about Gallger, and about you, and . . ." he groaned, "about the *Gambit*."

"They know everything?"

"Everything I know. I'm sorry, Murphy. I didn't want to talk, not after you tried to protect me . . . claimed me as your crew member." His voice drifted off, came back a whisper. "That was the first time anyone ever championed me. There were sycophants and hangers-on in the Company that professed everything from admiration to true love. For a while I believed them, but they were only attracted to my position and admired only what I could do for them. But you claimed me when I had nothing to offer but myself . . . I never belonged with anyone before."

His voice was charged with grief. Had he misinterpreted what it meant to be crew? Crew members often slept together on long flights to release tension and pass the time, but it had nothing to do with their working relationship.

"Then the door opened and I saw you and Spanner together—how can I have lived this long and learned so little?" He pounded his fist against his forehead. He lost his braced position. There was an awkward moment of limbs and touching before they settled back into opposite corners.

She stared at him, stunned by his forthrightness. This creature of secrets and silences she had traveled across dimensions with was babbling like a two-year-old, and making as much sense.

The truth drugs hadn't worn off.

She could ask him anything, and he'd answer her, in full and unedited detail. But it would be wrong, a violation; he was helpless.

The first question formed in her mind. Feeling dirty, she asked, "What do you know about Canodyne 4265?"

He glanced at her, hurt. Some part of him knew what she was doing. "That was a special project of Vivien's—"

"Who's Vivien?"

"My sister, the acting CEO of Gallger. Canodyne 4265 ran a small pharmaceutical manufacturing plant. It was shut down twenty years ago—something to do with the floater rebellion. The plant reopened a few years after that. When Vivien took over as CEO six years ago, she bought the station from Canodyne and closed it down again. I don't know why. Details about the acquisition were heavily secured."

Murphy's lips tightened. Confirmation, but not of anything she wanted to hear. "What about you? Why didn't you inherit the CEO-ship?"

Kyle laughed once. "Me? I'm a disappointment to the family. A throwback to humanity." His words were underlined with bitterness. "I was the youngest of three children. Vivien was the middle child. When

I was twelve, our older brother died in a shuttle accident. Vivien never relaxed after that." He met Murphy's eyes. "I think her guilty conscience worried I might follow her example and do likewise to her.

"The only thing that kept me alive was that I was bright and eager to please her. I'd hack into files so she could read the minutes of the boardroom, secret memos, and shipping billets." His voice drifted away, lost in memory. "I thought it was a game."

"If you and your sister got on so well, why'd you leave?"

"Vivien trusts no one." He paused again, shaking his head. "I was her tool, but I was also a threat—next in line should anything happen to her. I knew that. So did she. Three months ago, she hired a young cybernaut out of prison, bright, inexhaustible, and devoted to her. Then my personal chef of twelve years was replaced by someone from off-world. The implications weren't lost on me. I dined out after that, and began looking for a way to retire."

"The *Gambit*?"

"Yes." He stopped and didn't say anything more. The drugs must be wearing off.

Murphy could kick herself. Why had she wasted so much time? Damn. The *Gambit* was all she should have asked about. "Where did the *Gambit* come from?"

Kyle smiled, a look both attractive and predatory. "Now, that is a question several people have asked lately. In fact, I have been answering a lot of questions these past two hours. I'm tired of talking. You answer one—"

"The *Gambit*, who built it?" She nudged his ankle with her foot. "Tell me."

"No. Not until you satisfy my curiosity. Tell me about this other Murphy, the one floaters mention in hushed tones, your father."

"Why in space would you want to know about him?"

"Because I—" He shook his head. "No. Answer my

question. Or," he said, folding his arms, "if you're not in a talking mood, I could take a nap." He yawned extravagantly.

"I don't like to talk about my father."

"You didn't care whether I enjoyed talking about my fratricidal sister. If I'm going to tell you secrets about the most technologically advanced ship in the galaxy, I need to know more about you. Tell me of your father."

"He's not important."

"All the floaters we encounter grovel at the mention of his name, and you say he's unimportant." He snorted and crossed his arms, floating a little forward with the motion.

"Fine." Her voice hardened. "Ferris Murphy was a legend among floaters. A brilliant pilot that cared as much about his fellow man as about his ship—which, they tell me, was a lot. Over the last twenty years, floaters have come to consider him a patron saint of good luck. He survived more stupid, haphazard stunts than anyone had a reason to—or maybe he just talked big. Whatever the reason, he convinced a lot of folks that he was hot stuff. My mother too. Only he didn't make as good a father as he did a hero. He left us when I was five." She glared at Kyle.

"Where did he go?"

"No one knows. The story is he long-tripped. Left known space to explore new realms." Murphy kept her voice hard. "More likely he's dead or hiding out in a remote system. Mother and I never knew why he left. Maybe he wanted to get as far from us as he could. Maybe he just couldn't live up to the legend anymore."

She pushed Kyle back to his side of the cubical. "Your turn. Who built the *Gambit*."

"I have no idea." He held his palms open in front of his chest. "No one knows—not even Vivien. The ship turned up in Formalhaut."

"Formalhaut?" Murphy said. "Are you sure?" The asteroid belt where she'd grown up was in the Formalhaut solar system. The coincidence prickled her neck into gooseflesh.

Kyle continued, "A Gallger ship carrier was enroute to Lettinger station to pick up some rebuilt ships when they intercepted the *Gambit*. It was drifting without power. The captain assumed it was a lost launch. It's rare for them to turn up in inhabited space, but it happens. He sent a two-man tracer to stake a claim on the ship, on the chance it was worth salvaging.

"What they found was a mystery. The ship was a model no one had seen before. There was nothing like it, even in the projected prototypes listed in the shipbuilder's public records. The two crewmen could not fathom the controls, but they managed to tow it back to the station. The captain called Gallger headquarters, bargaining for a promotion in exchange for his unusual find.

"I intercepted the call. I had a habit of monitoring Vivien's private calls as a personal safety precaution. The ship sounded like a secret prototype. I needed money to escape Vivien, so I called the shipbuilder who could offer me the most."

"Avocet. Did *he* build the *Gambit*?"

Kyle smiled. "That's what he told me—but I don't believe him."

"How do you know he was lying?" Murphy asked.

"Years of watching corporate types dissemble. Communications is a specialty of mine." He smiled. "Computer skills aren't the only thing that kept me alive."

"So who do you think built it?"

Kyle shook his head. "I haven't been able to puzzle that out. The ship is too advanced for any other shipbuilder. It's impossible that a company could have developed the technology for such a ship in secrecy. The corporate spy network is too well entrenched." He shrugged. "Aliens? As good a hypothesis as any."

Murphy's breath caught. She said softly, "Impossible. Mankind's colonized half the galaxy without running into intelligent life."

"Maybe this was their first attempt at contact—and something went wrong, killed their pilot."

"Then, what—" Murphy stopped and cocked her head.

There was a sibilant hiss from the vent overhead, almost inaudible, but Murphy's trained ears registered the anomaly. She looked up. Just beyond the wire mesh was a dark knot of shadow. A ball of audio fabric. A microphone.

Murphy spoke to the ceiling. "Someone's listening to our conversation."

"*Jooking* feedback." Elma's voice echoed in the small room. "Still, I should thank you, Murphy. You thought of questions we didn't ask."

Murphy felt sick. She should have guessed the closet would be monitored.

"Let us out. You heard Kyle, he's got no more love for Gallger than you do. We're all on the same side."

"Maybe, maybe not. You two are resources. I must figure out the best way to allocate you. In the meantime, you will be fed and given quarters."

The door to the cell clicked opened. Louis hovered, holding an arclight. A personal reader was strapped to his thigh.

"Sorry about the wait," the floater said. "We had to check with a few people about what to do next." He waved them past.

Murphy pulled herself slowly along the handholds in the corridor. She followed the course Louis indicated with the welder's muzzle. "What are you going to do with us?"

"That door." He nodded to a beige oval with "10" painted in large russet numerals. "I can't tell you." The floater seemed embarrassed.

The room was crew quarters. Not large, but spacious compared to the closet she'd just left. Four sleep holes were built into the walls, two on each side of the wall toilet. The coffin-sized beds had a sliding mesh door that prevented nocturnal drift. She noticed one of the beds had been used.

Louis met her questioning glance. "Spanner will be joining you, after we've worked through some of the finer details."

Kyle pushed past her and wedged himself into the unused top bunk.

"There's fresh clothes in cabinet 36, food in 42." Louis pointed at a wall of drawers. "And 43 is a built-in reheater. Make yourselves comfortable."

Murphy climbed onto the toilet and, for Kyle's sensibilities, pulled the privacy screen around her. "As comfortable as we can be, knowing that Elma hears all?"

Louis winced. "It's a security precaution. For your safety as well as ours."

When she emerged, Louis unstrapped the personal reader and tossed it to her. It flipped end-over-end until she snatched it out of its trajectory.

"When we last cracked the net, there was a message waiting for you." Louis looked around the room. "If there's anything else you need, just let me know." He turned to go.

"Just tell any wall?" Murphy asked through the door.

Louis made no reply.

Murphy stared at the black clamshell in her hand. She didn't have a fixed address. Who'd broadband a message to her across the net? Avocet? Gallger? Kyle leaned half out of his coffin. "Are you going to play the message?"

Murphy frowned at the reader. "They must have read this already."

"Let me see." Kyle clapped his hands.

She threw him the reader.

Kyle tapped a few keys. "Looks unbreached to me. The security codes are intact. In fact, it's a rather complex algorithm. Clever. Maybe they weren't able to unseal it."

"Why bother, when they can just wait and listen to me play it." Murphy glowered at the walls. "Do you know any way to . . ."

He winked and said, "Did I ever tell you my favorite thing about light?" He pushed over to her, grabbing her shoulder hesitantly. A grounder's fumbling attempt at a point-of-reference grip.

They tumbled across the room. Murphy caught the wall by extending her good foot behind her so her head wouldn't slam into it, then she wrapped the other leg around Kyle for stability.

He blushed.

"Would you rather we wedge ourselves into a coffin?"

"No. This is fine." He opened the clamshell and held it between them. Then he wrapped his left arm around Murphy, hugging the sides of their bodies together to form a "V." The clamshell pointed toward them, its display hidden by their bodies. Kyle bowed his head over the top of the viewer, and the screen was complete.

"My favorite thing about light," he whispered in her ear, "is that you can't pick it up with a microphone." He set the reader to "text," instead of "sound."

She nodded and opened the file. It had been sent with full security encryption. A password, thumbprint, and retinal scan later—a face appeared on the palm-sized screen. The image was no larger than her thumb, but Murphy gasped in recognition.

It was Tali.

CHAPTER
12

Dark circles ringed Tali's cocoa-colored eyes, and her braids were wild and off center, as if she'd worked through the night. The dorm room behind her was dark, lit only by the safety strips along the floor.

"MURPHY, I HOPE THIS FINDS YOU." Tali's face blurred as she glanced over her shoulder. "I HACKED INTO THE UNIVERSITY'S COMMUNIQUÉS FOR THE WEEK BEFORE YOUR COURT-MARTIAL. NETCOM DETECTED ME AND KICKED ME OUT, BUT NOT BEFORE I FOUND THIS RECORDING."

"—THE MONEY? GOD—HATE THIS—YES, I'VE LOCATED—UM-HMM—GALLGER GETS HER—OSBORNE, THOUGH HE'S NOT—TONIGHT—SHE'LL SAVE—GOT A HERO COMPLEX YOU WOULDN'T BELIEVE—"

Murphy's hands tightened on the clamshell. On Tali's desktop screen, a voice-recognition subroutine identified the speaker: Haverfield.

Tali continued, "I ALSO FOUND AN UNDOCUMENTED DEPOSIT IN THE ACCOUNTING RECORDS. ONE HUNDRED FIFTY THOUSAND TRANSFERRED TO THE CEA'S GENERAL FUND THE DAY AFTER YOUR COURT-MARTIAL. ONLY A COMPANY—" The door behind Tali burst open. Light flooded the room.

A man shouted, "FREEZE! RAISE YOUR HANDS!"

Tali's eyes were wild with panic. In the background, MPs held assault-flechette rifles.

"STEP AWAY FROM THE COM!"

Her lips tightened into a thin line. "THIS IS A PRI-

VATE ROOM. YOU CAN'T COME IN HERE WITHOUT A
WARRANT."

The soldier moved his needler rifle to track her
movements. "WE KNOW IT WAS YOU WHO SABOTAGED
NET-COM AND UPLOADED BLUEPRINTS OF GOTTSDAMER-
UNG STATION TO TERRORIST FORCES. IF YOU ATTEMPT
TO TRANSMIT THAT MESSAGE, WE WILL FIRE."

Tali's face went through a series of contortions: outrage, fear, and disbelief.

Murphy gripped the personal screen so hard her
knuckles popped. "Tali—don't!"

On the tiny screen, Tali's eyes narrowed. "FUCK
YOU," she told the soldier and reached forward to
transmit.

"CRA-CRA-CRA," printed on the screen. Staccato automated rifle fire. The right side of Tali's face exploded in bone and blood. Needler darts impacted the
screen. The message went blank.

Murphy snatched the screen up to her face. "Tali!
No!" Her heart stopped, waiting irrationally for an
answer. But the message had ended. She held the
clamshell up to Kyle. "This can't be real. Surely Gallger, or Louis and Elma, someone, doctored this message. Tali can't be . . ." Her throat clenched, and she
couldn't get out the final words.

Kyle took the reader from her hand, tapped a few
keys. "The encryption seal's intact. As far as I can
tell, the message is real." He squeezed her shoulder.

She knocked his hand away and pressed the cold
metal of the screen to her forehead. She couldn't believe it. But, if it *was* true, there was no way Tali could
have survived needler fire at close range. Murphy
ground the viewscreen into her forehead. If it wasn't
for her, Tali would never have become involved. Murphy luck was a lie—everything in her life turned to
shit.

Haverfield was right, her desire to be a hero had
sent her out into the storm. He may have set the trap,
but she fell into it, and kept falling.

Murphy pounded the clamshell against her forehead. The pain helped her focus. It wasn't her actions alone that had killed Tali. There'd been an agency at work, starting the tumble, accelerating her fall. She growled, "Gallger."

"What?"

"Gallger. This is proof they were behind my expulsion. You read Tali's transmission. They were waiting for me when I stepped off the shuttle at Gottsdamerung. Gallger Galactic engineered my court-martial. They must have set up the terrorism frame that got Tali killed. She never would have committed treason."

Kyle shook his head, causing their linked bodies to oscillate. "It doesn't tally. Why would Gallger need you?"

"Someone decided only a Murphy could fly the *Gambit*, and the only Murphy around these days is me. They sent the flight simulator to the University—and insisted I test on it."

His brow wrinkled. "Maybe . . . but coercion and murder isn't Vivien's style. It's too blunt. She seduces people into following her, she doesn't bludgeon them."

"She does now." She poked his chest with a finger, adding a second harmonic to their motion. "Why did Tali have to die—why? Waste!" Murphy's hand clenched around the player. "I'm going to get this recording to the authorities—and take Gallger down."

Kyle paused before replying. "And just who are you going to turn the tape over to? You saw Vivien has the CEA in her back pocket. Who exactly do you expect to carry out this justice?"

Murphy released her leg lock and shoved him away. Recoil sent her into the wall. She spun and caught herself with her palms. Kyle thumped into the beds. The reader spun in place in the center of the room.

"Don't vent your frustrations on me," Kyle said, clinging to the sleep coffins. "I'm no part of Gallger Galactic."

Maybe not, but he was heir to the corporation that had ruined her life. And Vivien Gallger wasn't here right now. Nor was the bastard that had overshadowed her future the moment he helped conceive her.

Ferris Murphy had walked out on her when she was five and left her nothing but a legend that she could never live up to. Nothing she ever accomplished, no record she set, was ever good enough. And now her desire to live up to that legend had stolen her military career and Tali's life.

"Leave me alone," she mumbled, pulling herself into a sleep coffin. She pushed the webbing closed. "Just . . . leave me alone."

She stared at the padded ceiling of the coffin, breathing slowly to ease the pressure in her chest. She stuffed the emotional pain into a dark recess of her mind. It took all of her vitality with it. Each breath left her hollower, emptier, until she was nothing but a thin husk. The droning of the engine lulled her and, exhausted, she slept.

She sat, five years old, on the rough-hewn floor of her family's asteroid. The cold stone felt good against her bare legs. Her mother walked past. Murphy, her head at knee level, couldn't see her mother's face, just the wash of translucent filters she wrapped around her face when she worked in hydroponics. They trailed behind her in the reduced gee of the asteroid like brightly colored seaweed.

A sudden cold wind whipped the filters, and darkened them red. They blew away, wet and bloody, uncovering a face—Tali's face. White bone protruded through the flesh of her cheek. The left eye was a pulpy red mass. Tiny drops of blood bubbled from the wounds and jiggled in the air currents.

Murphy screamed.

A door opened, and light flooded the room. A man embraced Tali. Murphy didn't recognize his face, but his voice was like the beating of her own heart.

Then the stranger was before her, watching her out of brown eyes filled with concern. He held out a silver pear. No, it was a top, red and slick with blood. Tali watched as Murphy took it in a chubby hand. The man showed Murphy how to hold it against the floor with one hand, and pull the string with the other. The air rushed faster around the flared top of the toy, creating an area of lower pressure. In accordance with Saint Bernoulli's principle, the top rose into the air, spinning.

It flashed as it spun, darkening and shrinking into a black sphere, and then radiative fins sprouted from its sides. The *Gambit*.

Suddenly, the asteroid was gone. A wide field of stars engulfed her. Suitless, she was alone in its infinite expanse, except for the spinning *Gambit* and her father's face. As she watched, he aged. Wrinkles formed at the corners of his mouth and eyes. He spoke, his face contorted, but no sound came out.

She reached for him, and he dwindled away to nothing. He shrank into a grasshopper and leapt away.

The *Gambit*, still spinning, was almost full size. She stretched to touch it. A fin slammed down on her wrist—

The sleep coffin rang with a metallic echo. Her hand throbbed.

"Newton's apple! You all right?" Spanner pulled the webbing away. His face was scrubbed and his head shaved. The bacterial growth equations on his forehead gleamed.

Her mouth was dry. "Just a dream." There was something, though, she should remember. Something her father had tried to tell her, before the *Gambit* pushed him away. Like dust, the dream floated out of reach when she tried to catch it.

Then she remembered—Tali was dead. Murphy squeezed herself into a ball. No. She couldn't lose control now. Had to get out of the current situation— then she could fall apart. Murphy spoke around the lump in her chest. "How did your meeting with our hosts go?"

Spanner looked over his shoulder. Kyle was asleep in his bunk. "Not well. Elma wants to collect the reward on you. Louis and I talked her into taking you to the grapple first."

Murphy had been to a grapple once. Free-floaters, revolutionaries, and opportunists gathered off the space lanes. Some transport crews rigged their shipping schedules and manifests to attend. They docked their ships together to meet face-to-face, discuss the revolution, and trade goods. Grapples were rare, and illegal. "When is it?"

"Thirty-six hours. Louis sent directed-laser communications to tell them we were coming."

"Isn't that dangerous? The CEA might intercept the signal."

"Not likely. Space is big, and who but floaters are going to use the old technology?"

Kyle rolled over in his coffin.

Spanner lowered his voice. "I can get you out, Murphy. But the grapple'll eat Kyle alive. You have to reneg your crew-claim."

She shook her head. Once claimed, crew were only expelled for capital crimes. Throwing someone off your ship was a death penalty. For Kyle, it might be worse. "I can't."

Spanner's brown eyes met hers. "You've no choice."

Murphy floated with her hands clasped behind her head, listening to every sound on the ship. It was unnerving to be a passenger. That growling hum, Elma was lagging the engine. A high-pitched, nearly inaudible, squealing told Murphy the right and left reaction chambers needed balancing.

She was helpless. If Louis and Elma made a mistake, there'd be nothing she could do to save them, or herself. The engines slowed. She and other floating objects drifted toward the far wall. "We're turning," she mumbled.

"Stop listening to every noise," Kyle said. "A person would think you were the ship."

"I'm a pilot. I can't just turn that off."

"Evasion acceleration in twenty seconds," Elma's voice crackled over the com. "Strap down."

Murphy heard the hum of booster engines warming up. "Damn you, why didn't you give us more warning!"

"No time, honey. Been busy up here. Fifteen seconds."

"Into the coffins!" Murphy shouted.

Spanner caught the lip of a coffin with his left hand and whipped his body around, slipping feet first into the padded cocoon.

The hum had become a throbbing. Murphy grabbed Kyle's hand, shoved him headfirst into the lower coffin, and slammed the webbing shut. She dove into the coffin above Kyle's, snicked the webbing closed with her feet, and spun to face the direction of motion.

The hum changed to a roar as the boosters exploded small nuclear devices and kicked the ship into erratic, high velocity.

The back of Murphy's head slammed into the polyethylene padding. From below she heard gagging noises. Kyle must be facedown. Crushed by acceleration herself, she couldn't move to save him. The acceleration shouldn't last long, so he wasn't in real danger of suffocating. She hoped.

Finally, the pressure eased.

Murphy crawled out of her coffin and checked on Kyle. His face was red, and he was coughing, but he was alive.

Murphy raised her voice toward the audio pickup. "You can't collect the reward if you kill us. What kind of game are you playing?"

Louis's voice responded hesitantly. "Sorry. Couldn't be helped. The . . . situation required speed. Are you hurt?"

"We're fine. What's going on out there?"

Elma's voice, muffled, crackled over the com, "Why are you wasting time with them? Coordinate, damn it, that scout is still with us!"

The com clicked off.

"We'd better strap down," Murphy said.

The ship lurched and yawed in evasive maneuvers. Murphy stared at the padding in front of her face and re-created the scene outside. Yaw right, angle thirty degrees, pitch forty-seven. A sudden lurch right, then the spiral acceleration of a rollover. Tactics used to evade more than two, less than six pursuers.

Her fingers ached to touch controls, the *Gambit*'s controls. She had to convince the revolutionaries to help her recover the ship from Gallger. If its technology could be exploited, the universe would simultaneously open up and become a smaller place.

Long trips wouldn't be necessary for exploration. Fathers would have to find other reasons to abandon their daughters.

The ship jerked, Murphy slammed against the left wall. "What's happening?" She screamed at the microphone in the ceiling, but Louis and Elma didn't answer.

After interminable long minutes, the ship turned, slowed, stopped. They were in free fall again.

"Spanner, you okay?" Louis asked over the com.

"Ya—"

Murphy interrupted. "What *was* that?"

"A little unexpected company. Vargas and the boys scared them off. But it's a breached grapple. Negotiations will be swift and tense. Some ships are breaking off already."

"No. We have to stop them—they need to know about the *Gambit*."

"I'll tell them," Louis said and disconnected.

"Do you have to disclose the details of what the *Gambit* can do?" Kyle asked. "That's not the deal I negotiated with Avocet. I sold him a ship with secret technologies. If you tell half of known space—"

"It will only increase its value. Don't sweat it, Gallger, you'll get your money."

Elma escorted them to the control room, scowling. The forward screen displayed sixteen different squares, filled with faces. It was a real-time video link to sixteen other ships. Elma gestured with the arclight for Murphy to take a seat.

"What's this?" Murphy asked, locking her legs around the ergo.

"The grapple."

"But the ships aren't mated."

"Those trusting days are gone," Elma snorted. "The only handshakes around here are electronic. Besides, we don't have time to loll around. The CEA knows we're here. They'll be back with containment forces. If you're going to address the grapple, you'd better do it quick."

Sixteen bald floaters stared at her. Their marks covered every conceivable discipline: engineering, medicine, chemistry, physics, nanotech, astrogation.

Murphy opened with a ritual floater greeting: she touched her fingertips to her forehead. "Those that fly high, I, Thiadora Murphy, daughter of Jenevie Halliday and Ferris Murphy"—she paused to let her words sink in—"I bring news to change the balance of power in space forever. I swear, by the gods of physics, that there is a ship capable of self-launch."

The faces, each the size of her fist, reacted with various expressions of surprise and disbelief: some smirked, others scowled, most just stared, unconvinced.

One old man spat at the screen. "LYING GRONUGER FEM," his words scrolled along the bottom of his image. A man with a pockmarked face, asked: "IS SHE REALLY DAUGHTER TO THE MURPHY?" Other screens flickered with similar questions.

Louis sent Murphy's genetic code as confirmation.

"Six days ago," Murphy continued, "I piloted this ship into an alternate dimension. When I transitioned back, I had traveled forty-three light-years in seconds." She paused. "Without a launcher."

Mute questions sprung onto the bottom of the partitioned screens. "IS THIS CONFIRMED?—HOW CAN WE BELIEVE?—IS THERE PROOF?"

Louis uploaded the recording of Kyle's interrogation, confirming the event.

Murphy continued, "The ship was captured by Gallger Galactic two days ago. I have come to ask your help in reclaiming it, for all of us. With self-launch we could travel under our own power, go where we willed without the Companies approval and without paying their exorbitant launch fees."

A collage of voices asked: "WHERE DID THIS MIRACLE SHIP COME FROM?—WHO BUILT THE *GAMBIT*?—THIS TECHONOLOGY, WHO DEVELOPED IT?"

"The ship was found by Gallger, floating uncrewed."

Their expressions paled, and more than one screen displayed the word: *VERRAGUNG*, GHOST SHIP.

"No one knows who built it. What's important is that it exists. Gallger has it now. They will destroy the ship to bury the technology. We, the true inhabitants of space, must reclaim the *Gambit*, so that we can use its knowledge."

The videoed floaters reacted with various expressions of skepticism: "WHAT DO YOU NEED?—WE HAVEN'T RESOURCES TO BUILD SHIPS—DIZZY FEM, HOW ARE WE GOING TO TAKE A SHIP AWAY FROM GALLGER?"

"It is true, Gallger is a powerful enemy. I propose to take the *Gambit* from them not by force, but as my father would, by skill and cunning. With me"—she pulled Kyle into camera range—"is the Gallger heir. He released the *Gambit* from the hands of his company. He saw its value was more important than personal gain." She spoke as much into Kyle's ear as into the microphone, trying to impress upon him the need to play along. "With his help, I will infiltrate Gallger's stronghold and free the *Gambit*. All I need is a ship small enough and fast enough to slip into the Gallger system undetected."

BOLD WORDS—MURPHY'S GHOST RETURNED—ONE SHIP IS NOT TOO GREAT A PRICE—IF WHAT SHE SAYS IS TRUE.

They wavered. Her words were the stuff of legends, and it had been decades since floaters had a hero. Even the skeptics wanted to believe. Younger floaters, those who had grown up on the exploits of Murphy without ever knowing the real man, looked ready to follow her through Gallger's front door.

The man with a pockmarked face spoke. "EVEN IF WE GIVE HER A SHIP AND SHE ACCOMPLISHES THE IMPOSSIBLE AND BRINGS THIS SHIP OF WONDERS BACK TO US, WE HAVE NO WAY TO EXPLOIT ITS TECHNOLOGY. WE HAVE NO RESEARCH FACILITIES, NO MANUFACTURING PLANTS AT OUR DISPOSAL. THIS MAD PLAN WILL ONLY WIN US THE ENMITY OF ONE OF THE MOST POWERFUL COMPANIES IN THE COLLECTIVE. WE WILL BE WORSE OFF THAN WE ARE TODAY."

"It is true," Murphy said. "We don't have the resources to exploit the *Gambit*. But I know someone who does—Avocet." She gave them a moment to mumble and digest that information.

"BUT HE'S A COMPANY, TOO!—AVOCET? HE'S A—THIS IS BUT A GAME OF THE COMPANIES. I FOR ONE, WILL NOT PLAY."

"He was born a floater. Is a floater still. Both for his own gain and to do what's right, he will build ships that break Gallger."

"AT WHAT COST?—HIS SHIPS WILL BE BUILT AT *GRONUGERS*' PRICES—FOR THE ELITE, WE WILL BE LEFT OUT AGAIN!"

"There are more ship-using people in space than on all the colonized planets together, including Earth. We will show him the profit that can be made by selling to small-time floaters. It will be part of the agreement that brings him the *Gambit*."

The pockmarked floater spoke: "DOESN'T HE HAVE A PRICE ON YOUR HEAD, MURPHY?"

She stuffed down panic. "A misunderstanding. He doesn't know the *Gambit* was taken from me by force."

"WAS IT? YOU STAND WITH A GALLGER AT YOUR SIDE. PERHAPS THIS IS A RUSE TO ALLOW YOU TO ESCAPE ONCE MORE, AND WITH ONE OF OUR OWN SHIPS."

Spanner stepped forward. "Gallger *jooked* the *Gambit* from Canodyne 4265. Sent an exploration

launcher into a marooned system to get it. Spent a lot
of money to snatch that ship. And this one"—he
jerked a thumb at Murphy—"screamed like they'd
purged a lock on her. Man with her mewled that Gallger'd found him. They don't work for Gallger." He
looked back over his shoulder at Murphy. "She says
we must rescue the *Gambit*. And I believe her. I'll
dock with her."

Murphy stared at his face. Was he serious?

The man appraised Spanner. "WERE YOU ON BOARD
DURING THIS FABLED INTER-DIMENSIONAL JUMP?"

Spanner blinked. "No, but our tech examined the
launch reversal. Space unfolded with a strange radiation distort. *Gambit* folds space tighter than a Gallger
launcher. Verified."

"WHAT WE HAVE, THEN, IS THE WORD OF A WOMAN
RELATED TO A FAMOUS FLOATER, A LAPSED REBEL, AND
THE GALLGER HEIR. ALL OF WHOM CLAIM THEY WANT
NOTHING BETTER THAN TO HELP ALL SPACE-KIND."

One of the faces disappeared, replaced by four
specks that quickly resolved into CEA ships.

Louis transmitted: "CEA's back. Let's vote and get
out of here before we're IDed."

Numbers rolled in two lower corners of the screen.
Seven no. Nine yes.

"I need a ship," Murphy shouted at the distracted
floaters, some of which had already blipped off screen.

The man who had argued with her said, "YOU CAN
TAKE THE *DELTA-VEE*."

"Vargas, you brought that ship to sell for scrap!"
Louis shouted.

The other man shrugged. "A MURPHY COULD FLY
IT."

"Done," Murphy said.

"Are you insane?" Louis asked. "That ship's wreckage."

"I'll make do. Kyle, suit up."

"You'll never get away from the Corps. Vargas is
only dumping it for speed."

"Drop us near it, then get away." She pressed Louis's hand. "Don't worry, I've got a few tricks up my sleeve."

"Murphy, are you sure you can do this?" Kyle asked.

"You'd rather stay here?"

Kyle looked at Elma, his eyebrows raised.

Elma returned his inquiry with a sour expression. "I'll sell you the moment Louis gets tired of having you around," she grumbled. "You're a drain on my resources for no profit."

"Elma!" Louis protested.

"It's true. Our ship can't support a grounder's wasteful ways. And how are we to do business with that one on board?"

Kyle kicked hard toward the room that held their suits. "You won't need to. I'm leaving."

"Wait for me," Spanner said.

"No," Murphy said. "Louis is right. This is dangerous. I meant what I said. Kyle and I don't have anywhere else to go. But you've got friends among the rebels. Stay."

"No chance. You'll need me to pilot Vargas's ship back"—his smile was crazed and infectious—"when we recover the *Gambit*."

"*I'm* captain," she warned him. "There's no questioning that."

"I only ask to be your humble crew." She ignored his sly glance at Kyle, and kicked past him toward her suit.

The ship Vargas had dropped was a Thompson 543 interspace trawler. The plump wedge of its hull was reminiscent of an overstuffed scone. At some point the ship's reactor had been upgraded to fusion by a mechanic whose enthusiasm drove his skills past prudence. The doughnut-shaped Tokamak reactor and mass tanks were welded next to the old fission dome, not so much incorporated into the design of the ship as engulfing it.

Louis, piloting the shuttle, said, "Murphy, leave it. We'll find you another ship." His voice was muffled by his helmet speaker. They were flying with the ship's atmosphere evacuated, so Murphy and her crew could transfer without having to wait for airlocks to cycle.

"No. I've got a recording that transfers ownership of this vessel to me. I'm flying it out of here."

"You don't even know if it has power."

"Only one way to find out."

When the shuttle connected, Murphy climbed over handholds to her ship's airlock. Feet braced against the hull, she pulled up on the hatch with all her strength—frozen shut. The moisture leakage wasn't a good sign. It meant the ship couldn't hold atmosphere. She heated the hatch with a pen laser, working around the seal, and the hatch opened the next time she tried. The inside of the ship was as black as space. Not even emergency lights glowed. Full power off. The fusion reactor would be cold. She hoped the battery bank still held enough charge to reignite the plasma. There wasn't time to wait for the solar rechargers—if they were working.

Murphy started to work her way to the cockpit. She'd been in a Thompson 543 before. Her mother had traded biologicals with a man who flew one. The other floaters thought him crazy to fly a ship with a fission drive when he was successful enough to buy a new fusion-powered ship. But he had claimed his Thompson was easier to control, more reliable, and that the shielding for the crew quarters was more than adequate. Wouldn't give it up for the world.

She hoped he was right about the reliability of Thompsons. In about eight minutes, this one was going to have the stress test of its life.

She pushed herself into position behind the console and tested the battery bank. A quarter charge. Not great, but considering the ship's age, that might be maximum capacity. Murphy routed full current into the Tokamak's microwave heater and magnetic torus. The hydrogen isotopes wouldn't start to fuse until they reached 100 million degrees. If she couldn't get the reactor to ignite, they weren't going anywhere.

The IFOs passively transmitted ambient light from outside the ship. There was enough radiance from Latigos for Murphy to see the floaters dispersing from the grapple: some hiding farther out in the system until the heat was off and they could launch home, some slipping back to in-system jobs and posts before the CEA identified them, and others long-tripping to nearby systems that handled Latigos's launch-traffic overflow.

None of which would work for Murphy. The *Delta-Vee* didn't have supplies for a long-trip or extended hiding. She'd have to figure something else out. But first, she had to get away.

The reactor core was at eighteen million degrees. Trying to draw from the plasma now would snuff the reaction. The mass engines would eject tritium instead of helium, and she'd lose temperature and plasma mass. In the interminable moments of waiting, she thought of the Thompson's older fission drive. If the damn ship hadn't been upgraded, she could have just slipped the damping rods out of the core, and had instant power.

The IFOs flickered with movement. It was a dim view, with no electricity for enhancement.

A cruiser burped forth eight armored sentinels, each singleship armed with two ship piercers. These rockets penetrated a ship and blasted its atmosphere into space. While the crew scrambled for suits, and tried to preserve oxygen stores, the Destroyers moved in. Murphy smiled; her ship, quite literally, had nothing to lose.

Plasma temperature was fifty million degrees. She did nothing. It was an old floater trick. Drift like wreckage. A ship this old, they might consider it a decoy jettisoned for speed, as Vargas had planned. She wondered if it would fool the sentinels. All but one chased after the retreating ships; the last vectored toward the *Delta-Vee*.

Fifty-eight million degrees. Damn. Still not enough to power the engines.

She couldn't afford the electricity to send a transmission to the sentinel, but Murphy leaked a few milliamps into the com's passive receiver.

"Ship XRG-N3413D, we have you in our sites. Surrender, or face immediate destruction."

CHAPTER
13

Murphy's glance darted to the reactor's temperature gauge. Sixty-one million degrees. Still not enough.

"We must surrender, they—" Kyle began, pulling himself into the seat behind the captain's chair.

"Ssh. I'm thinking." Her heart pounded in her throat. If only the Tokamak didn't take so long to ignite from a cold start, she could be long-tripping out of the system. The conductive strips of the old fission controls were still mounted on the console—mocking her. The plutonium had probably been scavenged years ago. Damn. With it she could have brought the fission reactor up within seconds. She would have risked short-term exposure to the radiation.

Murphy stroked the antique reactor controls. She wanted a response so much she imagined the fission reactor display flickered. Tentatively, she touched the control again. It flashed. Murphy's breath caught, and she trickled more electricity into the display. A cross section of a sphere bisected by eight spokes appeared on screen. The spokes were green and met in a gray center. Below was a table indicating radiation levels and power.

The fission reactor *was* operational. The containment rods were pushed all the way in, dulling the reaction to background radiation, but if she pulled them out, the chain reaction would start. Instantaneously.

What kind of insane floater left a working fission

drive in a ship he had upgraded to fusion? It would be like living in a microwave oven.

"Incoming!" Spanner shouted from the copilot's seat.

The ship jerked right. Every object in the cabin jumped left. Murphy slammed into the side of the captain's chair. A hail of debris smacked the wall: empty food packets, pencils, and a palm-sized entertainment screen.

She calculated the damage quickly, port thruster guidance and perhaps the mass warning system had been affected. She needed power—now! The next bolt might hit the fission reactor.

Murphy diverted power from the Tokamak's microwave lasers to the fission systems. Then she traced her fingers along the reactor's control strip, easing out the containment rods.

The com speaker blared: "If you do not surrender immediately, we will be forced to board your ship."

"Board this," Murphy grumbled, turning on the engines. Heat licked up the conduits to the mass tanks, melting the frozen hydrogen. Murphy checked the levels in the mass tanks: twenty-eight percent.

The engine's pressure rose. The furnace of exploding atoms in the reactor superheated the hydrogen to nearly light speeds and shot it out the back of the *Delta-Vee* in a blue-white cone.

Murphy spun the *Delta-Vee,* aiming her exhaust at the approaching ship.

The blast melted the right side of the sentinel, knocking it sideways. The Thompson lurched forward. They were off! The sentinel tumbled in the rear IFO, dwindling in size.

Murphy moved ten percent of the fission reactor's power into recharging the battery banks and powered up the control systems at minimum.

"You getting anything on the com?" she asked Kyle.

He shook his head. The motion caused him to rock, and he caught the sides of the com to steady himself.

"A few stray signals from escaping grapple members. Garbage from Latigos. Nothing from the CEA."

"They must be using pulsed-laser transmission. We won't have any warning. You two keep your eyes on the IFOs."

"Murphy, that pilot back there, do you think he . . ."

"Look." The sentinel she had blasted appeared in the IFO, a tiny lopsided dot, growing larger. Three other dots followed close behind. Half the pursuit force. Blasting him, it appeared, had made this personal. Either that, or someone at the grapple had leaked information that suddenly made the tiny *Delta-Vee* the center of attention.

She couldn't outrun the sentinels using only a fission reactor. She needed more power.

The Tokamak's temperature was eighty million degrees. She pulled the containment rods out a little further and diverted additional power to the microwave lasers. Was this why Vargas had left the fission reactor intact—so that he could use it to jump-start the fusion engine?

"You insane?" Spanner hissed. "Fission reactor's close to critical."

A radiation warning siren bleated across helmet frequencies.

Kyle's head snapped up to find out what the noise was—saw the universal triple-diamond symbol flashing on the top screen—and blanched. "What is going—"

"I'm captain; this is my ship. I'll get you out of this, just hang on."

His mouth worked, but he said nothing.

The plasma ignited. Deep in the belly of the Tokamak, the heavy hydrogen glowed like a captive star. It churned in magnetic currents as it shifted phase, transforming into the fourth state of matter. She cut the electron skimmers off, pushing all of the Tokamak's power into superheating the helium by-product of the reaction.

Time to see if the upgraded engines were operational. The controls had been added to the console with as much attention to aesthetics as the Tokamak itself. A large metal and epoxy cancer bloomed from the left-hand side of the panel. A slide gauge curved along its top surface. Murphy traced the inductive strip to maximum.

An explosion shook the ship.

The *Delta-Vee* shuddered like a stone skipping waves. Murphy's teeth rattled as she fought her way back to the controls. One of the four add-on engines fired intermittently. Its jerking torqued the hull, straining already compromised metal. Murphy shut the malfunctioning engine down, and adjusted their vector to compensate.

Even with one engine offline, the acceleration was like a giant fist crushing the life out of her. Almost five gees. Murphy watched in alarm as their speed crawled over 100,000 kilometers per hour, but she kept full power to the engines.

The four sentinels dwindled to specks in the rear IFOs, then winked out. She eased the damping rods back into the fission reactor. The radiation siren subsided.

With the *Delta-Vee*'s small mass and dual reactors, she had outdistanced the CEA, but she still needed a plan. The closest inhabited solar system was four lightyears distant. If the CEA caught them now, they'd be tried as rebels and sold as indentured workers.

"Where are we going?" Kyle asked.

"Latigos. It's the only way to launch out of here— we don't have the power or supplies to long-trip."

"But the station is the CEA's home base!"

"Right. But they're on maneuvers now, breaking up the grapple." She gestured at the Thompson's speed on the display, nearly 180,000 kilometers per hour. "With two fully operational sets of engines and a tiny mass, we can reach the station ahead of the Enforcers and launch away."

"Latigos won't launch a rebel ship," Spanner said.

Kyle agreed, "Even if they did, the CEA can pluck our destination out of the launch computer."

"Don't worry," Murphy said, fine-tuning their direction again, "I've got a plan."

"You're crazy. You are absolutely insane!" Kyle said when she finished explaining.

"Can you write the program?" she asked.

Kyle sputtered, "Yes, but—"

"Then, do it." Murphy rattled off a set of launch coordinates from memory. In this much trouble, there was only one system she could run to: Formalhaut. Home. "Spanner and I will take care of the rest."

Kyle chewed his bottom lip, then came to some internal decision and started to tap controls, stopped, again, and said, "If this fails . . ."

Spanner leaned against the ceiling, arms folded. "What else were you going to do with the rest of your life?"

Kyle turned back to the display and mumbled, "Space-mad floaters."

"I'll scrounge parts from the tool room, Captain," Spanner told Murphy. He pulled himself hand-over-hand to the far end of the ship.

Between trial runs of his program, Kyle fidgeted with the com, amplifying and resolving signals from Latigos. They were mostly garbage, old EM entertainment broadcasts. "The sentinel's laser-pulse transmissions will arrive ahead of us," Kyle said. "The station will have time to launch in reinforcements. It will be crawling with CEA ships."

"It all depends"—Murphy pushed the containment rods in a bit more, slowing their acceleration—"on economics." She started calculations for their deceleration, figuring the mass she'd have left for maneuvering after she reversed thrust and braked. "If Latigos is willing to blow several million of its general funds renting emergency troops, you're right. But if they hesitate, or can't raise the credit, we're in. The *Delta-*

Vee's a small ship. Even with her add-on engines, she shouldn't pose a recognizable threat."

The navigation simulator bleeped. She'd set it to optimize their deceleration for a full stop before they hit Latigos space. Murphy read the display. Taking both engine systems and the remaining mass in the tanks into its calculations, the necessary turnaround point was fifty-eight minutes ago, twelve minutes before they powered up the ship.

Murphy changed a few parameters and ran the simulation again, same result: a negative turnaround point. She frantically pushed the containment rods all the way in, and funneled the Tokamak's total output into the battery banks. That stopped their acceleration—but they were still traveling at 216,000 kilometers per hour. "Newton's second law," she breathed. "Damn acceleration."

"What's wrong?" Kyle asked.

She clicked her helmet speaker to ship range. "Spanner, you copy?"

"Ya," he sounded distracted.

"We don't have enough mass to stop."

"What do you mean?" Kyle said. "I thought we had two working reactors."

"That's power," Murphy explained. "You have to convert energy into momentum to move the ship. Momentum takes mass, and the tanks are nearly empty."

"Backup plan?" Spanner asked.

Murphy wished she could reach through her helmet plate and rub her face—she squeezed her eyes shut for a long moment instead. "You two stay on task. I'll handle this."

The next two hours were filled with desperate calculations, analysis, and recalculating. If she didn't figure out a way to slow the *Delta-Vee,* they would blast through the Latigos system and keep going. Without the friction of an atmosphere, their velocity would remain constant, and they'd long-trip to whatever lay in their path.

"There." Kyle leaned back and stretched. "The program's finished."

Even in the dim red glow of the control panel, Murphy saw the dark smudges under his eyes. "How're you doing in that suit?"

He shrugged. "Everything that moves is chafed. Each square centimeter itches, and the air in here tastes like my own sweat. How are you?"

"The same." Even with the advanced filtration of the inertialess suit, the air was stale. "Why don't you crawl into the sleep sack in the hallway. If anything happens, I'll wake you."

He studied her for a long moment.

She wondered what he saw in her face and tried to smile confidently, but failed. "No solutions yet," she said.

Spanner returned carrying an empty radioactive-waste cylinder and a fistful of multicolored wires. He wrapped his legs around the copilot's ergo, and pulled a battery-operated soldering iron out of the canister.

Murphy watched the solder wick down the hollow tube of the tool toward the heat source. It fused the wire to the tank. Spanner fed more dull gray wire into the end. She'd never seen conductive electronics outside of history books. Modern electronics used transmitted-photon circuitry. "Where'd you learn to do that?"

"Rebels. Learned a lot in eight years."

She let him concentrate. The solder melted, wicking along the wire and fusing with the metal canister. He clipped three heat sinks around the area, long copper wires that curled into tight spirals along the canister. Then he set his handiwork on a wall magnet to cool by radiating heat.

Spanner's scalp gleamed in the low lighting as he tapped in calculations. Even through his suit, she saw the echoes of the grounder he had been in his wide shoulders and bone structure. Weightlessness and radiation had stolen his health and atrophied his limbs, but he was still an attractive man.

"Why did you come with me?" she asked. "You don't have any stake in finding the *Gambit*, not like Kyle and I do. You could have stayed with Louis and Elma."

He shrugged. "What else was I going to do with the rest of my life?"

There was more to it than that. Was it desire for her? The *Gambit*? "That's not good enough. If I'm going to trust you, I need to know why you're here."

He looked up. "I went into research to change the world. But working for a company wasn't about new tech so much as patent money. Joined the rebels for revenge on the Companies. Was enough, for a while. But now . . ." He clenched and opened his hands, searching for a word. "Rebels've something to fight against. You've something to fight for."

Yeah, Avocet Industries. Murphy was ashamed. She bit the inner corner of her mouth. How much of her inspiring speech at the grapple had been lies? What would she really do with the *Gambit* if she recovered it? Give it to Avocet? Or to rebel scientists? In either case, there was no guarantee its technology could be reverse-engineered.

"NOW ENTERING REGULATED SPACE." The monitor's chirpy voice startled Murphy.

Latigos wasn't yet visible on IFOs, but the automatic traffic beacon hailed her: "STATE YOUR SHIP'S IDENTIFICATION AND SUBSPACE DESTINATION." The *Delta-Vee* streaked past the beacon without answering.

Four CEA sentinels appeared on the IFOs, light, missile-launching, ships. Apparently they'd been left behind to guard the station while the bulk of the fleet dispersed the grapple. They were closing in fast.

Kyle drifted into the room, stretching. "So much for economics."

"Those are the least of my problems." She still hadn't figured out how to stop the *Delta-Vee*.

"Ship XRG-N3413D, you are intruding upon occupied space. Surrender, or we will be forced to fire on your vessel."

She stared at the piercers mounted to the four sentinels, and imagined them ripping through the hull of
the *Delta-Vee,* imagined the blossoms of metal as the
bolts tore through bulkheads. If one hit the fission
reactor would the core explode, or would the radioactive shielding be strong enough to stop the bolt?

An idea hit her: if she could catch the bolts, she
might be able to use their momentum to brake the
Thompson. "Spanner, what are the strongest bulkheads in a Thompson 543?"

"Control-room shielding and the reactor core. Why?"

Four sentinels, eight piercers. She quickly estimated
mass and velocities, thinking back to the times she'd
trained in a CEA sentinel. Yes. If she caught the bolts
head on, it might be enough.

"Kyle, watch for other ships. If this is all there is,
we may stand a chance."

She activated the com, wide-banding her message
so that the entire station would hear. "The revolution
will not be stopped! Murphy lives!" she shouted.

Every grounder lived in fear of a floater rebellion:
aware either at a conscious or unconscious level that
their well-being rested on the backs of the very floaters they despised. Guilt and incomprehension blended
together into a high-octane fuel for fear. Floaters were
erratic, untrustworthy. They lived by strange rules
under conditions no sane person would tolerate. And
all of the launchers, zero-gee manufacturing, and low-
cost shipping depended absolutely on these under-
paid workers.

Whenever this fear burned too low, the CEA
fanned the flames with interviews from border patrols
that had been attacked by rebel pirates. The floater
revolution was the threat the CEA existed to fight,
the threat that justified the CEA's huge budget.

This fear was droned into every lesson she'd learned
at the University. She hoped the sentinel's pilots had
taken the message to heart.

"They're closing to attack formation!" Kyle shouted.

"Good." Murphy brought up a schematic of the

Delta-Vee. It hadn't been updated to show the Toka-mak or the new engines. Estimating the fusion reactor's location, she marked a path through the ship to the control-room bulkheads. There was a target ten meters across the *Delta-Vee*'s nose that she had to get the Enforcers to hit. "Strap down—crash positions!"

Kyle glanced uneasily at the display. "Murphy, what are you—"

"I said I'd solve the velocity problem—I'm solving it. Strap down!"

Spanner stared at the IFOs, then the display. Comprehension blossomed on his face. He opened his mouth, stopped, closed it, and finished strapping down. "She's captain," he said to Kyle. "Do it."

Murphy shunted all power to the docking jets. She'd need fine control to make sure her enemies didn't miss. She melted into piloting, her suit seeming to expand until it filled the hull—was the hull. She twitched and the ship moved. There was no thought—simply being and reaction.

The first bolt launched. Murphy slid sideways, and the cone of the ship aligned perfectly. Right in the target zone . . .

The bolt struck, exploding the world in darkness and stars.

Murphy clawed her way back from unconsciousness. Her bones ached from the impact. Her teeth felt shattered. She opened her eyes just in time to see the second bolt fire. Heart racing, she pushed the ship directly into its path.

It kicked the breath from her lungs.

The third bolt hit. The ship shuddered as it tore through bulkheads.

The control panel buckled, and systems went dark. The IFO display was dotted with black patches where piercer bolts had penetrated. Murphy's luck, for once, held. The engine controls weren't damaged.

The fourth bolt caught them crosswise and passed through the ship. Murphy almost fell forward when the expected hammer blow didn't fall. The slight momentum it imparted caused the Thompson to spin right. She compensated.

The fifth bolt was softer, and for a moment she thought she'd lost that one, too. But no, the first bolts had hit hardest. Now the ship had slowed, and the impact was bearable. Murphy checked velocity: 162,000 kilometers per hour.

With the addition of the piercer bolts lodged in the ship's bulkheads, the *Delta-Vee* was harder to maneuver. The tiny docking jets strained to position the ship's increased mass.

The sixth and seventh bolts were aimed at her engines. Murphy ducked under the sixth and caught the seventh.

Latigos grew from a speck in the forward IFOs to a visible ring, gleaming in the brilliant light of its star.

The eighth bolt missed.

She fired both engines in reverse, full-brake. With the momentum they'd lost to the piercers, it might be enough.

The *Delta-Vee* skidded through the traffic path. Commercial tugs and private yachts veered out of her way. She tried to imagine what the Thompson looked like to them: a tiny ship, hunchbacked by a second set of engines and sprouting the tail ends of piercer bolts from its mouth, like so many broken teeth.

The tiny ship slowed, stopping a scant kilometer from the launch cone.

"Kyle!" She reached to the seat behind her and shook the grounder.

"Hmm?" his eyes fluttered open.

"I need you at the com. Get your program ready."

She shook Spanner. His head lolled. "You all right?"

Spanner groaned, ". . . 'll be . . . a moment." His eyes were glassy and dilated.

Even if she'd had a medibot, there wasn't much she could do for him through his suit. With a muttered prayer to the gods of biophysics, she swallowed around the lump in her throat and asked Kyle: "Can you patch us into the station news channel?"

"I think so—wait—got it."

"Good. On my mark, patch me through. I want both audio and visual. This will be more effective if they know who they're dealing with."

She breathed, composing herself.

"What if this fails?" Kyle asked.

One of her father's sayings came to mind: "Then it will be a breathtaking failure—better that than a mediocre success." She exhaled a last time. "I'm ready."

Kyle patched her through.

She didn't have visual feedback, so she imagined her audience: thousands of grounders, their entertainment, com messages, and work screens suddenly interrupted. All of the screens on Latigos, public or private, now displayed a single image: her face, too space-adjusted to be a grounder, too thin to be full floater, and wearing a strangely designed helmet. She hoped they could see the Murphy's marks on her brow.

"People of Latigos. My vessel is a Thompson 543, an old-style trawler powered by a fission reactor. If you do not clear me for launch within ten minutes, I'll expose the reactor core." With a slash of her hand, she signaled Kyle to end the transmission. "Loop that until we get an answer."

In minutes, the com bleeped. "Launch control, on line one, patching it through," Kyle said.

A tight-lipped grounder wearing a gray uniform scowled in the forward screen. "Who are you?"

"Thiadora Murphy. You have three minutes, ninety seconds."

"We do not accede to terrorist demands."

She glanced at the IFOs. All undocked ships, including transit shuttles, were moving away from the station. Including the ship in the launcher. Off camera, she whispered to Kyle, "Got the program ready to transmit?"

His face was slick with sweat. "Almost."

Murphy carefully positioned the Thompson above

the center of the launch cone and started easing it down into launch readiness.

"Your ship is damaged," the launch official said. "It won't survive a launch."

"You have two minutes, twenty seconds, to transfer control before my reactor core breaches."

He chewed on that one. Thoughts battled across his face. The sentinels had expended their artillery. Until the rest of the CEA fleet returned, his launcher was defenseless.

Kyle whispered, "He's trying to contact the Destroyers back at the grapple."

"You have less than two minutes—calling for help won't work. The CEA can't get back from the grapple in time to stop me."

She maneuvered the Thompson into launch position.

"One minute eighty. And to let you know we're serious . . ." Murphy gestured to Spanner, fist hitting a flat palm.

He tapped a hastily crafted remote control.

Twin jets fired on the canister bomb and blasted it out of the *Delta-Vee*'s empty airlock, past the lip of the launch cone, and toward Latigos's delicate spokes. A spark inside the tank ignited the pure oxygen inside, and it exploded—spraying radioactive by-products in a bright plume, a half-second's brilliant display. Nicely positioned, too. Murphy guessed the flames had been visible along the entire length of the windowed promenade.

Behind the launch official, a radiation siren blared.

Murphy grabbed the sides of the display screen, and spoke to her captive audience of thousands. "Hand over control of the launcher, or every man, woman, and child on this station will be exposed to a lethal dose of radiation."

The official held his expression for long moments. In the background, wall screens throbbed with connection requests, from executives, wealthy grounders, and the station manager. The steel bands holding the launch officer's reserve together snapped. He tapped something into his protesting com, muttering, "Useless CEA protection—"

The official's image vanished, replaced by the launch control screen.

"Got it!" Kyle whooped. "Downloading commands now."

Too easy. Murphy didn't trust it. "Is it going through?"

"I'm the son of the company that invented launchers," Kyle grinned like a boy with a mouthful of illicit cookies. "It'll go through." The launch screen flashed: trajectories, energy allocation, and calculations appeared and disappeared too fast to read.

Latigos's lights dimmed as the launcher drew enough power to fold space.

The Thompson's walls bulged inward, pressing Murphy, Spanner, and Kyle together. The hull, weakened by haphazard additions and piercer bolts, flexed. It might not survive the launch. Best hide in the safest part of the ship in case she broke up during launch.

"Lifeboat!" Murphy shouted.

They scrambled, pulling and kicking themselves down writhing corridors toward the cargo bay in the back of the ship. Hand over hand, Murphy pulled herself along crumpled walls, ducking under a piercer bolt that bisected the passageway. The only sound in the tortured ship was ragged breaths transmitted over helmet speakers.

The lifeboat was an olive-green metal bubble three meters wide with walls three-quarters of a meter thick. Murphy braced her feet and yanked on the hatch as the walls of the *Delta-Vee* bent and the floor fissured. Latigos's signature brilliance flooded through the cracks, piercing the hallway with walls of light. Spanner leaned into the handle with her.

The lid popped open. She shoved Spanner and Kyle into the heavily shielded lifeboat and crawled in after them, squeezing in and tugging the door shut behind her. The lifeboat was designed for two. She was crushed against the lead-impregnated steel. Seventy-five centimeters thick, it was intended to shield the pilot and copilot from lethal radiation leakage. She wasn't sure it would protect them if the core breached.

The lifeboat's antique coke-bottle windows flared with light as the Thompson crumpled around them. Brilliant blue-white light striped the twisting bulkheads of the abused trawler. The *Delta-Vee* launched.

The world exploded.

When the blinding light faded, she blinked and stared through the lifeboat's window. Pressed against Kyle and Spanner, she could hardly move. She had to cantilever her elbows between Kyle's shoulder and the wall in order to push herself into a better viewing angle.

Strips of stars and black space showed through the wreckage wrapped around the lifeboat.

Relief flooded Murphy, rushing up from her belly and exploding in her chest. Her mouth stretched wide into a silly grin. She was invulnerable. Once again a Murphy had defied the odds and survived. "We made it," she said, "we got away from Latigos."

"Aaaiiiyyy-haaa!" Spanner's cheer filled her helmet, resonating with the buzzing in her head.

Kyle's words were little more than a whisper as he said, "We made it?"

"Not yet." Being trapped in an undersized lifeboat wasn't saved. "Spanner, can you reach the controls?"

He grunted, and Kyle shifted, digging an elbow into her back. "Now I can."

"Are we there?" She hoped her memorized coordinates were correct. Otherwise, they could be a million kilometers from inhabited space, with no hope of rescue.

"Lifeboat doesn't have a nav-computer," Spanner said. "Designers never expected us to launch one. All I can say is we're near a white A-class sun, there's a belt about five AUs out. If there's a beacon, we're not picking it up."

"Try the ship-to-ship frequencies." If they didn't get out of the lifeboat soon, they'd die. Not being able to move was maddening. And she'd lived in cramped floater quarters most of her life. What must Kyle be going through? His breathing jerked and started in the helmet speakers.

"Sure these coordinates are right?" Spanner asked. "I'm not sure we've jumped to the right location—or that the CEA isn't right behind us."

"Not to worry." Kyle wheezed. "I transmitted the coordinates. My commands slipped through the launcher's back door. As soon as we jumped, the launcher's software erased. They are sitting on top of eighty million dollars worth of functional, but useless equipment."

"Unless, during the launch, the reactor did breach," Spanner said.

Forty thousand people lived and worked on Latigos. No one said anything for a moment.

"If it breached, we wouldn't be sitting here now," Murphy said. It was, at best, a hypothesis they could live with.

"Activating the distress beacon," Spanner said, tapping controls.

"How long will we be trapped in here?" Kyle asked. His voice held an edge. He shifted restlessly.

"Relax. Someone will respond to our call." She hoped. It had been years since she'd been to Formalhaut . . . years since she'd been home. A twinge of worry: had the Companies shut the system down? She said, "Think of something pleasant."

Moments passed. Kyle asked, "Like what?"

"Like being able to get out of these damn suits and scratch, for one!" Spanner said.

Murphy laughed.

"Stop that," Kyle said, pushing back on her quivering body. "You're crushing me."

Murphy choked her laughter back to chuckles. A pinpoint of light moved against the field of stars. "Someone's headed this way."

The pinpoint grew into a flat disk, then sprouted radiative fins. It was an Avocet Vagabond, a mid-class cargo ship. Painted on the side, beside the ship's registry, were the three dancing atoms of free-floaters.

Murphy felt her heart pound against her chest. Her face split into a wild grin.

The lifeboat's speaker fizzed and sputtered: ". . . XR-niner-four to wreckage, you copy?"

"Gods, yes!" she shouted. "Get us out of this sardine can!"

CHAPTER
14

Outside the lifeboat's porthole, beams of light washed across twisted support girders. Murphy surveyed the damage to the *Delta-Vee*. One wall had crumpled, and starlight gleamed through meter-wide rents in the hull, but the infrastructure of the ship was largely intact.

"Can you see them?" Spanner asked.

Murphy shifted, digging her hip into Kyle's side. "Two people in suits. I'm going out." She leaned against the inside hatch and twisted the handle. The door popped open, and momentum propelled her across the ruined cargo bay.

A spotlight fixed on her.

She raised her hand to shield her eyes. "Well met; it's a small lifeboat." She extended her other hand toward the light. "I'm Thiadora Murphy." Her eyes adjusted, and she saw the floaters. Their segmented suits gave them the appearance of anthropomorphized caterpillars. The photosensitive lenses of their helmets had adjusted to the dark hold; she could see their faces. Male, as she'd expected. One was in his fifties, with gray eyebrows and sun-damaged, leathery skin. His left hand held a recoilless pistol. The other couldn't be more than thirteen, the ink of his first professional tattoo barely dry, a tensor describing the kinematics of a rigid body with no fixed point. He must be a pilot in training.

"John Hroc," the old man said without lowering his gun, "of the cargo ship *Antigones*."

The boy whispered, "Murphy's ghost! See those marks on her head?"

"Don't mean nothing, Moshi. Young folk don't honor the Code anymore—that could be a fashion, or a CEA trick. She looks half-*gronuger* with that slim face."

Spanner reached out of the lifeboat.

"That's far enough," Hroc said, raising the gun. He asked Murphy, "How many are you?"

"Three," Murphy answered. "One woman, two men."

The old man told the boy, "Get any weapons they have. We'll test them in the airlock. If they're clean, I'll file a report. Arch'll know what to do with them."

Her heart pounded with joy. "Arch Kromhout?" she asked. "He still in this system?"

"What if he is?" the old man said. "We'll ask the questions here. Do as you're told. The rest of you, out of that hole, nice and easy."

Spanner pushed slowly out of the hatch, floated over to Murphy, and placed his hands on his helmet. Kyle shoved too hard and tumbled from the lifeboat in a blur of arms and legs.

The old man tracked him with the pistol.

Kyle grabbed a broken ceiling support and twisted around it until he slowed. Then he stared at the two floaters, and the gun.

They were equally transfixed by his unmarked forehead and the wisps of hair that streaked into his helmet.

"Gronuger," the old man snarled, trying to cover all three of them simultaneously with his pistol. "Told you we couldn't trust 'em."

"He's crew," Murphy said.

The old man looked her over. "You the captain of this outfit?"

She glared back. "That's right."

"Woman captain. That explains it."

The floaters led them through the *Delta-Vee*'s broken corridors. Scraps of dangerously sharp metal drifted in their path. Twice they had to climb around the crumpled shells of piercer bolts.

They stopped at a smooth hole. The welder that Hroc had used was tethered to the inner wall. A transit tube was magnetically fastened around the opening. Hroc and the boy crawled through first. Moshi opened the lock while the old man held the gun on them.

When the five of them had squeezed into the lock, the boy started the cycle. The external pressure reading in the bottom of Murphy's helmet display rose.

Hroc handed his pistol to the boy and unzipped a pocket on his suit's shoulder. Three transparent cubes floated out, each the size of Murphy's thumbnail.

"Suit down," he grunted, carefully snatching the cubes out of the air.

Spanner shifted behind Murphy. "In the lock? You trying to kill us?"

"I'll be damned if I'm going to take any untested folk aboard. Bacterial blooms, viruses, CEA spies— I'm taking no chances. Floater plague killed half my kin. You want transit, suit down."

Murphy felt Spanner's and Kyle's eyes on her, waiting for her move. In a fluid motion, she popped off her helmet and offered Hroc her neck.

Moshi's eyes widened when he saw her face. His glance slid along the Dirac function on her temple, with its delicately curved deltas and its sweeping integrals and tiny infinities, to the bold psi of Schrödinger's equation above her left eye. He stopped, as floaters always did, at the Heisenberg uncertainty principle that linked her arched eyebrows. It was the shortest of her tattooed equations, her family line . . . and her curse. "Blessed Ng and Curie," he said, "it's true. She's a Murphy."

"That's as may be," the old man grunted, lowering the cube to Murphy's neck just above her collarbone, "but she's still got to be tested."

The probe stung as it sank into her flesh, a cheaper, mass-produced version of the blood probe that Louis had used.

"No Murphy ever caught sick," Moshi argued.

"Murphy may be some minor saint to you, boy," Hroc said, "but he was just a man. He woke up with bad breath, and put his suit on two feet at a time, same as anyone else. There be no magic in a name. Even if this woman was Newton reborn, she'd still need the test."

The old man popped the probe off her neck and pushed it into a handheld reader. Antibody protein sequences and T-cell response rates scrolled across the readout. A light on the front glowed green.

The old man took blood from Spanner and Kyle. They were clean. He frowned at the readout from Kyle's test. The list of antibody identifiers was three times as long as either Murphy or Spanner's.

"The diagnostics are negative," Moshi said. "We're Code-bound to let them in."

The old man glowered at the traitorous green light. "Maybe so. But I don't like it. That one"—he pointed at Kyle—"watch him."

The cone-shaped ship was typical floater. Small, smelling of unwashed bodies and stale food. The wall around the air vents was stained a greasy brown, and the lights in the hallway flickered.

Kyle looked around nervously, as if he found the squalor disturbing. Spanner pulled along the handholds like a monkey. Both of them grounders, both so differently adapted. Which of their worlds did she fit into?

Hroc told the boy, "I'm going to let Lettinger know we've picked up survivors."

Relief washed through Murphy's chest and arms. Lettinger was Arch's station. He'd been a close friend of her father's. He could fix anything that broke, effortlessly. Be it UV ionizers, hydroponic regulators, or the waste compaction unit, Uncle Archie had repaired it sipping a beer bulb with one corner of his mouth and cracking a joke with the other.

It had been years since she'd seen him. There'd been tension between them when she enlisted in the

CEA. But she was desperate now, with nowhere else to turn. He'd have to help her . . . she hoped.

Formalhaut was a bright white star twenty light-years from Sol. Six planets and an asteroid belt orbited the A3 dwarf. Choice rocks in the belt had been broken up and ferried in-system, closer to Formalhaut's abundant solar power.

Murphy's chest ached when she saw the artificial belt spinning in the IFOs. She touched the screen. The names of the larger rocks came back to her: "Little Home. Tumbler's Remorse. Icarus." Even the sunlight seemed to welcome her.

As they flew farther in-system, she squinted against the sun's glare and saw the inner planets: Shi, San, and at last, Formalhaut-Ni, second planet from the sun.

The metal-rich planet's orbit was twice as fast as the artificial belt's rotation. In the span of a year, the planet and its satellite, Lettinger station, lapped the belt-bound floaters two times.

Formalhaut-Ni's surface was scarred with the parallel lines of earth eaters: huge machines that trundled along its surface, scooping in raw ore and spitting out waste. Titanium and vanadium were smelted in the furnace deep within their segmented bodies. Murphy counted eight of the huge machines. Business must be good; when she'd left, six years ago, Arch had only owned two.

Lettinger crested over the planet. It gleamed in the sunlight, a double cone connected at the points. A small living quarters at the juncture was the only pressurized area. Ships, in various states of repair, lined the twin cones. The station didn't spin. IFO crystallography and inertial balancing weren't possible in gravity; Arch and his technicians had adapted long ago.

The *Antigones* hovered near the opening of the space-ward cone. A swarm of tug drones erupted from the walls of the cone and engulfed the ship. She heard several far-off clangs. The *Delta-Vee* drifted away from the *Antigones*. The drones had locked themselves to its hull and were ferrying it to the station.

The nose of the tiny ship had been torn into a ragged cavern by piercer bolts. The frame was twisted, and the outer hull was split and torn. It was painful to look at.

"Where are they taking my ship?" Murphy asked.

"Don't worry," Hroc grumbled, "you're going with it. Arch wants to see you." He pulled a screen from the wall and opened a credit agreement. "Palm here for our tow-and-rescue."

The wording contained the usual family-obligation agreement. If she didn't pay off the help debt, her children and their children's children would owe her rescuers.

The screen was cold and slick under her palm. First Avocet and now this. How many more debts would she incur before this was done?

As she climbed into the airlock, Moshi clasped her forearm. "I just wanted to tell you what an honor it's been meeting you." He swallowed. "Your father was a great man, and I see his greatness in you. If you ever need help, call on me. Feynman bless."

She grabbed his forearm in return, completing the circle. "Thank you," she lied. His faith made her uneasy. He offered her trust and loyalty—but she'd done nothing to deserve it.

The station's transit tube had a row of handles built into one side. When Murphy grabbed one, it started moving. She dangled from the metal bar, twisting to look behind her. At the other end of the tube, she released the handle just before it folded back into the wall. Spanner and Kyle followed.

Murphy checked her suit's external pressure and air-quality readouts in the airlock. When the airlock was fully pressurized and Hroc's certificates of health had been approved, the inside door popped open. Murphy lifted her helmet. The air inside the station smelled of grease and the sweet tang of hydraulic fluid.

A repair technician lumbered in her direction, magnetic soles clamping his feet to the skin of the station. His ruddy face was crisscrossed with creases, and his eyebrows were startlingly white. He looked at Spanner and Kyle, then settled his gaze on Murphy.

The eyebrows exploded upward, and he launched himself at Murphy, crushing her in a bear hug. He clapped her on the back and touched his forehead to hers. "I'd but given you up for dead, Little Murphy."

Murphy's apprehension about her homecoming melted at his warm greeting. "Uncle . . . Uncle Archie?" Childhood memories of a lean, sharp-eyed technician stretched to fit the softened man before her. The nose was larger, but the same shape—and there was no mistaking the wide grin. She hugged him fiercely. When they broke, she said, "This is Spanner and Kyle. They're crewing for me."

"Two of them to get the job done?" He quirked one eyebrow up in a parody of scandal.

She punched him affectionately in the shoulder and drifted away. "It's not like that—strictly work."

"Ah. Too bad. Young people always waste their youth."

She smiled. "We can't all be as free-loving as you. No one would get any work done."

"True." He clasped Spanner and Kyle's hand in turn. "Well met. If you're her's, I'll take you aboard. Come now, I've orders to report to Maisie's rock. My whole harem would shun me if word got out that Little Murphy was in-system and got no woman's hospitality. The radio frequencies are fair to jammed with the news." He winked. "They'll be trying you on for a rock of your own, if you don't watch them."

"What is he talking about?" Kyle asked, frowning.

"Floater fems," Spanner said, "hollow out 'stroids and spin them up. Stone blocks ionizing radiation, gravity helps fetal growth. Fem pilots, like Murphy, are rare."

"This way," Arch said, turning and lumbering down the corridor.

Murphy activated the magnets in her boots and caught up with him. "What about my ship? I've got no money for re—"

"Shush. Have you forgotten your manners? Food before business." He glanced at her face. Something he saw there made him stop and mumble, "I'm guessing you want it fixed?"

"Yes."

"Good. There're twenty techs working on it now. Rush job."

Her eyes widened. An expedited repair cost double, and Arch's rates already reflected the fact that he was the best mechanic in the Milky Way. "I don't have money."

"Hush, child. I'm settling an old debt to your father. Damn *jooker* saved my life and then long-tripped to gods know where. Any other space-trash, I'd just forget the debt and be done with it. But that old man of yours, he'd be a one to come back and expect my great-great-grandchildren to build him a station or some nonsense to pay the interest." Arch winked. "Who wants that hanging over his descendants?"

The unexpected generosity blindsided her. Murphy's eyes filled with tears. For the first time in six years, she was home.

Arch's transport was a gleaming red-and-silver Avocet Corvair. The flattened oval of the hull had twin depressions on the top and the bottom surfaces, as if a giant hand had squished a ball of clay between its fingers and thumb. Radiative fins swept back from the sides of the top curve.

The seventy-eight-year-old cruiser had been lovingly restored and seamlessly upgraded. It was built to carry ten passengers in sumptuous comfort. The crash couches were covered in crimson microfiber, and when Arch accelerated toward the belt, thick aerogel padding cushioned the force to a whisper.

Murphy's eyebrows raised at the interior. "You've come up in the world since I was last here. Where's your old Wetherton?"

Arch chuckled. "Gone to the smelters, where it belonged years ago." He gestured at the Corvair, the station, and the drillers on Formalhaut-Ni. "Sa' matter of self-employ instead of working for a company. No one but me to leach off profits." He grinned. "You should see what Maisie's done with the old 'stroid."

Maisie's rock was an oblate spheroid, flattened at the poles. The near end was pocked with scorch marks from the asteroid's hollowing.

Arch dove the Corvair into the depression. The cylinder-shaped hole stopped abruptly at a flexcrete wall punctuated by a steel airlock door. Arch slowed the shuttle by pulse-firing the braking jets until the ship crept into the docking pad. Simultaneously, he fired the left navigational jets, spinning the ship to match the rock's revolutions. Acceleration pressed Murphy into the aerogel foam.

Arch paled, and sweat formed on his upper lip, the return to quarter-gee taking its toll on his aging body.

The ship clanged as the docking magnets activated. The door in the wall burst open. Three suited figures exploded from the airlock, trailing tethers and medipacks.

"Maisie!" he rasped, "didn't you trust me to land a'right?"

The largest of the figures bounded toward them. "Pish. Your pride don't keep me from my precautions. Where's that darling child of Jenevie's?"

"Aunt Maisie?" Murphy stepped forward cautiously, testing out her reactions in quarter-gee.

Maisie squealed and hugged Murphy until her suit creaked. Her eyebrows had gone salt-and-pepper, and her laugh lines had deepened, but otherwise she was the same Aunt Maisie from Murphy's childhood.

Another woman grabbed Spanner and Kyle, and the third took Arch's arm. Maisie clicked a control inside her helmet, and they reeled back to the airlock. The asteroid had two consecutive airlocks in keeping with Maisie's no chance, no worry, policy.

When the inner lock was up to full pressure, Maisie pulled out a blood cube.

"Love, is that necessary?" Arch asked. "Hroc's already tested them."

"One test is good; two is better." Maisie collected samples from Murphy, Kyle, and Spanner. When she was satisfied with the medical scanner's readout, she continued the airlock's cycle.

Once the second set of doors sighed open, Murphy popped her helmet and breathed in the fresh smell of hydroponic-cleaned air overlaid with the scents of hot oil, garlic, and ginger.

The room was a huge tube. The furnishings were laid out on its inside surface like a giant patchwork quilt. A green swath of plants colored the ceiling. Along the walls were stations for communication, navigation, hygiene, and cooking. The brightest spot of color was a pile of crimson pillows halfway up the wall. But the most inviting site was the collapsible plasticene Jacuzzi set next to the door. It was filled to the brim with steaming, frothing water—waiting to ease their transition to gravity and dissolve weeks worth of sweat and stale air from their bodies.

Arch inhaled the clean air deeply, his helmet under his arm. "Now you see why I love my Maisie."

Maisie skinned off her suit, purged and closeted it in seconds. Underneath she wore typical floater clothes: briefs and an elastic strap for her ample bosom. "Aye. That and the fact I'm the only woman in this eighth-arc that'll have you." She helped Spanner strip off the torso of his suit. Smiling, she said, "Hello there, you're a fine-looking lad."

Murphy stopped unhitching her suit, stricken. She hadn't introduced Spanner and Kyle.

"This is Andropolous Spanostani, my copilot, and over there is . . ." she hesitated. No. She wouldn't lie. If she couldn't trust her family, the universe was too far gone to save, anyway. "This is my communications officer, Jonathan Kyle Gallger."

"Murphy!" Kyle stopped fumbling with his helmet seal and glared at her.

The two other women looked closer at their fourth guest. "A grounder, huh?"

"A Gallger?" the other replied.

Murphy told Kyle, "If we're going to ask these people to help us, we owe them the truth."

Kyle's voice was hard. "That wasn't your truth to tell."

"The message is sent," Maisie chirped. "No recalling it. You two help the lad stow his suit." She waved at each woman in turn. "That's Dotty and Lisle, my co-wives from the closest arcs."

"Wha-at?" Kyle's helmet lolled against his right shoulder as the two women unlocked the suit's torso from the waist seal.

Maisie chuckled. "He is fresh from the well isn't he? His face isn't even filled out yet." She leapt delicately in the low gravity, settling her massive bulk like a ballerina, coming to rest near Kyle. She helped the other two women lift the suit's torso over Kyle's head.

Arch explained, "My station orbits Formalhaut-Ni. But the planet's orbit isn't synched with the women's belt. Formalhaut-Ni laps the belt once every two standard years. It's not feasible to visit a missus more than thirty-two thousand kilometers away. I'd spend all my time traveling with none left over for repairing, nor loving when I got there."

"And look which he regrets first," Maisie teased.

Arch continued, "A less attractive man would have had to settle for seeing his missus only four months out of twenty-four. But me and the ladies here, we solved it another way. Each of them owns me for an eighth of Formalhaut-Ni's arc around the belt."

"Arch's a right handy man to have around," Maisie agreed, "which reminds me, the third solar panel's not tracking properly. I think it took a meteoroid hit. Can you check it for me?"

The old man rolled his eyes. "Husband's work is never done." He gestured at the two other women. "And what're you two doing here?"

The dark-skinned woman grinned like a hunting cat. "Arch dear, if you think you can bring Jenevie's daughter within twenty AUs and me not come to welcome her—you are a bigger fool than a half-suit floater."

Lisle nodded. "Besides, we were visiting when Maisie got the news. And since you're heading my way next, I should tell you that my hydroponic system needs flushing. I've started the regeneration, but need your ozone generator. Make sure you bring it when you come."

"Is that all you fems love me for, the free repairs?" Arch protested.

Maisie stroked his shoulder lovingly, smiled deep into his eyes, and said, "What else is there?"

Kyle pulled off his last boot. "The arrangement sounds unfair to the women."

Maisie touched her hand to her mouth. "Now, aren't you a sweet one." She called over her shoulder. "Murphy, I like this grounder."

Arch leaned forward. "Would be, son, if I was their only husband. I'm not the only gent making the rounds on my eight beauties."

Kyle reddened, his eyes flickering to the smiling women around him. "So what they say about floater morality . . ."

Spanner placed a restraining hand on his shoulder. "Space requires certain . . . compromises in human law. Otherwise a person gets mighty lonely in the long stretches."

"Come to think of it," Archie said to Dotty and Lisle, "if you're here, where're Mack and Joe?"

Lisle rolled her eyes. "Joe's found a vein of germanium-rich copper in the asteroid he's mining. Nothing alive could tear him away until it's tapped out."

Dotty pressed her lips together. "And that Mack don't stop at my port anymore—not if he knows what's good for him."

Lisle sighed. "He gave Dotty chlamydia IV. He picked it up from some guy on Wallis Transfer."

"Cheated on us, the damn space-trash."

Lisle said, "There's a hole in our orbit until we find a suitable replacement."

Maisie looped her arms through the Arch's. "Just means we're ever that much happier to see you, Arch love."

Once the suits were closeted and their regen processes started, Maisie and Lisle pulled the lid off the steaming tub near the airlock.

Maisie splashed a hand in the water. The drops hung in the air, drifting slowly back to the water's surface. "Temperature's perfect. You four wash up and readjust to rock-gee while we finish the food."

Murphy shifted uneasily. She needed to tell them about the *Gambit*. It was more important than a bath or social niceties. But before she could speak, the women leapt away, each meters-long trajectory precise and controlled.

Watching them recede up the curving interior wall, Murphy sighed and stripped off her shirt. There wasn't anything that could be done until the *Delta-Vee* was repaired, and not bathing wouldn't fix it any faster. There'd be time after dinner to figure out how to save the universe.

Kyle was staring at her.

"What?"

He considered the steaming tub: Spanner stripping off his leggings and Arch lowering himself into the water. Then he looked back at her—or more precisely, her breasts.

Murphy pressed her lips together. "Haven't you seen a naked woman before?"

"Of course. Only never so . . . casually." His face flushed. "There's much about floater culture I don't understand."

"What's to understand? We live in small spaces. We need to bathe. There's no room for privacy on a working ship; it goes right out the airlock. I don't see the scandal in an unclothed body. In the CEA, men and women shared a locker room. Even on your precious planets, the aboriginals often go naked."

"But they are," Kyle searched for a word, "uncivilized."

Exasperated, Murphy sloughed off her leggings and eased into the water. In quarter-gravity, it felt fluffy, less compact. The water's heat loosened her muscles, and she melted into it up to her neck. She leaned back and watched Kyle squirm. "Who's uncivilized? You're the one that won't wash."

"Leave the poor man alone," Spanner said. "Maybe he's got, you know"—he glanced down at his own crotch with an exaggerated look of dismay—"something to be ashamed of."

She splashed Spanner in Kyle's defense.

"He'd better bathe," Arch said, stretching out. His plump belly bobbed above the water's surface. "Maisie won't feed an unwashed man."

"This is ridiculous," Kyle said, throwing his shirt against the wall. He skinned off his leggings and sat in the water. "Group marriages. Group bathing. Isn't there anything you people do alone?"

Underwater, Spanner stroked the inside of Kyle's thigh with his toes. "There is, but even it's more fun with someone else."

Kyle jumped. Water splashed out of the tub. He pulled his arms and legs together and sat balled up on the shelf that lined the tub.

"Spanner!" Murphy said. "That was uncalled for. Kyle's had a lot to adjust to in the last four days."

The floater's grin vanished. He held out his hand to Kyle. "Heya, sorry. It's just that—"

"Pass me the soap," Kyle said, ignoring Spanner's offer.

Arch said, "Antibiotic cleanser is mixed with the water. Wait-a-minute—" He fumbled along the outside of the tub. "There." The water rumbled as ultrasonics kicked in to knock off dirt and oils.

No one spoke for a few seconds, then Arch said to Murphy, "Thought you'd turn up sooner or later. Nets are covered with ads for your capture." He winked. "Woulda made your da proud."

A twinge of shame tightened her chest. Murphy

sighed. "I'm sorry to dock trouble at your port . . . I wouldn't have come, but I had nowhere else to go."

He appraised her with eyes that had ferreted out elusive mechanical problems for thirty years. "Just like your da, too proud to ask for help, even from those that are offering it with both hands."

Murphy said, "I didn't know . . . the way things were between us when I left . . ."

Arch leaned over and hugged Murphy. "Bless yer heart. You think feuding could break up this family? Gods, no. Feuding's what we do best. My only complaint is you haven't made the trip before now." He squeezed her one last time before releasing her.

Settling back into his submerged chair, Arch said, "Tell the truth, when John radioed Murphy was asking for me, I thought, well, it's just an old man's fancy, but I half expected your da."

Murphy went rigid. "Nobody comes back from long-tripping."

"Not in the lifetime of their kith and kin, no. Still, if anyone was to—it'd have been Ferris." The mechanic sighed, the grease-stained creases of his face folding into a wry smile. "But you're the only Murphy left to us now. How's your mother?"

"Jenevie's still hardscrabble shipping, last I heard. We haven't spoken in years. She didn't approve of my entering the CEA."

Arch chuckled, "No, I can see that. Don't blame her. The CEA gives that fem more than her share of harassing. When your father went beyond their grasp, the Companies took to punishing the ones they could reach."

"They never bothered me."

"That's true enough. Maybe it was your luck; maybe to woo you for their own. I suppose it was fate you enlisted. The young have to rebel, and with your parents, the only way was for you ta go straight and narrow. But imagine it, the daughter of Murphy—most rebelling space-junk ever—a CEA officer. Can't you taste the irony? No wonder the young ones don't have heroes."

Murphy felt her cheeks flush. She said tightly, "It's not my job to inspire floaters. My father was just a man, like any other."

"No." Archie leaned forward. "Ferris Murphy was a legend. And like it or no, fair or no, you're heir to that legend. You can live up to it, or you can disappoint it, but you can't escape it."

"Arch, stop bothering the child," Maisie said, landing delicately beside the tub, heated towels and fresh clothes in hand. "It's time to eat."

Dinner was dim sum. Tiny pastries had been baked, steamed, broiled, and fried into a bewildering array of sizes, shapes, and colors. Some of which, like the spiked *hum-bao* and the puffed tofu balls, could only be created in low gee.

Murphy bit into a pyramid-shaped curry pastry. It was buttery and flaked in her mouth. The curried tofu filling scalded the roof of her mouth with rich flavor. After the bland food of the University, it was heaven.

Kyle's face turned red, and he sucked hard on his water bulb.

"Something wrong?" Maisie asked.

The grounder coughed into his hand, regaining his composure. "The food's a bit spicy."

"We forgot," Dotty said, "he's not adapted yet."

Maisie searched through the plates of delicacies and passed Kyle a heaping bowl of white rice and a bulb of soy sauce. "I'm so sorry. I don't usually serve unadapted folk."

Kyle tried a forkful of the rice. "This is delicious. It has a delicate, nutty, flavor."

Maisie was delighted and proceeded to describe, in detail, how she had engineered the K-7 strain of Jasmine White.

When dinner was done and the dishes cleared away, Arch leaned back into Dotty's lap and said to Murphy, "So tell us how you came to be here and what's so

important that you bounced your way through supper
with the need to tell it."

Murphy drew in a deep breath. "There's a ship
called the *Gambit* . . . it can self-launch."

Arch raised an eyebrow. "Oh?" He was waiting for
the punch line.

"I'm serious. Gallger Galactic found it abandoned
near this system. Kyle embezzled the ship and sold it
to Avocet Industries. Avocet hired me to pilot it.

"Its controls are like nothing I'd ever seen. All the
text was written in a curving script. Sometimes I can
almost catch the meaning of it out of the corner of
my eye—but when I concentrate, nothing."

Arch leaned forward. None of the women moved
to clear the dishes.

Murphy continued, "Gallger found out about the
sale and tried to recapture the ship. In my panic to
escape, I set off the ship's self-launch. It was two-
stage, not like a straight jump. First we traveled
through a plasma state. I think it was a proto-universe.
The ship only moved centimeters before I jumped us
back to normal space, but when I checked our location, we'd traveled forty-three light-years."

Arch whistled. "Where is this ship now?"

Murphy glanced at Spanner. "We were betrayed.
Gallger found us and took the ship."

"So you've got this wild story, no ship, and only the
word of a turncoat Gallger to back you up?"

"That's the size of it." She sighed. "But don't you
see? Gallger Galactic's got a stranglehold on intersystem travel. It's in their best interest to suppress the
Gambit technology. Avocet, on the other hand, would
only profit by developing it. We've got to get it back."

Maisie's lips were speckled white with tension, and
she shook as she said: "And somehow this justifies
Jenevie's daughter shaming her whole line by turning *jooker*?"

"Auntie . . . I'd been set up and expelled from the
University. I was penniless with no one to turn to.
Avocet—"

Maisie cracked each word like a gunshot. "You-could-have-called-here!"

The back of Murphy's throat burned. "How could I? You and Mother put me through hell when I left. You wouldn't support my decision to attend the University—why should you help me when I was kicked out?" She inhaled deeply, "I'd dreamed of coming home in triumph . . . I couldn't come home a failure."

"No? But you could come home a filthy ship thief? Ach! And to think I fed you." She grabbed up a pile of dishes and stomped in enormous floating steps to the food-prep station. Lisle jumped up and followed her.

Murphy choked, "Aunt Maisie!" She rose to go after her.

Arch grabbed her hand. "No child, let Lisle talk to her first. Maisie's a hot woman, let her cool down a mite."

Reluctantly, Murphy sat.

"So that's the end of it. Gallger gets its ship back, and you're left with nothing?"

"No, it's worse. Gallger Galactic has a reward out for me. Meanwhile, Avocet thinks I've reneged on the original deal, and he's put a price on my head, too."

Arch patted his full belly. "Well, you're your father's daughter for sure. I've not heard of anyone in so much trouble of their own making in a long time."

Her chest clenched into a space barely big enough to contain her pounding heart. Avocet was convinced she'd sold out to Gallger—there was no one else she could turn to. Without Arch's support, she couldn't win back the *Gambit*. "You have to help me—don't you see?"

"No. I don't see. And that's the main problem of it." His face softened. "I know you're in a spot, Little Murphy, but I'm an old man, with a station and wives to look after. I have to be practical. I can't go haring after some fantastical ship when I don't even have proof it exists."

"Wait—" She leapt to her feet, ran to the suit

closet, snatched her suit from its port, and brought it
back to Arch. "This came from the *Gambit*. It's like
nothing you've ever seen."

Lisle offered, "Her suit is strange. I noticed that
when I hung it up to cycle. All the connections work,
but in secondary ports, as if they'd been kept for backward compatibility."

"It's probably next year's model. You're buying into
her game, sweets." Still, as he was talking, Arch unzipped a lens from his breast pocket and fitted it into
the orbit of his left eye. Winking to activate it, the
piezoelectric filaments lined up and fattened, magni-
fying the view. Arch studied the cloth and grunted
noncommittally. He winked twice more, and the lens's
power increased fourfold.

"This is . . . curious. It looks like the suit is a network of molecular machines. That's all I can see with
this pocket scope. I'd like to take a closer look at it
in the shop."

Murphy grinned. "Wait till you see what it can do."

She jumped up and shoved both feet into the pants
of the spacesuit before the quarter-gravity pulled
down. She finished suiting up, then stepped into the
airlock.

"What do you think you're doing?" Maisie asked.

"Proving something," Murphy said, her words
tinged with double meaning. She could have done it
inside the rock, but Maisie's accusations had cut her
to the core. She wanted to scare her a little bit. And
the more shocking the demonstration, the more
convincing.

"You're not going out that lock without a tether—"

The metal door slammed shut, cutting off Maisie's
warning. Murphy's breath was loud in her ears as she
finished closing seals and checking her suit's integrity.
Going for a walk without tether or backup was a fool's
errand, and her floater instincts urged her to go back.
She started the evacuation pumps instead.

Maisie pressed her face to the window, lips pursed,
her intention obviously to stop the lock's cycle and

keep Murphy from doing whatever suicidal thing she had planned.

Arch put a restraining hand on her shoulder. A fierce argument played out in pantomime. Maisie shoved on a helmet, and operated the com. "You get back inside here, you *jooking* daut-of-a-*shi'eel*. That suit don't have jets. No matter what you've done— you can't take the wild walk with no tether, not on my rock!"

Arch poked the rock-to-lock com set into the wall. "Murphy, have you gone over?"

"No. Just watch me."

Maisie and Arch stared through the tiny glass porthole.

"Trust me," Murphy mouthed.

He pressed his lips together and nodded. "Maisie, we got to let her go. The girl's not out of her head. Have a little faith."

The inner lock finished its cycle. Murphy stepped through to the exterior lock. She couldn't see Maisie and Arch through the window anymore. She hoped they had taken her advice and were watching the IFOs. She wasn't sure if she'd have the courage to do this demonstration twice.

Murphy's heart pounded while the outer lock opened. Intellectually, she knew it would work, but somehow that knowledge didn't extend all the way to her bowels.

Arch's Corvair was docked to one side of the asteroid's landing dock. Black stars and empty space lay beyond.

Every instinct told her to go back into the lock. Her feet slid along the rock, toes vainly working inside her boots, trying to grip its surface. The ultimate floater paradox: infinity viewed through IFOs was comforting; face-to-face it was a nightmare.

Breath clenched in her chest, Murphy jumped into the void.

The sensation of drifting was pleasant, comforting. Then she opened her eyes, and panicked. She flailed wildly, without a point of reference, until precession brought Maisie's rock into view. She kicked toward it. When the boot hit solid, as if on a wall, the shock of it vibrated through Murphy's body. It wasn't until that moment that she fully believed the suit would work.

She slapped her palms against an invisible wall to slow her motion. Then bumped her hip left, jogging the suit right. A jerk of her right hip slowed the motion. It still amazed her; without visible jets, this suit could shift position—an apparent violation of Newton's third law.

Kicking and climbing back to the asteroid, Murphy paused in front of a set of IFOs just below the main solar panels, and twirled like a ballerina.

Heart pounding with effort and spent fear, she crawled through the airlock. The inner doors cycled and opened. Arch and his wives stared at her.

"That's nothing like I've ever seen," Maisie said in a voice almost as pale as her face. "It ain't in the gods' plan." Murphy recalled that Maisie had been trained as a physicist and was still a very religious woman.

Arch patted Maisie's leg, Dotty rubbed her shoulders, and Lisle began to clear away the dinner dishes. "Even the laws of physics change, or at least our understanding of them, Maisie—everything changes."

She nodded her head, still trying to reconcile the behavior she'd just seen with years of indoctrination.

Murphy leaned forward. It was now, or never. "Uncle Arch, I need your help to recover the *Gambit*. If we can reverse-engineer its self-launch capability, floater life would be changed forever. The Companies couldn't trap us in-system anymore. We could be self-sustaining, free of their wage-slavery."

"No." Arch said. "Launch won't make us self-sufficient. Without the planets, we don't have enough biomass . . . but this ship of yours would give us a better bargaining position." He shook his head. "I don't know what they taught you at the University, but you've a healthy dose of your father's rebellion.

He was always wanting to change the shape of space, too. I know some boys with ships that have been waiting for just this kind of clarion call. Ten, maybe twenty, ships."

"Great!" Murphy grinned, her heart unclenching at last. "What they taught me at the University was military strategy and tactics. With your ships, and my knowledge—"

"It's not enough," Kyle interrupted. He re-crossed his legs and leaned forward. "Your strategy and a handful of ragtag floaters against Gallger Galactic?" His mouth pulled down at the corners. "It'll be a massacre. Gallger has the resources of the entire CEA at its disposal. If you jump into Gallger's home system, the automatic security would take care of you before you could scratch the paint on the main complex. The only trouble you'd cause Gallger is having to sweep the space lanes free of your wreckage, and they'll even turn a profit on that, in salvage reclamation."

Spanner pressed his lips together looking from Kyle to Murphy. Then he lowered his head. "He's right, Murphy. We've no chance."

She pursed her lips. "I know. That's why I'm going to ask for help."

"From who?" Kyle asked. "Half the galaxy has a price on our heads, and our only allies are poorer than we are. Who are you going to ask for help?"

"Damon Avocet."

CHAPTER
15

"You must be joking," Kyle said. "He has a price on our heads."

Spanner leaned forward. "Why would Avocet help us?"

"Because he wants the *Gambit*. He's put a reward out for us because he thinks we double-crossed him and sold the ship to Gallger. Once he learns that's not true, he'll help us get it back."

"Well, I've heard enough," Arch said. "Planning revolutionary attacks is for the young. I'm a respectable man with eight wives. I'll help you where I can. But these beauties"—he patted Dotty's bottom—"need my attention."

Maisie's lips twisted wryly. "What needs your attention is the pile of dishes in front of you." She grabbed one arm and pulled him half upright. He groaned, picked up a stack of plates, and trundled over to the kitchenette.

Dotty gathered the sip cups and sporks, Maisie got the bowls. Lisle started loading Arch's plates into the washer.

Murphy was stunned by their defection. "Don't you want to discuss the *Gambit*? It could change the socio-economic structure of the entire Collective."

Arch swiped a bowl with a towelette and handed it to Lisle. "This is your plan. Let me know what you need, and I'll help where I can. You want to change the world, fine, change it. But I don't want that kind of karma on my head." He didn't meet her eyes.

Was he afraid? She'd worshiped Uncle Arch as much as she'd worshiped her father when she was a little girl. But suddenly she felt like she was the adult and he the child. It was both exhilarating and frightening. The whole galaxy depended . . . on her. "All right," she said softly. "I'll let you know." She turned back toward Spanner and Kyle.

"How'll you prove we *didn't* sell the *Gambit*?" Spanner asked.

"I'll tell him Gallger took the *Gambit* from us by force."

Kyle shook his head. "Even if he believes you, he'll be unwilling to risk inter-Company war in a direct confrontation. Otherwise, he wouldn't have bought the *Gambit* from me."

"War?" Murphy asked.

"Yes," said Kyle. "The Collective isn't a cohesive faction. There's no overt aggression; no one Company is strong enough at this point. But there are forays to test each other's strength. If one Company could overpower the others, the whole system of government could change overnight." A slight smile escaped him. "I assume this was not taught at the University?"

Murphy's eyes lit up. "If the Collective is that unstable, maybe we can get other Companies to—"

"No. Avocet, possibly. Obtaining the *Gambit* provides him a real business advantage. But no other Company will join us. They are too afraid of reprisals or of setting a dangerous precedent. Besides, many of the Companies share trade interests with Gallger. The Collective is tightly woven together by strands of paranoia and mutual self-interest."

"But if I prove the *Gambit* is capable of self-launch, that makes it worth the risk."

Spanner ran his palms over his scalp. "How? We've no physical evidence."

In a single leap, Murphy bounded eight meters to the airlock, grabbed something out of her locker, and returned. "I'll send Avocet this." She held out the left glove of the spacesuit that she had discovered on the *Gambit*. Its spade-tipped fingers gave it the appearance of a frog's hand, only much more dexterous and supple.

"Your suit?" Spanner asked, unbelieving; a floater without a suit was a dead floater.

"Just the glove. The seals are backward compatible. I can borrow a spare from Maisie. Once Avocet sees for himself the advanced technology that's at stake, he'll have to join us."

"Even if he helps," Spanner said, "we don't know where the *Gambit* is."

Murphy turned to Kyle. "Do you—"

Kyle shook his head. "Vivien has thousands of remote research facilities. It might be at any one of them. It took me eight weeks, with full access to the Gallger computer system, to find it the first time. From here—impossible."

Murphy rubbed her face. Think like Vivien. What did she want? To destroy the *Gambit*? No, if that was the case, it would never have survived long enough for Kyle to sell it.

Like Avocet, Vivien must want its technology. She had tried to bribe Murphy to leave the University. When that didn't work, Vivien had set Murphy up and tried to hire her again when she stepped off the Gottsdamerung shuttle. Previously unrelated details snapped together in Murphy's mind.

She grabbed Kyle's shoulders. "Vivien needs me to pilot the *Gambit* for her. That's why she offered two hundred thousand dollars for my *safe* return."

Kyle opened his mouth to speak, apparently thought better of the idea, and closed it. He shrugged.

Spanner looked doubtful. "At that price, Vivien could buy twenty pilots."

Murphy ventured, "But not the only pilot who's ever gotten the *Gambit* to self-launch."

Kyle said in a weary voice, "That is true. The test

pilots Vivien hired either couldn't get it to initiate launch, or didn't survive if they did."

Murphy's chest swelled with optimism. It was simple. "Then it doesn't matter where Vivien's hidden the *Gambit*. She'll take me there herself—after Kyle turns me in for the reward."

"Wha—at?" Spanner's eyebrows contorted. "You insane? She'll not let you waltz in and *jook* it again. You'll be guarded, possibly sedated."

"But Kyle will be helping me from the inside."

"No. I refuse." The grounder's voice was as cold as space. "I won't go back there." His voice lowered. "You don't know what you ask."

"I need you in that compound with me. Spanner's right, I won't be able to reach the *Gambit* without you." She touched his arm. "Please. I'm not asking for me." She activated the com screen. Lettinger appeared. Tiny floater ships swarmed around it like a hive of bees. Murphy pointed at the station, at the asteroid around them, at Arch and Maisie in the kitchen. "The lives of a whole people are at stake."

Kyle moved his face so close to hers that she felt his shaky breath on her chin. "I betrayed Vivien. If I go back, she'll kill me."

"Can't you convince her you've recanted long enough to help me?"

He shook his head. "She was already planning to replace me. That's why she hired a tech out of prison."

"But if you pretend, she might leave you alone long enough for you to—"

"No."

"I won't leave you there, you'll launch with me, in the *Gambit*—I promise. Please. I need you."

He looked her straight in the eye, the tips of their noses nearly touching. "I. Said. No."

Murphy's blood heated. "What choice do you have? Has Avocet paid you for a ship you didn't deliver? Will that executive card of yours support you for the rest of your life?" Her voice lowered a notch. "Or were you just planning to live off the charity of floaters?"

"Murphy!" Maisie chastised from the kitchenette. Murphy ignored her.

"I can work," Kyle said. "I have skills."

"Skills good enough to keep Vivien from hunting you down? Or are you relying on her forgiving nature?"

That barb hit home. Kyle's face drained of color. Murphy moved in.

"You can't run away from the second-largest Corporation in the galaxy. Your only safety is in helping me expose its corruption." She grabbed him by the shoulders. "You must!"

He smacked her hands away and said, "This is your insane war. Not mine." He stalked off toward the hygiene unit.

Spanner slapped her on the back. "Nice recruitment technique. Think you've really sold him on the idea."

She pushed him away. This was no time for joking. Without Kyle's help, it would be nearly impossible to recover the *Gambit*.

"Fine. I'll go without him."

"You crazy?" Spanner asked.

"No. It'd be unthinkable not to try. You know what it's like to be trapped in-system. If ships like the *Gambit* were available, that couldn't happen anymore."

"What we really need to know," Spanner said, "is who built the *Gambit*. Someone already has this technology. Why dump it near Formalhaut? Why stay quiet all this time?"

"I don't know. What am I supposed to do, send a broad-band message? If they wanted to be known, they'd have made contact by now. Whoever it is must have a pretty good reason for hiding." She scratched the stubble on her scalp. "I'm going to call Avocet and see if he's willing to help us, or at least call off his manhunt." She turned. "Maisie, can I use your com?"

Arch patted his hands dry on a towel. "You're not sending any messages to Avocet from here. I won't have you endanger my girls."

Maisie dropped the dishes into the sink and turned, hands on hips. "Arch love, I'm already an accessory for harboring these dangerous criminals. And if the CEA comes looking for Murphy, where would they go first but Murphy's raising-rock? It's too late to keep me out of it. Besides, this is my war, too—or have you forgotten?" Her eyes fixed Arch in place like a docking pin. "Murphy, honey, send whatever chips you need to. The local launcher frequency is 320.9."

"Thanks, Auntie, but I only need your recorder. I'll be launching the chip from my meeting place with Vivien."

Murphy shaved her head and oiled her scalp until Heisenberg's uncertainty principle gleamed between her eyebrows. She wanted to remind Avocet of their shared floater origins and of her family line. Last time he'd seen her she'd been a failed cadet running from the past and trying to hide her identity in a CEA uniform. This time she'd face him looking proud, as a floater. As a Murphy.

Maisie smiled when Murphy stepped away from the hygiene cubical. "Now that's the woman you were born to be." She kissed Murphy's cheek. "Show that Company man what it means to be a floater. Maybe he's not forgotten everything."

Murphy felt a pang of guilt when she sat in front of the com. Despite her preparations, she didn't feel like either a floater or a Murphy. She felt like a fraud. What right had she to claim the identity she had thrown away six years ago? But she *needed* Avocet's help. So she'd use whatever symbols would make her point. Murphy turned on the recorder, exhaled, and spoke into the microphone.

"Avocet, this is Thiadora Murphy. The *Gambit* has been taken from me by force. Before Gallger recaptured the ship, we proved it is capable of self-launch." She inhaled deeply and continued.

"The ship appears to dimension shift to a proto-universe. In eight seconds, I traveled forty-three light-years. As proof of the advanced technology the *Gambit* contains, I am enclosing the glove from the suit I found on board. It appears to violate inertia by using micromachines built into the fabric."

Strictly speaking, that didn't prove the *Gambit* was capable of self-launch, but she hoped the glove's advanced technology, combined with rumors he picked up about what happened on Latigos station would convince him that the *Gambit* was worth the gamble.

"I plan to recapture the *Gambit*, but need your help. Cancel your reward. Once that is done, I will send further instructions."

She clicked off the recorder. The datachip popped out of the slot next to the com screen. Murphy wiped her sweaty palms on her thighs and removed the centimeter cube of iridescent plastic from the recorder. It was still warm from the molecular burn-in. She tucked it in her belt pocket and zipped it closed.

Dotty walked in from the kitchen, drying her hands on her pants. Sweat beaded the equations carved into her chocolate-colored skin. "I, for one, am exhausted by all this revolutionary fervor. I'm headed home. Matt said he would stop by my rock early if Tisha could spare him."

"I need to go, too," Lisle said, stretching. "I'm growing a new strain of antibiotics. I need to check its division rates—make sure I got my money's worth."

Maisie slipped her arm under Arch's and said, "Aye, and it's nearly time for lights out."

"But the *Gambit*—"

Maisie cupped the younger woman's chin with both hands. "Murphy, love, you're as dear to me as my own child, and I do realize the importance of your task, but lights out is in fifteen minutes. Whatever planning you're going to do after that, will have to be done in the dark."

Murphy looked at Spanner and saw dark circles under his eyes. She felt a dull pounding in the base of her skull. But wasn't freeing floaters more important than sleep?

Maisie said, "You're exhausted, child, and not thinking straight. Save the universe tomorrow, neh?"

Murphy bit back a reply. It was Maisie's rock; her decision was final. She grabbed one of the crimson pillows and flung it at the center of the asteroid. It left with enough force to carry it through the null-gee center and down to the other side of the 'stroid. Coriolis forces swept the pillow in a helictical arc, and it settled near the hydroponics bank. "I'll sleep there."

Spanner, standing next to her, asked, "May I join you?"

"Whatever."

Kyle exited the hygiene unit. His face was ruddy, as if he had tried to scrub the skin raw.

She called to him, "You want to sleep with me and Spanner?"

His brow wrinkled and he said, "I have no wish to . . . intrude."

Murphy sighed explosively. "Why do *gronugers* think everything revolves around sex? Maybe if you loosened up your taboos, you'd be a lot less obsessed with the whole process." She glanced him up and down. "Don't worry, I've got bigger concerns on my mind. Your virtue is safe."

Kyle hesitated.

Throwing a pillow at him, Murphy said, "Fine, then. Sleep with us, sleep with Maisie and Arch, sleep in an open airlock for all I care!" She jumped straight up, her recent years in gravity giving her enough strength to punch through the null-gee zone. She twisted her body like a diver in reverse, and landed feet-first next to the pillow she had thrown.

Maisie's comment to Arch followed her from across the rock, "Sure has Jenevie's temper, doesn't she?"

Murphy punched the body-sized pillow into submission and lay down on it, the quarter-gee settling her weight into it. When would people stop measuring her by her parent's meterstick?

Spanner, lacking her gravity-born strength, walked the long way around the rock's inner surface. He was breathing hard by the time he reached her. "You had to pick the farthest point from your aunt's bed?"

She moved over to make space for him next to her, between two rows of edible ferns. "I was angry," she whispered. "Where's Kyle?"

"Over by the airlock. Said he'd a lot to think about."

"The airlock? You don't think—"

"No. Even so, your aunt has triple-ID checks on that thing. He'll be all right. Come on," he said, rubbing her shoulders, "lay down. You need a good turn's rest if you're going to save the universe in the wake-up."

"You think my plan is insane, don't you?"

He was silent a long moment before he answered. "Basically. But you mean well." He stroked the side of her neck. "Want to relieve some tension with me?"

After six years of celibacy at the University, his intimate touch jolted her. For a second, she froze, unsure how to respond. Finally, she lifted his hand to her lips, and kissed it. "Sorry. Like I told Kyle, I have a lot on my mind right now."

He squeezed her hand. "Okay, Captain," and rolled over to sleep.

Murphy lay with her hands folded behind her head. She could feel the hum of atmospheric recyclers through the metal floor. With effort, she could make out the curled forms of her uncle and aunt in the darkness ten meters overhead. They nestled together on a multitude of pillows, the soft gravity rendering a mattress unnecessary.

She let her eyes unfocus. The whole interior of the asteroid was lit by constellations of status lights and indicators. Tiny pinpoints of white, green, and blue. The heavy scent of hydroponics rolled over her, and fern fronds shimmied in tune to the atmospheric recyclers. She could almost believe she was planetside and that none of the recent past had happened. No Companies, no expulsion, no mystery ships.

Beside her, Spanner's breathing settled into a regular pattern.

He was so trusting, so willing to follow her direction.

Was that because he had nowhere else to go, or did he believe in her vision? Did Kyle? She didn't blame the grounder for blowing up. She'd pushed him hard.

Breathing in slowly, Murphy forced herself to relax. It was easy to pretend the future of floaters didn't depend on her. Why should she risk so much? If she didn't recover the *Gambit,* the future wouldn't be any worse than it otherwise would have been—it just wouldn't be any better.

She pulled the datachip out of her pocket and rolled it in her fingers. Perhaps she should give up trying to recover the *Gambit,* and use the *Delta-Vee* for in-system cargo runs. It was unlikely that Avocet or Gallger would ever catch up with her if she settled down in some backwater system.

The fern fronds shivered and parted.

"May I join you?" Kyle's face was pale in the meager light from the hydroponics automatic controls. "I've had enough of being alone."

She scooted over, making room for him under the row of ferns. "What changed your mind?"

He sighed and settled beside her, fastidiously avoiding skin contact. "Your aunts and uncle. I have never seen a . . . family so happy. It's a strange arrangement—I could never be involved in anything like that—but still, hearing their laughter during dinner, and seeing how they look at one another . . ." His voice trailed off.

Murphy waited until he spoke again.

"I want to help you get the *Gambit* back—whatever it takes." He dragged the fingers of both hands through his tangle of curls. "I can't stand the thought of Vivien having life-and-death power over people like Arch and Maisie."

Murphy grinned. Impulsively, she leaned forward and kissed him on the cheek. "Welcome to the revolution."

Arch's booming voice shattered Murphy's sleep. "Oho! Just crew, she says. Not likely!"

Murphy struggled up from sleep and a tangle of

arms and legs. Kyle lay on her left and Spanner on her right. She pushed herself to her feet, overcompensating a bit and bouncing up a meter before floating back down to the rock.

Kyle and Spanner sat up and blearily regarded each other.

"Thought you were sleeping alone," Spanner said in an unfriendly voice.

A smile flickered over Kyle's lips, and he said, "Apparently I don't sleep as soundly as you."

Spanner's eyes widened and he looked at Murphy.

"Come on," she said, extending a hand to Spanner. "We've a message to record. Kyle's switched sides."

As she hauled Spanner to his feet, a wry grin touched his lips. "So that's all it takes."

Murphy smacked the back of his head. "I'm captain, remember?"

Spanner rubbed his head, grinning. "Not here you're not."

He was right. It was Maisie's rock. The woman's infectious familiarity had broken through Murphy's reserve, causing her to act more freely. Had she been a CEA officer, she would have been reprimanded for being so familiar with the crew. But here, grounder rules didn't apply. The floater's Code didn't fit her anymore, either. So whose laws should she live by?

When they reached the galley, Arch was alone at the table. Three tan-and-white insta-packets were grouped around a note. Maisie had already eaten, and was running diagnostic tests on the tweaks Arch had made to the solar panels earlier this morning—double and triple checking his work against failure.

"Sounds redundant," Kyle said.

"In space, you survive on the narrowest margin of error," Arch said. "I don't mind her checking behind me. Maisie's a smart girl to be so cautious. Tedious redundancy and paranoia are long-term survival traits." He stretched. "I'll be heading back to Lettinger after I finish readjusting the tracking on those panels."

As she watched him leave, Murphy snapped the activation disk in her insta-pack. She massaged the plastic package, mixing and heating the oatmeal. The contents of the food pouch tasted like cinnamon-spiced paste. When the three of them were done, and the bags rinsed and in the recycler, Murphy led them back to the com unit.

"It's not safe to launch a chip to Vivien," Kyle said. "Every jump, down to the smallest datachip, is logged. Once a day, launchers transmit their log to Gallger central. That's how Gallger maintains an up-to-date listing of inhabited systems."

"Gallger maintains a private list? Why not use the CEA map of systems?"

"That only records registered colonies. Vivien has a list of every jump destination attempted. Unless you long-tripped to a system, she knows where you are."

Murphy whistled.

"If we send her a datachip, she could trace it back to this system within thirty hours."

Murphy shrugged. "So we'll launch it from our meeting point."

"You don't understand. *Every* jump is logged. She'll be able to trace the datachip to the meeting location, and from there, the *Delta-Vee*'s launch from this system."

"You covered our tracks when we jumped from Latigos."

"Yes, but I had to destroy the launcher's software to do it. Gallger's sure to send a rescue launcher to a central spaceport like Latigos. I doubt they would extend the same courtesy to Lettinger."

Murphy frowned. "Can't you just erase the ship's launch from the log?"

Kyle thought about it. "Possibly, but that whole section of the code is triply protected. Trying to hack in might trigger an alert, or worse, totally disable the launcher."

A chill crossed the back of Murphy's shaved neck. If the launcher was disabled, Lettinger would become a one-way trip, a dead system. Formalhaut was home

to a repair shop and small mining operations—nothing
worth the billion-dollar expense of sending a portable
launcher to investigate the problem. For a few months,
cargo shipments would arrive and people seeking repairs. But they would never return. Lettinger was
eighteen light-years from the nearest inhabited solar
system, too far to long-trip for help. It would become
a ghost system, banned from the star charts. The people trapped at Lettinger would starve. The colony
would collapse, devouring itself for life, as Lil's people
had done.

What was more dangerous, risking being cut off from
the galaxy or letting Gallger know where they were?

Murphy swallowed, and said: "If Arch and Lettinger's crew agree, I want you to try."

The crew's argument raged for five hours over secured beam-to-beam transmissions that bounced all
over the system. It came down to a vote.

When it was done, Arch ran his hands over his
scalp. "They've agreed, not unanimously, but enough
to make it stick. Do what you have to, boy." He swallowed and looked up the curve of the asteroid to
where Maisie worked in her lab. "But do it right."

Arch pushed himself away from the com.

"Aren't you staying?" Murphy asked.

"Nope. Can't watch this." Arch squeezed Kyle's
shoulder. "Good luck. A lot's riding on you—everything, in fact."

After Arch had left, Kyle opened the programmer's
tool kit. A series of planes and hemispheres appeared
on the screen. He fumbled under the edge of the surface. "Where's the holo trigger?" he asked loudly.

Maisie called back from her lab, ten meters away.
"Think a floater like me could afford holo? Sorry, flat
screen's all I have."

"Can you crack the program with a flat screen?"
Murphy asked, leaning over his shoulder.

Kyle watched Maisie. The floater woman put down

her spectroscope and embraced her husband. Kyle's expression softened.

It wasn't hard for Murphy to guess what he was thinking. In their talks of family he'd never mentioned his mother. What had happened to her?

"I can do it," Kyle said, bending over the controls. "It'll take me a moment to switch paradigms." Hands flickering over the toolbars at the sides of the screen, he started knitting planes and curves together.

Blue squares wiggling with hundreds of connection interfaces merged with pale yellow surfaces that Kyle teased into impossible topologies. A half hour later, sweat beading on his forehead, he was finally satisfied with the code. He transmitted a request to the launcher. A log-on screen appeared.

"I didn't know you could shell connect to a launcher," Murphy said.

"Not many people do. It's one of the few advantages of being a Gallger." He palmed the ident screen to authenticate his account and then downloaded a section of the application.

It appeared as a mass of translucent yellow spikes that protruded in every direction from a set of blue-green cubes that overlapped and engulfed each other. It looked identical to Kyle's object.

"See the difference?" he asked.

"No."

He pointed at two extra interfaces on the launcher's object, tiny wiggling strings among hundreds. If she hadn't been looking for them, she'd never have seen them. "Those transmit information to the destination log."

He opened the two logging interfaces on his own object, then typed in an obscure command. Raw code scrolled across the interface.

Murphy inhaled. "You read code?" Production programmers used modeling software. Code was an obsolete language known only to hackers.

"Small changes are harder to find. And code changes are the smallest, nearly impossible to catch—unless the person looking can read code, too." He popped the scrolling text with a finger, pinning it in place. "There, that's the address we want." He changed six pairs of numbers on the screen and saved the object. "Now all we need do is get this back to the launcher without the system realizing this is a new version."

"All that to change twelve numbers?"

"Those numbers are the address where the system stores its destination buffer. I moved it to a different location in the launcher's memory.

"Since we've moved the temporary data location, the logging program won't be able to archive it. Our launch destination will be overwritten the next time anyone launches.

"The only real dangers are if the launcher realizes this object is a new version and transmits an alarm to Gallger, or if the location in memory I blast the data to is already in use. If that happens, the launcher's system could become corrupt—we won't know until after we launch."

Murphy's stomach churned. If anything happened to Arch and Maisie because of her, she'd never forgive herself. "Please, gods," she murmured, "let this work."

The *Delta-Vee* was primed and ready. Its surface was smooth again, and gleamed in the starlight. Two turrets had been added to either side of the back edge of the scone-shaped spaceship.

"What are those?" Murphy asked.

"Ion cannons. You've got nearly 360-degree coverage with that placement. With what you're up to . . ." Arch shrugged. "They were just laying around the shop."

She knew damn well that 450-TW ion cannons didn't grow on asteroids. She appreciated the gesture, but—"I can't fly into a monitored station with those!"

Arch pulled a thumb-sized cylinder from his waist pocket. He clicked the button on the end, and the turrets retracted into the ship. Metal shields slid over them, blended seamlessly into the hull.

Murphy howled with joy and jumped into the air.

She bounced once and then hugged her uncle. "You're a genius!"

"So I've been told." He handed her the control. "Thought you'd approve, military type like you. Takes up a bit more of the hold than a cargo shipper would want, but then you seem hell-bent on avoiding that dull fate."

Murphy went on board and stepped through the *Delta-Vee*'s systems, assuring herself everything was operational. All was ready for transport: Avocet's package contained the glove and Murphy's sealed message. Suits were checked and rechecked; the air and waste systems fully recycled. All that was left was for Kyle to record his transmission to Vivien.

Kyle rubbed his hands on his leggings and said, "Are you certain you want to do this? If we walk into Vivien's power, there's no guarantee we'll be able to leave again. I may not be able to help you."

"You see any other way to get me on the *Gambit*?"

Kyle shook his head. He closed his eyes and took three deep breaths. When he opened them, he was another person: calm and confident. He sat up straight and started recording.

"Vivien, my plan worked. I have acquired the pilot. I will deliver her to you after you deposit five hundred thousand to the following account." He rattled off an eleven-digit number from memory. "Once I have the money, I will send coordinates and a delivery time." He stopped the recorder.

"What plan?" Spanner asked, his voice edged with suspicion.

Kyle's mask still firmly in place, he swiveled to look at Spanner, his eyes hard. "Vivien's more likely to believe my actions are a labyrinthine scheme than believe I've had a change of heart. She doesn't understand those kind of emotions."

"Five hundred thousand?" Murphy asked.

"Pocket change," Kyle said. "Vivien will spend that much just to satisfy her curiosity. If I asked for less, she'd be suspicious."

Spanner asked, "How'd we know this wasn't the plan all along? You might *be* working for Vivien. How do we know you're not?"

Kyle considered the question, his face empty. Finally, he said: "You don't."

Spanner, Murphy, and Kyle launched to Gottsdamerung, the spaceport where it had all started. Murphy thought it fitting to end this where it began. Also, as the Collective's seat of government, Gottsdamerung was a busy way station; no one would question the comings and goings of one more small ship.

Once she had piloted the ship through jump, Murphy exhaled a long-held breath. So far Kyle's code was solid; they hadn't wild-jumped. She murmured a quick prayer to the gods that Lettinger's launcher was still functional, and that her plan hadn't stranded Uncle Arch and her aunties.

So much was at stake. Her next step was to leave everything behind, the University, her loved ones, even the tiny ship that had served her so well. Murphy sighed and stroked the *Delta-Vee*'s controls. It might be the last time she flew it. She unlatched her belt and drifted to the back. "She's all yours, Spanner."

He wriggled into the pilot's chair and called the station. Between spats of flattened transmissions from the tower, Spanner asked, "Why hand me the controls? Thought we'd storage the *Delta-Vee*."

"No." Murphy pressed Kyle's executive card into Spanner's hand. "Use this to launch her back to Arch's system. If we don't come back, we won't need it. And . . ." She paused. "Vivien might take us anywhere, we don't know what kind of environment . . ."

Spanner stared at the card in his hand. "Meaning full-gee. That I'm too weak."

Murphy sighed at the despair in his voice. "Well, yes."

The station blurted confirmation of the ship ID and directed Spanner to docking berth one-sixteen.

Spanner set the ship's course and then turned around in the captain's chair. "Murphy, I need to go—

to make up for not protecting Jan from the Companies, for not saving our baby."

She put a hand on his shoulder and squeezed. "Help us from Lettinger—"

He slapped her hand away. "It's not enough!"

"Look, there's nothing more you can do here. If you go, you'll just be one more handle that Vivien can use to control me. She might torture you; she doesn't care if you die. To her, you're expendable."

He muttered, "Like any other floater."

"Exactly. Kyle is family, she'll have a hard time killing him—"

Kyle said, "Hardly."

Murphy ignored him. "And she needs me, but you . . ."

"Once she knows all the *Gambit* data in your head, you're just as expendable."

Murphy met his gaze. "I know. That's why I'll be long gone before that happens."

Spanner looked away. "Used to be a grounder scientist, researching bacterial genetics. Used to be someone. Now I'm adapted: floater trash. Weak, obsolete, disposable."

"Not if we pull this off. That's the whole point of the revolution." Murphy caught Spanner's gaze again and held it. "I know you want to help, but this is something that Kyle and I have to do—alone."

"I wish it was something you had to do—alone," Kyle muttered.

Murphy ignored him and clasped Spanner's forearm. "I need you to take the *Delta-Vee* back to Arch's system. Wait for our call. You're our safety net."

Spanner pounded the cracked plastic of the captain chair's arm. "More hole than net, I'd say."

"Don't talk that way. She's yours."

Spanner's head snapped up.

"I've made an entry in the log, transferring ownership." Murphy looked him in the eye. "I mean it. If this doesn't work, start a new life for yourself."

Spanner didn't say anything. He nodded curtly, eyes blinking, and started the final approach.

Murphy leaned against the wall of the spaceport, watching the crowd swirl and ebb around her: a pack of first-year CEA cadets on leave; spice traders in flowing multicolor robes, whose passing flavored the air with scents of clove and cinnamon; grounder tourists, who goggled at everything and directed their recorder bees to shoot terabytes of holo they'd never watch; bureaucrats, speaking into wrist coms while their entourages wedged into the crowd, pushing tourists and traders out of the personage's way. No one sought her out. No one looked at her and Kyle for more than a moment.

Fear squeezed her belly into a tight ball. She shouldn't be doing this. What had seemed a brilliantly simple plan in the safety of Maisie's rock now seemed the sheerest stupidity. She should have waited for Avocet's reply. He might have believed her, might have sent help. On the other hand, without the *Gambit,* he had no proof she hadn't sold him out. He might have captured her instead. She wondered what Kyle thought of their plan.

Kyle's face was unreadable. His eyes scanned the crowd coolly, as if he were waiting for a friend to get off shift. Was Spanner right? Was Kyle playing the part of betrayal a little too well? For five hundred thousand, he could retire to an obscure planet and live out the rest of his days in relative luxury. Was that his plan? Murphy didn't think so, but then, she'd only known him five days.

Kyle stiffened. Murphy scanned the crowd, following his gaze.

Four tall men strode toward them, not in uniform, but with a bearing too precise to be civilians.

Panic seized her chest, and for a second she couldn't breathe. A firm hand grabbed her elbow. She looked up into the eyes of a man who, with two weeks growth of beard, looked older than the last time she had seen him, but was unmistakably Haverfield.

CHAPTER
16

"Haverfield!" Murphy jerked away. His grip was as tight as a docking clamp; she struggled at the end of his arm.

Of the mass of people swirling about them, only two patrolling CEA officers looked up. Inscrutable in black MP helmets and uniforms, they stared for a moment, and then angled through the crowd toward Murphy and Haverfield.

"You're weak," Haverfield whispered. "Been out of gravity, haven't you?" He pulled out an injector cube.

Murphy tried to kick it—with both feet. The instant her second foot left the ground, she realized her mistake. The last two weeks in zero-gee had reset her instincts to floater. She was used to thinking and acting in three dimensions; she'd forgotten about gravity.

Her hand twisted out of Haverfield's grip. She fell, landing hard on her right ankle—the one she had fractured stealing the *Gambit*. The weakened bone cracked. Pain blocked out any other thought.

Haverfield pressed the cube onto her upper arm. Agony faded to discomfort, then a suffusing warmth.

"It's all right, officer," Haverfield told the CEA patrol, "she's just had a bit too much recreation." Haverfield palmed their report book.

The patrolman scanned his name and snapped to attention. "Sorry for bothering you, sir."

"Not a problem. You're just doing your job." Haverfield slumped Murphy over his shoulder and hefted her weight.

Her broken ankle jangled with his walking, pain mumbling through the drug's effect. From a galactic distance, Murphy saw Kyle tuck a credit card into his jacket.

Haverfield carried Murphy into a sleek Avocet Ultra cruiser and strapped her down. During the launch, she blacked out.

Her next sensation was the sharp smell of antiseptic. Murphy opened her eyes. Everything more than two meters away was lost in a gray blur. Thick nylon webbing on her chest and legs strapped her to a medical examination table. An IV ran into her left arm.

A dark-skinned man with a pointed nose leaned over her.

"Who're you?" she slurred.

He checked her right leg. It had acquired a cast that ran from her heel to mid-shin. Piezoelectric wires snaked out of a battery pack at the top of the cast, down to her ankle. "Doctor Singh. Are you comfortable?"

Murphy grunted.

"Good. I am going to ask you a series of questions. You must answer them truthfully. Do you understand?"

His words echoed down a long hall to her brain. After a moment to decipher them, she said, "Yes."

"What is your full name?"

It bubbled up through her lips. "Thiadora Murphy."

"What do you fear most?"

A sigh: "Failure."

The doctor paused, making a note on a lap screen. "What was your password at the University?"

The words rolled out her mouth of their own accord. "F equals p dot of x."

"Where does your Aunt Maisie live?"

She wanted to hold back the answer, but before she could finish that thought, she said, "Lettinger."

The psychologist consulted his screen. "Okay. That

checks." He set the pad down and adjusted the IV running into her left arm. "How did you first learn about the *Gambit*?"

"Damon Avocet."

"What did he tell you about the *Gambit*?"

"That Gallger had salvaged a ship, and he wanted me to steal it."

"And were you able to decipher the controls?"

"No."

Singh leaned back and steepled his fingers. "But you did pilot the ship?"

She hesitated. "Yes. I couldn't read the controls, but they were somehow familiar. I guessed—used intuition—to pilot her."

"You had never flown a ship like the *Gambit* before?"

"No, just a simulator. Williams . . . at the University."

"What caused you to disappear from Gallger space?"

"Gallger attacked, I hit controls I thought would maximize propulsion. Instead, the ship jumped."

Dr. Singh tapped a note on his screen. "What happened?"

"I don't know. I think the ship crossed into another dimension. Red and orange plasmas swirled outside. The ship's hull temperature was 17,000 degrees Kelvin and cabin temperature started to rise."

"What did you do then?"

"I had to get the ship out of there. We were starting to burn up. I hit more controls, trying to duplicate what I had done the first time—and we jumped back to normal space. Near Canodyne 4265."

"You traveled forty-three light-years in a few seconds?"

"Yes."

A holo of the *Gambit*'s cockpit appeared around Murphy. "Show me the controls you used to jump."

Murphy reached out, her left arm trailing the IV line. She slid two fingers along both of the projected throttle strips. "Like this." Holo bees flew orbits around her, their hairlike fiber optics recording every nuance of her motion.

"Show me again."

Murphy repeated the motion, and the bees snapped more data.

The interview continued for an interminable amount of time: the psychologist asking her to manipulate the virtual controls, and Murphy, half dreaming, piloting the *Gambit*. When he was done, the psychologist said, "You may go back to sleep."

And she did.

Murphy woke in a room with high ceilings. Gravity compressed her chest like a giant palm pushing her down. Her ribs ached, her ankle throbbed, and each breath required effort. Groaning, Murphy pushed herself into a seated position. The effort exhausted her. She looked around in a haze of pain and nausea.

The room was overwhelmingly beige. Everything was the color of sand or dried grass: the marble floor, the stucco walls, the drapes, even the beams in the ceiling. Rough-woven cloth draped in sinuous curves along the walls, punctuated by hand-crafted baskets. The only color in the room was the bench Murphy sat on, which was upholstered in tan-and-coral raw silk. No electronics were visible in the room, not even a light switch.

Moving slowly, Murphy picked up a cushion and threw it. Its trajectory arced left. A strong Coriolis force. This must be a gravity ship, or a station. A planet's rotation was too slow to produce that much deflection in such a short distance.

She reached down to touch the tile. It was cold, like marble would be, but the texture wasn't as slick as she would have guessed from its appearance. Then she saw that the foot of the bench joined seamlessly to the flooring. Stone flowed into raw silk upholstery. She glanced at the joins of wall and floor, wall and ceiling. The entire room was a single surface—without a visible door. How had she gotten in here? Had they built the room around her?

"Thiadora Murphy, quite possibly the best pilot in the galaxy." One wall dissolved, its projected draperies fading into sunlit porch. A woman reclined in a chaise lounge, like a visitor outside a glass door. "At last we meet. I am Vivien Gallger."

Adrenaline shocked Murphy fully awake. This was the woman who had ruined her military career and hounded her halfway across the galaxy. Murphy's face heated as she examined her captor.

The woman's hair was not as bright as Kyle's, and where his was a dandelion explosion, hers was a carefully teased lion's mane. Golden eyes completed the predatory picture. Well-defined muscles rippled under her silk sheath when she moved. Graceful, Murphy thought, and dangerous.

"Where's Kyle?" Murphy said, then stopped, unsure. The memory of his tucking away payment played again.

"Kyle has been paid. He has no further interest in you."

Because he had betrayed her, or because he was a captive in his sister's house? "What's your interest in me?"

Vivien touched her chest with one elegantly manicured finger. "I want the same thing as you. I want you to fly the *Gambit.*"

"Is that why you paid Williams, Haverfield, and Jenks to destroy my University career? They work for you, don't they?"

"Haverfield is a pilot of some small skill—though nothing to match yours," Vivien said. "I hired him to fly the *Gambit* for me after you refused my offer, but he could do no more than start the engines."

"But you did have me set up."

Vivien shook her mane, a lioness brushing off a biting fly. "No. I sent Williams to recruit you. The deception was Commander Osborne's idea. They acted without consulting me. A regrettable choice. I *am* sorry."

Murphy rocked back on the bench. She knew that Osborne resented her presence at the University, but to use illegal means jeopardized his own career. His hatred of her must border on the psychotic.

"You could have waited until I graduated."

Vivien sighed. "No. Once you signed your commission papers, extracting you from the military would have been . . . complicated. And other interests, Companies like Avocet, were moving in to take the *Gambit* from me. I had to act swiftly."

"I thought Gallger was all-powerful," Murphy said.

"Regrettably, no. We are only one-twelfth of the Collective. Other interests, such as WearHaus and Intellix are much stronger than us. We're quite vulnerable."

"Not compared to the average person."

"Average people do not have my adversaries. I must gather what influence I can, just to survive." Vivien leaned forward, pressing her palms against the virtual glass. "That is why you must work for me."

"What about my contract with Avocet?"

"Nullified by the fact he asked you to perform an illegal act. As a near-graduate of the University, you know that. Ship theft. Even floaters consider that wrong, do they not?"

Murphy's eyes narrowed.

Vivien continued. "Your only opportunity to fly the *Gambit* is as an employee of Gallger. After all, it is our lawful salvage."

Murphy snorted. "I saw your interpretation of the law on Canodyne 4265. How do I know the *Gambit*'s pilot was dead when you *found* the ship?"

Vivien raised one eyebrow. "So, there are things about the *Gambit* you do not know. The craft was empty when Gallger salvage discovered it. There was no wreckage, no bodies outside. Only a pile of ashes floating around the command cabin."

"Then, how did it get there?"

"No one knows." Vivien pressed her palms against the screen. "Whoever, or whatever, created the *Gambit* possesses a technology beyond anything we can fathom. Working for me, you could make history."

A chance to create her own legend? It was tempting. "I thought the only thing that you wanted to make was money."

"Don't believe everything Kyle tells you." Vivien brushed aside an errant strand of golden hair. "He has his own agenda."

"Why do you need me? Dr. Singh's already wrung all the secrets from my brain. You've recorded everything I know about the *Gambit*."

Vivien's eyes glittered. "But not everything you *will* know. Of the fourteen top-ranked pilots I tested for the *Gambit,* only you could fly it. Only you."

"Having Dr. Singh take me apart hardly makes me eager to join your side."

"I had to have accurate information. The *Gambit* represents an advance too important to leave any aspect of its understanding to chance. I hope you will forgive my means of obtaining it. I do not have the luck of a Murphy on my side." A brief smile flickered on her lips. "At least, not yet."

"What are you going to do with the *Gambit* once you've understood it? Destroy it to keep your launcher empire intact?"

Vivien steepled her elegantly manicured fingers. "Business is not that simple. Now that engineers know a ship like the *Gambit* is possible, it is only a matter of time before someone puzzles out the how of it. No. The time of launchers is over. The only question is who will control the business of self-launching ships."

"And floaters? When will they have access to such ships?"

"Ships like the *Gambit* will be available to floaters in time. Perhaps if you work for me, that time can be shortened." Vivien caught Murphy's gaze. "But that is not the reason you will work for me. You'll fly the *Gambit* because, like me, you would do anything to possess its secrets."

Was that true? Had her desire for the ship blinded her to her methods? She'd *jooked*, run from the CEA, illegally entered Latigos station, threatened innocent lives, and consorted with rebels. Worst of all, she'd put Arch and Maisie at risk. But that had been because she'd wanted to free floaters from Gallger's oppression—wasn't it?

The memory of the *Gambit*, its responsive—near instantaneous—propulsion, self-launch, alien script that writhed with hidden meaning, and a EVA suit that promised other alien wonders, suffused her with guilty pleasure.

Murphy needed to think, but her head was full of cotton. She scratched at her forehead. Her face was feverish and dry.

Vivien leaned forward. "Are you in pain?" Her voice was the concerned whisper of an art investor whose painting is scratched.

"What did you shoot me up with?"

"Haverfield sedated you at the station, and Dr. Singh administered a pain reliever and truth-inducing drugs. Nothing toxic. The symptoms you feel are probably due to withdrawal."

Murphy looked at her trembling hands. "Withdrawal?"

"Yes. The truth drugs Dr. Singh administered are highly addictive." Vivien examined the polished nails of her smooth right hand. "Some would consider that a liability. I've found it quite useful." Her glacial eyes pinned Murphy's. "So much of reality depends upon one's attitude. Don't you find that?"

Murphy's chest tightened. "Why go through all this"—she waved at the lush room surrounding her—"if only to turn me into an addict? I thought you wanted me to work for you."

"I do. Your addiction does not preclude my offer. Rather, it is insurance you will not run away. After all, you did steal the *Gambit* from me once before."

"How is ruining my health going to ensure my cooperation?"

Vivien's lips twitched, a last convulsion of a dying smile. "Every twenty-four hours, Dr. Singh will administer another dose of the drug. Run away, and a day later you die."

For a moment Murphy considered it. Death might not be too high a price to get the *Gambit* out of Vivien's hands.

Vivien laughed delightedly. "Your thoughts are so transparent. How refreshing. Kyle warned me that self-preservation alone wouldn't be enough to control you." She steepled her fingers. "I offer you a second incentive. You will not run away, because if you do, I shall shut down the launcher system at Lettinger."

Murphy's heart froze. Arch, Maisie, and all their crews, dozens of floaters, would be stranded in a non-self-sufficient solar system.

Vivien leaned forward. "Swear fealty to me on your crew's name—your marks to be laser erased if you betray your oath."

Murphy's hand crept to the equations on her scalp.

"See, I do know a bit about floaters. Will you swear?"

Murphy's heart pounded. What Vivien asked was tantamount to life servitude. Murphy knew that at some point she would have to pretend to work for Vivien, in order to get on board the *Gambit*. But this! *Jooking* was bad enough, she couldn't break a crew oath. Crew defined who you were. *F'kup*, to betray crew—those you worked with, those who depended on you for their very survival—was unthinkable. Vivien didn't depend on her like normal crew, but even so, Murphy didn't think she could break her oath once it was given. She was scared, for herself and—how could she help Arch and Maisie if she wasn't her own person? "No. I won't."

"Ah, typical floater stubbornness. The cause of much suffering. When the revolution first started in the Tau Ceti system, we quarantined them—shut down the launchers. It was an isolated system; the revolt should have died out there. But who could predict floaters would be so tenacious?" She stared at Murphy. "Someone long-tripped."

"The conditions that fueled the revolution aren't

limited to one system. If you cut off one station, ten others will revolt."

"The CEA does not share your view. With proper isolation and quarantine, the planets and stations will be safe from the revolution. It will die out."

"Along with the floaters that are rebelling. You need cheap floater labor. You can't kill us all."

"Can't we?"

Murphy swallowed. She felt as if local gravity had increased tenfold. Her chest clenched. If she didn't swear fealty to Vivien, everyone on Lettinger would die.

She tightened her hands into fists, her whole body rigid. The words formed in her mind, but she couldn't force them through her clenched teeth. She exhaled loudly. "I . . . can't."

Vivien stepped back. "Perhaps I have someone who can change your mind."

Murphy's hands began to sweat. "Who?"

A door behind Vivien sheathed open, and a slender brown woman filed through. She approached Murphy, tentatively, half turned away. Her movements were stiff, with none of the flowing exuberance that she'd possessed at the University.

"Tali!" Murphy shouted. "You're alive!" She clumped to the screen, ignoring her ankle's protests in her desperation to touch her friend, to somehow verify this miracle was real.

Tali flinched. Her shoulders hunched and a hundred tiny braids fell over her face. "Oh, Murphy," she whispered, "she doesn't have you, too."

Vivien walked into the background of the scene and reclined on a chaise lounge. Watching.

Murphy touched the part of the screen that projected her friend's face. "I thought I saw you die. The MPs needlers . . ."

Tali shrugged. "I almost did die. Sometimes I wish I had." She flipped back her braids. The left side of her face was clear and smooth, thinner than she had been at the University, with more worry lines and less

laugh lines, but still Tali. The right side was a mass of
needler scars. They streaked like raindrops in a high
wind from her nose to her ear. Her right eye, a watery
blue, clashed with the warm chocolate of her skin. Tali
touched her cheek below the new eye. Her hand was
gnarled with scar tissue, and the smallest finger was
missing.

"The needles stopped three millimeters short of my
brain. That's how close it was. I owe my life to Vivien.
She paid for the transplant. And what reconstructive
work was necessary for me to do my job."

"You work for Vivien?"

Tali inhaled deeply. "Information systems security.
I couldn't continue at the University. They trumped
up charges of treason. I was tried and convicted,
sentenced to death. Vivien saved me. She worked
with the judge to commute my sentence to life indenture, working for her." Tali touched a scarred
hand to the screen. "Vivien's been good to me. I
owe her everything."

"Including the frame-up that nearly got you killed."
Murphy held out her hands, pleading. "Don't you see,
Tali? Vivien had you set up."

Either Tali didn't hear, or she ignored the question.
"Vivien took me in, gave me employment." Tali's eyes
glowed. "I get to work on Diamond III systems. I'm
the best communications security operative in the
Collective."

"What kind of life is that? You wanted to be a
navigator. How can you work for Vivien? She had you
shot." Murphy looked over Tali's shoulder at Vivien.

Vivien cocked one eyebrow, not denying anything.

Tali closed and opened her hand stiffly. "My dexter-
ity isn't good enough for navigation anymore."

"You could use a prosthesis—"

"*You* did this to me, Murphy." Tali lowered her
face, until a curtain of braids hid her eyes. "They shot
me to keep me from helping you. If you hadn't been
obsessed with proving you were better than any
grounder, we'd be graduates on a CEA ship right now.

If you had accepted Vivien's offer of lawful employment, instead of pirating for Avocet, none of *this*"—she scraped her wounded hand over her scars—"would have happened."

Murphy took a step back. She couldn't breathe. Did Tali, who'd stood staunchly by her through the taunts and hazing of the other cadets, hate her now? Murphy whispered, "I was set up. By Gallger. You know that. That's what you called to tell me."

"You were set up, but you didn't have to take the bait. If you hadn't been so wrapped up in your pathetic need to live up to your father's legend, you would have seen that."

Murphy's stomach clenched. Emotion, or another symptom of her addiction?

Vivien stretched with the satisfied ease of a well-fed cat. "This interview has gone on long enough." She placed her hand lightly on Tali's shoulder. "It has been a long day for you, Thiadora. Tomorrow will be even longer. You will teach Haverfield to pilot the *Gambit*. If you succeed, perhaps I will reconsider the profitability of mass-producing *Gambit*-like ships. Fail"—Vivien cocked her head—"and certain launchers will suffer mechanical difficulties: Gottsdamerung, Latigos . . . Lettinger."

Murphy held her face in the rigid mask that had gotten her through so many taunts at the University.

"Now, rest." Vivien tightened her hand on Tali's shoulder. "Much depends on your performance tomorrow."

Tali clasped Vivien's hand, either unaware of or accepting the implied threat.

Murphy had a sudden urge to throw up.

The screen switched abruptly to a patio garden at sunset. Willow trees swayed in a virtual breeze and simulated crickets began to whine.

Murphy prowled the room. It was large and comfortable, beautifully decorated, but still a prison. Everything, down to the baskets and the cloth draped on the walls, was part of a single surface, as if the room had been cast from a giant mold, furnishings intact. There was no door. The only screen was the wall-sized one projecting the garden. There were no touchpads or controls anywhere.

A twinge in Murphy's groin reminded her that she hadn't emptied her bladder since Lettinger. Vivien apparently hadn't thought of everything. Staring at the willows swaying in the far screen's virtual reality, Murphy grumbled: "If I was sure this was a constant-gravity ship and not just temporarily spun up, I could pee in the corner."

A sudden movement in her peripheral vision caused Murphy to whirl. Growing out of the left wall was a seat as plush as a captain's chair, complete with head-and-foot rest. It was also a toilet.

Gingerly, as if the porcelain might bite her, Murphy touched the new fixture. The surface was slightly warm. For her comfort, or from friction as its molecules flowed over each other during its creation?

Murphy had heard of programmable plastic, an array of molecules that could be electrically induced to take on a variety of forms. It was generally used for lightweight multipurpose hand tools. But one fist-sized tool cost two months of floater pay. An entire room of the substance? She looked at the room in awe—and not a little fear. Vivien, with a single command, could cause its volume to compact, crushing her. Could cause spikes to burst from every surface and impale her. Despite the high ceilings and wide expanse of floor, Murphy felt claustrophobic.

She used the toilet and then climbed down and stared at its bulk. "I'm done," she told it. It receded back into the wall, leaving no trace it had ever been there.

What else in this room was voice activated? "Door open." Nothing happened. "I want to leave." The walls remained smooth and unresponsive.

So she didn't have complete control over the room's furnishings. No surprise. Murphy faced the wall-sized screen. She stared at the sunset garden scene and said: "Dawn."

The rich oranges and cobalt blues of the night sky were replaced by pinks and grays of dawn. Morning glories opened, and night-blooming jasmine closed.

"Communications."

The screen blanked to the spinning atoms of Gallger's corporate symbol. "USER?"

Murphy grinned. She'd bet her marks this room wasn't just a prison, that it also served as a guest room. If that was so, the right user-name and password might give her access to a fully functional communications center.

"USER?"

"Guest."

"INVALID. USER?"

Murphy seethed with frustration. Who would have access to this account? She didn't know. Or did she? "Tali."

"PASSWORD?"

She tried: "Floater's bible."

"INVALID. PASSWORD?"

This pitiful attempt at hacking must be sending up alarms all over Vivien's system. What had been Tali's password at the University? Something historical . . . "Ganymede four tilda two."

A com screen appeared, a gray box bordered by controls that would let her call a person on the ship's network. The launch-chip controls were grayed out. She was cut off from the outside world. Damn! She had to warn Arch about Vivien's threat to the Lettinger launcher. Tali wouldn't help her, but there was one other person on the station who might. It was a risk, but what choice did she have? "Call Kyle Gallger."

Kyle appeared on the screen. The room was dark, only the light of the screen illuminated his face. His curls were flattened on the right side of his head. "Uhmm?" He stared blearily at her.

"It's me," she whispered, "Murphy."

He bolted upright. "Why are you calling?" He glared at her. "Our business is concluded."

Murphy pressed the heels of her hands to her forehead. "I need your help. I have to get a message out—"

"That is none of my concern. Vivien paid me to deliver you, and I did. What I said last night was a lie. Regrettable, but necessary to bring you here. My allegiances lie with Vivien." He stared into her eyes, his right hand clenching and opening. "They always have."

Murphy's face flushed. "So that's the way it is." She shook her head, both to clear it and in disbelief at her stupidity. "I should have known. The drugs your sister pumped into me must have confused my thinking."

Kyle said, "She injected you with Veradine?"

"Ye—"

Kyle's image was abruptly replaced by Tali's. She looked tired, perhaps embarrassed. "Murphy, did you really think such a simple hack would work?"

Murphy mumbled, "Can't blame a floater for trying." But there was something about the conversation with Kyle that worried the back of her mind. Something not right, or something she had missed. Murphy wished she could replay the transmission.

Vivien walked from offscreen and put her hand on Tali's shoulder. "Thiadora, you should be resting."

Murphy's arm trembled, whether from fever or adrenaline, she couldn't tell. "What are you going to do with me?"

Vivien smiled sadly. "Not to worry. This changes nothing. I do not expect fealty from you, merely compliance. In fact, your communication was a useful test of Kyle's allegiance." Vivien leaned closer to the screen, examining Murphy over Tali's shoulder. "She looks bad. The truth drug must be wearing off. Tali, go to her and administer another dose."

Tali nodded, and the screen blanked to a star-filled evening in the garden.

Ten minutes later the wall parted. Murphy lunged

through it, only to crash against a hard surface. She
was in a vestibule. Tali must have opened a pocket in
the wall, like an airlock, closing the way behind her
before she opened a door into Murphy's chamber.

Tali picked up the hypospray she had dropped.
"You can't escape her. Accept that."

Murphy stared at the ruin of her friend. She reached
up a hand to cradle Tali's chin.

Tali flinched and turned her scarred side away
from Murphy.

"What happened to the woman I bunked with at
the University?"

"She was a stupid girl who thought she could
change the world. She died trying." Tali pulled the
sheath off the hypospray and set it for subdermal in-
jection. She grabbed Murphy's arm. "Do what Vivien
asks. It'll be easier for you. Easier for all of us." She
jabbed the hypo against Murphy's upper arm and
pulled the trigger.

A flash of cold numbed Murphy's flesh.

Tali resheathed the empty hypo.

Murphy followed Tali into the vestibule, grabbed
her, and whispered, "I need you to help me get word
out about the *Gambit*. Its technology could change the
financial structure of the Collective."

"Then, work for Vivien, she has promised to try—"

"Try isn't good enough. Hundreds of floaters die
each day, trapped on stations with inadequate
shielding simply because they can't leave the system
without Gallger's permission. Help me, Tali."

Tali sighed. "I can't."

"Can't or won't?" Murphy tightened her grip.
"What if I don't let go? What if I won't let you leave
this room without me?"

"Don't you get it? The whole complex is bugged.
Either I'd stay locked in here with you, or they'd
pump knockout gas in through pores in the walls. You
are in the belly of the beast." Her voice caught. "And
not even the great Murphy can get out of this one."

Murphy stepped back and watched the vestibule
close around her onetime friend. Tali might be right.

CHAPTER
17

A steady chiming woke Murphy. She opened her eyes. The wall screen flashed: blue—white—blue—white.

"I'm awake—I'm awake!"

The screen shifted into a morning scene. Mockingbirds called tunes to one another, and bluebirds twittered.

Murphy smelled food. A table extruded from the floor, piled high with gleaming covered plates, a coffee carafe, and a portable screen. She lifted a cover and found slices of butter melting between layered sheets of pastry. Others revealed strips of real bacon, crisp and curled around wafers of *tamago*, biscuits and gravy, tofu cubes swimming in a ginger broth. More food than she usually ate all day, smelling delicious and hot and steaming.

After gorging herself, Murphy opened the screen. It displayed a test pilot's employment contract.

The terms were better than Avocet's; the rate of pay was double, and its duration was only two years—not five. She felt a twinge of guilt, but really, what choice did she have? Murphy pressed her palm against the warm plastic, registering her employment with Gallger Galactic.

She felt better than last night. The fever was gone. Her ankle was nearly healed, thanks to Dr. Singh's piezoelectric treatment.

"Shower," she told a wall. It obligingly extruded a water stall, sink, and full-length mirror.

After a deliciously scalding shower, the stall re-shaped into a convection tube. Warm gusts of air buffeted her body. A prison, but a luxurious one.

When she emerged, her tights and tank top were gone. In their place was a neat blue pile. Murphy picked up the cloth. It was a flight suit, emblazoned with a Gallger patch. She dropped the garment and kicked it. Considered going naked. No. In grounder terms, naked was vulnerable, and the last image she wanted to present to Vivien was weakness. Grimacing, she slipped the jumpsuit on and zipped up the front. The fit was, of course, perfect.

The wall behind her irised open, and Haverfield entered. He threw a pressure suit and helmet at her. "Suit up. It's time to fly."

She caught the helmet aimed at her head and stared at Haverfield. He was already dressed in a pressure suit, and beneath that he wore a Gallger jumpsuit identical to her own.

"You really hate that I can fly the *Gambit* and you can't."

Haverfield narrowed his eyes at her. His hands clenched into fists.

Murphy tensed.

The screen flashed on, displaying Vivien. She sipped from a crystal mug of a honey-colored steaming liquid. How long had she been listening?

"Haverfield," Vivien said between sips, "if you cause Thiadora Murphy injury, I will suspend your wages—permanently."

Haverfield dropped his hand. "Sorry, sir."

"As you should be. You fly with Murphy to learn from her. I can easily replace *you*." Vivien's golden gaze turned. "Thiadora, you will fly the *Gambit* to the best of your abilities. Remember"—Vivien traced a square in the air before her. It filled with tiny replicas of the *Gambit,* and a station—Lettinger—"much depends on your good behavior."

Murphy's temperature rose. "Lettinger is a well-known repair port. You can't—" But the words fell

from her mouth, a lie as soon as she said them. Of
course Vivien could, she was a Company, above the
law. Murphy bent down and picked up the flight suit.
"Why don't you let me leave Haverfield here? You
don't need him now that I'm in your employ; I've got
a contract and an addiction to bring me home."

"You trying to get rid of me?" Haverfield growled.

Vivien laughed. "Don't worry Haverfield, your position is safe." Her gaze swung over to Murphy. "Certain acquaintances of yours inform me you are too
idealistic to trust to your own sense of self-preservation.
You might even be willing to risk the lives of your
loved ones to possess the *Gambit*'s technology."

Murphy shook the pressure suit. "Then, at least get
me decent equipment. This thing's junk. I need the
suit I was wearing."

"The suit on board the *Gambit* when we salvaged
it?"

"Yes."

Vivien studied Murphy through the wall screen.
"Why?"

"The suit interacts with the control systems. I can't
fly the *Gambit* without it." A lie, but a plausible one.
She wanted that suit. Its capabilities might give her an
edge when she needed it. And with Haverfield's gaze
boring a hole through the back of her head, she might
need it soon.

"Interesting . . ." Vivien pursed her lips, looking at
something above the boundaries of the garden interface. Her eyes moved left to right as she read from a
secondary screen. "A glove is missing."

"It was destroyed in the first self-jump—during an
onboard explosion." Murphy didn't want the glove
traced back to Avocet. Jumping ship on him was one
thing, starting an inter-Company war was another. She
hoped Kyle had seen some personal advantage in
keeping their message to Avocet a secret. These days
she had great faith in Kyle's self-interest.

Vivien considered, then said, "The laboratory's

analysis of the suit is nearly complete. It will be brought to you."

The screen clicked off.

"I won't forget you tried to get rid of me," Haverfield said.

"Neither will I." Murphy met his hostile stare with a look filled with six years of failed aspirations.

The tension broke when the wall irised open. A technician wheeled in a regen cabinet. It contained the *Gambit*'s suit. Murphy slipped into it and checked status. Perfect, all systems regenerated, and except for the missing glove, fully operational. Next to the over-size frog-fingers on her right hand, the normal replacement glove on her left looked shriveled, drawn in.

Murphy followed Haverfield out of the room, through endless corridors, to the docks. Glancing out one of the IFO portholes, Murphy saw that the constellation Orion had stretched into a thin snake. Wherever they were, it was thousands of light-years from the center of commerce.

Then Murphy saw a sight that made her heart leap.

The black sphere of the *Gambit* lay just outside the airlock, docked to the rim of the station like a drop of ink hanging from a silver bracelet.

Built into the wall next to the airlock was a series of lockers. Haverfield palmed one and pulled out a polypropylene case. He tucked it under his arm, closed the locker, and started the airlock cycle.

When it was at pressure, Murphy and Haverfield stepped inside. Once the doors closed and the pressure started to drop, Haverfield unzipped the case he had retrieved and showed her an Aulinc 4032, fully automatic. Its matte-black plastic body was barely visible in the shadow of the case. During training at the University, she'd fired needlers like this one. The plastique charges loaded into its chambers projected thirty-two hair-thin needles a second. Fast and brittle, the projectiles shattered inside the target. It was the same kind of weapon used to shoot Tali.

The needler had been modified for zero-gee use.

A reaction spring coiled like a sleeping snake along the wristguard.

Murphy's assessment of Haverfield's stupidity doubled. If he shot the needler on board the *Gambit,* the razor-sharp fragments would work themselves into every crevice, doing gods-know-what damage to the ship's controls.

He touched his helmet to hers. "You pull anything funny when we're on board—anything at all, I'll use this."

Murphy swallowed and murmured, "Discharge that thing on board, and you'll kill us both."

The cycle finished and they climbed down into the Gambit's central chamber. Organically shaped, it was a rough dome, four meters across. Titanium walls bulged with lockers and drawers. Equipment encrusted every surface. There was no up or down. Controls were oriented every which way. The room looked more like a cave than anything man-made.

It was an efficient design, every square centimeter of surface area used. Murphy found it soothing. It reminded her of Maisie's asteroid.

"Ugly," Haverfield said. "They may have advanced technology, but who designed this place? Cramped, controls look like they were spatter-painted onto the walls, it gives me a headache."

She tried to see it with grounder's eyes: a chaotic hole with little empty space, no white walls or ceilings to provide perspective.

It was obvious to her that the *Gambit*'s designers were floaters. Human or nonhuman, whoever built this ship didn't spend time in gravity.

Murphy caught one of the hand straps near the airlock and lowered herself carefully onto controls that had never meant to be walked on. "Let's undock from the station rim before we step on something important," she said.

Haverfield dropped with a thud. "Afraid I'll break a critical system and you won't be able to impress the boss-lady?"

Murphy grit her teeth. "No. I'm afraid you'll kick the fusion rods control and we'll be reduced to atoms." She pointed at the slider bar under his feet. The script was impenetrable, but she guessed it might regulate the cabin temperature.

Haverfield stepped lightly over the bar, and tiptoed around the other controls in his path to the front of the ship.

The pilot's spherical chamber rose from the top of the living quarters like a head above shoulders. Inside was perfectly smooth. The controls here were delicate touchpads set into the wall like mosaics. Sliding windows protected the controls of vital systems.

The pilot's crash couch dominated the room. It ran from the middle of Murphy's thighs to slightly above her head. The couch was thickly padded with a cobalt gel that oozed into the curves of her body. It was attached by a steel bar that ran through the pivot of the seat and back and into the curving walls, allowing the couch to swing in the direction of acceleration.

Next to the pilot's couch, Vivien's workers had welded in a copilot's seat for Haverfield.

The air was filled with nine holo bees; they dipped and spun, intent on recording everything in the cabin from every possible vantage point, all at once.

Haverfield waited for her to strap in, then loaded himself into the trainer. She noticed he kept the pouch holding his gun free of the safety restraints.

The forward viewscreen was a hemispherical depression set into the wall in front of the pilot's chair. When she sat down, it expanded into a spherical holographic projection of the view outside the *Gambit*. By focusing close up, she could see what was behind the *Gambit;* with normal focus she could see what was in front of it. There was a tiny red dot just off center in the sphere. What was that? Center of mass?

She didn't see any way to set the com frequency, but hoped the system auto-negotiated with the station's transponder. She spoke into the forward screen. "*Gambit* ready to undock."

The radio blurted the singsong of a traffic controller who'd repeated the words a hundred thousand times. "Granted. Release and slow to three hundred meters off counterclockwise."

"Do my best." She scanned the controls in front of her, trying to make sense of their labels. There, that one. Trusting to intuition, she tapped the pad. The *Gambit*'s docking pins retracted, and the ship hurled tangentially off the station's ring.

Freed from the station's centripetal force, gravity lifted like a curtain going up. Murphy felt the vertebrae in her back expand.

She slid a gloved finger along something that looked like thruster controls. Green-and-yellow script scrolled in the screen next to it. Their speed didn't change. She tapped other controls. The lighting flickered on and off, and something boomed in the far reaches of the ship.

"What was that?" Haverfield asked.

Murphy tapped the control again. Red script changed to green. "Still feeling my way around."

Haverfield's right hand lingered over the pocket that contained his weapon. "If you try anything, I'm authorized to stop you."

Murphy whirled to face him. "Look, the reason Gallger tracked me down to the ends of the galaxy was because no one else could figure out how to fly this ship. Excuse me if I make the occasional mistake."

Haverfield's features relaxed, became almost a smile. "By all means, make as many mistakes as you want."

How to stop the ship? If Vivien had to send tugs to bring the *Gambit* back, she might decide Murphy wasn't worth keeping around. And Murphy knew too much for Vivien to risk letting her go.

Murphy's chest tightened. She had been sure that slider was the right control. She slid open one of the covered panels and touched it.

The control room vanished. Murphy drifted in a field of stars, the Gallger station spinning like a top.

Her heart stopped. What had happened to the *Gambit*? She jerked left—

Every item not attached to the interior surface slammed against the right wall. Murphy and Haverfield smacked against the right side of their chairs.

Murphy's perspective swam with double vision: stars—controls—stars. If she unfocused her eyes, details of the control room fuzzed into view: mosaic walls, Haverfield swearing, a portable screen drifting off the right wall. If she tried to look at anything directly, she saw only stars.

The suit. It must interact with the controls. Her lie had been true after all. Delicately, she swiveled her head right. She felt the inertia of her body resist the change of motion. Incredible. The ship's motion was tied directly to her body.

She marveled at the simplicity of it. A floater child could fly this ship.

"What the hell are you doing? Trying to shake the ship apart?" Haverfield asked.

Haverfield couldn't see the stars surrounding her. He had no idea her suit controlled the ship. She had to use that advantage to disable him. "Sorry, I thought those were the fine controls."

"Damn floater. Bank left around the station at 105 degrees azimuth and 42 degrees altitude. Keep a distance of no less than 4500 kilometers."

Murphy struggled to unfocus her vision. She reached for a new set of controls, holding her fingers a millimeter off the surface and miming their activation. Relaxing her eyes, she fell back into the kaleidoscopic stars. She couldn't help smiling as she arched her body to bank around, feeling the gentle tug of acceleration.

Haverfield's voice cut through her reverie. "Enough fine control, show me how to start the launch process." Murphy unfocused her eyes and started the procedure that had launched the *Gambit* before.

Haverfield tapped in notes on a hand-held screen. While he was distracted, she entered a second set of numbers, then leaned forward so he wouldn't see the change.

Haverfield finished his notation and nodded at her. "Start the prelaunch warm up."

She wondered what controls her hands had pretended to manipulate while she maneuvered the ship. One thing was certain. Haverfield wasn't going to come out of this flying lesson with any useful information. For that she was fiercely glad.

She stared at the controls. "The configuration is different. Controls that were lit last time I entered the cockpit are dark now. What happened?"

Haverfield's lips tightened. "Tried to start it up. Damn ship shut down on me." He glared at her. "Nothing an ace pilot like you can't fix."

"I'll try." Murphy said, touching twin bands of throttle strips.

Haverfield leaned forward until his helmet pressed against hers. Through the privacy of helmet-to-helmet sound transmission, he said, "You'd better do more than try, or your home system dies a slow death."

He jerked his helmet back, and said loudly. "Of course, if you don't think you can . . ."

Murphy couldn't concentrate on his words, the aside he'd whispered to her was spinning around in her head.

He pushed hard on her shoulders. "Start the self-launch." He tapped his portable screen, and Vivien's image appeared.

Her face was dark. "What's taking so long?"

"Sorry, sir. Murphy's still trying to get her bearings. I was helping her figure out the controls."

Murphy noticed that Haverfield's face was flushed, and he was sweating—like she was. Vivien didn't take chances when it came to ensuring people's loyalty. She'd bet the *Gambit* Haverfield was addicted, too.

Murphy wheeled the ship away from the station, and initialized both sets of engine controls, transferring power from the docking thrusters to the main engines. She slid the *Gambit* left and then fired jets on the underbelly. The acceleration made her slightly dizzy.

Haverfield said, "It's easy for you isn't it? Everything's easy. Got your Murphy hardwires at birth, and you've just used them ever since."

Murphy didn't argue. The man was unpredictable and armed. She had to figure out some way to get the needler away from him.

The launch systems weren't ready. Distracted, she touched two controls simultaneously and an alarm sounded. The ship shuddered, jets firing out of phase.

"Vacuum-head"—Haverfield leaned forward in his seat—"you've misaligned the thrusters, let me—"

Murphy slapped at his hands. "I'm pilot. Get off my controls."

He looked down. The numeric symbols were recognizable, even if the script wasn't. The coordinates on the screen were a magnitude larger than the ones he'd given her. "That's not—"

Murphy drove an elbow into his solar plexus; he tumbled backwards.

Out of the corner of her eye, she saw him reach for his needler. Not yet—waste! Murphy frantically pushed the controls, trying to get the launch powered up—now.

Vivien's voice over the com: "What's going on—"

Haverfield had the gun free. "Send reinforcements. She's trying to steal—"

Murphy focused her eyes on the stars and slammed the ship hard right. Haverfield hit the left wall.

The gun swung off target, but he snapped it back into line.

One of the holo bees dive-bombed Haverfield's face. He swatted at it with the hand holding the needler.

It went off.

Murphy's right side jerked, then pain blotted out sensation. A fierce throbbing in her arm pulsed her back to consciousness. She looked down, expecting to see blood bubbling from her sleeve. An area on her spacesuit as big as her fist had turned black, but the

strange fabric was whole. It had stopped the needles.
A thousand plastic fragments dusted the air.

Reflexively, Murphy checked the position of her
ship. The *Gambit* had moved left 4500 kilometers.
How? She straightened and the ship moved with her.
Of course! She was still synched with the ship. The
needles's explosive impact had thrown her sideways,
and because her suit was synched with the ship, the
Gambit had mimicked her motion. But 4500 kilometers in a few seconds?

Murphy glanced over her shoulder. The improvised
copilot's chair hadn't survived the strain. The restraints had snapped. Haverfield drifted limply, the
right side of his helmet crushed, blood bubbling
around the edges of the fractured plastic.

She checked the ship's direction and position. Everything was clear. Then she tapped the control that
synched the suit with the ship, and suddenly found herself reduced, trapped once more in her own flesh. She
unbelted and crawled back to check on Haverfield.

His breathing was noisy, but even. She lifted the gun
out of his limp hand and unloaded it, storing rounds of
ammunition and the weapon in separate pockets of
her flight suit.

Using the tether cord from Haverfield's own suit,
she strapped him to the chair. In his current condition,
she probably didn't need to bind his arms and legs,
but she wasn't taking any chances.

By the time she finished tying his limbs down, the
cut on his face had stopped bleeding. She used a disposable towel to wick away the bubbled blood from
his mouth and nose to prevent him from suffocating,
and returned to the pilot's couch.

Vivien's voice shouted over the portable's com.
"What the hell was that? What's happened? Kyle,
focus those holo bees forward!"

Murphy's head snapped up at the mention of Kyle's
name. She glanced over her shoulder. All but the rogue
bee drifted in lazy circles, shooting footage of the ceiling,
the floor, anything but Murphy and Haverfield.

Kyle was helping her!

Memory flooded back: during their video conversation, his fist opening and clenching. The floater hand signal. He'd been telling her he was on her side.

Murphy wanted to shout and cry at the same time. Then a panic grabbed hold of her mind. How was she going to get him off the station? She had promised—

The rogue bee slammed itself into the spherical navigational control. Dazed, it drifted back, then pivoted to dive-bomb deep space again.

Kyle was telling her to leave. But without the drug, she might die—and she couldn't leave him. She'd promised not to leave without him.

In the spherical navigational hologram, a dozen ships disengaged from the station's ring, ship-catchers: tugs armed with magnet cannons and refitted for speed. They accelerated in her direction. Vivien must have pulled the plug on today's exercises. The *Gambit* no doubt would be treated gently. Murphy held no illusions that order applied to herself.

The bee started another buzzing assault on the forward screen.

She could launch. If she got to Lettinger before Vivien transmitted the shutdown commands, Arch might have a way to stop it—or the floaters could launch away and escape. She started the first stages of powering up the launch controls.

What about Kyle? If she left him behind, Vivien was sure to trace the bees' behavior back to him. What would his life be worth then?

The ship-catchers closed in; grapple magnets swung to bear. Two moved to intercept her path of acceleration and cut off her route of escape.

Around her the ship hummed as the launch systems powered up. The green script on the launch controls blinked impatiently.

Gods, what should she do?

Slam! The tiny robot cracked open its case, scratching part of the front IFO control. It drifted back, useless.

"Kyle, you stupid grounder—you're not supposed to sacrifice yourself—that's my job."

She tapped the launch controls. Acceleration slammed her back into the gel of the pilot's chair. The stars in the IFO compressed into a single point of blinding white light. The *Gambit* shuddered as a grapple magnet hit it—

—and jumped into hell.

The cabin temperature rose immediately. The stars in the IFOs were replaced by red-orange gases that swirled in magnetic eddies. Behind the *Gambit,* a white light flashed. The ship-catcher that had locked onto the *Gambit*'s hull had ruptured.

Murphy wasted no time looking for survivors in that plasma hell. She pushed the ship icon to the center of the navigational sphere, and the *Gambit* jumped—

—into the blackness of deep space. Murphy checked the navigational calculations. She'd jumped farther than she'd intended. Losing the mass of the ship-catcher halfway must have thrown off the launch— the *Gambit* had jumped 35,000 light-years. Even the forward edges of known space hadn't pushed that far. She was farther from Sol than any human had ever gone, halfway across the Milky Way.

No reason to stay here. She had to get back to Lettinger, figure out some plan to rescue Kyle and stop Vivien.

She touched the navigational sphere. It blinked yellow, then red, and disappeared. Murphy activated the self-launch control, but the holographic display wouldn't stay up. Pages of unreadable text scrolled by, no doubt detailing the problem.

Gallger's engineers had studied the ship for weeks since Murphy last flew it. No telling what they'd done to its systems, intentionally or otherwise.

In all directions, Murphy and Haverfield were surrounded by unforgiving vacuum. If she didn't figure out how to reactivate the launch system, they would die of withdrawal from Vivien's truth drugs.

CHAPTER
18

The navigational sphere flickered on again, then went blank. Murphy slid her finger along the power strip for the launch engines. Nothing she had tried in the past hours had worked. The sphere wouldn't stay lit.

What was wrong? This control had always launched the ship before. Murphy touched it again.

More text scrolled by. The ship stayed inert.

Maybe a needle from Haverfield's gun had worked into the electronics. Murphy cursed. She searched the cabin and found a portable vacuum. She sucked glassteel slivers off the instrument panel and out of the air.

Murphy tapped the power strip again. Still nothing. The now-familiar symbols rolled by. Murphy felt illiterate. The information she needed was right there, but she couldn't read it. She pounded on the control panel in frustration.

This wasn't helping anyone. She should take a break and cool down, check on Haverfield again.

He was still unconscious, his breathing shallow. Murphy popped his neck seals and gingerly pulled the helmet off, keeping the shattered faceplate away from his scalp.

The ship didn't have an autodoc. Aside from keeping him warm, Murphy didn't know what to do. Haverfield had been unconscious for hours now. If he didn't get expert medical help, he might slip into a coma . . . or die.

Haverfield had helped Gallger destroy her career, but she didn't want to see him dead.

When Murphy checked his pulse, her hand trembled. How long had it been since she'd eaten?

She looked at her suit's clock. She'd been working on the navigational controls for twelve hours. Fourteen hours since breakfast and twenty-two since Tali had administered her last shot of Veradine.

Her head felt clogged by engine oil, and her muscles ached. She'd done all she could for Haverfield. Now she needed to take care of herself. There was no time for sleep, but food—that was worth investigating. Gallger had no doubt stripped the galley of food, but maybe they had missed a powerbar or javacup.

She propelled herself through the hole in the floor to the galley. The room was exactly as it had been when she and Kyle had explored it: a cramped multipurpose area with galley, toilet, and sleeping quarters squeezed into a space barely three meters across.

Murphy opened the pantry. Her eyes widened.

The endless packages of pasta were gone. In their place were freeze-dried banquets: Beef Wellington, Crystallized Shrimp, Pad Thai, and Multi-Protein Wraps. Rich food Murphy had never tasted before.

Murphy touched a packet of Mu Shu pork. "Kyle." He must have reprovisioned the *Gambit,* for their escape. Unshed tears welled in Murphy's eyes. How could she have left him behind?

He'd told her to go—she'd had no choice. But the only thing Kyle feared was his sister's revenge. Vivien had to know he'd helped engineer the *Gambit*'s escape. What retribution would she exact for this second betrayal?

Was Kyle even still alive?

She had to get out of here. Kyle's sacrifice would be pointless if Murphy ended her days trapped in space.

After she'd downed a javacup and a cup of Pad Thai, Murphy propelled herself back to the control room.

She tapped the launch control again. This time she studied the error message as it scrolled by.

If she couldn't figure a way around the error message, she would have to work through it. Cracking codes and ferreting out information wasn't her specialty. But Kyle and Tali weren't there. She was.

"Time to learn your secrets," Murphy told the computer. She activated a control pad, studying the text that scrolled by. Murphy sketched the symbols on a personal reader and organized them by size and repeated shapes, then touched the next control.

An hour later she was stiff and sore. She toggled the launch engines, and more text flowed down the screen. Most of the characters were familiar to her now. But then—Murphy's breath caught in her chest.

In the center of the alien message, one human word had flashed by: MURPHY.

It couldn't be.

She reactivated the control. The text rippled again, but the message was different. Murphy tried several combinations but couldn't get the anomaly to repeat.

She worked for another hour without seeing any more human characters. Had she imagined it?

Her eyes were bleary with exhaustion. She had accumulated a set of a hundred and fifty symbols. One she understood: a spiky set of inward arrows. It was the first character in the messages that popped up when she did something wrong: ERROR.

Haverfield groaned.

Murphy Velcroed the portable reader to her thigh and floated to him. She was glad he would live, but having him conscious presented a whole new set of problems.

"My head," he moaned. "It's killing me." He struggled in his bonds. "Wha? Where . . ." His voice trailed away as his eyes focused on Murphy. "You . . . I remember you."

"You remember that you almost killed us both by shooting that damn needler?"

"Where are we?"

Murphy shined a penlight in Haverfield's eyes. They contracted equally. No concussion. "About 35,000 light-years from home."

Haverfield tried to sit up. "Why am I tied up? Release me."

"I don't think so." Murphy met his gaze. "I'm not as trusting as I was at the University."

Haverfield flushed. "That wasn't personal. Gallger offered me a lucrative position as a test pilot. All they asked in return was my cooperation at the trial. Osborne and Jenks set you up—Not me. I swear."

"Maybe not. But you didn't stand up and speak the truth at the trial, either. That makes you just as guilty in my eyes."

"I didn't think the University would expel you," Haverfield said. "Censure, yes, but with your flying record, I didn't think the CEA could afford to lose you. I just wanted to see you knocked down a peg. You were always in front of me, always the top flier."

"You're either lying, or incredibly stupid."

"Now, wait-a—"

"You listen. We're lost in uncharted space. The *Gambit* won't launch. I don't know if it's something I'm doing wrong or if the *Gambit*'s damaged." She grabbed the collar ring of his spacesuit and leaned her face close to Haverfield's. "You're going to tell me all you know about the ship."

"I'm not saying anything until you untie me."

"You don't understand your position. You screwed me over once; I'm not about to hand you a second chance. If you won't help me with the *Gambit,* I'll pitch you out in the big dark now. Saves me food, power, and irritation. Talk now. Or you walk home."

Haverfield glanced at the IFOs and then back at Murphy's face. "Okay, I'll talk. But please, at least get me an analgesic. My head is killing me."

Murphy popped open the medipak and fed him two aspirin.

Haverfield dry-swallowed the pills. "There's not

much to tell. Gallger was picking up some rebuilt ships in a remote system, and noticed a metallic mass floating outside the orbit of the asteroid belt. They investigated and found the *Gambit*. Random impact damage suggests the ship was drifting for at least twenty years."

"No one else found it in all that time?"

"Space is big and the *Gambit*'s matte-black. No radiation or reflective surfaces makes detection difficult. Maybe someone spotted it and took it for space junk. I don't know. It was abandoned when Gallger's crew found it. The only trace of a pilot was ashes."

"Did they run DNA-vacuum tests on the ship?"

"If they did, no one told me." He struggled in his bonds. "Won't you untie me? My muscles are on fire."

"Later . . . maybe. What else do you know?"

Haverfield stared at Murphy. "Just one other thing. No one told me this, but I can read between the lines. Gallger found something on board the *Gambit* ship that tied it to you. Something makes them think you're the only one who can fly it." He licked his cracked lips. "From the way the *Gambit* shut down on me when I tried to pilot it, they may be right."

What Haverfield said made sense. Gallger and Avocet had been after her ever since the *Gambit* was found. She was good, but there were other pilots just as good that the Companies could have hired more easily.

A chill prickled Murphy's spine. She remembered the name she'd seen—or imagined—in the display. Did the ship know who she was?

Haverfield's face was white and sweating. "You want a drink?" she asked.

"Please," he croaked. "My mouth feels like a desert."

Murphy got a water bulb from the galley. She pressed it to Haverfield's lips, and he sucked greedily. "One other thing . . ." Haverfield broke off. His eyes became huge and vague. "Do you see them?" He stared intently behind her.

Murphy turned and looked, saw an empty corner. "See what?" Her hands started to tremble again. She looked at them, surprised. What was happening? From her floater upbringing came a word: *Verragung,* ghost ship.

"No!" Haverfield drew in a great shaking breath. His back arched, and he strained against the bonds that held his wrists and ankles. "No—no—no—" He broke off into incoherent wailing.

Murphy broke open the medikit on her suit, looking for a sedative. As she opened the case, Murphy's skin blurred and started to flake off. Hundreds of tiny scabs with wire-hair legs pulled themselves out of her arm and burrowed under her skin.

Every cell in her body cried out. If she was still she could feel individual cell walls shriveling, dehydrating . . . she was thirsty—dying—

She sucked in great gaping breaths. Then scratched at her cheeks until they bled. The pain brought instant clarity. The drug, Veradine. She had to get back to Vivien and get more of the drug.

Murphy caught the edge of the pilot's seat and climbed into it. Had to pilot the *Gambit* back. Had to!

Murphy's throat hurt and she realized that she was screaming, too. Faces of people she'd failed floated past her: Tali, Carmady, Spanner, Kyle.

Had to get back to Vivien. Only then would it stop. Vivien said Murphy would die without the drug.

Murphy pounded the launch controls. The now-familiar error message scrolled by.

"No!"

Murphy tore at the controls, pounded cabinets. She pulled the gel cushion from the pilot's seat. Had to find a way to get back. Had to find a way.

Had to.

The wall she was staring at lost its fascination. Murphy snapped awake. She had no idea how long she'd been mesmerized by its smooth blankness.

She looked behind her. The room was madness. Gel

stuffing bobbled beside pieces of cabinet doors. Some of the control-panel tiles had been snapped off and danced colored whirligigs in the air. Everywhere she looked, something was moving. The room was filled with debris.

And blood.

Murphy's heart stopped at the sight of the red jiggling globs. They centered around the prone form of Haverfield.

"No!" Murphy pushed through them, ignoring the mess and the blobs that clung to her suit. "No."

Haverfield's right arm was free. There were marks on his suit from where he'd snapped the bonds. His right hand clenched a utility knife. His boots were sliced up from where he'd cut the restraints. He must have panicked at the end, trying to get free. His left wrist was nearly severed.

Murphy pulled the glove off her hand and touched Haverfield's pale neck. His flesh was cold.

"Gods no." Grief choked Murphy's throat. Haverfield had helped get her expelled from the University, but he hadn't deserved this.

And what was she doing alive? Vivien had said the drug's withdrawal would kill. But it hadn't. Not directly. Another lie?

Murphy looked at the chaos around her. If she'd been able to pilot the ship back to Gallger she would have. Better to compel than to kill. The cold efficiency of it was Vivien all over.

Murphy bandaged Haverfield's arm to keep it from leaking further. She stowed his limp body in an empty suit cabinet, then vacuumed blood and debris out of the air.

Murphy prayed she hadn't damaged the *Gambit* in her drug-induced frenzy. Losing control and tearing up the cabin was inexcusable. Floaters had been spaced for less.

Murphy set about making repairs. She snapped tiles into place, taped cabinets closed, and wiped cushion-gel off the IFOs.

The pilot's chair was a loss. The gel-filled seat was ripped in several places, as if it had been torn with nails and . . . teeth? Yes, those were crescent-shaped bite marks.

Shame burned Murphy's cheeks. She sopped up more of the gel, then rotated until her head was under the chair, and unzipped the gel-filled pad from the chair's steel frame.

The zipper stuck halfway through its run. Murphy reached into the opening and pulled the obstruction free.

She stared at the object in shock. It was a floater's bible.

The book was old, bound with metal hinges and memory-text pages. Who had stashed it here? One of the Gallger salvagers? A test pilot?

Murphy opened it. Inside the front cover, scrawled in pen, was a signature: Ferris Murphy.

Her father's bible.

"It can't be." Murphy stroked the cover. Memories flooded back: clinging to her father's knee while he read to her about the saints and prophets, the stain on the back cover from when she'd touched it with a jam-sticky hand, the expansive swoops of her father's signature that she'd tried to emulate as a child.

Murphy's hands trembled. She turned the page. Text filled the left frame, a line-drawing the right. The picture of Newton had been replaced by a hand-drawn sketch of a woman and child, a girl, about five years old. The lines were shaky, but Murphy recognized the woman as her mother. The child must be herself. The words opposite the picture read:

12-27-2197, ship's time / 1-12-2198 Lettinger time
Trying to change the world is a mug's game. I know that now. Thought the rebellion could make the Companies sit up and take notice. At least realize floaters were human. Thought I could help people.

What a fool . . . I can't even help myself.

The Companies are too big to fight. They captured us at Canodyne 4265. Thought that would be it for me, a short trip into the big dark. But no, the Companies were afraid to make me a martyr. So they came up with something much more slow. They killed everyone I loved . . . of old age. They killed me, too.

The official story is I chose to take a one-way exploration trip to systems never before charted. The truth is the Companies knocked me out and stuffed me into this self-sufficient tin can, an Avocet Explorer LT. The thing's been accelerating at one gee for the past ten months. I'm traveling at half the speed of light, and speed's still increasing. There's no spacesuit on board, and no way for me to EVA and turn off the propulsion without one.

While I've stewed in here, a whole year has passed for my family. My daughter's almost seven now. My wife . . . what must Jenevie have thought? Did she believe the Company's lie? Or did she know that I'd never leave her willingly? I like to think she knew.

It's an efficient revenge. The Companies get rid of a troublemaker, the rebels think their leader sold out for a chance to explore the universe, and the Collective gets valuable exploration data. Or at least, they did until I woke up. The first thing I did once I got my bearings was destroy the long-range communications laser. A petty revenge, but you have to take what you can get.

Don't know why I'm writing this. To stay sane? Something to do besides look out the window or immerse in vids I've seen thousands of time? It started with a picture of Jenevie and little Thia. I drew it to remind me what they looked like. Their memories are starting to fade— couldn't let that happen. I'm no artist, but I remember the curve of my little girl's cheek.

> *The crooked smile of my wife. It helps. I drew*
> *the picture, then more pictures, and then the*
> *words poured out.*

Murphy's heart skipped a beat. Was this one of Vivien's tricks? She touched the cover of the book. It felt old, brittle. She pressed the book against her forehead. Its cool plastic soothed her.

If the bible could be believed, her father hadn't abandoned his family. He'd been shanghaied.

Her mind whirled as the facts she'd built her life on suddenly rotated 180 degrees. Murphy read on.

> *5-18-2199, ship's time / 3-2-2217 Lettinger time*
> *Strange to think that millions of kilometers*
> *away, my daughter is a grown woman. My*
> *speed is fast enough now that the effects of Saint*
> *Einstein's verses of special relativity are*
> *noticeable. While two years have passed for me,*
> *twenty years have slipped away on Lettinger.*
> *Does my little girl have children now? What*
> *kind of person did she grow into? Did she ever*
> *forgive her father for disappearing when she was*
> *a child? Jenevie might be dead. I know that*
> *I'll never see her again. The laws of physics are*
> *jealous gods and don't make exceptions for*
> *sentiment. There's too much space and time*
> *between us now. But it hurts . . . hurts to know*
> *the young woman I married is gone.*

The diary went on to describe the monotony of Ferris's daily life: making observations, maintaining the Explorer LT, struggling with depression and isolation.

In contrast to these bleak writings were the descriptions of how his life had been: adventures he'd shared with his rebel friends, the passion of his courtship and life with Jenevie, and his pride in his young daughter. He wanted the revolution to make the universe a better place for little Thia, so she wouldn't grow up as a second-class citizen.

Seeing in his own words her father's love, Murphy
wept. Softly at first, then long raking sobs. When they
were done, she was weak and drained.

There was more, lots more. A lifetime's worth of
her father's observations. She believed in the little
book now. There was too much there that was personal. Events between her and her father that she'd
never told anyone about. Details too inconsequential
for the Companies to have discovered during questioning. It was improbable to the point of impossible, but . . .

Her father had written this journal.

But how had the bible gotten off the Explorer LT
and onto the *Gambit*? Murphy skimmed ahead.

6-21-2202, ship's time / 8-11-2272 Lettinger time
Checked the IFOs against the metallic scan. It's
true. There's a non-natural construct up ahead.
I'd say man-made, but I'm 100 light-years out, 60
farther than any human's gone before.

My hands are sweating. First contact, and who
represents humanity? Not an ambassador, not
a general, but an exiled floater with a talent for
getting himself into trouble.

I sent greeting messages on all communication
frequencies the com can transmit. No reply. Of
course not. There's no way they could decode
English from such a small sample. I set up the
com to play all the videos from the library:
Shakespeare and pornography, nature
documentaries and situational comedies. All in an
endless loop.

It's six hours later and I've just gotten a reply.
A series of pulses: one, two, three, five, seven,
nine. Prime numbers. I respond in kind with the
next set.

Static on the incoming video resolves slowly
into an image. For the first time I see who I've
been talking to. She's beautiful. Or maybe that's
just the reaction of a man who's spent five

*years alone in space. I don't know how or why,
but she looks human. Cocoa-butter skin with
neon-green eyes. She blinks and I see a second
set of sideways eyelids flash by. Her hair is
silver strands braided into tight helixes, like
stainless-steel springs that hang down from her
head. Her skin is unlined, her face ageless.*

"Who are you?" I ask.

*"Tangent Fourier," she says, her voice strange.
Clipped, and with harmonics that sounded as
if multiple vocal folds vibrated at once. "I am a
historical anthropologist. Your communication
protocols are antique. The language samples were
most interesting. Your speed, however, and its
effects on the frequency of your transmission,
complicates communication. Will you slow
down so we may discuss normally?"*

*I explained to her my situation and the fact that
I couldn't stop.*

*She said, "Then may we decelerate your ship?
I would be most interested to interview a
person from the Collective, circa 2202."*

*I laughed and wept aloud. She said it so matter-
of-factly, relegating the expenditure of two
million tera-Joules of energy—as much energy as
a space station uses in a year—to a matter as
simple as setting up an afternoon snack.*

*"Hell, yes," I said. "If you can slow down this
one-way rocket without killing me, I'll tell you
everything you want to know about the twenty-
third century."*

*A black bubble of a ship suddenly appeared
behind the Explorer. It caught my ship in a
magnetic field, slowing it marginally before I sped
out of range. Then suddenly, the black ship
was behind me again, and again slowed the
Explorer. It skipped through space like a stone,
catching up to my faster ship by jumping over the
space between. A launcher that could bootstrap
itself? I stared at the rear IFOs, facinated.*

*   *   *

9-21-2202, ship's time / 1-18-2275 Lettinger time
Even with their advanced technology, it took
three months to slow the Explorer LT without
killing me in the deceleration. I've got bruises on
my bruises.

9-29-2202, ship's time / 4-6-0068 Principia time
It is now eight days since I met Tangent. To
me it seems as if I have been traveling for only
five years. But on Earth, seventy years have
passed. Tangent's people were physicists that
fled the Collective three years after its inception.
They pooled their resources and bought a
portable launcher. Their destination was an
uninhabited system outside of Collective-
controlled space, farther than anyone had dared
launch before. As a further precaution, they
rigged the launcher to self-destruct after their
jump, so no one would know where they had
gone. Their colony, Principia, has flourished ever
since. All resources and time not needed for
survival are committed to scientific study. Their
government is a true democracy. Citizens who
pass competency tests vote on which experiments
to fund, the proper education curriculum for
children, and so on.

10-3-2202, ship's time / 4-10-0068 Principia time
During Tangent's physical examination of
me—necessary before I can board their
station—she commented on my reflexes and
spatial perception. I told her I was a test pilot
before the Companies exiled me. This excited her.
The young people, no longer content with
isolation, have been working on a ship to launch
them back to populated space—the same matte-
black bubble they used to decelerate my ship.
They gave me a tour inside the prototype. Its
workings are wondrous.

Her father's entries over the next month described in detail the *Gambit* and the various tests he put it through. It was fascinating, but Murphy flipped ahead. She wanted to know how and why the *Gambit* appeared in Lettinger space.

> *5-23-2202, ship's time / 12-3-0068 Principia time*
> *Tangent is very upset. She slept in her own room last night. My theories, she said, are irrational and suicidal. But I proved to her the* Gambit *is capable of time travel. I saw it in her face. Any spacer child knows time and space are two sides of the same coin. You can trade one for the other with velocity. If you can fold space, then by extension, you should be able to fold time as well.*
> *"Look at the energies involved," she argued, pointing to the equations on the wall screen. "It doesn't matter whether it is theoretically possible. Even if you only travel back a week, you'd burn up. There's no way to manufacture a material that could stand up to hundreds of millions of terawatts." She took my hand. "You can't go back to them, Ferris. They're dead and gone."*
> *But her cousin, Pohl, doesn't agree. He grew excited and began correcting and expanding on my theories.*
> *I'm glad to be alone tonight. There's too much to think about. Jenevie and little Thia are dead. I've tried to reconcile myself to the fact that I'd never see them again. Tangent helped me forget, for a while. But if there's a chance—even a fraction of a chance that I'll be able to go back to them, I have to try.*

Murphy skipped past descriptions of the theory behind how the *Gambit* could fold space and time. She found:

Tangent cried all night in my arms. "We're sending you to your death," she said.

"You don't have to work the control room," I told her. "You don't have to watch."

She kissed me then, slow and thorough. "This might be the last time I see you. If our positions were reversed and I was Jenevie, could you turn away?"

There was no way to answer that, so I hugged her to me and smoothed her hair. "I'm not going to die," I said. "They call me Lucky Murphy. I'll come through this all right."

"It doesn't matter," she snuffled into my shoulder. "Either way, I'm losing you."

Pohl ran through a last systems check before the time-launch. The coordinates were set to Lettinger, 12-25-2197. Home. After that, assuming I survive, I'd map course to Canodyne 4265, to see what's left of the revolution, and then a jump back to Lettinger.

Jenevie, I hope that you'll help me write the next entry. Principia is a beautiful place, and I confess there were nights I let myself be swayed by Tangent's arguments that you were decades dead. But if home is where the heart is, mine is 100 light-years and seventy years in the past.

Pohl says all systems are go. He's about to start the countdown. I'd better stow this journal in a safe place, it might be a bumpy ride.

I love you, Jenevie. Tell little Thia her daddy's coming home . . .

That was the last entry.

Murphy hugged the bible to her chest. Tears burned in her eyes.

"No," she whispered. "Don't."

But he already had. She was sitting in her father's coffin. His ashes were on file in Gallger's laboratories. His Murphy-luck hadn't been enough to overcome the laws of physics.

She'd rather think of him loving Tangent in some far-off scientocracy. Or exploring somewhere between the stars. Death was so final, so immutable, so unforgiving.

But he wasn't really dead. Not yet. At this moment, he was somewhere out there. Traveling between the stars. He wouldn't reach Principia for fifty years. He was traveling, timeless, toward his doom.

And she didn't know where in infinite space he was. She had no way to stop him, to slow him down, no way to help him. But maybe—she pulled the book away from her chest and looked at it—maybe she now had a way to help herself.

Murphy spent three days studying her father's journal, reading and rereading the technical details of flying the *Gambit*.

The diary didn't explain the graphitos. It simply described it as a compact linguistic code. The scientists invented it as shorthand because serial letters were bulky and inefficient. But with Ferris's detailed observations and instructions, she didn't need to be able to read the controls to use them.

The problem was simple. She was trying to launch the *Gambit* without setting destination coordinates. Ferris had programmed in three launch destinations, but only lived to use one. Murphy's first two launches had succeeded using his coordinates. That was how she'd ended up at the abandoned station Canodyne. If the extra mass of the ship-catcher hadn't thrown the last launch off, she'd be at Lettinger now.

She set the controls to jump back to Lettinger, then suited up. Murphy took one last look at the bible. The last page held a line drawing of the three of them: Jenevie, Ferris, and Thia. A picture of happier times. Murphy touched her father's image.

"I've missed you." She tucked the book into the thigh pouch of her suit and punched the launch control. The *Gambit* quivered and jumped—

—into swirling red and orange. She twitched the ship forward and up a few meters, and then jumped—

—a burst of ions exploded over the *Gambit*'s front bow. Two clangs jolted the tiny ship sideways. The IFOs were chaotic with ships. A CEA Drone Escort released battalions of drones and remote-piloted squad leaders. Battle-modified cargo ships, tugs, and shuttles engaged the CEA fighters.

One of Lettinger's cones was crumpled and oxidized black.

Murphy synched with the *Gambit,* her body dancing to evade cross fire and collisions. She tongued the controls in her helmet, and transmitted on the Lettinger station frequency: "This is *Gambit.* Lettinger, please confirm." Radio silence. "Arch, are you there? What the hell's going on?"

Another pause, then a crackle of static. "Murphy?" Seconds later, Maisie's image resolved on screen. A bandage wrapped her head and left eye. Her right eye was red-rimmed and glassy. She looked as if she hadn't slept for weeks.

Behind Maisie, the interior of the asteroid was disheveled: plates smashed, portable equipment strewn across the floor, plants tumbled out of the hydroponics racks. It looked as if the rock had been struck by an earthquake, or projectiles.

Maisie jumped when the image resolved. "Gods alive! It *is* you."

Murphy dodged a shuttle retrofitted with a Luger ion cannon and asked, "What is happening?"

"Gallger Galactic has shut down 98 percent of its launchers. Thousands of systems are stranded. It's triggered a Collective-wide war."

CHAPTER
19

"War?" Murphy said incredulously. She jinked the *Gambit* to avoid a formation of drones. The coffin-shaped automatons formed a three-dimensional wedge, surrounding their leader. Twice as large as a drone, the remotely piloted lead ship bristled with radar dishes and antennae. It controlled the formation and coordinated its movement with the rest of the fleet.

Maisie spoke in a rapid staccato, "Gallger disabled the launchers. Gave us seventy-two hours to surrender. Spanner—"

Static. Then dead silence.

"Maisie!" Murphy toggled the com—nothing.

The wing leader broke formation, circled the *Gambit*, and strafed her starboard side with twin high-wattage lasers. Fiber optics on that side of the hull scarred over and went dark.

She pivoted the *Gambit* into a left-hand spiral, rounding the left side of the wedge. The drones caught up and converged on her. She dove through the hole in their formation her maneuver had created, accelerating. Before they could retarget and fire, she was out of range of their heliarc lasers. The drones followed, closing fast.

From her new vantage point, she saw the attack wasn't limited to Lettinger station. Tiny motes of silver flashed among the asteroid belt. Rock melted, bubbling and bursting as air exploded outward, flinging the rock's contents into space—beakers, hydroponics, and human figures, some too small to be adult.

The drones were firing on the women's rocks.

Ignoring the drones pursuing her, Murphy dove toward the ships attacking the rocks, colliding with one drone and scattering others. Maisie's rock was a third of the way across the rim.

She pumped propulsion up to maximum, streaking between the fighting ships, but the drones were already dispersed throughout the belt. Please, Einstein, let her get there in time.

When she was within visual range, Murphy lensed the fiber-optic display to enlarge the image of Maisie's rock. The asteroid was shattered.

Grief tightened around Murphy's throat like a band. She was too late. Her eyes burned. Maisie. The woman who had raised her, never done harm to any, and gave food and a kind word to all she loved. What kind of monsters would attack the women's rocks?

Murphy pivoted on her attackers. The *Gambit* wasn't armed, but it out massed the drones and their remote-piloted leader. She smashed the sphere of the *Gambit* through the lead ship. The crunch and shudder as its hull impacted and flattened against the *Gambit* was satisfyingly violent.

The drones attacked her, now running off onboard AIs. Their response times were quicker than when they were under human control, but they no longer moved as a unit. Without coordinated attack, this six-ship squadron of drones posed little threat to the *Gambit*. Unless they combined fire, their lasers didn't have enough power to punch through the *Gambit*'s hull. They could only blind her by scarring the IFOs.

Murphy's lips pulled back from her teeth in a snarl. She pushed the *Gambit* to full throttle, aiming at the carrier ship. As she rocketed through the system, more and more drones turned from fighting the floaters to pursue Murphy. Floaters in retrofitted tugs and reengineered shuttles made good use of the drones' distraction and launched missiles, destroying dozens.

Murphy, trailed by drones who in turn were trailed by floaters, carried the battle to the carrier.

Someone hailed her. Murphy punched it on screen. A man with close-cut brown hair appeared. He didn't look any older than a first-class cadet, but he wore lieutenant's bars. He said, "*Gambit*, this is *Potemkin*. Surrender yourself and we will call off the attack on Lettinger."

She set the com to broadband her reply. "The only surrender this system will see is your own. You've got thirty seconds to power down the ion cannons and recall your drones."

The young officer looked perplexed. This wasn't a situation covered in the CEA negotiations manual. He said, "Our reports state the *Gambit* is unarmed."

"Unarmed does not mean weaponless. Call off your drones."

"I am under orders to—"

"*Stow* your orders. You are killing women and children. Stand down your weapons."

Her answer came in a salvo of ions from the upper cannon. The golden beam hit the *Gambit* port-side and melted the left docking clamp.

Drones and their wing leaders barraged the *Gambit*. Back and side fiber-optic screens darkened. Six drones concentrated their fire and breached the aft hull. Automatic bulkheads sealed the area.

So they wanted to fight. Good. The destruction of Maisie's rock had left her craving vengeance.

Murphy ignored the alarms, her eyes fixed on the carrier's ion cannons. On raised turrets to either side of the ship, they offered near 360-degree coverage. But near was not absolute. There was a patch, six meters in diameter, on the underside that was beyond cannon reach. Normally, this area was guarded by drones held in reserve. Murphy was betting the inexperienced lieutenant had discharged them all.

She had spent years in a simulator, learning to protect the carrier's weak point from enemy fire. Now she used that knowledge to attack it.

Murphy dove under the plane of the ship, bobbing the *Gambit* from side to side to avoid ion bursts. The belly of the ship was pocked with drone bays. Empty now, they were silver holes that could do nothing to defend the carrier.

Murphy slipped into the unprotected zone and nestled up to the ship. She popped the grapple. The right side of the *Gambit* magnetized. The ships clanged together.

"Do you surrender?" she asked.

The officer replied, but not to her, "Wing leader Alpha and Bravo defend the *Potemkin* drone bay. All others continue operations."

"I'll take that as 'no.'" Murphy programmed coordinates and initiated launch. For a second, she thought the carrier was too much additional mass. It was four times as big as the ship-catcher she had accidentally dragged into a jump.

A high-pitched whine buzzed in her teeth. The *Gambit* rattled like a seventy-year-old Thompson. Then the disk of stars spun. Slowly at first, picking up speed until they blurred together into a white singularity and the *Gambit* and *Potemkin* launched—

—into red-gold plasma. The cabin temperature shot up. The hole the drones had shot in the *Gambit*'s hull melted wider. Plasma flowed into the ship's interior, dissolving walls and bulkheads as it seethed through the rooms.

An explosion boomed in the back of the *Gambit*. Status lights flashed red.

Murphy checked the ship holo. One of the interior bulkheads had blown and the breach was spreading. Plasma boiled through the projected black sphere, moving toward the launch generator. If that went, she'd have no way out of this plasma hell. Automatic bulkheads dropped, temporarily halting the flow of plasma into the ship. But the metal barriers were heating, and would soon melt through. The *Gambit* couldn't take much more.

The *Potemkin* was in worse shape. Never designed

for a plasma environment, meter-thick glass view-screens fractured and exploded, jets of oxygen ignited. The main parabolic communication dish folded in on itself, like a burning rose. Part of Murphy wanted to watch the *Potemkin* disintegrate. The bastards had killed Maisie.

But if she didn't get the ship back to Lettinger, more women like Maisie would die. She had to launch the carrier back while it was still able to recall the drone's attack.

They hadn't officially surrendered, but communication was impossible in this electromagnetic soup. Murphy prayed they'd had enough. She punched in Lettinger's coordinates.

The high-pitched whine returned, and red symbols flashed by the screen too fast for her to parse. The *Gambit* shuddered once, twice, then the plasma coiled into a spinning white disk. It unrolled into stars dotting velvet-black space. Lettinger.

A sharp report jarred Murphy's spine. A second crack. The *Gambit* was radiating heat—too quickly. The metal was cracking as it contracted. Another ping, and the lights went out.

Murphy flicked on her helmet light and pounded the com. "*Potemkin*, do you copy?"

No answer.

Murphy pushed out of her seat and surveyed the carrier ship as best as she could through heat-warped fiber-optic screens. The view was distorted but available. Thank the gods IFOs weren't affected by power outages.

The *Potemkin*'s drone bays had melted into a single undulating landscape. The ion cannons were retracted into their housings, and all but one of the glass windows was gone.

Had she done her job too well? If the crew and commander were dead, no one would be able to call off the drones. Come on, she prayed. Returning to the com, she transmitted, "*Potemkin*? This is *Gambit*."

Static.

She'd let anger drive her. The CEA wasn't the enemy. The crew of the *Potemkin* were just people, like herself, like the cadets she'd trained with. People trying to do a difficult job.

The *Gambit*'s cabin lights flickered, and Murphy heard a whump as life support returned. Power was coming back online. Come on. She hit the com again. "*Potemkin*!"

A crackle, then softly, "We hear you, *Gambit*." Video wavered in and out of focus, jittery lines of static sliding down the picture in an endless loop. The left cheekbone of the lieutenant's face was swollen and already darkening to a yellow-and-black bruise. Another burst of static, then "—have your surrender. All units return to—"

She lost the signal. Drones broke off their attack and sped toward the carrier.

Murphy set the com for broadband transmission and said, "Floaters, hold your attack. The *Potemkin* has surrendered."

A flurry of response hails competed for her attention. Murphy displayed them as tiled images on the forward screen. Dozens of faces shouted and spoke at once. Some, she recognized, like the old cargo runner John Hroc. But there were dozens of faces she didn't know, all looking to her, waiting for guidance. Only one was silent—the pockmarked Vargas, who had given her the *Delta-Vee*. He studied her intently.

When the commotion died down, Murphy said, "The *Potemkin* has surrendered. But they are badly wounded. I need people to board the ship, offer aid to survivors, and disable the *Potemkin*'s weapons."

"My crew will do that," said Hroc.

The coms began to babble again, questions about her status, the launchers, and what to do next.

"Assist those who are in need. And listen to the station's channel. I'll send information as soon as I have it."

It struck her how arrogant it was for her to command these people. In the University she was trained to lead, yes, but people under her authority. These floaters owed her no allegiance. And yet, here she was barking orders at them, and they seemed perfectly willing to obey.

She opened a hail to Lettinger. An eight-year-old girl with a round face and sad brown eyes answered and, with quick efficiency, told her to dock at port twelve.

When the *Gambit* was locked in, the airlock extruded to meet the outer hatch. She pulled herself along its accordion folds to the pressure chamber and waited while it cycled and processed her blood sample.

The inner door popped open, and an explosion of arms and legs grabbed Murphy and held her in a suit-crushing squeeze. "Child, I worried for you. Don't scare an old woman that way!"

"Maisie!" she screamed, and returned the woman's bear hug matching it, if not in mass, in intensity. "I thought you were dead. Your rock was destroyed."

"I'd suited up and packed myself into the shuttle the moment that carrier hit the system. No offense to your training, but the CEA rarely comes to a system to do floaters any good."

Murphy pushed away and held her aunt at arm's length. "You're *yar*, Maisie, I knew I could count on you." Murphy hugged her aunt again. "And Uncle Arch, where's that reprobate?"

Maisie's smile disappeared. "In opps. The doctors said he should leave the command room, but he wouldn't hear of it while Lettinger was in jeopardy."

"He's injured?"

"The old coot was working in the repair bay when Lettinger was hit. Corley patched him up as best he could, but he's only trained for emergency response."

"Where's Doc Pederson?"

"On a 'stroid with his wife and son. Couldn't get him to the station when the attack hit. Now he's half a rotation away."

"We've got to get Arch to a medical facility."

"Can't. Gallger disabled the launcher."

"I'll take him in the *Gambit*," Murphy said, then wondered if it would withstand the launch.

"No, that ship's too useful. He'll keep. It's the launchers' destruction you've got to stop. Be a lot more than an old man's pain if those go down."

"There's time for both. Vivien gave you seventy-two hours."

"We had seventy-two hours when the launchers first went offline. That was sixty-nine hours ago."

Murphy shook her head. "This is insane. How could Gallger expect you to turn over the rebel leaders if the launchers are disabled? Even if you wanted to, there's no way to get mass nor message out."

"Not true," Maisie said. "There is exactly one way. Gallger is holding the entire galaxy hostage to draw you and the *Gambit* out."

Murphy exhaled. Was the *Gambit* up to another jump? It'd have to be. Lettinger had neither equipment or expertise to fix a ship as advanced as the *Gambit*.

"Gallger will get its wish. But first, I want to see Arch."

The walls of opps were alive with screens displaying the space around Lettinger. Shuttles and tugs puttered through the women's ring, rescuing survivors and belongings. Drones swarmed past the station toward the *Potemkin*, bees returning to a busted hive.

Red emergency lighting gleamed off the autodoc wedged into the corner. Tubes trailed from it to a crumpled figure sitting in the headman's seat.

"Uncle Arch?" Her voice echoed, magnified, from a speaker at Arch's side.

The old man turned, pulling half out of his ergo. His left hand clung to the armrest, holding him in place; his right arm floated limply. Tape held a respirator tube to the corner of his mouth. The silicon snaked through his lips and down his throat. Arch spoke around it. His words were too soft to make out. The

sound system magnified his leathery whisper:
"Murphy?"

"I'm here." She drifted toward him and touched his
arm, grabbing the back of his chair to stop her forward
motion. "It's all over now. We've won. The station's
safe. Let someone else take over for a while. You
need rest."

Bruises of exhaustion lined his eyes. Arch swallowed several times before he replied, "Rest and en-
tropy catches up with you." He breathed laboriously.
"I'll stay here. Doesn't matter much . . . whether I
live or die." More breaths. "Station's dead . . . Galaxy's gone to hell . . ."

Murphy squeezed his arm, "No. I'll stop Gallger.
I'm taking the *Gambit* and launching to Gallger's
headquarters in ADS 17062."

Arch's eyes watered. "You think the *Gambit* can
make a difference?" A few more breaths. "The CEA's
attack proved the Companies are big. We're small."
He sighed. "We no longer have the resources to do
anything with the *Gambit*. Go ahead. Give it to Gallger." His chest labored. "Save the galaxy back to its
old rotten status quo."

The despair in his eyes squeezed her heart like a
vise. She leaned close to Arch and murmured too quietly for the sound system to pick up, "My father was
the original pilot of the *Gambit*. It was built by humans—rebels like us who ran away from the Companies." Murphy leaned back to gauge his reaction.

Arch glared suspiciously.

Murphy told him about the bible she'd found and
her father's journal. When she was finished, she said,
"He died coming home to us. He never gave up. Neither should we." She kissed the old man's forehead.

Arch paused a moment, as if judging whether to
believe her, then said, "Maisie, send Corley around."
His whispered words reverberated through the speakers. "And Hawkins, someone needs to take over
opps."

Murphy squeezed Arch's arm one last time, and kicked off from the command chair toward the door.

There were tears in Maisie's eyes. As Murphy passed her, Maisie said, "I don't know what you said to him, Child. But gods bless you."

Murphy touched her forehead to the old woman's. "Where I'm going, they'd better."

Murphy examined the damage from outside the ship, clinging to magnetic handholds and leaning into the rent. The inner bulkheads were too warped to slide open. A third of the *Gambit* had been destroyed by plasma. Interior walls hadn't melted so much as sublimated, leaving irregular edges.

She whistled when she saw the extent of the damage. Plasma had boiled through the interior of the ship, dissolving walls. Where the walls had ruptured or evaporated, she saw the black-and-silver lattices of solid-state circuitry. If it ran throughout the entire ship, the onboard computer must be incredibly complex.

It was a wonder that the *Gambit* was still functional. Either the ship was full of backups or it had reprogrammed itself around the missing electronics.

"Behind you," Hroc transmitted.

Murphy moved away from the hole, walking up the *Gambit*'s hull.

Three men in power suits wrestled a curved plate of tungsten-plated titanium over the hole. Magnets welded to its underside clamped it onto the ship. It was a kludge. But even if it only held for seconds, those would be seconds the *Gambit*'s damaged bulkheads wouldn't have to hold fiery death off her back.

Murphy continued up the spherical hull to the hatch, her magnetic soles clanking with each step.

Both doors of the airlock were wide open. Murphy stepped through.

She had pumped the *Gambit*'s remaining air into the reserve tanks. Safer to run the ship unpressurized. That way a hull breach wouldn't explode the ship as

escaping air increased damage and created an uncon-
trolled propulsion.

Inside, the ship was dim, as if power from the lighting had been transferred to vital systems. It wasn't her
doing; the *Gambit* was a smart ship.

She settled into the pilot's chair and radioed Hroc.
"How are repairs going?"

"Won't hold atmosphere, but it's better than flying
bare-arsed."

Hroc's crew finished, then jetted back to the station.

She released the dock pin and eased away. The
missing mass threw off the ship's balance. Murphy
compensated with thrusters. Half of the fiber-optic
screens were dark, the previously panoramic view replaced by portholes fore, aft, and left. Twenty-seven
percent of the ship's surface was bandaged with titanium patches.

Could it self-launch?

Stories of floaters who launched and never returned
had haunted her childhood. About one in ten thousand launches never arrived. Usually data or cargo,
but sometimes people went missing, and no one knew
what fate awaited them: instant oblivion or creeping
death as their life support failed somewhere in uninhabited space.

Murphy stared unblinking at the stars a long moment, then tore her gaze back to the launch controls.
This was no time for superstition. Either she'd make
it or she wouldn't. That thought, however, did nothing
to ease the knot in her chest. She increased acceleration out of Lettinger-space while starting up the
launch systems. She didn't want to take anyone with
her if the reactor exploded.

Murphy touched the spherical mapping control, setting the launch translation to take her to ADS 17062.
The status graphitos blinked and turned yellow, but
the secondary systems powered up. Murphy felt a sub-
sonic vibration through the bar of the ergonomic. The
Gambit's engine strained. She tapped the launch
control.

The *Gambit*'s whine rose to a chatter. The vibration expanded to a bone-loosening convulsion.

Murphy thought the ship would shake itself apart, then stars swam in her vision, and compressed to a bright ball—

Her suit's environmental systems kicked in as the temperature climbed. A quick glance at the fiber optics showed the titanium plate buckling. Its edges curled up, like paper in a fire. The *Gambit* shrieked and—

—darkness, lit by a thousand stars. In the distance Murphy saw the clustered lights of a CEA fleet.

The *Gambit* provided a small profile, and the fleet was tens of thousands of kilometers away. Unless they were sweeping the entire system with laser sonar, she doubted they'd seen her. To be safe, Murphy cut the cabin lights to minimum to avoid back-leakage through the fiber optics. She prayed they weren't scanning her with infrared. The *Gambit* was built to quickly radiate away launch heat, but for the first few seconds she'd be as hot as a small star.

She increased the fiber-optic lens power. Between the two main sequence stars, one red and one orange, glittered CEA warships: four Drone Carriers, two Destroyers, and a dreadnought, the *Armstrong*—but no *Delta-Vee*. Where was Spanner?

Hovering over the planet nearest the sun was another ship, a troop transport. Why would Gallger requisition planetary defenses? Certainly not to fend off an attack from floaters.

It was quite a show of force for a backwater system like ADS 17062. The only thing in the habitable zone was a dense iron-rich planet two AUs from the sun. Murphy guessed Gallger's installation was there, underground.

She checked the clock. Eighty minutes remained until the launchers were destroyed. Her first plan was to rescue Kyle and jump away with him—if the *Gambit* could handle another launch. Surely he could countermand any destruct order Vivien transmitted.

If rescue wasn't feasible, she'd have no choice but to turn herself in. There was too much at stake. Murphy smiled grimly. If it came to that she would take comfort in the *Gambit*'s less-than-pristine condition.

In addition to the troop transport orbiting ADS 17062-ichi there were three moons. If she timed it just right, she could come in behind the smallest one and keep it between her and the bulk of the forces.

Cutting the engines to minimum, Murphy eased the *Gambit* toward the small planetoid.

Hundreds of drones filled space between the moons and the planet. They were running a search pattern, spiraling outward. Murphy was fairly sure no one had spotted her jump in. So what were they looking for?

Status indicators for the left side of the ship flashed red. Someone had fired a short-range ion cannon and hit the *Gambit*. Murphy scanned the area. No drones. Not even a remotely piloted scout. She located the source: below her. Someone was already down there. With her ship spotted by Gallger forces, the game was up. The *Gambit* was in no shape for a dogfight, not with the entire galaxy riding on the outcome.

She opened a channel to the ship that had shot at her. "The *Gambit* won't be much use to your *jooking* mistress if you blow the damn ship up before I surrender."

Spanner appeared on screen. "Murphy?" His eyes were red-rimmed, as if he hadn't slept for a week. When he saw her face, exhaustion was banished by a wide-toothed grin. "Gods, it's good to see you!" He tapped the com, opening private channels to the other floaters. "Hold fire. That's not Gallger. It's the *Gambit*. It's Murphy! Let her land."

"What are you doing on the moon?" Murphy asked.

"Same as you." He winked. "Hiding."

Spanner transmitted rendezvous coordinates. The *Delta-Vee* and two other floater ships were parked on the moon.

As the *Gambit* neared, she saw the tail fins of the *Delta-Vee* tucked beneath an overhanging ledge. The other two ships lay in the shadows of stone peaks, hidden by the inky blackness.

Murphy tightened the focus of her transmission, targeting the *Delta-Vee*'s receiver. With luck, the laser wouldn't scatter. "What's going on?"

"Jumped in-system three days ago, and've been playing hide-and-seek with the CEA ever since. Vivien and Kyle're somewhere on that planet."

"You've verified that?"

"Aye. Received a message from the Gallger bosslady. She said surrender or she'd disable the launchers. We didn't buy it. As if Gallger'd cut off their money-making empire to spite—"

"She's done it. Everyone's trapped in-system. And if you and I don't hand ourselves over in the next hour, she'll send a self-destruct command to the launchers and blast the galaxy back to intrastellar days."

Spanner's brow furrowed. "Gods, the fem is mad."

"Agreed. Are you sure Kyle's there with her?"

"Ya, hidden in the base signal of Vivien's transmission was a message from Kyle. He'll steal a shuttle and escape. We're to pick him up."

"When?"

"Eighteen fifty-two."

"That's seven minutes from now, why aren't you massing in-system?"

"The others think it's a trap. A ploy to draw us out."

"What do you think?" Murphy asked.

"I believe Kyle." Spanner shrugged. "But can't rescue him alone."

"You're not alone any longer."

An ironic look passed over his face. "Been waiting for you to say that." He looked down at a second message screen. "Murphy, before we suicide run, I need you to launch the wounded back to Lettinger. Louis and Elma's ship took heavy damage. Louis's chest was crushed during acceleration. He's the worst, but there're others, Joe and Ilya. The Rafferty twins."

Murphy's chest clenched. "I can't. The *Gambit*'s wrecked. I doubt she's got another jump in her. I'm at the end of my tether."

"Damn." Spanner's eyes glazed over for a moment, then he bit his lip. "Well, no reason to linger. Either way, better for the wounded if we're quick."

Murphy fired the *Gambit*'s jets, moving away from the Moon's surface, and switched her com laser to the dreadnought *Armstrong*. As the flagship, it carried the mission commander. "*Gambit* to *Armstrong*, this is Thiadora Murphy. Spanostani and I are coming in. Do not fire. I repeat. Hold your fire."

She was surprised to see captain's bars on the shoulder of the man who answered her hail. Then she recognized him, a specter that had haunted her all through her University days. Murphy's breath froze in her throat.

It was Osborne, in command of the CEA flagship. War had been good to his career.

He said, "*Gambit*, we read you." His eyes narrowed. "So this is what comes of allowing floaters into the University. I always knew you would turn your back on the law."

"If the law is a woman so insane she'd destroy the galactic infrastructure to get her way, then, yes, I reject it. The CEA isn't in the service of humankind; it's the private fleet of the member Corporations."

Osborne's eyes narrowed. "I won't listen to your revolutionary propaganda."

"I'm not asking you to. Vivien wants Spanner's and my surrender. She's getting it. Just don't shoot us down before we can be captured. Agreed?"

"Agreed." He turned as if to log off—then snapped back to face her. "Murphy, don't try any floater tricks. Every weapon in my fleet is targeted on the *Gambit*." The expression on his face showed both scorn and fear.

She said, "I expected no less." Murphy clicked the com to transmit to Spanner. "Welcome party's set up. You ready?"

"Be there."

A cadre of twenty drones met the *Gambit* and *Delta-Vee* as they entered the zone between the moon and planet. Hair on the back of Murphy's neck stood on end. Status lights winked on the drones and sunlight glinted on their human-sized hulls. It was like being followed by a pack of malevolent dogs that were quiet now but could attack at any moment. Destroyers and carriers loomed at a respectable distance. They did not fire, but their cannons tracked the *Gambit* and *Delta-Vee* in a deadly salute.

As much as Murphy disliked this phase of her surrender, she feared more what Vivien would do to her once she was on the planet. The woman who had terrorized her brother out of his inheritance, maimed Tali, and poisoned Murphy to ensure her loyalty, would have free reign.

But there was no choice. If she didn't hand herself over, Vivien would destroy the galactic infrastructure. And there was Kyle. She could help him only if she were on the planet.

They were 85,000 kilometers from the planet's surface when a missile fired at them. Murphy jerked the *Gambit* left, then saw what it really was, a shuttle. She opened the receiver to all frequencies.

CEA personnel screamed orders.

"Intercept that—diving to cover—shuttle incoming— sites locked ready to—"

Vivien's voice rose above the din. "Capture that shuttle. I want him back alive."

A voice that made Murphy's heart swell with triumph said, "Shuttle one-nine to *Gambit*. Shuttle one-nine to *Delta-Vee*. Copy? Over." The words repeated in a desperate mantra.

Kyle had stolen a shuttle and escaped from the planet. Murphy could've kissed him. It gladdened her heart to see Kyle defiant at last.

"I'm closest," Spanner said on tight beam. "Cover me."

Murphy maneuvered the crippled *Gambit* between

the two Destroyers and the *Delta-Vee*. Its hull wouldn't last long, but it might buy enough time for Spanner to rescue Kyle and . . . then what? The thought of the *Gambit* and *Delta-Vee* fighting through the military to the launcher was ludicrous. Even if they could, Vivien would simply shut the launcher down. They were trapped in-system.

The cadre of drones following Murphy and Spanner changed course to intercept the shuttle. The com spouted a new flurry of communications.

"Target one—intercept the shuttle—with no casualties—on it, get the—"

Vivien's cultured tones were abandoned; she growled, "Get that shuttle. If necessary, shoot to kill. He must not escape."

No longer asking for a live capture? Murphy wondered what Kyle had with him in that shuttle. Something powerful enough to stop Vivien? Murphy aimed her com laser at the planet. "*Gambit* to Vivien Gallger, come in."

Vivien's face appeared on screen. Her neatly coiffured hair had come undone and flared around her face like a halo of yellow flames. "So. You've come to turn yourself in. I knew you would."

"I'm here to bargain. I offer you the *Gambit* and my full cooperation as a test pilot if you allow Spanner and Kyle to launch out of this system."

Vivien grinned, the skin tightening on her skull. "Gallger didn't become a major power in the Collective by making unprofitable bargains. You have nothing to offer me. I will have the *Gambit*"—her eyes widened—"and I will have your full cooperation. Your way, or mine."

Murphy looked at the screen. The shuttle approaching the *Delta-Vee* wobbled feebly, as if an untrained pilot attempted evasion maneuvers. Drones swarmed around the small craft.

The hidden ion cannons of the *Delta-Vee* extended. Drones evaporated as the beam of the industrial 450-

TWs caught them. Spanner fired continuously, opening a path for Kyle's shuttle. It wasn't enough.

As she watched, six drones converged on the thin-hulled shuttle and fired. Their concentrated attack cracked the hull, and it exploded in a puff of humid air that crystallized as soon as it hit vacuum.

"No!" Kyle was a grounder, born to an environment that promised pressure and atmosphere. He hadn't had Maisie's paranoia of vacuum drilled into him since birth. He wasn't trained to always wear a spacesuit, even in a pressurized ship.

The *Delta-Vee* clamped onto the shuttle—too late. Too late.

Murphy slammed her fist into the console. All Kyle had wanted was escape, and life on a quiet planet. It was her aspirations, her dreams that killed him. He had given his life in her cause; then let her actions be his eulogy.

She set the com to record and flung her message out to all assembled: floater and military ship alike. "I . . ." Grief and anger choked off her voice. She inhaled deeply and restarted. "I once dreamed of being an officer in the Collective Enforcement Agency. Enforcing the laws of all people. It was the height of morality—or so I thought." Her upper lip wrinkled. "But the CEA is nothing more than the lapdog of the Corporations. You're not here serving the common interest; you're the rented army of a despot. Vivien Gallger has shut down all launchers in the galaxy—not just rebel launchers—all launchers. That's why you haven't received new orders from command—they can't launch the datachips.

"Unless Spanner and I surrender, Gallger will transmit a destruct message that will blast the galaxy back to intrastellar days. Think of it. Interstellar travel will be nonexistent, because of the whim of one insane executive. Will your family, your loved ones be able to survive in the system they inhabit without resupply? Billions of people will die. Why? Because one person, Vivien Gallger, has that much power. I once wanted to be an officer. Now I'd rather die than serve in the Collective's corrupt service. Know this. If you ever see your loved ones again, it won't be because of the heroic officers of the CEA, it will be because of the sacrifice of *floaters* like me."

The com erupted in shouting and chaos—captains issuing rapid-fire orders, seeking verification of Murphy's claims, and Osborne's condemnation of her speech as propaganda. Murphy clicked the transmitter off.

She closed her eyes and drifted, mind and body. Kyle was dead, and with him the last chance to stop Vivien. It was all over.

Spanner's voice brought her back. ". . . recovered Kyle. Bruised, but alive."

Murphy gaped at the screen. A man in a full spacesuit, latest executive model, clung to Spanner's chair. She couldn't make out a countenance behind the polarized faceplate, but the figure lifted its right thumb in salute.

Murphy's heart raced, and she grinned uncontrollably. "You ground-hugging, son-of-a-*gronuger*!"

Kyle leaned toward the com and said, "Learned a few precautions from your Aunt Maisie, such as when to suit up. Maisie is an amazing woman."

"That she is. I'm sor—"

Vivien's transmission broke in. "Kyle, what do you gain by siding with these malcontents? You were born to better things."

"I gain my freedom. And the companionship of people I can trust." Kyle shook his head as if freeing himself from her reins. "You can't control everyone, Vivien."

"Yes. I can." She lifted a datachip into view. One side of the opalescent plastic was numbered 000000.

Kyle shouted, "No!" and lunged forward.

Vivien slapped the chip into place. Lifting her eyes to the camera, she smiled as cold a smile as ever touched human lips. "You don't know the first thing about power, Kyle. You can't get away from me. Gallger doesn't lose. *I* don't lose. Ever." Vivien punched transmit. A pulse of coded static wiped the screen.

The launch-cone glow brightened from yellow to green as it powered up.

The destruct command. Vivien was transmitting it.

Full throttle, Murphy plunged the *Gambit* through a wall of CEA ships, toward the launcher.

Cannon fire scored the *Gambit*'s sides. The ship spun wildly. Fiber-optic screens went dark.

Kyle's disembodied voice screamed over the com, "Vivien, no! There's no profit in this! You will destroy civilization!"

Murphy pulled out of the spin and ducked under the hull of a Destroyer. The launcher's main cone glowed violet. In seconds, the datachips would launch to two or three launchers. Each in turn would launch the message to two or three others. Standard wideband transmission, an efficient method of transmitting the galaxy's death.

Vivien's reply was unearthly calm. "Not civilization, brother, just democracy. Power is for those strong enough to take it."

The *Armstrong* reared into position between Murphy and the launcher.

"Osborne, you gods-damned fool. Stand aside!" Murphy shouted.

"You are in violation of—"

The *Gambit* accelerated. The *Armstrong*, swift despite its bulk, moved between the *Gambit* and her target. Murphy jinked left. The *Armstrong* swung to block her. She tried to spiral under the massive ship. It slipped sideways, back into position between her and the launcher.

The launcher's glow intensified to brilliant white.

Murphy glanced at the backward IFOs. The other floater ships were kilometers behind her. She was the only one who could reach the launch cone in time.

She flailed the *Gambit* through space, darting and faking like a fish on a line. Acceleration bruised her as she fought to pass the *Armstrong*. But the larger ship had the advantage of location. She couldn't fly past its bulk faster than it could pivot to stop her.

Through the link between the *Gambit* and the *Delta-Vee*, Spanner moaned, "Too late. Never get there in time."

In the launcher, space rippled as it reduced the distance between here and there. The datachip was transmitted. All over the galaxy, launchers were starting to destruct.

A sudden thought struck her. There was exactly one way to stop that message before it was sent. It was an insane plan—the same one that had killed her father. It probably wouldn't even work. The *Gambit* was damaged. But as things stood, she had nothing to lose. "Spanner," she asked, "would you give up your life to save the galaxy?"

After a pause he said, "Ya."

Murphy initiated the *Gambit*'s launch sequence. The ship shook as the overstressed engines kicked into higher output. She said, "So would I."

The launch-status icons flared red. Murphy cut off all other systems, and the symbols faded back into yellow. She aimed at the launcher, ignoring the fact that her path would take her straight through the *Armstrong*. If the *Gambit* didn't launch, the *Armstrong* was as good a target as any.

Murphy set the launch coordinates to overlap the transmit tower. The time coordinates she set to the instant before Vivien transmitted the destruct message. Time wasn't a problem. Murphy could beat Vivien at her own game, strand the *shi'eel* before she marooned a civilization.

Energy was a problem. According to Tangent's theory, even a time jump of a few minutes would generate trillions of Joules. Murphy could stop Vivien, but in doing so, she'd burn up like a unshielded ship in reentry.

The *Gambit* quivered, the galactic circle shrinking and growing as the launch field powered on, then faltered. Come on—*Gambit*—come on, she prayed, rocking in her seat. We've got history to make—come on.

The *Armstrong* loomed in front of her, seconds before impact—

—Red swirling hell. Plasma flooded through the *Gambit*, dissolving interior walls away like the film of a soap bubble. The *Gambit* shuddered, then—

—Occupied the same space and time as the reception antenna. Where matter overlapped, nuclear forces ripped the atoms apart. Like father, like daughter.

It was her last thought before the explosion ripped through the *Gambit*.

PART 3

". . . An object in motion shall remain
in motion . . ."
—Mechanics, Book of Newton 1:1

CHAPTER 20

Murphy soared through a space-black tunnel. At the end was light, white-hot and as bright as a supernova, the only light in this new universe. Murphy reached for that unrivaled brilliance.

And every nerve in her arm screamed. Shocked fully conscious, Murphy saw the light was attached to the arm of an intensive-care station. Gravity was about a quarter-gee. Pillows were like whipped cream beneath her, but even that slight pressure stung her damaged skin.

Murphy strained to lift her head and look at her body. Her torso was wrapped in white. She blinked, but her eyes did not clear.

Flashes of the explosion played against the fuzzy backdrop of her blurred vision: the *Gambit*, launching forward in space and back in time, the instantaneous dislocation of looking out and seeing another *Gambit* launch away. For an instant, there had been *two Gambit*s. Had anyone else noticed? Then white-hot detonation as, in that same instant, she overlapped the launcher's communication antenna with a centimeter's worth of the *Gambit*'s hull.

The heat and force of the blast played itself over in her mind. Time after time the crushing impact threw her backward, heat engulfed her, and she writhed away from the scalding inner surfaces of her suit.

"Murphy?"

She jumped, startled out of recollection, and peered in the direction of the voice, squinting.

A blurry yellow-and-tan shape lumbered closer. Kyle's voice repeated, "Murphy? Can you hear me?"

She tried to answer him, but her lips and throat were parched. She wheezed around a tube that ran down her throat.

"Don't try to talk." He gripped her right hand. "You're out of danger. The suit we found on board the *Gambit*—the one you were wearing—it saved you, barely. If the explosion had been any stronger, you would have ended up like the *Gambit*'s first pilot."

Murphy pushed away the thought of what her father must have endured, jumping back not seconds, but seventy years. She croaked, ". . . where . . . ?"

"The hospital bay of the CEA ship, *Glasnost*."

Murphy's eyes widened.

"We're free." His voice was soothing. "Gallger is under military control; Vivien's forces surrendered. After you intercepted the destruction message, the Collective mounted an assault on Gallger. Telesto Terraforming had hoarded three disposable exploration launchers—the kind used to scout new systems. Telesto launched two of the launchers to the CEA's home system. The CEA attacked Gallger—and won." His voice paused for a second. "But if you hadn't stopped the destruct message, it would have been too late. The entire galactic infrastructure would be in ruins."

"Sor . . . ry." Murphy's voice broke. ". . . sorry I left you behind . . . promised . . ."

"Shh. That's not important. You had to leave. I knew that." He kissed her forehead. "Don't think about it."

". . . Spanner?"

He hesitated a heartbeat. "Spanner is fine. You'll see him soon."

Murphy sank back into the cushions. "Can't see . . ."

Kyle stroked the side of her face. "Don't worry.

The best physicians in the galaxy are working on your case."

". . .'s destroyed . . ."

"Ssh. Ssh. Not now, later. Rest. The Collective has called a tribunal to investigate Vivien's actions. They're holding up the proceedings for your testimony. We need you. Rest."

She wanted to get up—find out what was going on. It wasn't over yet, not by a long shot. As long as Vivien still had power and influence, none of the people she loved were safe.

Murphy lifted her head—and stars swam in her vision, their light slamming into her skull like piercer bolts. She sank back into the pillows, and darkness.

The next time she woke up, the breathing tube was gone. A thick-bodied grounder woman stood next to the bed. Her short cinnamon-colored hair was streaked with gray. "Woke up for treatment?" The nurse lifted Murphy's chin and rubbed both sides of her neck with disinfectant.

The cold feel of evaporating antiseptic cleared away the remnants of sleep. "What . . . are you doing?"

The nurse held a cube, like the one Elma had used to extract blood for testing, but full of clear liquid. "You took a dose of more than four thousand rads."

Four thousand rads? Murphy's heart froze. Uncle Lucius had taken 3500 when the reactor on Vega blew—he only lasted twelve hours. "How long . . . do I have?" Her voice cracked uncomfortably.

The nurse patted Murphy's bandaged right hand. "It was touch-and-go the first six hours: cerebral edema, vascular damage, loss of intercellular fluids and electrolytes. But the CEA launched in the best physicians in the galaxy. You'll survive." She efficiently stripped the synth-skin and gauze from Murphy's chest and groin and placed more cubes.

"What are those?"

The nurse held up one of the loaded cubes. "This contains a hunter adenovirus. It circulates through your bloodstream and kills mutated cells." She pressed the cube into Murphy's neck.

While the injectors released the virus into Murphy's body, the nurse inspected her, mumbling notes to a holo bee buzzing over her left shoulder: "Burns healing, down to thirty-two percent of surface area. Patient's weight down. Now that she's regained consciousness, recommend solid food, high caloric. Faculties seem unaffected." She looked at Murphy's face. "How're the eyes? Any blurring?"

"No. Not anymore"

"Good." She said over her shoulder, "Patient reports no blurring with lens implants."

"Implants?" Murphy wheezed.

The nurse tapped the holo bee on the back. Its wings folded and it fell into her pocket. "Yes. Even with that high-tech suit to protect you, enough radiation penetrated your faceplate to burn your eyes." She nodded at Murphy's left arm. "The hand giving you any trouble?"

Murphy flexed her fingers. "They're stiff. What hap—" Then she knew. She'd sent the left glove of her suit to Avocet. Her hand had been protected only by standard spacesuit technology. It must have vaporized when the blast hit her. If the *Gambit*-suit hadn't sealed the breach in time . . . she exhaled shakily. "My hand . . . is an implant, too?"

The nurse shook her head. "No, that's cloned tissue. Don't worry, the tightness will pass with physical therapy." She plucked off the empty viral injectors. "How's the pain?"

Murphy closed her eyes and inventoried her nervous system. A few twinges and a dull throbbing in the back of her skull. "Not too bad."

"Good. Dosages for floaters are always dicey. It's easy to overcalculate."

Murphy opened her eyes. "When can I leave?"

"That's up to you. The cancer's nearly gone. Your lenses are attaching nicely. Any time you're ready, you can start physical therapy."

Murphy raised her arm. It felt as if needles were suspended in her flesh. Every motion drove them deeper.

"No." The nurse tucked her arm down and deftly slipped the hospital gown back over Murphy. "Let the virus run its course. I'll make a note to schedule you for next week. I don't have time now anyway. Do you think you're my only patient? There's a whole radiation ward filled with forty-two men and women too critical to jump." She snapped the covers over Murphy and tucked them in with firmness. "They were the launcher crew."

Murphy sagged against the sheets, guilt exhausting her as much as the quarter-gee. Her actions had wounded and killed dozens of people. But what choice had she had? Hadn't those same actions saved billions of lives? Wasn't that worth a few dozen deaths?

Not if it's you doing the dying.

And what had she accomplished? Vivien would buy her freedom from the tribunal, unless Murphy convinced them otherwise. She had to testify, and soon.

When the nurse left, Murphy wiggled her arm free of the coverlet, and lifted it, flexing the screaming muscles and joints. She would get better. This wasn't over yet.

Twelve agonizing days of physical therapy left Murphy strong enough to sit in a gravity chair. "I'm ready," she announced during Kyle's next visit.

Kyle placed his hand on her shoulder. "Not yet. Take time to recover. What's the purpose of jumping to Gottsdamerung if you don't survive the trip?"

Murphy's pulse raced. If Vivien wasn't stripped of wealth and power, there would be reprisals—against Kyle, Murphy, and floaters everywhere.

"I have to go," she said, squeezing his hand. "They've already taken Osborne's deposition, and my testimony is crucial. I endured test-piloting the *Gambit*, jumping across the galaxy and back again, and leading a revolution. I'm not going to fail now."

He looked directly into her eyes. "They won't close proceedings without you. The entire galaxy is waiting to hear your testimony. The Collective didn't move fast enough to suppress witnesses from spreading accounts of your actions. The only reason this medical facility isn't flooded with reporters is that your presence here is a military secret. You're a hero. A political force to be reckoned with. The Collective can't reach a decision without hearing from you."

"I'm ready to jump." Murphy said with finality.

Despite a host of medical precautions, the launch did not go well. Murphy went into shock and had to be revived by paramedics. After resuscitating her, the medics fitted her into a gravity chair. They deemed it necessary considering her weakened condition and the 1.5 earth-standard gravity of the capital planet, Varuna.

Murphy felt shame as the medics attached catheters and strapped support-gel packs around her waist. A gravity chair was the ultimate symbol of floater weakness.

On the shuttle ride from Gottsdamerung station to Varuna, Murphy had an expansive view of Ares, the brownish-red planet that housed the University. At this distance the only visible features were the snaking scars of Jagg's Canyon and the illuminated runways of the spaceport.

Had she really lived six years on that rock? The memories flooding her seemed artificial. She looked at her reflection in the shuttle's window: tattoos blazing black against her newly shaved scalp. Perhaps she *was* a different person. Or simply restored to the person she had been before she joined the University. In trying to escape floater culture, she had come full circle. Now she was poised to become her people's greatest advocate.

But she felt like a fraud. Could she call herself a floater after rejecting that heritage for six years? More importantly, did she want to?

Murphy turned away from Ares and looked forward to Varuna, looming green and blue in the shuttle's window. The capital planet was lush and massive. Sixty-three percent ocean, with a wide equatorial belt, it was one of the few fully terraformed planets in the galaxy, and certainly the most massive. Murphy's bones ached just thinking about the one-and-a-half standard gravity.

But it was on that planet that her future, and that of the Collective, would be made.

The council had never before entertained testimony from a floater. Murphy had to exploit this opportunity to its fullest, not just to convict Vivien, but to make the tribunes understand the waste and deprivation that fueled the revolution. She hoped she was up to it.

The shuttle landed. Murphy grew light-headed in the increased gravity. Then the bladders in her gravity chair expanded, squeezing her lower body and forcing blood back into her brain. The tightness of the pressure bladders was uncomfortable, but was nothing compared to the grinding ache in her neck and lower back. The chair injected muscle relaxants into the spasming areas. Numb and compressed, she felt distant, like an observer to her traitorous body.

As the paramedics unbolted her chair from the shuttle floor, Murphy looked out the window. The spaceport was a flexcrete lacework. Ambassadors from a thousand worlds wandered the pathways between arches, meeting travelers and being met. All the myriad breeds of human were represented: broad-bodied heavy-worlders, dark-skinned people from tropical zones, subterraneans wearing voluminous clothes and eye shields, ocean-dwellers in pressure suits. All the peoples of the Collective except floaters.

Murphy rolled down the ramp from the shuttle. No floaters . . . until now.

Two CEA paramedics, a man and woman in their thirties, accompanied Murphy to her rooms. Her quarters occupied the central building, one of many suites in a long curving hallway. Murphy pressed her palm against the wall plate, and the door opened.

Inside, the floors were white marble, the walls a softly glowing alabaster. Murphy's lips compressed into a line. The understated opulence reminded Murphy of her imprisonment by Vivien.

The female medic saw her expression and said, "I've worked Varuna before. This is the default decor. If you don't like it, tell the host system." She addressed the empty room, "Host, change style to Tropical Gardens." The alabaster walls darkened into green palm fronds. The ceiling painted itself with the pinks and oranges of a tropical sunset. "There are hundreds of preprogrammed styles," she told Murphy. "Or you can describe your own."

On the left was an enormous bedroom in which the *Delta-Vee* could have docked with room to spare. The paramedic said, "Host, remove bed," and the elegantly draped canopy bed vanished into the floor. When it was gone, the medics assembled the gel bed they had brought, adjusting viscosity to her weight. When the gel set, they covered it with a thin rubber membrane that would keep the emulsion from sticking to her skin while allowing the gel to mold to her body.

The male paramedic said, "Meals are served in your room, or if you wish, you can dine in the council restaurant. But be sure to call ahead for a private room, otherwise tourists and reporters will hound you. Your testimony starts at nine hundred hours tomorrow."

"Who's testifying today?"

He unclipped a portable screen from his belt and considered it. "Dr. Andropolous Spanostani." He clapped it shut and reattached the portable to his belt. "In the morning, I or one of the other medics will assist you into your chair and escort you to the court room." He paused. "Do you require anything further?"

"No."

The medic bowed curtly. "If you change your mind,

call us through the room's host. We are at your disposal around the clock."

A few minutes after they left, Murphy drove her chair into the hallway, exploring. She ran into Kyle, exiting the room next to hers. He was wearing a conservative navy suit with inch-wide lapels and a black undershirt. His blonde hair was pulled back into a sleek ponytail.

Murphy had never seen him in corporate clothing before. The change was alarming, like a dandelion transformed into a shark.

Kyle grimaced. "It's awful, I know," he said, holding out his arms and looking down at his clothing. "But it's all that was in my closet. Rows and rows of suits."

"It's not so bad," Murphy lied. "This your room?" She pointed at the door behind him.

"Yes, I'm on your right. Spanner's on your left." An ironic smile touched his lips. "It reminds me of Maisie's rock."

Murphy looked down the hallway. Additional doorways continued up the hall and around a bend. "Which one is Vivien's?"

"None. The council has her sequestered. She has been arrested and formally charged with obstruction of free trade and a host of lesser crimes."

"What'll happen if she's convicted?"

He shrugged. "They will dissolve Gallger's corporation and sell its assets to reimburse the damaged parties. Currently unrepresented corporations will bid for the empty seat."

"Wouldn't that destabilize the Collective?"

"Of course. The Bankers' War was fought over an open council seat. Similar political situation."

She nodded. Though it had lasted only days, millions had died. Murphy studied Kyle. He looked amazingly at ease in the corporate suit. But why not? He had been raised to be an executive. "Why don't you take over Gallger Galactic?"

"Me?" Kyle arched his right eyebrow. "I don't have the killing instinct. Find someone else."

"It's your duty. If you don't claim your birthright, the blood shed in the ensuing wars will be on your hands."

Kyle shook his head. "I don't want the responsibility."

She grabbed his wrist and prevented him from leaving. "Don't you see, you already have it."

When Spanner returned from giving testimony, Murphy wheeled herself to his door and asked the host system to announce her.

The door opened. The lighting in the room was dim, and the walls twinkled with artificial ship readouts. It looked like an enlarged version of the *Delta-Vee*'s cockpit.

"Nice," she said.

Spanner wheeled out of a shadow. His eyes glittered in dark bruises of exhaustion. He said in a soft voice that was half sigh, "Can only take so much wood paneling and velvet cushions."

She drove as close to him as their chairs would allow and clasped his arm. He bent his head until their foreheads touched. "Hard week?" she asked.

"Between the gravity and the cross-examination by Vivien's lawman?" He grimaced. "And you? You look terrible."

She held up her wasted arms and looked at them. "Not bad for a survivor of a nuclear explosion."

"Saw that. How'd you trigger the explosion? The *Gambit* was unarmed."

"I jumped to overlap part of the *Gambit* with Gallger's launcher."

He whistled low. "You *are* Murphy to have lived through that."

She silenced him with a finger to his lips. "That's the past. I want to talk about the present. And the future. Will Vivien be convicted?"

"Hard to say. Tribunal is a closed hearing. Only time I'm allowed in is when giving testimony."

"Do the judges listen to you? Have you convinced them Vivien needs to be removed from power?"

He sighed. "Doesn't matter. Vivien is just a part of the system. If they dispose of her, another company'll join the council. Floaters still won't have any representation. Nothing ever changes."

His words triggered an idea in Murphy. She gripped his forearms tighter. "Are you willing to change the system? Even if effecting that change became your life's work?"

His brow furrowed. "Of course, but what can I—"

"I've got an idea." Without further word, Murphy left him.

In her own room, she recorded a datachip message and transmitted it to Lettinger. The rebel leader Vargas had worked as a corporate lawyer before emigrating to space. She needed his legal advice.

The next morning, a medic helped Murphy into the gravity chair and escorted her to the council chamber.

The walls were paneled in black-veined ironwood. The heavy planks darkened the room, giving it a close, secretive air. It was, in actuality, a large room, twenty-by-twenty meters, octagonal. The far end was populated by a large semicircular table that surrounded an island of chairs and tables from which the witnesses delivered their testimony. The other end of the room was a smooth expanse of flexcrete. No audience during this part of the hearing; trials of council members were sealed. Only the verdict and sentencing were open to the public.

Above the floor were the loges owned by the member corporations. Set halfway up the wall, they faced the tribunal. The boxes were shielded by polarized-velvet curtains, allowing the inhabitants to observe without being seen. In the Gallger box, a curtain fluttered. Was Kyle watching? Or one of Vivien's people?

The flesh between Murphy's shoulders tightened, anticipating an assassin's bullet.

Ahead of her, on the right-hand side of the witness stand, was Vivien. She was exquisitely coiffured, hair swept up into a French twist so smooth it could have been sculpted from golden ivory. Her face was a mask of calm assurance. She watched Murphy wheel forward into the left-hand side.

Only a ceremonial waist-high wall separated them.

Beside Vivien sat a thin man in a crisp silk suit. His black hair was slicked back from his forehead. He stared briefly at Murphy, a calculating gaze, then whispered to Vivien. Murphy guessed he was Vivien's attorney.

Murphy rotated her shoulders to release some of their ache. She must be perfectly focused and persuasive.

The tribunes were arrayed before her, eleven of the most influential people in the galaxy, each of them CEOs or high-ranking representatives of the Collective member corporations. In front of each representative was a banner displaying the logo of their company.

The chairman, a dark-skinned man with sunken eyes, sat in the center. He wore a maroon turban edged in gold. The empty chair next to him was draped with a blue cloth bearing the interlinked atomic shells of Gallger Galactic.

Avocet's bulk occupied a gravity chair to the right of the chairman. He breathed heavily, studying Murphy. Was Damon Avocet friend or foe? As a floater, he might sympathize with her cause. Or not. People who escaped low status didn't always feel obligated to help those still in it. She remembered her own attitudes on Ares. It wasn't until she became a floater again that their cause became hers.

The other council members were a mix. Telesto Terraforming was represented by a black-bearded man with a purposeful glint in his eyes. A doughy man sat behind Canodyne's double helixes. The woman behind the tragedy and comedy masks of Joyco was round, but tautly so, her red cheeks and bright eyes giving her the appearance of an apple. To her left was a square-headed man with epicanthic folds, his fingers absently tracing the quartered diamond of Lübeck, the software conglomerate.

University political training put names and business specialties to the symbols before her. How strange to meet the leaders of power and find them to be merely human, with all of a fallible person's foibles and prejudices.

Murphy's hopes sank. Vivien had served on the council with these people for years. How could they judge her impartially? Spanner was right. Nothing would change.

Vivien's attorney rose to his feet. "I object to this witness." He pointed at Murphy. "This woman was expelled from the University for insubordination, reckless endangerment, and theft. Since that time, she has engaged in rebellion against the Collective and committed acts of terrorism."

The pudgy, balding man sitting behind the double helixes of Canodyne said, "I agree with council. The witness is unreliable. Why waste our time hearing her testimony?"

"Ms. Murphy was at the center of Gallger's attempt to strangle free trade," the Telesto agent argued. "Her testimony is vital."

The Lübeck tribune said, "She is a rebel, unheeding of the law. She belongs on the defense stand, not with the witnesses."

Avocet countered, "That rebel is the only thing that prevented the fracturing of the galaxy and total economic chaos."

The Canodyne member said, "Avocet and the witness share a mutual upbringing. Perhaps he sympathizes with the revolution."

Avocet whirled. He said in an even, friendly, dangerous voice, "Perhaps Gallger's investments in Canodyne have influenced your sympathies."

"It is a provable fact this witness is under contract to Avocet Industries," said the Joyco representative.

"How can we trust the impartiality of a witness you pay?"

"Tribunes," the dark-skinned chairman said, "let us not be distracted from the issue at hand. If we disallowed testimony of those paid by, or holding interest in, a member corporation, only the destitute and unemployed could address this court. Avocet has presented a detailed report of the actions taken to coerce Ms. Murphy into signing his employment contract. Actions that include conspiring to prevent alternative employment and economic threats. Because Ms. Murphy signed the contract under duress, it is null and void. The witness is no agent of Avocet's."

"A point of law only. How do we know where her allegiances lie?" said the Joyco representative.

The chairman banged the gavel. "Come to order. I rule we hear the testimony of this witness. The amount of relevance given to such testimony will be determined during deliberation." To Murphy he said, "Please describe, in your own words, the events leading up to the attack on ADS 17062."

The council listened intently as she described the strange simulation, Gallger's offer, her betrayal and expulsion from the University, stealing the *Gambit*, and self-launching across the galaxy during her escape.

At mention of this last, the chairman said, "You claim the *Gambit* self-launched?"

"Yes, sir."

"How is that possible?"

"I don't know, sir. The *Gambit* appears to launch into an alternate dimension, one in which small distances map to large ones here. For example, if you travel a meter in that dimension, you may jump back 500,000 meters from your starting point."

"Interesting. Who built this ship?"

Murphy hesitated, then said, "I don't know, sir."

The Canodyne representative leaned forward and pointed to something beneath the council table. "She is lying, look at the flush-response readings."

The chairman said, "Ms. Murphy. It is pointless to

tell falsehoods before this tribunal. Your physical condition is completely monitored." He leaned forward on his elbows. "The penalty for perjury is five years indentured servitude. Would you care to retract or correct your previous testimony?"

"I haven't lied to this tribunal," she said. "Although I have theories, I don't know how the *Gambit* was created."

"What are your theories?"

Murphy hesitated. The concept of self-launch had thrown the galaxy into chaos and near destruction, but that was nothing compared to the fear and paranoia that would arise if the Companies learned there was a secret race of dissident scientists with superior technology on the other side of the galaxy. "Nothing that can be proved. They are irrelevant."

The chairman's eyebrows rose. "It is not your place to judge what this court considers relevant."

Council for the defense leapt to his feet, pointing a finger at Murphy. "Objection, this witness is defiant and unreliable. I demand her testimony be stricken from the record!"

"Denied."

Murphy continued, "Sirs, everything I have told you about the *Gambit* is true. However, there are things about the *Gambit* I cannot tell you."

"Why not?"

"Because to do so, would endanger the future of the entire Collective. If that condemns me to perjury, so be it."

"This is preposterous," defense council said, "the witness is in contempt of court. I demand she be—"

The chairman cut him off with an impatient wave of his hand. "You will demand nothing. There are hundreds of reporters outside, representing thousands of worlds. This remarkable young woman has done them and us an incalculable favor at great personal cost. With such considerations in mind, I am not going to cite her with contempt of court. We shall drop this line of questioning."

The Canodyne tribune half rose out of his seat. "Your honor, this is an outrage! The rules of law should not bow to political pressure."

The chairman cut him off, "The tribunal, however, reserves the right to reopen this line of questioning at a later time. Now tell us, Ms. Murphy, what happened next to the *Gambit*?"

Murphy described her trip to ADS 17062, and how she had deliberately self-launched so the tip of the *Armstrong*'s communication tower occupied the same space as the *Gambit*'s rear hull. She left out the detail about launching back in time. "The *Gambit* was destroyed."

"Are you certain of the ship's destruction?" asked Avocet.

"Yes, sirs. The hull was breached, and plasma from the launch process dissolved many interior walls. It could not have withstood the subsequent explosion.

"The action I took to prevent Vivien's transmission resulted in the destruction of the *Gambit*." She held up her withered arms, covered with skin grafts and radiation treatment patches. "It was very nearly the end of me."

The chairman glanced down at the response monitor. He sighed, "A loss to us all. But at least we will not have to decide the disposition of that unparalleled ship."

Avocet looked near tears. Or murder.

"What happened after that?"

"I woke up in a military hospital. Then I came here."

"That will be all for now, Ms. Murphy. The tribunal thanks you for your testimony. You are excused. Note, however, you may be recalled to provide testimony on Vivien Gallger's alleged imprisonment of you and others. Please keep your host system apprised of your location at all times." He tapped the gavel against the bench. "This witness is dismissed."

Exhaustion boiled off her like waves of heat. Just

as well. She didn't have any more energy for speaking. She pivoted the gravity chair and met Vivien's gaze.

Those glacial eyes followed Murphy as she wheeled to the door.

She was woken from sleep later by the host system's soft whisper. "Kyle Gallger and Dr. Spanostani to see you. Shall I let them in?"

Murphy rubbed her eyes. "Yes, please."

Arms trembling, she lowered herself into the gravity chair. She hooked up the connections and filled the pressure bladders surrounding her legs.

Spanner rolled in, Kyle walking beside him. Their eyes were dark, and Kyle's face sprouted fine yellow stubble.

She clasped forearms with Spanner and shook hands with Kyle.

"What time is it?"

Kyle said, "Ten a.m. You slept through the afternoon and evening. We were unwilling to wake you."

"What's the news on the trial? Any verdict?"

Spanner said, "No. They're still sequestered."

"More than that," Kyle said. "The ISR representative's assistant is a friend of mine. She told me the tribunal is deadlocked. Half want to convict Vivien, but there's no concrete evidence against her, only conflicting eyewitness accounts. Without proof of intent to unfairly compete, they'll have to release her."

"What about her records?" Murphy asked. "Surely there must be notes, transactions, messages that were logged."

"Those are personal property. The tribunal has no right to search and seize them."

"But if *we* did it, if we found evidence of criminal intent, would the tribunal ignore it?"

"Probably not. But Vivien's files are locked."

"As the Gallger heir you can demand access."

"It wouldn't help. They are encrypted."

"You were her computer wizard, can't you—"

He shook his head. "I've already tried. It was easy

to download the file using my executive card, but Vivien has re-encrypted the files. I can't crack the key."

Murphy ran her tongue over her teeth, thinking. "Tali. Is she here?"

"Yes, but she's Vivien's creature."

Murphy said, "I think I can get her to remember when she belonged to herself."

She wheeled toward the door. "Host, what room is Talibah Hamadi in?"

"Fifty-two."

Kyle followed her into the hallway.

She raised her hand to stop his progress. "This is something I have to do alone."

"Murphy, Tali blames you for all that has happened to her. She despises you. In your weakened condition, she might do you harm. At least let me accompany you."

"No. My only chance of success is to make her recall our University days. You were no part of that. Stay here."

"You're taking an enormous risk."

Her mouth quirked into a lopsided grin, the one Maisie claimed was the mirror image of her father's. "Don't I always?"

CHAPTER
21

Murphy knocked on Tali's door. The host system asked: "Name and reason for calling?"

"It's Murphy. We need to talk." After long moments without response, Murphy turned her chair to leave.

The door slid open.

Murphy glanced through the entrance and froze. The room was the twin of their quarters at the University: the same prefabricated beds and desks molded from the floor, student screens flickering with class assignments, even their first-year cadet portraits on the wall. Murphy rolled in.

Tali lay prone on the right bunk, propped up on her elbows. One dark-skinned foot dangled over the edge of the bed. She studied a portable screen.

"Tali?"

She turned. Her face was as smooth and beautiful as it had been the day Murphy left the University.

"Is this what you wanted?" Tali touched her cheek with a hand miraculously restored. "Things the way they used to be?" She walked with smooth grace to Murphy's chair, bent down to Murphy's level, and kissed her cheek.

The surface of Tali's face flickered.

Murphy recoiled, then held up her hand to block the overhead light. In the hand-shaped shadow, Tali's flesh was scarred and puckered. Elsewhere, it was unblemished.

"How did you—"

Tali knocked Murphy's hand away. She ducked her head. Her braids fell like a curtain, hiding her face. "That was always your problem," she said. "You had to know the truth. No matter how ugly it was. No matter who got hurt." She gestured at the walls. "The host system. With a little programming, it can do more than the designers intended."

There was menace in those words. A challenge. In her mind, Murphy saw impaling spikes extrude from the walls.

"Drop the illusion. I came to see you, Tali. Not this make-believe."

The room's lighting wavered. In that instant Tali's face was maimed.

The right side looked as if it had been mined by a thousand tiny augers. The scars had thickened and darkened the skin, lying like horizontal ridges on the cliff-side that was her face. Above the foreign landscape was the pale blue moon of her transplanted eye.

Murphy found Tali's appearance startling, but not repulsive. She rolled her chair closer. "It doesn't make any difference. It doesn't change who you are."

"Don't be stupid. Of course it does." Tali flipped her braids out of her face. "Why are you here?"

Murphy sighed. "I need you to crack a personal file."

Tali's lips tightened in self-mocking knowledge. "Vivien's? You want me to find something to help you win the case."

"Yes."

"I heard the court was deadlocked for lack of evidence. Knew you'd turn up." She shook her head. "I can't help you. I need Vivien—"

"Vivien sent the assassins who maimed you!"

"I know." Tali's voice was hollow. "But it was an accident. After I was convicted of treason and sentenced to death, she saved me. No one else—"

"If she wanted to help you, why didn't she pay for full corrective surgery? She can afford to hire the best doctors. And why were you accused of sedition in the first place? Because Vivien set you up—just like she did to me." Murphy caught Tali's hand. "She used your disfigurement and criminal record to hold you. To keep your skills. Somewhere under all that propaganda she's filled your head with, you know that. She's not your friend"—Murphy stroked Tali's injured fingers—"I am."

Tali pulled away and reclined on the bed, hands behind her head. She was a juxtaposition of memories. New Tali in an old setting. "What happens to me if Vivien is convicted? If I'm not indentured to her, my old sentence will be reinstated. I'll be executed for treason."

Murphy rolled her chair over to Tali. "No you won't. The evidence proves Vivien framed you; the judgment against you will be overturned. And with your programming skills, you could work for any company in the Collective." She touched Tali's arm. "Vivien *is* going to be convicted. Her actions are too extreme for the Collective to ignore. It's not in their self-interest to exonerate her. Either way, you're not going to be working for her much longer. Your best chance is to break free now. Help us convict her."

Tali pulled away. "I didn't spend six years and all my scholarship money to become a freelance hacker."

"And I didn't spend ten months in centrifuge and endure six years of harassment to end up back where I started, a shipless floater. Life doesn't always work out the way we intended."

Tali wrapped her arms around herself. "I don't know what the future holds. It's too far gone from the plan. I can't program or predict it." In a low voice she said, "I'm scared."

Murphy touched her shoulder and whispered, "It's all right."

"Don't be nice to me," Tali whispered. "Hating you is the only thing that kept me going after the accident. If I don't have that . . ." She hung her head and cried silently.

Murphy ignored her gravity-strained muscles and leaned forward to take Tali into her arms. Tears pooled in and overflowed the dams of scars on Tali's cheek.

"Will you help me?" Murphy asked.

There was a long pause.

Hot tears soaked into Murphy's collar. Tali clutched her, as if she were holding onto the emergency handholds of an opening airlock. Then Tali's body shuddered, with dread or relief, Murphy couldn't tell.

Tali croaked, "I don't seem to have any choice."

"Thank you," Murphy said. "You're not just helping me, but millions of floaters."

Tali wiped her eyes. "Just my luck to end up working for the one group that can't afford to pay."

"Think of breaking into Vivien's files as a galaxy-wide audition. What company in the Collective wouldn't pay an executive salary to have you on their side—even if only to make sure you didn't work for their competitors." Murphy squeezed Tali's shoulder.

Tali shrugged off the gesture. "You'd better go back to your room," she said. "Figure out how you're going to get my sentence repealed. I'm not doing this for free."

A message waited for Murphy in her room. Vargas' reply. It had been routed through eight different high-traffic, politically neutral, launchers to hide its origin. After sixteen years of revolution, paranoia was second nature to him.

She read the message twice. When she was done, she clenched the datachip in her fist. This was it. She could change everything. All she needed was a hearing.

"Host, get me a link to the chairman."

The system said, "He is busy at the moment."

Murphy thought of all the floaters who'd ever suffered at the hands of member Corporations, the Company-engineered floater plagues, the children who'd been born in unshielded stations. "It's an emergency. I have vital information. I *must* speak to him."

The screen displayed, "PLEASE WAIT," and a soft ululating raga began to play.

The chairman's image appeared on screen. His wavy black hair fell past his shoulders. He wore a maroon silk dressing gown. His face was flushed. "This is highly irregular. Witnesses are not allowed to contact members of the court outside of chambers."

Murphy guessed that only part of his irritation stemmed from the breach in protocol. "I must address the tribunal."

"You have additional testimony?"

"No, but I must speak—"

"Then I advise you to petition the council for a hearing. This court is convened to decide the guilt or innocence of Vivien Gallger. It is not a platform for personal or political speeches. Because I permitted you leniency in the courtroom yesterday does not give you license to ignore protocol."

Murphy narrowed her eyes. "I will have my say. Either in the tribunal tomorrow, or by addressing the reporters on the courthouse steps." She shrugged. "I assumed you would prefer the former. It's all the same to me."

The chairman licked his lips. "You could be imprisoned for such an act of contempt."

"Then, lock me up. I'll make my speech from the prison cell."

"No," he said. "We cannot allow that. You will be given an opportunity to speak tomorrow." He frowned. "You are a most intractable negotiator."

"Coming from you, I take that as a compliment."

The chairman inclined his head toward her. "Indeed." The screen went dark.

The council room was encrusted with chairs and filled to capacity. A newly extruded balcony overlooked the proceedings. The air was alive with conversation and holo bees.

Murphy rolled over to Spanner, who sat at the end of a reserved front row. Crossing the space from the door, Murphy felt exposed and vulnerable. In gravity she was weak, crushed in the hand of an invisible giant. But that same force was nothing to the thousands of grounders thronged around her. Strong muscles, dense bones, any of them could attack her and she would be defenseless.

Kyle joined them, edging easily into an extruded seat.

Vivien was alone in the witness box. Her face and body so motionless she could have been carved from alabaster. Her eyes surveyed the room without seeing it, like the empty-eyed statue of a voracious goddess. A corporate Kali.

The chairman said, "Vivien Katerina Gallger, please stand for the verdict of this tribunal."

Vivien rose, her back to Murphy, Spanner, and Kyle.

"The tribunal has received evidence that incriminates you. Datachip messages clearly state your intention to monopolize the intersystem transportation industry by destroying the *Gambit* and—"

Vivien's face was red. "Those are personal records!"

"I object!" her lawyer said. "Collective law 34, section 9, states personal records cannot be subpoenaed by the court. Neither can the court employ individuals to crack the defendant's file security."

"This court has done neither," the chairman intoned. "As I said, these records were provided to the court by an anonymous source. If your client stored these records on her system in such a manner that any interested individual could easily gain access to them, they are hardly private."

"A code-cracker could break into private files." The attorney met the chairman's eyes. "Or create them."

"The validity and authenticity of this data has been verified by our security experts. Their findings will be made available to you. Your objection is overruled."

The chairman straightened and glanced at the

screen built into his desk. He continued. "Ms. Gallger, after deliberating on this newly revealed data, the council has reached the conclusion that you are guilty of attempting to monopolize the intersystem transportation industry; guilty of repressing technological discoveries, in the form of the *Gambit*; and guilty of entrapment of former Lieutenants Thiadora Murphy and Talibah Hamadi."

Vivien's shoulders were straight and stiff. Her hands strangled the banister.

"The tribunal will now deliberate on your sentencing." The chairman paused, then asked, "Do you have anything to say in your own behalf?"

"Hypocrites," Vivien said in a whisper that carried across the room. Her voice grew louder. "I have done only what was necessary to protect Gallger, the Corporation built by my great-great-grandfather. I suppressed knowledge of the *Gambit* not to hold the galaxy back from a technological advance, but to prevent competitors from beating me to the market. Trade secrets are a legal and fully protected commodity." Vivien met the gaze of each member of the council. "Shutting down the launchers was a mistake. But my property had been stolen, and my company was at risk. If a rival corporation had acquired the *Gambit* and developed its technology, Gallger would be bankrupt. There isn't one among you that wouldn't have done things *exactly* as I have."

The chairman said, "Your statement will be taken into consideration. Please remove the defendant from the courtroom."

As Vivien passed Murphy, she spoke over her shoulder in a low voice that carried no further than Murphy's ears. "This is not over between us. No matter how deep they bury me, I will come back for you."

The hair on the back of Murphy's neck prickled. Could Vivien make good on that threat?

Two CEA guardsmen moved to grasp Vivien's arm. She stared them down. "There is no need. I am finished here." Vivien stalked out of the room, the men beside her seeming more an honor guard than restraint. She left not in retreat, but as a predator seeking better ground for an ambush.

The chairman raised his gavel. "Are there any further statements?"

"Yes," Murphy said, rolling forward. "I would like to speak before the tribunal."

Canodyne said, "I object. This witness flaunts Collective protocol and has already taxed the patience of this council. Testimony is ended. Nothing she can say will have any relevance to our sentencing."

The chairman said, "Your protest is duly noted. Any further objections?"

No one spoke.

"Ms. Murphy, please proceed."

"My statement regards how your sentencing will affect the Collective. The crimes committed were those of an individual, not a corporation. Dissolving Gallger and removing it from the council would destabilize the Collective." She stared up at the chairman. "Instead, I recommend you appoint a person to take Vivien's place as CEO. One who has a legal claim to Gallger, experience in intragalactic dealings, and who had no part in Vivien Gallger's crimes."

"And who might that be," Canodyne asked, "one of your revolutionaries?"

"No, not a rebel. He is one of your elite. He is poised in times of crisis, resourceful, and worthy of trust." She pivoted her chair. "I recommend, as CEO of Gallger Galactic, Jonathan Kyle Gallger."

The spectators buzzed and holo bees dive-bombed the witness stand, each jockeying for the best shot of Kyle's expression. His face was stiff, but composed.

Murphy wondered if she was pushing him too far. His only goal when he met her was to escape the fate she now thrust upon him. But there was no time for self-recrimination, she had to finish this while her words had momentum.

Murphy held aloft a datachip—the one Vargas had transmitted.

"Finding a new CEO for Gallger will only solve half of the instability problem. This is the other half of my proposal. In my hand I hold the end of the rebellion."

The audience hushed. Holo bees abandoned Kyle, his story already ten seconds stale, and converged around Murphy.

"I hold the authenticated signatures of more than one hundred thousand floaters, on a petition to incorporate under the laws of the Collective and to establish a thirteenth council seat."

"A corporation?" asked the apple-cheeked Joyco representative.

"Of floaters?" echoed Telesto.

"Exactly." Murphy jabbed the air with the datachip. "The rebellion has long been a drain on the financial and military resources of the Collective. But that need not be the case."

The Canodyne representative said, "The Collective is a council of *businesses*. Private citizens cannot serve on its board."

"These signatures represent holdings in excess of three hundred million dollars. A small corporation, to be sure, but Telesto, when it joined the council forty years ago, was even smaller."

"You offer yourself as representative for this new power block?" the Telesto member asked.

"No. For that honor, I nominate Andropolous Spanostani."

The holo bees left Murphy and swarmed around Spanner. His face was frozen somewhere between delight and terror. "Me?" he gestured, pointing at himself.

Murphy opened and clenched her fist, signing back an affirmative, then continued to address the council, "Dr. Spanostani holds a Ph.D. in biology and has lived both as a grounder and a floater. He has a strong character and will be able to withstand the pressures of council life."

"But he's one of the most notorious instigators of the revolution!" argued Canodyne.

"Precisely. He has already proven himself a leader. What better way to keep an eye on him than in your meetings? What better way to ensure floaters' adherence to the laws of the Collective than to give them a say in creating them? It is unprofitable to continue the war against the rebellion when it is so much less expensive to subvert them."

Avocet steepled his fingers in front of his chin. "She makes sense."

The chairman said, "Ms. Murphy, you have raised interesting points. We will take your comments into consideration." He spoke to one of the uniformed guards positioned along the wall. "Bailiff, please file the datachip as exhibit 234."

She closed her fist around the chip. "No. This list contains the names and locations of rebels and rebel sympathizers. I will not hand it over to the Collective until the council seat is ratified, and Company immunity provided for its shareholders."

"You tax the patience of this court," the chairman said. "You ask for our cooperation, and yet withhold your own. How can we be sure this chip contains the data you say?"

"I will allow it to be audited by an independent analyst. That person can compile a summary of its contents."

Kyle and Spanner ambushed Murphy outside the hearing room, pushing through crowds of reporters. Kyle swatted a particularly persistent holo bee out of his face and stamped on it.

"We need to talk," Kyle said once they were out of earshot of the crowds.

In Murphy's room Kyle scanned for bugs. When he was satisfied the room was clean, he sat down on the bed and said, "I hope you know what you're doing."

"It's the only thing to do."

Spanner grabbed her arm. "When you asked me if I wanted to help floaters . . . that it might take up the rest of my life doing so, I thought you meant fighting, not politics." His eyes were filled with wonder.

"Aren't you pleased?"

"I'm not sure. I think fighting would be safer. Why not you Murphy, you're the obvious choice."

Murphy held up her hands. "Not me. I can fly any craft built, but handling people, that's beyond me. Spanner, you've been a grounder. You know what they're like. You're the perfect bridge between the two cultures."

Spanner grinned widely. "Dr. Andropolis Spanostani. CEO of Floater Inc., member of the Collective council. I rather like the sound of that. I think I could shake things up around here, do some real good."

"Then, you'll take the chair?"

"If given the chance, I will. But warn a man next time you plan the course of his life for him, eh?"

Kyle snorted at that. "Yes, do."

"You'll be a great CEO, Kyle," Murphy said, touching his shoulder.

Kyle didn't flinch, but he didn't respond, either. "I told you I didn't want to be CEO of Gallger. I don't have to take the appointment."

Murphy held her breath. They needed Kyle. A sympathetic ally within the council would be essential for the nascent floater corporation's survival. "Are you going to?"

Kyle put his hand over Murphy's. "You want me to accept, don't you?"

"Yes, of course."

"Then, ask me. For once in my life, I'd like to be asked, instead of told what to do."

Murphy met his eyes and saw the pain there. He'd been stoic in the council room. Breeding and decades of social training had held, but here in private, she saw the strain of what she was asking of him, the raw fear in his eyes.

She glanced at Spanner for help, but he wheeled his chair to the other side of the room and pointedly studied a faux painting on the wall.

"Please," she said. "Agree to lead Gallger Galactic. We need you Kyle, I need you, to do this."

Kyle inhaled sharply at her words. After a long pause, he patted her hand, and said, "All right, then. I will."

Spanner wheeled back to join them, and grinned. He touched his equations in salute. "As one potential CEO to another, glad to have you on our side."

"Am I," Kyle said, looking pointedly at Murphy, "or am I just on her side?" Kyle and Murphy locked eyes.

"It's one and the same," Spanner said, interrupting the tension. He cocked his head at Kyle. "Come on. The lady's tired from testifying all day, and us future magnates have plans to make." He tugged on Kyle's sleeve, pulling him to the door.

Kyle rose from the bed and followed Spanner, but he looked over his shoulder at Murphy and said, "We'll wait and see what the council says. Perhaps all your machinations will be for naught. Either way, this isn't over between us."

Murphy held her breath until the two men had left her quarters. When they were gone, she sighed and slumped in her chair. Kyle was different in gravity, in the corporate surroundings he knew so well. In his own world he was intense, formidable. Somehow she felt responsible for his changes. And she wasn't sure she'd done him a service.

After three days of deliberation, the council reconvened.

The council room was filled with lights and human reporters. Murphy's speech had been transmitted to every system in the galaxy. Debate wars flamed across data channels. The trial had become a media event, history in progress.

Every seat on the floor and balcony was occupied. Standing crowds lined the back wall. The boxes were filled with the elite: executives and celebrities wearing improbably architected grounder hairstyles, glowing tattoos, and clothing of the rarest cut: silk-and-velvet formal wear, leather suits millimeter-tight, and coruscant microfiber-optic dresses that glittered with ever-changing color.

Extra guards stood by each exit, armed with net cannons and needlers.

For all the people, the room was relatively quiet, as if everyone held their breath, not wanting to miss a syllable of the proceedings.

Vivien wore a synth-silk sheath so purely white that it shone with pale blue highlights. Her hair tumbled over her left shoulder in a cascade of ringlets. Her face was a calm mask, save for an unaccustomed emotion that flickered in her pale eyes. Was it fear?

Murphy's body hummed with adrenaline. The council's decision would not only decide Vivien's fate, but her own. If Vivien was set free, there would be no corner of the galaxy where Murphy would be safe.

The chairman spoke: "Vivien Katerina Gallger, in consequence of your criminal actions, this court has judged you be stripped of council status and your position as CEO of Gallger Galactic, forfeiting all assets and personal wealth. You will be sent to Tiberus-san, a primitive colony in a launcherless system. There you will live out the remainder of your life, contributing to the well-being of the colony by working the soil with your hands."

Vivien's legs buckled and she fell, insensate, to the floor.

The crowd stood, roaring with one throat, necks straining to get a better view. The front guards pushed them back.

Kyle ran to his sister's side and took her hand. Two medics Murphy didn't recognize pushed him out of the way and checked Vivien's vital signs. They loaded her onto a stretcher and whisked her out of the courtroom.

Kyle returned.

"Is she . . ." Murphy asked.

He gripped her hand tightly. "She was breathing—

I couldn't see more than that." His eyes were blank. He whispered, "After all she's put us through, I shouldn't care. But . . . she's the only family I have left."

Murphy squeezed his arm, wanting to say something, anything, to comfort him. But her words were cut off by the chairman's gavel.

"Order! Order! This court will come to order, or I will clear the room!"

The room quieted and the chairman continued, "In addition, the tribunal has decided how best to dispense with the assets of Gallger Galactic. We resolve to keep Gallger Galactic intact, and establish Jonathan Kyle Gallger as CEO." The chairman looked down at Kyle. "Welcome to the council, Executive."

Kyle exhaled a shaky breath, then stood and nodded his acceptance. "Thank you, sir."

The audience murmured. There was scattered applause. A woman in the ISR loge waived a red fan at Kyle and whistled.

Murphy raised her voice to be heard over the background noise. "What about the new council seat?"

The chairman regarded her with his dark liquid eyes. "Order." He tapped the bench lightly.

When the room quieted, he said, "It would be highly irregular for the council to consider a petition for incorporation during the trial of one of its members."

Murphy opened her mouth to protest—

"However, these are unusual times. Because the Collective owes a debt of gratitude to the petitioner, an exception was made. Bailiff, will you read the results of the council's vote?"

Murphy held her breath. This was the moment that would—or would not—change everything. There were thirteen votes in the council, one for each Corporation, and two for the chairman. She needed seven.

A burly woman stood, and intoned in a rich alto voice: "Petition for incorporation of the Floater's

League. Voting for the measure: Avocet, SysFirst, Telesto, and ISR."

Murphy's limbs went leaden. Joyco, five—no, six—SysFirst counted twice. But even with Gallger's abstention, it wasn't enough.

She exhaled, hope draining away with the air. Spanner was right. Nothing ever changed.

The bailiff continued. "Voting against: Canodyne, Maxard, Wardstrum, Gamble & Wicks."

Murphy's heart flip-flopped. Only four?

"Abstentions: Gallger, Lübeck."

Murphy's chest felt like it would implode. So close! But it wasn't enough. New measures had to be approved by a majority. A tie meant she, and floaters everywhere, lost.

Murphy closed her eyes and wished a black hole would consume her. Failure. It seemed her destiny to disappoint.

When she opened her eyes again, the chairman was looking at her with compassion. He raised the gavel and said, "This court is adjo—"

Kyle sprung to his feet. "Objection!"

The chairman paused, still holding the upright gavel. His lips twitched with consternation. "To what exactly, do you object?"

"I am the chief executive officer of Gallger Galactic; appointed with due process and a preponderance of witnesses." He gestured grandly at the packed gallery and balconies. "You cannot close this incorporation petition. Not without my vote."

Murphy looked up at Kyle, astonished. His mouth was pulled into a feral grin, his blue eyes hard and unwavering as he stared the chairman down.

The chairman looked back to Kyle. "How do you vote, Gallger?"

"*For* the petition."

Relief and joy exploded through Murphy's limbs. She'd won! They'd won! She hugged Kyle's waist, and nearly toppled him over.

The chairman's last words were lost in the roar of

the crowd. In silent pantomime he banged the gavel to close proceedings.

Kyle placed a hand on Murphy's shoulder to steady himself.

Spanner whooped with joy. He hugged Murphy and kissed her cheek. "We've won!" he shouted. "We've won!"

Murphy's eyes flooded. Something *was* different, and she was the agent of that change. A council seat wouldn't end prejudice against floaters, but for the first time in history, floaters would have a say in government.

It was the opening move in a game Murphy intended to win.

EPILOGUE

That night, space was filled with celebrations. In every artificial atmosphere: stations, asteroids, singleships, cargo tugs, miners, even shuttles, floaters broke open hoarded intoxicants and toasted the future and Murphy, their hero. Her mail cache overflowed with messages of congratulations and adoration.

Avocet launched six of his finest yachts to Varuna orbit and docked them together, forming a hexagonal station. He invited the council members to join him in a zero-gee celebration.

The walls twinkled with iridian stars and neon comets. Music and conversation filled every crevice. Floater acrobats clothed in iridescent skinsuits shot like meteorites between the guests, passing out drink bulbs of wine and flat champagne.

Murphy's spine expanded, her worries and stresses easing with the gravity. Council members, executives, and ambassadors congratulated her. Awkward in zero-gee, they clung to the walls and each other. She showed them how to clasp arms and touch foreheads, explaining that the floater greeting was safer in weightlessness than shaking hands.

Exhausted by pleasant conversation with people she didn't know, Murphy sought out Tali, Kyle, or Spanner.

She found Tali talking to a man with black hair pulled up into a ponytail and a SysFirst emblem embedded in his right ear. He whispered to Tali and extended three fingers. She shook her head slightly and extended five.

A business deal, Murphy guessed. She pushed off silently into the crowd.

Kyle clung to a handhold near the airlock. Alone.

Taking his elbow, Murphy steered him to a quiet corner of the suit storage room.

"It appears you've got what you wanted," Kyle said. His face was pale.

"I'm sorry about Vivien."

He grimaced. "Absurd, isn't it? I suspect she killed our older brother. She autocratically controlled my life. I don't know why I should miss her. But I do."

"Is she going to be all right?"

"I don't know. Life on a colony planet, toiling with her hands? She's not prepared for that."

Murphy squeezed his shoulder. "It'll work out. Vivien controlled one of the most powerful companies in the Collective. She's a fighter. She'll survive." Perhaps too well, Murphy worried.

He sighed heavily. "You're right." He rubbed his hands together. "Murphy, I don't know if I can do what she did. I don't know whether I can run Gallger Galactic."

Murphy touched his elbow. "You'll be fine. It's in your blood."

He clutched her arms like a drowning man. "I know I could do it . . . if you were at my side. Murphy . . . stay with me. I . . . I . . ."

He leaned in and kissed her. His lips were warm and firm. His body pressed against her with mute entreaty and yearning.

Murphy jerked back, sending them into a quick spin. She caught the wall and slowed them. "Kyle," she whispered, "what are you doing?"

"I think . . . I love you. Please don't leave."

"You don't know what you're asking."

"We could run Gallger Galactic, jointly. You talk about helping floaters. With Gallger's money and launcher technology, you could make a difference. We could. Together."

His face was sincere and pleading. Her heart

twinged. She could happily make love to him, but he would read too much into it. Culture separated them. What he wanted—a sister, a mother, a wife—she wasn't able to offer. She closed her eyes, then opened them. "Kyle, I can't."

"Are you worried about the gravity? We could run the business from a null-gee station—"

"It's not just my body that's adapted to space," she explained, touching his cheek, "it's my mind. I'm sorry Kyle, but I can't be what you need."

He sighed. "Then, I'm alone."

She cupped his chin and looked into his eyes. "No. You're not. I'll always be your friend. Spanner, Maisie and Arch, even Avocet. We're all on your side. Just don't ask us to be more than what we are."

He licked his lips, tried a smile on for size. It didn't fit, not yet. But Murphy thought he would grow into it. "As you wish," he said.

"Heya, heroes of the revolution!" Spanner said. He kicked off from the wall and launched toward them. "There you are, I've been look—" He saw Kyle's red-rimmed eyes and grabbed a cabinet handle to arrest his forward motion. "I interrupt something?"

"Unfortunately, no," Kyle said. He pushed clumsily off the wall and propelled himself through the door. Spanner raised a hand, too late to prevent his leaving.

"Don't," Murphy said quietly. "Let him go. He needs to be alone."

Spanner exhaled. "What'd he want?"

"I don't want to talk about it. How are you doing?"

"Wonderful." Spanner stretched his arms out expansively. "You're right, Murphy. Things can change. First time in years, the good guys've won." He clasped his right arm around her shoulder. "We'll make so many things right."

Murphy squirmed out of his embrace to look at his face. "What do you mean, 'we'?"

"You, me . . . floaters everywhere!"

Murphy relaxed.

Spanner waved a dismissive hand in the direction

Kyle had gone. "Grounders're always trying to lock things down, scared of motion, of change. Don't have to worry about me. Won't try to maneuver you into hard dock. But you'll stay with me, neh?" He smiled a little shyly. "After all, you got me into this council position."

The corners of Murphy's mouth twitched. It was too much. For six years she had lived in near-celibacy because none of the students, with the exception of Tali, would have anything to do with her. Now in as many minutes she had two offers of coupling.

"Spanner," she said gently, "if I'd wanted a council position, I would have taken it myself. You're the martyr to this particular cause. Not me."

Spanner looked stunned then recovered his jovial mask. "Hey, you have to help me. What else're you going to do with the rest of your life?"

She'd been wondering the same thing. Murphy kissed him softly on the cheek and pushed off toward the door. "That's what I have to figure out."

The night was filled with propositions. Everyone wanted something from Murphy. Everyone had something to give. Wickmont cornered her and offered her reinstatement with the CEA, captain's rank, and a University teaching position. When she refused, he said the CEA would give her command of the newly commissioned *Sallal*, a Destroyer, fast and heavily armed. The SysFirst chairman wanted to take her to lunch the next day and discuss an account for the new floater corporation's assets. Others simply wanted to talk to her, touch her, so they could say they'd met Murphy, hero of the revolution.

And through it all, Murphy wondered what she would do with the rest of her life. The *Delta-Vee* was Spanner's, the *Gambit* destroyed, the University like an old spacesuit that pinched and didn't fit anymore. She didn't seem to belong anywhere. Had she saved the Collective, only to lose herself? Murphy watched the people around her laughing, drinking intoxicants, smiling and clutching one another. She was surrounded by admirers, but had never felt so alone.

After a time, the floaters and grounders separated out, clusters of like-minded people gathering at opposite sides of the room. Murphy sighed. A lot had changed, but more stayed the same. You couldn't change a people's prejudices overnight.

Murphy wanted to socialize, but which group? She was neither floater nor grounder, her experiences drew from both cultures. She wasn't sure what she was anymore. Which set of values should she live by?

The answer lay inside of her, as much a part of Murphy as her bones. She'd live by the values that had carried her to the edge of the galaxy and back: Her own.

Why hadn't she decided that years ago, instead of trying to cram herself into other people's molds? Murphy took a drink bulb from a passing acrobat and sipped reflectively.

Not that she could make a career out of following her own mind. She'd seen enough of the underbelly of the CEA that she had no illusions about its serving justice. And the last week had put her in the spotlight enough that she knew she wanted no part of political life. What would she do with herself? Follow in her mother's flight path, pilot cargo? The thought repulsed her, but there wasn't much else she could do other than fly a ship. But any other spaceship would seem backward and ponderous after flying the *Gambit*.

Murphy watched Avocet at the bar, smiling and offering inhalants to the apple-shaped Joyco woman.

It snapped together.

She knew what she wanted, and who could help her get it. Murphy waited until the Joyco representative drifted off, then cornered Damon Avocet.

Suited construction crews swarmed like flies over the four cones of the new Avocet Industries research station. Yellow sunlight gleamed off the service bays.

Inside the one nearest her, Murphy could see the beginnings of a matte-black spherical ship.

She tapped the com. "*Phoenix* to Lettinger II. Request permission to dock."

"Welcome home, Murphy," Hroc's voice replied. "Cleared for port 16."

Murphy aimed the Avocet Comet at the docking pin. The tiny, wasp-shaped ship was a pleasure to pilot: fast and responsive. She dove toward the pin, braked furiously at the last possible moment, and docked with a precise click.

Arch met her on the other side of the airlock and swatted at her helmet. "I don't care if you are the galaxy's hero, you dock like that again at my station, and I'll lay you out."

"Don't mind the old bear," Maisie said from an overhead tunnel. She maneuvered her body with a twist of her waist and floated down between them. "He's as happy to see you as I am." She crushed Murphy in an enveloping hug.

When she could breathe again, Murphy asked, "How's progress?"

Arch said, "In bay two, we've developed a ceramic alloy that closely matches the fragments of the *Gambit*'s hull we collected from ADS 17062." He ticked off items on his left hand. "Bay three is working on a fusion engine compact enough to fit in a singleship. Investigation of the suit you were wearing during the *Potemkin* explosion continues. There's been nominal progress in developing a counter-inertial microfiber." He squinted his eyes. "But the hardest part is going to be bridging space time. The work in bay seven is going slowly."

Murphy said, "You can do it, Uncle Arch, if anyone can."

"Sorry to interrupt such a hearty round of self-congratulations," Maisie said, "but this arrived for you a couple of hours ago." She flicked a datachip toward Murphy. The plastic cube spun, iridescent colors flashing off its surface.

Murphy snatched it out of the air. "Who's it from?"

"Kyle."

"Ah," Murphy said, stowing the cube in an upper-arm pocket.

"There's also a package. I've had it delivered to the *Phoenix*."

"Was it ticking?" Arch asked.

Maisie elbowed him. "Seal it. The boy's soft on her."

Arch shrugged. "And what's wrong with that? We've had cross-gravity marriages in the family before. A little interbreeding with that set strengthens the genetic cash flow."

"You daft bugger. She's not soft on *him*."

"Oh."

Murphy waved away Arch's forthcoming apology. "It's all right. If you don't mind"—she tapped her shoulder pocket—"I'll read this in my ship."

The *Phoenix* was custom-built to Murphy's measurements. It fit her like a skinsuit, consoles within arm's reach, captain's chair molded to her curves, touchpads optimized for her reflexes. It was a joy to pilot. Avocet had loaned it to her indefinitely, or until Arch's *Countermove* was ready for test flights.

Avocet had tried to talk her into letting someone less valuable do the initial flights. Her memories of the *Gambit* and the few scraps they were able to salvage were the only blueprint they had.

But Murphy insisted on test-piloting. It was the only nonnegotiable condition of her employment: the *Gambit* had been her ship; the *Countermove* would be, too.

Murphy wrapped her legs around the pilot's ergo and popped the cube into the reader.

Kyle's face appeared on screen. Six months of power had changed him. His soft mouth had hardened into an uncompromising line and fine wrinkles were forming between his brows. Gravity tamed his dandelion curls into shoulder-length waves. His image smiled, the fit better than it had been at Varuna.

"I trust you and the project are doing well," the recorded image said. "I've followed Avocet's reports to the council. Arch's work is amazing. Give my regards to him . . . and to Maisie." He paused. "You will be glad to hear Spanner pushed the radiation shielding standards through. Seventy-two thousand Company stations, mostly floater-operated, will be upgraded over the next five years. The man is an indefatigable negotiator." Kyle broke off, as if fumbling for more small talk, then he said, "I enclose what you asked for, the ashes of the pilot that Gallger discovered on board the *Gambit*. Our labs were able to do a limited DNA profile, despite the incineration. It's human, as I suspect you already knew. Perhaps someday we will meet again, and you will feel free to tell me what you learned that time you long-jumped to escape Gallger station."

Murphy grasped the golden cylinder Kyle had sent along with the chip. She started it spinning and heard a soft whisper of abrasion inside.

She listened for a moment, straining to make sense of the sound. Her mind searched for words, some kind of message in the low shush-shush . . . foolish.

Murphy secured the canister and radioed the station. "I need to undock. Got an errand to run. Save supper for me."

"Cleared. Proceed away from the station on niner-five."

"Copy."

She released the docking pin and eased away from Lettinger, following the specified trajectory. Once away, she pivoted the ship and accelerated at maximum speed toward deep space.

When the sun had faded to a fiery ball, Murphy set the autopilot and pulled free the package stowed at her side.

She pressed the smooth, cold, cylinder against her forehead. It was all she had after twenty years. Just ashes, and the knowledge—however belated—that he had loved her. The modified floater's bible she'd found on board the Gambit was gone, disintegrated in the explosion at ADS 17062. Unless she and Arch succeeded in re-creating the *Gambit*, this is all she would ever have of Ferris Murphy.

But his wasn't the kind of soul you could hold onto as a keepsake.

She tucked the golden canister under her arm and pushed off toward the suit room. She suited up in the Maxard special Avocet had provided. After checking and rechecking the suit's seals, Murphy stowed the canister in a hip pocket. She looked down once more at it, then stepped into the pressurized airlock.

Murphy unstrapped the emergency air canisters from the wall and tied herself in their place. Torso and legs pinioned, she could just barely reach the lock controls. She overrode the safeties, and without cycling, cracked open the airlock door.

Air hissed past the space-side seal. Murphy was pulled toward the opening. The straps tightened around her.

Murphy unbelted the canister from her hip and opened it. Gray-and-white powder swirled out of the canister and through the seal in the airlock. She opened the door wider, and the powder became a tornado, particles flying toward freedom, exploding out of the *Phoenix* with enough velocity to carry them to the ends of the universe. Exploring forever.

Tears bubbled along the edges of Murphy's eyes. "Good-bye," she said, her voice breaking. "Goodbye, Father."